A BLAST OF

David Rix is an author, editor and artist from London—specifically from the East End, where the canals, railways and wild areas of street art and alt culture have had an immense impact on his work. His published books include *What the Giants were Saying*, the novelettes *A Suite in Four Windows* and *Brown is the New Black*, and the novella/story collection Feather, which was shortlisted for the Edge Hill prize. He also runs Eibonvale Press, which focuses on unusual new writing in the area of Slipstream, Speculative Fiction and Horror. He has been designing the covers of Eibonvale Press books since the press was founded in 2004.

DAVID RIX

A BLAST OF HUNTERS

THIS IS A SNUGGLY BOOK

Copyright © 2019 by David Rix.
All rights reserved.

ISBN: 978-1-64525-003-6

With grateful acknowledgements to Quentin S. Crisp and Lynda Warwick-Hynes for providing the initial spark. Also to Nadine Buchmann and Alexander Zelenyj for their invaluable thoughts and assistance.

A BLAST OF HUNTERS

This melancholy London—I sometimes imagine that the souls of the lost are compelled to walk through its streets perpetually. One feels them passing like a whiff of air.

William Butler Yeats,
*Letter, August 25, 1888,
to writer Katharine Tynan.*

SATURDAY

The moon in London always has competition. Against the orange city haze and outshone by every streetlight, it seems to come through from another layer of reality—a world behind or beyond what we know. This was one of those nights when the still air hangs heavy with the day's heat—a dull, quiet texture that you can almost smell. And for me, those nights are always associated with a moon coloured red or brown. Pollution—dust. White moons like dead skin are moons of cold. Summer moons are moons of dirt.

On this night, in the dark place where I was lying, the moon seemed much clearer than usual—a pale disk that burned itself into my eyes. My head was uncomfortable but relaxed against cold metal; rough stones were digging into my back. My field of view mostly consisted of ancient brick, steel, rubble, wire, overhanging trees, scrubby plants, black, distant city lights, silence . . . a very specific mix of the antique and the modern utilitarian. There was an illusion that the rest of the city was a hundred miles away and the darkness that surrounded me felt precious. Something rare in the city.

Guess where I am yet?

Out there, beyond the dark, this was one of those nights when people still swarm, even into these small hours. When the busses are packed with a dizzying mix of excitement and despair. When the city is filled with tipsy Londoners babbling in many different languages, streaming in every direction—with the only obstruction being the endless shadows of the homeless. The skirts are never shorter, the bustle never wilder, the smells and sounds never more vivid, the tears and rage never stronger than on these hot summer nights.

And who among those crowds cries to the moon? Who remembers its existence? When you run through the world, you see nothing. When staring down at the concrete, waiting as the minutes pass in complete stasis, maybe there is nothing to see.

I didn't really mind the passage of time. I knew precisely how long the wait would be. 23:08 the train would arrive at its destination—the terminus a few miles further into the city—so 22:56 passing here. Still about seven miles down the line now, I estimated—speeding in fast and heavy. I felt full of a sense of calm and almost tranquillity, my only discomfort being the chill of the metal rail against the back of my neck. I was lying there and dreaming gently. And soon hopefully that peace would be permanent.

Dark . . . rubble, steel, brick, turning wheels, drunkenness . . .

There was a skittering sound as some animal passed by somewhere not far off. Then another. I didn't bother looking round though—probably a fox or rabbit or something on the move. Green corridors, they called these railway lines. The long threads of wild land where humans feared to tread were perfect for other lifeforms that didn't care about laws and fences. London was a surprisingly living city, I knew that much—and not just the pigeons and the foxes. Right then though, I didn't care even slightly. I didn't want to disturb the cloth I had wrapped round myself.

Cloth—ah yes. Why was I wrapped head to toe in a black sheet? No—it was not some weird costume or ritual. I just . . . didn't particularly want to traumatise the train driver, though honestly you'd think they would be getting used to it these days—their hearts would be hardening through sheer over-exposure. I had draped myself with a black sheet from my old bed. In the darkness, hopefully I wouldn't even be noticed—nothing more than an amorphous black shape, one end leaning barely visibly over one of the gleaming rails—just a slight bump as the train passed by . . . that was how it should be.

And what was I thinking about? Well—it's not always as dramatic as some might imagine. It doesn't have to be hot and wild—sometimes it's pure weariness, sometimes the cold realisation that it is the only worthwhile choice. I would describe it more as a dull and rancid sense of displacement and disconnect. In a tranquil procession, faces were drifting through my mind. Faces of old friends—loves—momentary encounters. None of them particularly loved or hated now though—not even my neighbour Tea, who had been a focus of pointless and unrequited attention for far too long. Indeed, in some ways, I found the sad rotting of all that more disturbing and desolate than those past times when it had blazed bright enough to burn the world to white-out. These faces, without exception, seemed a long, long way away, in another world that only brushed mine through the thorniest overlap. They: far, far away and possibly not even real—me: here and now, equally yet differently unreal. I was drunk of course, which helped these thoughts. You will understand why. Almost an entire small bottle of gin, enough to defeat even the cold of steel and the ticking of time.

There was another sound approaching now. It was surprising how active this forbidden space of the railways was at night. But I suppose anywhere humans can't or won't go, other things will. And you know what? I envied them. Why is it that in this world we have created for ourselves, it is only other creatures that can ever seem free, while we ourselves are bound tight like trembling masochists awaiting the touch of a whip? They—if they can, they climb or fly over fences or borders as though they weren't there. So which then is the more advanced? It didn't matter to me though—I would soon be free too. I lay there listening—no idea what it was. I could hear the repeating skuff skuff of moving ballast, the sound approaching quickly. Running steps. Larger than a fox surely—but still light. I lay still, hoping the invisibility of my black sheet would hold—hoping I would not be seen by whatever it was—hoping that my presence would have no impact on the course of its life. That's all I wanted now—non-existence, even to some passing animal.

Then suddenly a heavy blow on my leg.

It was a hard blow. A contact unexpected to both of us, and there was a scree of ballast and then a crash as whatever it was fell down hard. There was a yell, and my skin prickled in shock—it was not an animal yell at all, it was a human one, complete with a very clear swear word.

I sat up sharply and she gave a great hiss of terror. My eyes, used to the darkness that never really was darkness in this city could make out a figure sprawled on her face, her legs tangled in mine. She was wearing what looked like black trousers and a tight black pullover, her hair tied back with a hairband, the strands painfully taut around her forehead.

Something gleamed in the stones by her hand and I dimly focussed on a long knife . . .

She hauled herself up onto all fours in a panicked scrabble, kicking herself free from my cloth-covered feet and stared at me with huge eyes, looking feral and terrified. I guess it was no surprise. My concealment had been good and how is it not shocking when a human being turns up somewhere you are fairly sure there wasn't one?

"What are you doing here?" she whispered with a shrill tone to her voice. She had caught up the knife again and was holding it warily. I couldn't make out whether it was aggression in her eyes or fear. Sometimes it's hard to tell those apart—I suppose they always were kissing cousins. I just gawped at her. I really was too drunk to deal with this. Indeed, faced with an unexpected human being, my drunkenness seemed to have expanded massively, leaving me virtually incapacitated. My peace had been shattered—my steady and quiet waiting for the world to no longer matter was gone. I was left swimming and blinking.

She sighed, apparently shaking off some of her shock, and stared away up the line in the direction she had been running. But whatever it was, it appeared that she could only give up on it. She gave me a cross look, which I didn't understand. Aside from a few bruised knees, what had I messed up here?

Then there was a thrumming from the tracks behind me. 22:52. The train was due.

"Gawd," she muttered. "Come here."

I stared round, making a vague motion towards the rails again. That's where I should be. Cold metal—hidden—peace, rubble, dark, steel, concrete, train, *train, train, TRAIN* . . .

"Get over here, you stupid twat," she yelled under her breath. "We'll be seen."

Yeah—seen. My cloth was thoroughly disarranged now. Tangled round my waist. The driver would see my white face . . . uselessly slam on the emergency brake . . . and a hundred late night commuters would mutter about my selfishness while I was cleaned up from under the train wheels . . .

She caught me by the arm and hauled me into the bushes with a massive yank. Such was the force that I plunged down there like a fish on a line, stumbling and landing almost on top of her with a painful crash that made her hiss.

And there was a blaze of light behind me. And a rising scream. The roar of the train coming out of the night with a terrifying crescendo. The light was dazzling. Dark vanishing, steel screaming, ultimate illumination . . .

Wheels flashed past—just a few feet away.

I stared at them. Train wheels are big things when you are up close. Like a procession of revolving guillotines moving at over sixty miles per hour. And now all I could see was that gleaming yet grubby metal cutting through flesh with the efficiency and inexorability of a butcher's saw. It sent chills across my skin. I clutched at myself as though my stomach was going to fall out of my body.

And it passed.

As the mass of metal faded into the night, I realised I was still crouching half on top of the woman in black, most of my weight channelled through my hand onto her chest. That was not a good place to be.

"Sorry," I muttered, pulling myself to my feet and standing arms out, unsteady. I studied her for a moment, but there seemed little to suggest that she was any more real than any of the other faces in the world so I turned away and tramped back up onto the tracks. The darkness had returned now—as dark as it ever could be here. I stood and stared after the vanished train, feeling water like an ocean swirling inside me. It was heavy, but it wouldn't manifest as tears, I knew that much.

No more trains here now until the 23:37 local service . . .

"Hey," she called. I ignored her. No—'ignore' is too deliberate. She wasn't real, remember.

"Oh gawd," she muttered scrambling out of the bushes beside me. "You cost me tonight's dinner, you know that?"

I had no idea what that meant.

"And nearly made me shit my pants, I might add. So—what's it going to take to get you off this railway line and cheer you up a bit? Want me to say, 'There there, it might never happen'?"

There was a silence.

"Probably not," she said. "Need a shot or sniff of something to feed the turkey?" she asked dryly.

I watched her, feeling puzzled—wondering why this person was standing there. Her mouth was moving and that meant communication. And communication meant that I would be called upon to talk—to somehow extrude words out through the frozen-up pipe of my mouth. I tried to marshal my thoughts.

"I could just fuck off and leave you to it, you know," she added with a hint of impatience.

"My name . . ." I began, then gave up. It just wasn't important. "Sorry, I am a bit drunk so I could . . . wouldn't lose my nerve. I didn't expect to meet anyone here."

My voice sounded slow but polite—extremely polite and extremely normal. An accent almost verging on the posh, which I didn't like much. Something to do with being drunk, no doubt. It certainly seemed to surprise her.

"Yes," I said. "You can leave me to it."

She frowned.

"Forget it," she said dryly. She looked up and down the tracks a moment, then gestured me to follow her.

"How did you get up here? Through the cemetery I suppose?"

"Yeah."

"Come with me. Let's go back to—to my place. Maybe the others will have had more success than me."

"I don't want to go anywhere," I slurred, but she grabbed the cuff of my sleeve and yanked.

"Come on," she snapped. "I don't want to read about you on the news tomorrow. Assuming the world still cares."

"But . . ."

"Don't worry—I ain't trying to fucking pick you up or pinch your wallet. Frankly you don't look as though you would be worth much for either. I am just trying to be your basic Good Samaritan here, you get it? Now will you shift your arse?"

With a mental shrug, I shifted it. I was in no state to resist. We walked along the tracks a short way and hauled ourselves back through the busted fence into the cemetery that clung to one side of the railway—on the other were sterile industrial buildings and yards. In the cemetery, the darkness was far more intense but never total—the city produces too much light for any kind of real dark. We picked our way through the trees and old tombstones towards where the old metal kissing gate let us out onto the road.

What followed was actually quite a long walk, as far as the passage of time meant anything to me. Normally I never went out at night, except maybe a quick nip to the shops. In this city, one tends not to, right? But this was what you might call a special occasion and I was too drunk to care. We headed south and west, I knew that much. My eyes were squarely on the feet of this unexpected companion as they paced over crumbling tarmac or wonky paving slabs, with everything else peripheral vision. Just pace, pace, pace, almost hypnotising, like a minimalist artwork— glancing back every so often, possibly to make sure I was still following and not showing signs of rebellion. Quiet city streets were passing with dreary apartment blocks and houses jumbled up together—the duller side of north-east London. The railway was not far away either, now rearing up high onto a parade of arches. Massive brick. Concrete. Curves. Fences. Trees. Old posters plastered on top of each other, and graffiti of various kinds. Most illegible, but I do remember one large scrawl in white spray paint—*BE READY!* Though 'ready' was the last thing I was feeling. Posters for gigs and events, political messages—down with or death to someone or other. The same old rotten stinking politics that benefitted nobody. There were even a few of the old 'Meat is Murder' stickers from the bad old days when you could still legally get it in a few places in the city. When that was still an issue that needed shouting about.

Pace, pace, pace, over the cracks in the pavement, negotiating the occasional pothole or broken area, neatly sidestepping a pile of shit on the floor that might have been human or animal. Either way, it didn't look too healthy. But then—who is?

I came to a stop then, breathing heavily. I was exhausted by this forced march at a time when my head was spinning and swimming. Why was I moving? I hated moving. Moving hurt. My feet, my lungs. I shouldn't be moving—I had hoped never to have to move again.

"Get a move on," she said roughly, but with a not-unfriendly edge to her voice. "Not far."

"But—look, I really . . ."

"Come on," she repeated with emphasis. "Otherwise I'll bash you in the face and see if I can wake you up a bit that way."

But where was I being taken? Wasn't this rather . . . weird? This sort of thing just didn't happen out in the city at night. The night was a world to pass through as quickly as possible—its people merely ghosts.

Pace, pace, pace—and a second sidestep, this time the remains of some chips and half-chewed battered meat substitute in a yellow food tray. Mycofillet I think they called it. Whatever it was, this was the diametric opposite end of the previous mess, I thought. This is a sickly world.

Where I was being taken turned out to be the New Sea Wall—that monstrosity topped with yet more railway tracks, yet more razor wire, yet more fences. And beyond this there was nothing but ruin. The fences were starting to feel oppressive. Fences of grey metal, filled with overblown functionality. The feeling of a prison was only reinforced—but what side of the fence were we on? Need I even ask?

This, plus the glistening water of Regent's Canal nearby, told me that we had made it all the way to Limehouse—somehow. Don't ask me how. The massive watergates or tidal lock that allowed boats to pass through the sea wall was centre stage here—a similar functional construction.

"Nearly there," she said, hustling me along a narrow and claustrophobic path. "One more climb."

I gave her a blank look as we came to a stop facing crumbling concrete and ancient brick. This was the remains of the old Accumulator Tower, now a ruin up against the viaduct. "Okay," she said. "Up here—you see the way?"

I opened my mouth.

"But I thought . . . your place?"

She grinned. "Fuck yeah, my place. And it's over there."

She gestured at the wall. Nothing was visible down here, but the dark ruined buildings that filled the land beyond were legendary.

"Just one little climb, and you can sleep, or pass out . . . or whatever."

She reached up one foot and scrambled upwards. I couldn't see how she did it—couldn't see how I did it either. Maybe the fact that I was drunk helped or maybe it wasn't as hard as it looked. At any rate, a few moments later I was up and gasping for breath by her side.

And beyond the tracks . . . devastation. And more than that, a devastation that London tried to pretend had never happened. The city hadn't really lost dozens of postcodes to the rising sea. There had never really been Thames views here for the millionaires to gawp at. Things had just . . . rearranged themselves slightly and it was generally better if we didn't talk about it, you know. Just accept the sea wall as the city's event horizon.

For those that did talk, however, the abandoned areas on the wrong side of the wall were known as Soaks, and now Limehouse Soak stretched out before me from this rather unusual vantage point, a chaos of buildings, some as standing ruins, many bulldozed completely. A few warning lights gleamed among them—a few other lights too, suggesting that some were still in hazy non-public use. And below . . . hints of black water lapping here and there where it had pushed in. Mud and sand. Sea. Scraggly sea grass and stains of algae forming darker shadows on the darkness. A few sombre and mysterious boats were still moored in the old Limehouse Basin. And of course, looming over everything in the middle distance was the vast constellation of lights of Canary Wharf Island, one of London's two sterile and glittering financial districts. To my drunken senses, the whole scene could have been a vision from a nightmare. Or an ultimate symbol of humanity's doom.

My companion didn't let me stare for long though. She grabbed my arm to support me and tried to bundle my exhausted body down the tracks. But something was ticking in my head and I glanced at the clock on my phone. This was not right. Not a good idea. These four tracks were the lines out of Fenchurch Street Station and the New London Ring, so that meant . . .

"Wait," I managed.

"Hm?"

I staggered across the lines to the seaward side, staring up and down, and waved vaguely for her to follow me.

"What the fuck . . . ?" she demanded, but then the inside track suddenly woke up under her and began to thrum.

She muttered something and darted after me and dropped down into a tight crouch up against the brick and concrete parapet, her head almost between her knees.

"Fuck's sake," she muttered. "Get down." But I already was, trying to copy her position, scrunched up like some pile of sacks or debris, face hidden. Then with a rush and a roar the train was passing in a flurry of lights.

"You get used to that," she said, unfolding herself again and standing up. "And in the dark the drivers can't see much."

I made a meaningless sound. To be honest, that last bit of activity and drama had been a final straw. That quiet world of watery ruin beyond the wall was feeding into my head like a dream in the dark—in the orange-tinted luminous darkness of the city. Water seemed to be everywhere—even the concrete seemed fluid and swirling. I was seeing flickers and flashes of red at the edges of my vision. Somewhere between afterimage and ethereal vision. Winking lights that came and went.

"Oh boy," she muttered, grabbing at my arm again. "Come on—up—get up. It's not much further. You can't crash here, you stupid . . ."

I suppose I must have followed her. I remember the heavy railway ballast under my shoes, then some downward scrambling over slippery concrete. Then I was inside. There was a flicker of candlelight and faces were staring at me in astonishment, again registered as nothing more than an uncomfortable dream. Then I was allowed to drop down onto something soft and almost immediately I was swallowed, sinking down backwards and head first into universal blankness, helped by another deep low train-rumble from somewhere. I have a memory of someone asking a question, which my addled mind remembers as "Is he one of us?"—and something inside me cringed at that. That is never a good question to hear. Whatever that question meant, the only possible answer was *no* and that brought with it a crashing sense of fear and failure. I had been diverted from the only thing in the world that was right—the feel of cold metal and impending peace. It was gone—in fact it had been stolen. And that was a tragedy . . .

SUNDAY

There was a glimmer of grey light, dim but still painful to my eyes. Day. A dull painful freshness that I never liked much. I stared at it, trying to work it out. Mundane London daylight. Not some kind of afterlife I had never believed in. The patch of light was framed by old brick, in which a few tough plants had taken root—tufts of grass and a small buddleia sprig. And the brick was curved. It arched above me beautifully and in London that suggested one thing—the railway. I was underneath the arches of a viaduct. I was in bed, under a railway arch. A glance around revealed that both I and the light source were quite high up in this railway arch. It was also enclosed on all sides, the two arched openings bricked up, as many of the London arches are, to create a useable space. Shops, storerooms, warehouses, garages—almost anything. But what I could see of this place looked more like a home, and that was somewhat stranger. I suppose in London, in the grip of the housing crisis, people would be living on the Heathrow runway if they could. Anywhere—any little scrap or hole in London, legal or otherwise, there would be people trying to pass their days in it. So no, this wasn't surprising.

As if to underline the point, a rumble came echoing in from above that seemed to shake the bed I was lying in. It rang round my aching head and I screwed up my face. I was filled with that dull half-sick feeling of hangover, and memories of gulping down gin last night came back to me, of cringing as the burning liquid went down far too fast. The bottle lay somewhere on the tracks, I remembered. So did my black sheet. And of course . . . I had failed.

I need to describe this place without messing around, don't I? My swirling head and woolly brain slowly put it together in some muddled order that would only annoy you. I was indeed in a railway arch that had been converted sometime long ago into an enclosed space. Below me was a floor of concrete, but I was on a sturdy wooden platform that had been erected to give the place a makeshift second storey. A ladder gave access and it looked a fairly recent construction. The light that was razoring into my eyes came from an oblong hole in the brickwork a few feet above the platform. It was glassless, but a thick black curtain had been hung there, now pulled aside. A glance down revealed more of these holes at ground level, roughly where you would expect windows and doors to be. However, these other ones were filled in with concrete. Also down below were chairs, a table, a small bookcase—and on the wall a huge scribble in white spray paint, looking more like an unfinished sketch than an artwork. Another ladder leaned nearby. Several screens stood around, shaping the room. Lots of candles were in evidence—unlit at the time. I saw a small stove attached to a gas canister and a long chimney duct that snaked all the way up to the window and outside. There were various wicker storage baskets filled with unknowable stuff. On the table were kitchen utensils and mugs.

I scrambled out of bed, forcing my limbs to move. I quickly went to the window and leaned out, hoping for more insights—and outside was the bleak ruined land of the Soak, transitioning from a concrete marsh riddled with mud to glimpses of the gently heaving Thames. So that meant . . .

That meant, surreally enough, that I was inside the London Sea Wall. I could see it stretching away in a curving line of metal and brick, topped with the heavy electrical gear of the railway. The sea wall itself, built from hefty metal sheet piles, had basically been slapped on the front of the old railway viaduct and the whole thing concreted in like a kid playing with putty. The sheet piling reached up to about six feet below the viaduct wall and I could see the old brickwork of the bridge rising above it. The hole I was leaning out of was only a short distance above the metal, which formed a rough shelf. It looked precarious, rang-ing from over a foot to just centimetres from the brickwork and filled with geological-looking concrete. Had I somehow walked along that last night? I could see no other possible way to access this place, so I must have. It was a realisation that came with a certain sinking feeling.

In the daylight, the Soak in front of me was much clearer. Buildings rose up out of mud and concrete, with well-defined bands of seaweed and algae on the lower levels. Windows and doors were boarded up, barred with heavy metal bars, or covered with rusty mesh. In some places these had been broken open again and lively graffiti covered the walls, which meant that in spite of the isolation, some people must have been coming here. Much of it was tags and daubs but some areas were much more elaborate. Rolling waves covered one wall—obviously inspired by Hokusai. Another featured a bleak cityscape populated by some seriously strange and rather creepy figures—black circular faces in which a single orb of white was placed, seemingly at random. Art always finds a way. I had seen pictures of places like this before on urban exploration websites, taken by carefully masked and anonymous wanderers and artists, or river travellers, but I never expected to end up in one.

I was interrupted by a slither against concrete directly in front of me and a pair of legs blocked the window. I flinched away as the legs squatted down and a figure slid in. I recognised her as one might dimly recognise something or someone dreamt about a long time ago.

"Hello," she said, brushing at her clothes. "I was starting to wonder if you had decided to insure the job with poison as well."

". . ."

"You were asleep for fourteen hours," she said with a grin. "Do you feel better?"

I put a hand to my head.

"Maybe not," she murmured. "Perhaps I should get you a painkiller or three?"

"Please," I muttered. It hurt to talk—and even more so to marshal all the thoughts needed to talk. I watched stupidly as she dumped her bag on a small table and extracted a water bottle, poured some into a mug (with the slogan 'mad cows' on it) and pushed it in my direction, along with a few white pills. I sat down as well with some relief. In the daylight I could at last see her in more detail and her appearance was striking. What had seemed in my hazy drunken darkness to be normal black trousers and a drab top were actually green and covered with complex shapes of dark and light, brown and grey, forming something close to modernist abstract patterns. It was not military camo but it reminded me of a subtle version of the old dazzle camouflage they used on warships long ago to break up the outline. The patterns flowed elegantly around her—almost seeming to change her shape. Not literally but in an illusory way—something to do with the way the eye followed curves and edges. It must have been stitched by hand rather than printed and it rather countered the severe way her hair was tied back.

Her accent had an ever so slight hint of cockney about it—nothing overt but it was there.

"So," she said, leaning back in her chair and looking at me with thoughtful eyes, "wanna talk about it?"

For a moment I wasn't sure what she meant.

"You know," she said encouragingly, "spill the beans, get it off your chest." She patted her shoulder. "It's here if you need to cry on it—and hopefully it's not so hard."

I stared at her, feeling frozen. If there was any pipe between whatever words whispered exhaustedly in my head and my lips then it seemed totally clogged with ice. Talk about it?

"Thank you," I murmured, but then my tongue literally stuck to the roof of my mouth. "Nnnyug. I—I . . ."

"Something go wrong for you?" she asked. "Something break your heart? Or life just become impossible?"

"N-no," I managed. "Not really . . ."

She gave me another thoughtful look.

"It was . . . something I had to do . . . but . . ."

Her eyes looked very deep and dark and I quailed in terror. Please, I was begging silently—don't make me talk . . .

"It's just a 'thing', then?" she asked with a small smile. "It seems a rather drastic 'thing'."

I hunched down over my glass of water. Time ticked past very loudly, its progression like a heavy snake moving round my shoulders as I scrabbled to find some words that weren't there in the totally eroded-out depths of my mind.

She looked puzzled, obviously taking in my rigid posture and helpless silence.

"Hey—no bother, don't worry about it."

I nodded unhappily.

"Come and meet the others instead."

"Others?" I wasn't at all sure I wanted to meet any others. I glanced round at the window that was presumably the only exit, wondering how I could make my escape and get out of here—back to the peace of loneliness . . .

She rose to her feet and crossed to the ladder on, which was fastened securely to the edge of the platform with new-looking rope. She swung herself onto it and scrambled down, indicating with her eyes that I should follow. I did so and descended to the concrete floor. And now I could see a new feature of this space—a small opening, an arched doorway in the leg of the viaduct itself that presumably led through into the next great curved space. A curtain hung across it, hiding a faint murmur of voices. She twitched that aside and ushered me through—almost a tunnel in the massive brickwork—and into the eyes that awaited me beyond.

At the time I was frozen by the presence of other people watching me, but I eventually realised that this second arch-space was almost the same as the first save for two major differences. The first was that there was no platform here, just a concrete floor with a disparate range of comfortable furniture—chairs and beanbags—as well as more candles on tall elegant candlesticks, lit now and providing a warm and mobile illumination. The second was that there was no window. Instead, a grey concrete wall stretched from floor to ceiling on both sides.

But yes—awareness of all this came later. It was the people that held my attention to begin with. Whenever I was brought into the presence of strangers—others—it sent ice through every muscle of my face in what I can only call stage fright, so much so that I could barely take in the details. They were nothing more than an amorphous blob of otherness that hammered at my eyes and brain. And if it wasn't for the flow of movement created by the girl in abstract green washing me forward, I might well have come to a stop in the doorway, unable to move in either direction.

"You probably don't remember anyone from last night," the girl said. "But we were all here to look after you."

Is he one of us? Someone had definitely said that. And it didn't help.

There were four of them seated comfortably—that was all I got to begin with, but the green lady was cheerfully performing introductions.

"This is the Philosopher," she said, indicating a somewhat older man who was wearing an incongruous top hat (seriously) and what had once been a quite elegant black coat—now faded and tatty. The weirdness of that got my attention rather and I began to focus. He inclined his head gravely in greeting.

"This is the Butcher," she continued, gesturing at a second elegant-looking guy, tall and slim in a green waistcoat. He gave me a boyish grin.

"The Beggar," she said, and this was a small but strongly built woman dressed starkly different from the others in well-patched jeans and a jacket. Her hair was brown and rather unkempt and her eyes gleamed at me with curiosity, a tiny candleflame in each of them.

"Clay Man, the street artist," she continued, indicating another youngish guy in what I can only describe as an ordinary semi-casual suit of dreary city grey, his hair a severe and regulated black that must surely have been dyed.

"And I," she concluded, "I am Star Girl."

"Okay," I said. "Um—hello."

To this day I am not sure what was going through my mind at that introduction. Maybe it even helped me cut through my frozen brain a little. There was something so strange about it, such a sense of unreality that it paradoxically made things easier. After all, in dreams one can function—it is reality where things break down. And were these people real?

"Welcome to our strange little house," someone said. I think it was the Philosopher.

"Yes," Star Girl agreed. "Come and sit down—and let's make you at home. I have been trying to get him to explain why he was lying on the railway in a black sheet—but not getting very far yet."

"Well don't force him," someone said. "He can tell us when he's ready."

"Humankind has committed many crimes," the Philosopher said with a sonorous theatricality that went well with the candlelight. "It has done things and not done things, many things, many unforgivable. It has prohibited the harmless and encouraged the harmful—and one of the worst things it has done is lost the will to listen. Even to itself, but especially to others. But we are here to atone for that if you wish." He gave a low laugh. "That's the funny thing—all too often you have to search for reality between the cracks—when the mundane has lost all sense of it. Am I right?"

"Too fucking right," Star Girl said. "Those wankers up there," she gestured to the curved ceiling, "don't care one single solitary shit about any of this. You could die on the railways a thousand times and they still wouldn't pay any attention."

There was an uncomfortable silence. Star Girl swallowed. "Sorry—I didn't mean to be blunt . . ."

I finally settled into a vacant armchair, trying to fold my body into it while still remaining rigid. "Don't worry about it," I murmured. It was true enough.

"Would you like something to drink?" someone asked. I think it was the Butcher. His gesture encompassed a bottle of wine standing on a box nearby, but the thought of more alcohol made me cringe.

"Just some water would be nice," I said. "I had rather too much gin yesterday so . . ."

There was another awkward silence, but the Butcher quickly grabbed a bottle of mineral water out of a cooler and poured me a glassful.

"Yeah—I forgot. Get this down you."

In contrast to Star Girl, his voice had a slightly posh twang to it, which felt a little out of place down here in this candlelit cave. Indeed, in appearance, he looked like an overgrown kid—still a hint of the schoolboy about him, visible in the roguish grin that sometimes flooded his face under neat pale hair. The sort of face that might still be happy to get up to mischief or snigger wildly at the cruder kinds of joke.

As I sipped, part of the conversation shifted away from me, much to my relief. The Butcher and the Beggar were soon talking about something among themselves, but Star Girl seemed to feel the responsibility of the host.

"So who are you?" she asked me at last.

"Well . . ."

"Ah—not your name. We don't have names here—you will have noticed. I mean really, who are you?" The Philosopher also leaned over with interest and I stared at them wondering what to say.

"I am . . ." I managed, then broke off, staring at the nearest candleflame. "Well, not much really . . ."

"It is so hard for people to define themselves," he said. "If you say, I am a this or I am a that then it's probably a lie—but on the other hand, if you define yourself with nothing then it's also going to be a lie."

"What do you love?" Star Girl prompted, taking a glass of wine for herself.

I had no idea what to say. There is little love left at times like these. It's hard to even remember what it feels like.

"There must be something," she prompted with a smile.

"Trains?" I suggested rather lamely, then paused. No no no. "I love exploring the city," I said shyly. "Mapping it. I love the backstreets—the places where you see the arse ends of buildings rather than the facades. The crevices where you can . . . almost hide. The places where you can really . . . taste this . . . place . . ."

I broke off. That was quite a speech to come out of me and I was genuinely surprised to hear it. Both of them were staring at me curiously.

"The arse ends of buildings?" Star Girl repeated, a small mischievous smile spreading across her face.

"You like the reality that lurks beneath the public façade?" the Philosopher tried. "That is interesting. And maybe with people too? What people really are rather than the performance they put on?"

But my eloquence had dried up again now. As far as people were concerned I really couldn't find any words or phrases at all.

"I dunno . . ." I stammered, withdrawing behind my glass of water.

"Are you hungry?" the Butcher asked.

"Yes of course," Star Girl chimed in. "I was forgetting. You want some food?"

I wasn't sure actually—my stomach still felt as fragile as my head, in spite of the pills.

"It might help settle you a bit," the Beggar said, reading my mind—and I nodded in agreement. Her voice was soft and pleasant—a little on the deep side and very gentle. It soothed me.

"Yeah—thanks."

"What kind of food?" someone asked. It was Clay Man. He hadn't said much at all since I came in—sitting there in a silence that felt a bit discomforting. Where the others seemed larger than life, he was the opposite—a grey blank that one could almost forget existed, the reason for his name a complete mystery. Now, though, I focussed on him anxiously. That question had seemed mundane, but the pause that followed caught my attention. Significant. His eyes looked very intense, burning out of that grey like obsidian in the candlelight.

Then the Philosopher smiled a small smile. "I think," he began, "we should trot out our best for our esteemed guest, who so loves the cracks in the world. I think he may find it interesting."

"Well . . ." I began.

"Through the cracks, my friend, remember . . . through the cracks."

"Yeah," Star Girl said. "Why not?"

"I dunno if that would be a good idea," Clay Man said, looking distinctly uncomfortable.

"Yeah—but that's all we . . ."

"And why not?" Star demanded. "For fuck's sake it's not that big a deal."

There was a really weird atmosphere in the room now and I stared round from face to face, trying to find some clue as to the reason. But then the Beggar answered my question by reaching into the cooler and producing—something wrapped in a clear plastic bag. As far as I could tell in the warm light, it was a dull pink. It took me a moment to realise what it was, and when I did I felt my skin prickle.

"Is that—meat?" I asked, feeling stunned.

I shouldn't have been so surprised, really. After all, it was common knowledge that meat still circulated in shadowy places beneath normal attention—which this place certainly seemed to be. In fact, things were finally beginning to make a little sense—the anonymity, the concealment—perfect for illegal activity. A carnivore ring, as the newspapers called them. But it was still a shock to come face to face with it. I just stared at it—dull pricklings of emotion coursing through a mind that was totally exhausted emotionally.

"I told you it was a bad idea," Clay Man muttered, staring at me intently, but the Philosopher only shrugged.

"You never had it before then?" the Beggar asked.

"No. Where did you get it?" I asked, curious in spite of the instinctive reaction of uneasy revulsion. Clay Man smiled thinly, but that was all.

I glanced around at the faces that surrounded me, wondering what the heck I had got into. Should I be nervous?

"But look," Clay Man said, leaning closer. "Don't tell anyone about this. Otherwise your life really won't be worth living."

There was an immediate sense of discomfort in the room. "Oh come on," the Beggar protested. I just stared at him in silence. Given that only the previous night I had been waiting to die on the railway line, his threat meant almost nothing. It did derail my train of thought though and I glanced round, quietly analysing again whether it was time to leave.

Who would I tell anyway?

"Okay okay," Clay Man said crossly. "I'm just trying to be careful."

"We need all the friends we can find," Star Girl said with a frown.

"Yes but . . ."

"You took a risk with me as well, remember," the Beggar said. "I don't remember you threatening me. Aren't we all, sort of, in the same boat here?"

"The fewer people involved, the less chance of things going wrong," Clay Man grumbled.

"Oh for gawd sake," Star Girl snapped. "The state he was in, I doubt he even knows where we are. And why the fuck would he be a problem?" Then she gave me an apologetic look.

I made up my mind.

"Hmmm," I said standing up, "excuse me—I think I should probably just go. And you needn't worry." Any thought of staying here had faded now. In my head I was analysing the route I would have to take—back down the railway line, which I vaguely remembered, and then a short walk to a certain bus stop. But everyone was looking at me with a whole range of expressions on their faces.

"Sit down," Star Girl ordered. Clay Man was looking a little sulky, the Beggar worried. Then the Philosopher coughed politely.

"I would just like to point out," he said gently, "that whether you are rude or friendly, he is here before us and you cannot alter that fact. Therefore, if our new friend is here, he will presumably leave again at some point in the future. And as this is a practically inescapable fact, it would be preferable if he leaves us with a good impression. And therefore," he stood up in a flurry of black coat and extended a hand in my direction, which I reached out and shook dazedly, "we may as well let our true natures reign—and be welcoming."

"Seconded," Star Girl said with a laugh. And to my amazement, she also reached out and shook my hand, then glanced pointedly at Clay Man. He pulled a face.

"Okay," he mumbled. "Yeah . . . Yeah. I suppose . . ."

He also gave me a rather fumbling handshake and sat down again.

The Philosopher quietly poured glasses of red wine, handing one to me and one to Clay Man.

"The world is a much simpler place when a little drunk," he said softly. "Both of you. And possibly more real sometimes, given the unreality of the world around us. What a pity it is that this new reality cannot be dragged forth into our sober lives, though at least we get the chance to see it better."

"Maybe it can," the Beggar said, taking a glass herself.

The Philosopher shrugged. "It is possible of course, but relaxation often requires a majority consensus. And that's the hard part."

I took a drink—a little reluctantly since I still felt sick, but at the same time not wanting to be unsocial. The wine was rich and warm—a Shiraz. Many times nicer than the cheap gin I had forced down last night. I still felt wary, but it almost immediately seeded a hint of warmth inside me.

But still—I found my eyes being drawn back to the meat on the table. It sat there incongruously—a strange touch of the macabre in all this conviviality. Pink and bloody.

"What is . . . what was it? Is it?" I asked awkwardly.

"Rabbit," the Beggar said. "Would you like to try some?"

"I—"

It didn't look very appetising. Not even slightly.

"It's good eating," she said. "And you look hungry."

That last was true enough, I realised. It had been a long time since any kind of food had passed my lips. But however hungry you are, food has to be, well, edible. Something of that must have appeared on my face for Star Girl gave a slightly impatient grunt.

"Ach—all these same old arguments," she said, "over and over. Just forget the crap. It's not radioactive. It's food—always has been."

I smiled, feeling very awkward, but prevailing wisdom always stated that if you eat this forbidden substance, your lower intestine will tie itself into knots and eject itself through your anus in sheer revulsion . . . or something.

Star Girl held up the packet. "Okay, okay," she said, still frowning slightly. "Never mind. No one's forcing you to eat anything of course, but while you're agonising, let's get cooking, Butcher. I'm hungry even if no one else is."

The Butcher grinned and stood up. "With pleasure," he said, taking it. "I will cook up something that goes down well after a heavy night." He whisked it away and into the other room, where I remembered the stove was located. Star leaned back in her chair and I watched her uneasily. Such a tone of voice pretty much shut my mouth as sure as duct tape, though I wasn't quite sure how I had managed to annoy her. I guess she must have been able to read that in my face though, for she sighed.

"Fuck," she muttered. "Sorry. I didn't mean to have a go at you. The whole situation just gets on my wick, it really does. It's so stupid."

"'s okay," I mumbled, still confused. I wanted to ask what. To try and work out precisely what was bugging her—but I didn't dare.

"You going to try some then?" she asked. "If not we have other things. No worries . . ."

". . . Yes. Sure." Still mumbling.

"Excellent," Star said with a grin, then jumped up and followed the Butcher to the doorway. "And please don't mind me. I am just an angry bitch."

I suppose some people might be shocked at me—but why exactly would you expect me to refuse? It's not that I was especially rebellious back then, I just didn't care much what anyone thought. The world was barely real to me, after all, and the only thing I cared about was my own death, which is a surprisingly liberating state, so it seemed utterly irrelevant to me to justify myself in my head to any external opinions. I had reached a place where norms and standards of behaviour only retained the most superficial influence, with the deeper emotional levels entirely severed. If these people wanted to feed me a forbidden food, then I really couldn't bring myself to care.

The Beggar stood up and slid herself into the chair that Star had vacated. Next to me. This was the first time I had taken a real look at her—and the impression I got was of surprising gentleness. No particular rough edges or darkness, as I might have expected from her name. Grey eyes that felt unexpectedly haunting under a tangle of carelessly trailing brown hair—and one of those rather angular faces that seem ever so slightly stretched forwards, her sharp nose becoming a probe that led the way wherever she went. A simple, unadorned face that, in a quiet way, seemed to glow slightly. I watched her nervously—disproportionately pleased that she had decided to sit by my side, but nervous that I would be compelled to converse—and the possible consequences of that.

"If you don't mind me asking," she said, "and tell me to shut up if you like—but why did you . . . want to . . . die?"

It was a different kind of question to the one Star Girl had asked. She finally got that last word out as though it was something dirty that her tongue clamped down on. But that was superficial—a basic taboo that most of us probably share. That which must not be talked about, like so many things that are actually good to talk about.

"You seem wounded somehow," she said, and I stared at her with my eyebrows up. "I mean—almost physically?"

Was I? In the past I had definitely been wounded. I could remember that. I remembered times when I had raved and stormed about my apartment, punching walls until my hands were bruised—when I had cut my arms and had lain there in blood-soaked sheets—when I been physically unable to talk for days at a time. But more recently that had all faded rather. It felt as though the wounds had healed a bit, but looking back at those dark days, I now wonder whether I had only gone lower—to a place where the pain of existence was so crippling that I had broken through into a flat serene numbness. A death in all but actuality.

Of course, I couldn't say much of this aloud, and I have no idea how much might have been conveyed anyway. Suicide was a matter of logic, I said, or something like that. Not emotion, not damage. It was just the quiet realisation of what was inevitable.

The Beggar watched me. Those grey eyes. Curious and sad. The sort of eyes that felt as though they could read down to my soul. Maybe it didn't matter what stumbling phrases came out of my mouth. Maybe it was all unreal. Looking back on it, it must have been dismaying to her, because I was as good as saying I would try again—that it had to happen. Maybe the fact that I can't remember her response is because she had no response to give to that.

And all the while I was aware of the Philosopher listening in unselfconsciously as well. He, likewise, didn't say anything.

Also, a smell was filling the room that I couldn't ignore. A pungent warm cooking smell, the likes of which I had never smelt before and that gave me a very strange mixed feeling inside. There was something about that smell that chilled me, but at the same time there was the warmth of cooking that was reminding me how long it had been since I had eaten. I frowned—reminding myself just what this was, another part of me yanking hard with hunger. Think of your own least favourite food, one that really makes you cringe, being cooked in the most appetising way you can imagine and making your stomach rage . . .

"It's okay," the Beggar said at last. "Talking is good—maybe silence is as well sometimes. Just—well . . . just know that either option is fine. If it helps."

I smiled, and then there was a flurry of movement as the others twitched the curtain aside and stepped back in.

"For our honoured guest," the Butcher said with a grin, suddenly appearing behind me and leaning over, causing my eyes to flicker upward sharply. He placed a warm plate into my hands. The smile went awkward and I stared at it, something turning over inside. I had accepted this without much thought but now I came to see it I felt a clench somewhere in my chest and stomach. This was meat then. Seared, brown, slightly fibrous-looking—flesh.

The Butcher had done a good job cooking it—that much was clear. It was accompanied by a light salad and what I eventually worked out was lightly fried bread, not filled with oil but moistened with some kind of sauce that smelled beautiful, before being crisped on the outside. The whole thing looked easily as good as anything you might see in a fine restaurant.

Except for the meat.

I was aware of everyone's eyes watching me—the Beggar anxiously, Clay Man sharply and a little warily, the Philosopher with clinical interest.

"You'll feel better," the Beggar said with a smile.

Maybe. I wasn't sure though. I didn't want it. Everything in me rejected the thought of eating flesh—almost with a physical clenching of all my internal organs. It was flesh that equated too well with the flesh of these people around me—even of myself. Of Star Girl as she dropped her arse heavily back into a chair with a well-filled plate of her own. It was hard to define why, in spite of all the shouted ideologies that filled the world on all sides—but it came with a huge **no** that filled every fibre of my being. And yet—you remember what I said earlier about imagining your least favourite food? It was a war. And what tipped it, I am sorry to say, was the self-effacing feeling of not wanting to fly in these people's faces—a nervousness—a simple desire to avoid confrontation, even to fit in. In spite of any amount of careless due to utter despair.

I cautiously forked one of the gleaming chunks and dipped it in the sauce.

"Remember," the Philosopher said, his voice with that same theatrical and sonorous tinge. "That," he pointed, "that is a primeval thing—a thing that brought us out of the trees, that brought us up onto two legs, that maybe even helped bring us culture and community. It is a part of what we are—a part of our deepest natures. It lurks at the depths of our intelligence and our social lives."

I stared at him in amazement, fork suspended somewhere between plate and mouth. Some of that went straight over my head, but enough didn't to confuse my emotions completely. He was performing—of course he was. He was being playfully dramatic. He sat there as though delivering a lecture, a slightly self-satisfied smile on his face, eyes gleaming under his battered old top hat.

And meanwhile the plate on my knees was steaming gently, its smells confusing my nose.

Star Girl giggled rather harshly, grabbing a chunk and shoving it in her mouth. "Ban this, ban that," she said, with a similar sense of theatrics. "Ban everything. If we work hard enough and ban enough things, we might stop being human entirely—and wouldn't that be just great. Fuck them."

"Please don't," the Butcher put in dryly. "That would be just . . . wrong."

"Alright sod them," Star Girl corrected with a grin. "Screw them. To hell with them. A plague on them." She chomped her mouthful and chewed. "Fucking delusional cunts," she said with startling bitterness.

"That tends to be how Star contributes to these discussions," the Butcher said with a teasing smile. Star gave him a sour look. "Star has what you might call some fundamental philosophical differences with the official position in this matter," he explained, flicking a handsome eyebrow in my direction. "As do we all, I suppose. Star does not like absolutism and . . ."

"Who the fuck does?"

". . . and she is sore that the powers that be decided to fix all our problems by following some, shall we say, rather questionable ideas. That's about the size of it, right?"

"I guess so," Star said with a shrug. "I mean, are these veggie vegan whatever morons seriously trying to tell me that our natural diet is somehow 'wrong'?"

"Oh," I said with a frown. Part of me was wanting to try and argue but unable to find the words in the face of her sharp expression.

"Fuck that," Star growled, but with a dash of humour now. "It's fucking insane. What they did—the stupid laws I mean—it was never really about fixing anything. That was just an excuse. You don't fix things by going all absolutist and arguing over whether eating figs fits your ideology or whatever."

"People have always wanted to believe they are above nature," the Philosopher ploughed on. "Or—that the moralities that clothe us are somehow superior. One can maybe trace that back to certain Christian beliefs that see nature as something vile and base that we must strive to rise above. Or . . . maybe not. It is a pretty universal feeling, when you consider it. Our animal natures—sex—food—some of our instincts—all must be invalidated as far as possible. I speculate, however, that when nature and ethics start to contradict, there is a certain arrogance about assuming the ethics are correct."

The Beggar coughed politely. "It's getting cold," she murmured.

That was true enough. I let all that talk come and go—confused but with no particular agreement or argument in my mind. As I said, it may be that under other circumstances I might have reacted to it differently. Like everyone else, I shared the instinctive revulsion against meat that is hammered into most of us from an early age. But if they were trying to seduce me with philosophy, it wasn't going to achieve much. It hardly seemed relevant. Not here at road's end. Some strange new drug, some bizarre or obscene activity, a forbidden food, it would all have been nothing more than glimpses through the window of the sealed train I rode through life. So if you readers are expecting me to gag and spit it out in trumpeting horror and revulsion, forget it. As it was, I simply ate and it didn't even seem that significant.

It tasted nice.

So yes—I finished that plateful of rabbit, tasting the unfamiliar material on my tongue and deep in my mind. You who are reading this probably haven't much idea what it was like—unless you have been to an underground party or college dorm, maybe, where some little plate of precious meat has been shared around. Or assuming that the government ban hasn't been lifted yet by the time you read this. But comparing one thing to another is hard. What does blue sound like? What colour is someone sobbing? I might compare it to certain fruit, with a quiet subtle flavour that contains great depth. Or, if you can't switch from sweet to savoury in your head, maybe think of certain mushrooms that have the same trick of subtlety and depth. And yet nothing like either. Not much help, is it?

By the time my plate was finished, the wine was starting to get everyone relaxed. I was still slowly making my way through my first glass, but even so, the warm mood was compelling.

"What do you think?" the Beggar asked.

"Um," I said—that was about all I could come up with. But the Philosopher gave a knowing grin.

"It's a kind of reality," he said again. "A small kind. Maybe we can find a few more for you, if you like. It's what we are here for."

"Sure," Star said. "When you have danced naked on the railway line, or had a good roll in the mud, or primal-screamed from the top of a ruined tower block, or tried a sweaty wrestling match in some dark crevice of the city, or fucked on the beach, or lived in a hole in the ground . . . And why do we have to be so fucking sneaky about everything?" she finished, her voice suddenly going furious again. I stared at her warily. There seemed a lot of rage flowing through her. Considering how kind she had been on the railway line and afterwards, that was slightly surprising—but then, emotions are never simple.

"I don't understand," I murmured—a rather surprising admission to come out of my mouth.

Star Girl leaned forward, her eyes gleaming.

"Reality is what you are missing, Mr Haven't-Thought-of-a-Name-for-You-Yet. Those gaping holes in your reality are why you were fucking lying on that fucking railway line."

The Beggar shifted in her chair at that, slightly uncomfortable, but I didn't really mind Star's blunt talk. I only wished that my brain would function more clearly so I could decide what on earth I made of it all. What even *was* reality?

Before things could get any more complicated though, overhead came the boom of a train—a long one. Out of pure instinct I glanced at my phone. The 20:30 out of the terminus heading east. But it did remind me of the time, and I shifted uneasily, hesitating to speak but left with no choice.

"I am really going to have to go," I said. "I need to get to bed again ready for work in the morning."

Everyone turned to look at me.

"Hmm," Star Girl said reluctantly. "You going to be okay?"

"Yes," I said—though as you can imagine, I wasn't exactly certain about that.

"You should come back," she continued. "And prove it."

"It's your choice of course," the Beggar put in, "but—yes, come back and visit. We'll probably be meeting again on Tuesday."

"Thanks," I said awkwardly, aware on some level that I owed them a lot more than could be covered by that word. "I mean . . . it's been a nice evening, and . . . well . . . and somehow I am still alive, so . . . I don't really know what to say."

Star Girl grinned. "I had better show you the way," she said. "I don't suppose you really know where you are?"

"Actually," I said with a smile, as we all moved back through the curtain and into the dim daylight of the adjoining arch, "I think I do. Overhead is signal LSW85 if I remember right. We are looking down towards what used to be Limehouse Cut before the sea wall was built—with the old Basin somewhere a little to the west—so about four hundred yards from Limehouse Station. Therefore, just the other side of the wall, a little way away, is Commercial Road and where we are at the moment, well, I'm not totally sure which arch it is but I presume we are in what was once either arch seven or eight."

There was a startled silence in the room. Everyone was looking at me with various different expressions on their faces. I should probably not have said all that—I wasn't even sure why I did. Some small need to assert myself and stop playing the pathetic victim? Normally I just keep quiet and wait to move away and onwards. Star Girl in particular looked astonished.

"I almost had to carry you here last night," she said. "How the fuck do you know all that?"

I shrugged. "I just . . . know London I suppose."

The Beggar laughed quietly and Clay Man drew a deep breath.

"Oh boy—now I really do have to kill you," he said. But there was a humorous twinkle in his eye.

"For what it's worth," I said, "the rest of the world doesn't exist. You guys—well, maybe you exist, I'm not sure. So who would I be able to talk to about this except you?" I remember grinning—an unfamiliar muscle motion to me at the time. It was a joke, though I admit a somewhat weird one. Clay Man looked at me with a puzzled expression on his face.

"Well, I'm coming with you anyway," Star Girl said. "Just in case." She stepped over to the ladder, scrambled back up onto the platform, and I followed. Then we made for the hole in the wall.

"See you sometime, right?" the Beggar called after me. I gave a slightly awkward nod and wave back.

Sometime during our talk, the darkness had descended again outside and the curtain was now closed. Star Girl pushed through, taking care to let as little light escape as possible, and scrambled out onto the narrow concrete and metal ledge. I followed her, trying not to worry about the height. I watched her pace away along the top of the sheet piling, heading west, stepping from wide part to wide part with long unconcerned strides. I couldn't see how we were supposed to get off this ledge again, but I followed without a word, and a few tens of metres down, she came to a stop. Here, the smooth brick wall of the viaduct itself that had been looming over us was disrupted—no doubt where some structure had been demolished to make way for the sea defences. Star Girl stared up thoughtfully and I realised that this must be the way up to the level of the rails, about six feet above—with the help, I now noticed, of a strong knotted rope. Again, the question of how on earth I had managed to make this journey while drunk close to insensible was hammering at me.

Even as we stared up, a long intercity train came screaming in from the distance and we ducked down again into a crouch. "Fuck me," Star Girl muttered, "I never checked the timetable. I suppose we will just have to run for it and hope we are not seen, unless you want to go back?"

"Give it a few minutes," I said with a grin. "That was the 20:54 arrival—the 20:45 departure will be along in a moment. Then we have a quarter of an hour gap before the 21:00 comes by."

She looked at me in surprise.

"So—ummm—you know the times of all the trains on this line? Seriously."

I couldn't resist boasting a little. After the pathetic show I had put on earlier, I felt I almost had to. "I know the times of every passenger train in the city," I said quietly—trying to be casual. "And a good many of the regular freight trains."

"Wow," she said. "Okay—that's a fucking weird skill. Are you a trainspotter or something then?"

"Not really—"

She gave a low laugh. "I think we shall call you Train Man," she said. "How the fuck do you know all this?"

Train Man? I thought with a smile. I kind of liked that.

"I just . . . know how the city works. I know the buses as well, as far as you can—and the roads themselves. I guess it's my 'thing'—you remember the Philosopher trying to get me to define myself with something?"

"The roads?"

"Yup."

She grinned with a hefty dose of mischief. "Okay, this is fascinating. So directly over there—on the other side of the tracks—is what?"

"Ummm—Island Row and Wharf Lain I think. Am I right?"

An incredulous look. "I'm not actually sure—but I think so."

I flinched as she dropped down casually, her arse landing on the concrete and her feet dangling into space. I joined her in an uncomfortable crouch. It was a long time since I had cared enough to be embarrassed about anything, but now I wondered whether I should be—the contrast of her seemingly perfectly functioning body and me, worn down, fat and unfit. Her relaxed legs that folded her in half without effort and me stiff and awkward and frosty . . . I found myself studying those legs, relaxed and slightly flattened against the concrete but I guessed ready to move in ways I had never been able to move in my entire life.

I chased that thought away and stared out at the buildings, the constellation of lights of Canary Wharf beyond, the abandoned and ruined places like black standing stones in the mud and sea grass.

"So what do you think, Train Man?" she said at last. "Dare I ask?"

"About?"

"About us," she said with a doubtful smile that didn't disguise her seriousness. "I wonder—are you shocked?"

"Well . . ."

"I think you are. After all my blather. But you know—maybe that's not such a bad thing. I like shocking people. The world needs a shock. Really really fucking needs it. Pow!—right in its dreams and delusions. Right where it hurts."

She gave a grin that was decidedly non-humorous. Then she reached out and plucked a small plant from where it was growing in the wall. It came up by its roots in a scattering of soil and concrete fragments. I had no idea what it was—just some city weed, as far as I was concerned.

"Do you feel connected to nature?" she asked at last, twirling the plant under her nose.

"I suppose not," I said reluctantly. "But surely, in this city . . ."

She shrugged.

"Not many are," she said. "And I mean the nature in yourself as well as anything outside. Maybe that's even harder. Any fucker can sit in a field—but to get within your own head and find your own identity, then to be it without fear . . ."

She abruptly bit down on the plant, removing about half of it and chewing gloomily.

She held it out to me.

"Chickweed," she said. "Try it."

I stared at the little green sprig for a moment, then took it gingerly. She gave a sudden laugh. "You look almost as dubious as you did when the Beggar first shoved that meat under your nose."

That was a discomforting remark and I took a very cautious nibble. It had a mild salad taste that was not at all unpleasant, but even so, I settled for the absolute minimum tentative amount that politeness would allow me before handing it back.

"All I want is to reconnect with what I am," she said with a shrug. "It's not just about food. I am sick of other people trying to tell me what to be. I need to be honest with myself. I need to say *this is what I am*, not a continuous shitstorm of *this is what I ought to be*."

"I . . . suppose," I said softly.

She stared sourly down into the Soak, and the remains of the chickweed fell from her fingers into the mud below.

"I apologise if I get a bit defensive sometimes," she said. "But . . . it's kind of hard not to, you know. Our bodies, our food, our attitudes, our interests, what turns us on . . . we're told to be paranoid about this, guilty about that, afraid of something else. Censorship—prudery—laws—repression . . . blah blah. These people are essentially saying there's something wrong with you. *Me*. I am defective. Repugnant. How else can you respond other than . . . getting furious?"

It was quite a speech, delivered in an intense mutter staring out into the darkness. I didn't know what to say.

"Sorry," she said with a half-smile on her face. "As I said, sometimes it gets me wild."

She was staring at me, her eyes almost glowing now.

"That is why everyone is so angry, whether people know it or not," she said. "You can feel the rage here in London . . . flowing down every street, or behind every conversation. Online, offline. Of course, some people blame the wrong targets—that's far too easy. But the rage is there. Can't you feel it in this city, since you seem to know so much about it?"

I was silent. In all honesty, I couldn't say I had—but I could here and now. The sense of rage in her seemed completely alien to me—so much so that I wanted to retreat back down the wall a little way. Instead I watched her, feeling riveted.

"Maybe it will erupt one day," she said, her voice going quieter. "Maybe then . . . well it would be nice to be what we are for once . . ."

She paused and stared out at the darkness of the Soak. She seemed deflated now, her moment of anger past. "I can dream, can't I?" She sighed, looking rather unhappy now. Behind us there was a rising roar and a small commuter train came past, accelerating out of the city.

"The 21:00?" she asked.

I nodded.

"Okay, this way," she said, scrambling back up and grabbing the rope. She hauled herself up and over the parapet and then stood watching anxiously as I followed. Then she took my arm and we hurried along the tracks towards the west. The sight of the dark rails, gleaming threads of silver, inevitably brought back memories of the previous night. Or was it two nights ago? I honestly wasn't sure. But I remembered the sense of calm and correctness as I lay there, metal ice-cold against my neck—and in my head was the question: now what? Maybe it was still the right destination in spite of the delay. I wasn't sure though—there was a question mark that hadn't been there before. And I looked forward to getting home and trying to work that out.

A few dozen yards down the line, she paused and took something from inside her coat that gleamed in the dark. It was her knife—the same blade she had been carrying since way back when she fell over me in the dark. I watched curiously as she took it by the blade and slung it as far as she could out into the deep water of the old Limehouse Basin.

"I buy a new one each time," she said with a smile. "Better than being nicked for carrying. Then it can be still in its blister pack with a packet of mushrooms until I actually need it. People have been hassled and arrested even for carrying screwdrivers on the streets of this fine city."

Then we crossed the tracks. Here a second viaduct, ancient and abandoned, branched off inland—the old Limehouse Curve. And it was here, in the narrow wedge between the two, where other structures had been demolished, that the way down was possible. It was considerably less friendly this side of the line with massive fences wherever a fence could possibly be. But an unobtrusive hole let us through and then it was little more than stepping or lightly jumping from one ruined mass of bricks to another until we found ourselves in the claustrophobic darkness of the footpath that had been built directly along the landward side of the sea wall viaduct, presumably to make up for all the routes that had been severed so brutally. Then it was only a short walk to the Regent's Canal towpath, emerging by the huge watergate or tidal lock. I stood for a moment, catching my breath again, gritting my teeth in self-hate. How she managed to move with such agility was beyond me. Like many other things on that day, anger was not something I had been overly familiar with, but now I did feel a bit angry. The comparison between me and her was so blatant that it was farcical and my mouth turned down at the corners.

"You going to be okay now?" she asked. "Go down that way a little to the next road and you will come to a bus stop."

"Yes, definitely," I said. "The number 135." Star Girl gave a wry smile.

"Okay—why I thought you needed any directions, I have no idea. Any trains coming that I should know about for the return trip, Mr Train Man?"

I glanced at my phone. "Wait until about 21:32," I said. "Then you will have a thirteen minute window before the 21:40 comes past from the terminus. Then hopefully nobody will see you."

A quiet laugh. "Okay then—I will wait in a little place I know back up there in the bricks. You get along home, but don't go living up to your name any other way, will you. I don't want to fall over you again on any bloody railway tracks. Especially in pieces."

I found myself smiling. It was a macabre joke, some might think, but I appreciated her attitude.

"And come back here," she said. "I'm not really such a menace—I'm just the fucking dewy-eyed revolutionary that the wingnuts all love to hate so much."

I had to chuckle.

"Come back on Tuesday and prove to me you are still alive."

Then to my surprise she gave me a quick hug and a kiss on the cheek. I stood rather frozen as she ruffled my arm, then she seemed to disappear almost instantly into the dark of the footpath.

I slowly turned away, feeling that hug glowing gently in the darkness. However, it was beginning to dawn on me that I was now alone in London, in an obscure place, at night. The fear of the night these days was probably mostly media-generated—a whipped-up unease as the ratio of homeless to homed people increased and increased, easily transformed into an 'underclass' whom one could reasonably expect not to be very friendly with the city that had spat them out. After all, I had neighbours at home who were always out at night, up to all sorts of things from street art to scavenging. I had never heard of anything happening to them. But it was still a little nerve-wracking and I quickly started walking, looking around the silent towpath and making for the busier, more illuminated areas. Whether the rumours were true or false, I was fairly sure it was not very sensible to stand still in obscure corners of London and run the risk of being checked out by either the law enforcement or the people they were theoretically supposed to be enforcing it on. So I got moving, leaving the towpath and entering the streets. Here was a world of what had once been rather drear and ordinary urban houses now succumbing to decay—badly maintained streets, scattered rubbish and apartments even more depressing than my own. A darkness dwelt here—a stale whiff in the air. Windows seeming black with grime. Very little sign of life or movement, save for the occasional throb of music from some indefinable direction.

It seems that as you increase the depth of your home below sea level, you also increase the depth below humanity. That is probably a new measure of social inequality around the world that never existed before the sea started rising seriously. House prices, which had always been essentially irrational and commodified, suddenly tied to elevation? How proud we can be that human nature reacted to the crisis so efficiently as to make everywhere above the waterline more expensive. And conversely, everywhere below became the domain of the dregs—the underclass, or at least so the media would have us believe.

Somewhere overhead, a single red light gleamed. I watched it for a moment, trying to work out what it was. It didn't move—and there was no sound of engines. Maybe it was a tower crane hidden in the darkness? Though if so, it was a bright one. It watched me like an eye as I fled that place—then quietly winked out.

And a few minutes later, I was on a train heading north through a tranquil procession of city—trees, looming buildings, glimpses of streets filled with restaurants, shops, bars, fast food. People. There was still a bustle of life down there—people passing in and out of restaurants offering a huge range of vegetarian cuisine. It was good to lay back in the seat and watch the world going past. I enjoy riding any form of London transport—anything that gets me around the city. But trains, of course, are king. I like travelling, you see—I like travelling and watching—I like knowing London. It's my thing, as I said. I don't have any spectacular motive for my obsession other than that I want to know this city—to understand every crack and crevice. But these days I must admit it is more fun if I don't have to walk. I never used to be this unfit—it crept up on me, motivation destroyed by stress and gloom. I even owned a bike, currently lurking somewhere in the storage area at home, but I hardly ever used it.

I didn't put the light on when I arrived. Private darkness is darker than public darkness, but even here familiarity and the city glow outside was enough to help me find my way up and through, past the sleeping figures of Kate and Aceline on their beds, screens left open again. In spite of my care, Kate moaned under her breath and rolled over, so I hastily bolted for my own room on tiptoe and slipped inside.

MONDAY

I . . . think . . . I am sure I was tied down.
  Tied . . . ?
  Yeah—straps. On my hands and feet. Maybe one around my waist. I must have been. I vaguely remember struggling against it but I couldn't move. It was probably to stop me thrashing around and damaging anything. I . . . was lying there in wet sheets. I must have . . . wet myself. I think. It was pretty horrible.
  So what they gave you was making you . . .
  I thought I was being eaten. (Laugh)
  I'm sorry?
  Yes. Things were—all over me, burrowing into my body. Like those hyperactive little Amazon fish that get inside you and eat you from within. Such vivid dreams. I don't know what that stuff was supposed to do—but it sure had a weird effect.
  So the test was a failure?
  I suppose. I hope so. Though maybe they learned something. It was three days before they let me go. And then I had to limp across the city on the tube. I was so wet with sweat by the time I got home that I looked as though I had been in the Thames. And it wasn't until the next day that my girlfriend spotted the small scars on my back.
  Surgery?
  Yes—tiny. Keyhole. Though I don't know what for.

You mean—you underwent surgery in the London Labs . . . without knowing about it?

It must have been when I was out of it. Maybe those things that were eating me were . . . well, maybe it caused me to dream.

And didn't you have to sign some sort of agreement? Surely . . .

I might have—there was so much paperwork and I was rather bewildered when I first got there. And then high the rest of the time.

I see. Can I ask . . . in general, were the London Research Laboratories careful? Did they do their best to keep you safe?

I suppose so—in an impersonal sort of way. They gave me a very thorough check-up. They even gave me the report to take home, which was nice of them. Though I am sure there's better ways to discover that my blood pressure is a bit high. (Laugh)

And now? How do you feel now?

Well—more or less back to normal I guess. I can go out again without feeling exhausted . . .

So—how do you feel about all this? I mean . . . this is a controversial area. Technically it's all voluntary, but . . .

I . . . dunno. I mean . . . there's no good options when you get in that situation. All the possibilities can ruin your life. It honestly might as well be a death sentence once you get chucked out of the basic job market and housing becomes impossible. So this one . . . well, the element of chance feels weird. As though they are playing some kind of game with you. But at least you might come through it okay.

And is it hard to talk about now?

It's hard because . . . I know that a certain portion of your listeners won't care. They will have already written me off as worthless. They'll be glad I was lying there in my own piss. Maybe even wish the test had *gone worse . . . so maybe I would never have come home. That's what they say. I see it all the time on the internet. Same old, same old . . .*

Um . . .

But . . . I suppose one always wants to communicate. You always want to tell your story, right?

Yes. That is true. And one last question . . .

Yes?

If you don't mind . . . what crime did you commit?

I made a noise that was half way between a groan and a wail and shut the video off, shut the social network down, filling my world with merciful silence. This was the morning after to end all mornings after and the last thing I needed was sickly miserable reality barging in with its attendant sense of dread and despair. I was still in bed, my eyes prickling with tiredness, every part of my body feeling heavy and painful. I looked round the room without much happiness at everything I had hoped never to see again. According to all my plans, I should be dead now—asleep in a vast infinity of nothingness. Switched off. The candle out. Asleep perchance never to dream again. And I very much hoped there was no afterlife to interfere with that oblivion. But here was the familiar room, recently tidied up and organised but still far too mundane and normal. And that normality stretched in front of me as though the road I was supposed to follow had been engulfed by a dust storm. I would now have to get up surrounded by normality—eat normal food, go to normal work, pass normal people, feel normal things . . .

I have failed.

And the whole road would now have to be walked a second time. I just closed my eyes again and those three words repeated over and over.

Failed.

Leaden thoughts. It seems a fundamental flaw in the human animal that suicide should be so hard when as a culture we make so sure that it is inevitable.

- A plate of meat.
- A glitter of rage in a pair of eyes as their owner ranted at me, while the cold of the concrete ate up into both our arses on the nighted sea wall.
- A hug.

A dream of drunkenness as I waited on the railway for a train that presumably never came. Strange dreams for strange days.

Home is something I suppose I am going to have to describe to you, though you will have to forgive me for keeping quiet about the actual location, of course. I wish I could tell you which little area of the city I lived in, so I could go off on long flowery descriptive and analytical passages about what it is that makes it individual, just as every little patch of London seems to have its own soul—but instinct insists on paranoia and the secretive as the default, so I must refrain. My own place wasn't so individual though. It was situated in a small blind road-thing in a deep city canyon about fifty metres long hemmed in by old buildings and street art. I live at the end of it, okay? It's not a Street, certainly not a Road. Certainly not a Place or Avenue either. It's a stub. A withered appendix to this part of the city's digestive system. And I say that without any massive hatred. I lived in one room in one apartment on one floor of an old building that certainly hadn't been designed to be lived in. I have no idea what it once was. Old office space? Warehouses? Both? But at some point in its history, the ingredients of private residences had been shoehorned into it. Rooms were subdivided, new doorways knocked through—or not as the case may be. Corridors were long and empty because nobody really wanted to take responsibility for beautifying them. Even the edgy and paranoid graffiti seemed scarce here. A nasty smell came drifting in from the communal toilet and a faint hint of old brick and stale clothes pervaded the place. That all sounds unappetising, but to be honest, it was not something I cared about much, or even noticed. There is something comforting about mess, after all. Especially when it is not your own. It exonerates you from the need to spend your life worrying about appearances or feeling guilty when housemates whinge.

One of the basic rules of life: always live with people slightly messier than yourself.

My own room—well, what can I say? It was one of the more awkwardly placed ones, opening onto another occupied room rather than the corridor. There was a bed in it, a table, a small microwave oven, a rail on poles that someone for a joke had called a wardrobe and which I had hung with elegant lengths of fabric in an attempt to disguise its basic end-of-any-meaningful-kind-of-civilization vibe. Indeed, there was quite a lot of fabric randomly hanging around the place, on the principle that anything is better than a blank cube. A small computer by my bed, which could be turned to face either chair or pillow, provided a connection to the outside world considerably more than the door did. I had kept that machine going for a long long time in a way that reminded me of the old (false) saying that the human entity replaces literally every cell in its body every seven years. So are we still the same person? Is it the same computer? The Ship of Theseus paradox or something.

I could have lain there forever, until civilization crumbled, until London faded to dust. *Oh you lazy fucker,* the alarm clock said reproachfully. *Do you know you've slept right through work? That's the second day you've missed without telling them.* Did it matter? Very little mattered when the railway lines beckoned. Not even having the life support system that is your job switched off. That is one of the nice things about it.

Get up, the clock said.

"No," I said aloud. "What's the point?"

The point is that you need the effing bathroom, it explained patiently.

I drew a deep breath, then reluctantly obeyed orders. I didn't leave either my bed or my room very much usually. The bed was the only really comfortable place in the room and the room was the only private place in the entire world. Or so it pretended anyway. In fact, you might even say I was an expert, even a virtuoso at remaining in this room practically indefinitely. But there was that one problem that the clock had so cheerfully outlined. The bathroom was somewhere outside in the hall—beyond where

Kate and Aceline slept. There were ways round this, of course, using bottles and things—and my virtuosity easily encompassed dealing with it with the help of a small sloping roof and a gutter outside my window in ways you probably don't want to know the details of. But even so, it wasn't a permanent solution by any means. So up I got—clothes on, a quick glance in the mirror studying myself briefly and without love, taking in a fat face that seemed permanently set in a grim and off-putting scowl. Hair brush. Some underarm deodorant where underarm deodorant is supposed to go—mustn't frighten my neighbours too much after all—and I stepped out into the gaze of the two pairs of female eyes that always stood between me and the outside world.

My roommates, housemates, buildingmates, people-who-lived-outside-the-door-mates were sprawled on the sofa watching the news quietly burbling on a laptop. It was a scene of domesticity—the floor-standing screens that surrounded their two single beds dragged back, a few used dishes cluttering the table between them, the dregs of a bottle of wine from some vague moment in the past, fag ends in the ashtray, mobile phones cast aside, a vase of flowers, books and papers scattered around . . .

"Morning," Kate said affably enough. "I was wondering where you had got to. You were out bloody late last night."

I smiled, remembering tiptoeing past her in the very large hours.

"Yeah—and then I was sleeping for a long time," I said, truly enough.

"You want to be careful. London isn't safe out there at night. Want some breakfast pasta?"

I glanced at the empty bowls, filled with yellow remnant.

"Thanks," I said, hiding a hint of caution. "Just a little. I still feel a bit rough." Kate waved vaguely in the direction of the kitchen and shifted comfortably. Yes—they had a small kitchen attached to their room. I didn't. I suppose we were supposed to share it, though I rarely liked to exercise that right. It was all a matter of territory, you know. Special treaties allowed me access to their space for the purpose of reaching the hallway, but treaties tended to break down where utilizing the kitchen unit was concerned. Regardless of leanings, food always seems to excite strong opinions.

"Help yourself," she said. "And don't forget your pills."

"I won't."

. . . the [?]-o'clock news, came from the laptop following a suitably garish fanfare. *At least three people have been injured after renewed unrest broke out in Brixton last night with . . .*

I went back for my pills, kept in my bedside cabinet in little batches, each for one day, then slipped into the kitchen, which smelt of a blend of fried mycofillet, fruit and rotten vegetables. I found a bowl—then investigated the ominous-looking saucepan on the stove. The contents were yellow and rather wobbly. It reminded me of a certain bizarre art project I had once seen in which the artist threw up onto a canvas after swallowing various coloured dyes, presumably in some kind of aesthetically relevant way and who am I to argue?

"Just heat it up in the microwave," Aceline called through. I was not sure what the ingredients were since it had all homogenised into an oily cheesy sauce. There were a few mushrooms, and certain squidgy objects might have been slices of courgette. I tried a spoonful. It was salty but edible—cheese can make almost anything edible, I suppose. At the back of my mind though, irritating me with tantalisation, was the memory of the sauce that a certain green-waistcoated gentleman had prepared the previous night.

There had been a touch of the divine in that flavour.

"Hey," Kate said as I rejoined them, swallowing the last of the pills and perching my arse on the very end of the sofa in front of the laptop, "why aren't you at work?"

I frowned at that, then immediately hoped it had gone unnoticed. Good question.

"I—took a few days off to . . . try and recover," I lied.

. . . we are getting tired of living in fear, someone declaimed from the laptop. *Can nobody do anything about these hooligans? Does the law not apply to the underclass or something? Are they allowed to go around raping and mugging everyone? Why doesn't the police do something about it? If they can't or won't then maybe we will . . .*

"Yeah," she said, without much interest. "You seemed a bit . . . down lately. We were getting worried."

I didn't reply to that. 'Down' seemed the only possible state to be in—the only state that made any sense. It was happy people I didn't trust. They had to be either delusional, mentally blind or somehow lying. Probably they had taken government-sponsored acting classes in order to perpetuate the mythology that the world actually worked, that we could all continue slaving away in blind hope—and then had looking happy tied in as a clause on their housing benefit. *Well sir, and now I will just confirm that you have met the required target of public grinning this month. Just give me a moment while I call up the surveillance camera data . . .*

"So what have I missed?" I asked.

"The fucking mice have been having a party in the kitchen," Kate said. "Who left the bread out on the worktop last night?"

"You did," Aceline said with a smile. "We're going to have to get some poison or something. That's all."

Kate gave her a doubtful look. "That's . . . you're not supposed to use . . ."

"Oh come on—everyone does," Aceline snapped. "And I am getting sick of finding mouse shit all over the worktops. That sonic repeller is useless. I swear I can hear them singing along to it some nights." She paused. "I know someone who can get us a good strong poison—I will ask."

The mice never bothered me that much, though I occasionally heard them in my room at night. Maybe it was because I had more or less surrendered the kitchen so it really wasn't my problem. Maybe it was because they seemed to lead better lives than we did.

"Could try foam," I suggested.

"Hmm?"

"Find any holes in the walls and stuff them full of wire wool—then shoot some building foam in there. That ought to block them."

There was a news-infused non-silence for a moment—a presenter talking in front of images of a London building suffering from vaguely police-like symptoms.

. . . the unrest centred around here after the arrest of a young man alleged to have . . .

"You know Tea-Cup in number sixteen?" Kate said, reaching idly for a doughnut and chomping it in a sprinkle of sugar.

"Is she back?" I asked, sitting up.

"Yes she is—a day or so ago. But you know what happened?"

"Hm?"

"Someone burnt her bike last night."

That was strange enough to almost be interesting and I stared in astonishment.

"Yeah," Kate said. "Right in the corridor outside her flat. Outside our fucking flats."

"How can you burn a bike?"

"Must have doused it with something. And nobody knows who did it or why."

"They are going to be for it if anyone finds out though," Aceline put in. "Maintenance are furious. The floor is going to need redoing and the walls repainted. The police were in—criminal damage—which is the last thing we need."

She drew on her fag wearily and I had to smile. Even though this was a rather extreme case, the bickering and weird clashes in this old building were continuous. Inevitably so, I suppose. Personally I preferred to remain well below them and keep quiet and neutral. And watching.

A meat farm in Hackney has been closed down by police following a dawn raid, the news continued in the same totally ordinary end-of-the-world tone of voice. Kate was still talking about something, but at that point I suddenly refocused my attention. The presenter, a dangerously upright-looking woman with plastic hair and a suit I really wanted to throw an egg at, was as emotionless as ever.

Police raided a property in Hackney Wick where several unlicensed animals were kept for the underground meat trade. Police described the conditions as 'appalling' and 'inhuman' and . . .

Kate gave me a reproachful look, finding herself suddenly ignored, and repeated something.

"What's that?" I said.

. . . believe the meat was intended for Turkish and Balkan communities in . . .

"I said, Tea's looking fucking great since she came back," Kate said. "I don't know how she does it."

I bet she was. Though I suspect my judgement in such things was rather clouded.

"Hmmm."

. . . appalling conditions with no daylight and no space to move. Viewers are warned that they may find the following images disturbing . . .

On the screen, the camera was showing an ordinary-looking city building, like many others in Hackney Wick—run down but enlivened with hints of art. I slotted it into my encyclopaedia of the city as being on a certain street I won't tell you near the canal. I swallowed uneasily, for obvious reasons. My mind had frozen, my brain uselessly trying to remember what it could of the place instead of thinking about . . . other stuff. But there was no escaping it. Suddenly yesterday seemed a lot more real. I could remember the taste and texture of flesh in my mouth—the juiciness and, well, meatiness of it . . .

"Horrible," Kate murmured, without paying much attention. The screen was showing a montage of small rooms plastered in mud—or maybe it was animal shit—and pink meat cut up on a table.

"They don't look so different to our place," I said without thinking.

"Well—yeah. But you can't keep animals like that . . ."

Everyone who eats meat, some prominent activist with eyes like a predatory bird said, *deserves to have an equivalent portion of flesh surgically removed from their bodies. I don't expect the government to legislate that, of course, but I consider today's action to be another small step in the right direction.*

"That's the mountains," Aceline said.

"What is?" I asked in bewilderment.

"Tea—so fit."

Kate sighed and glanced down at her somewhat pudgy body.

"I couldn't walk in the mountains to save my life," she muttered gloomily.

Aceline grinned. "You could always join my exercise class."

A different voice: *. . . actually, a fairly obvious consequence of our legislation criminalising the production or consumption of meat was to drive it underground like this, like prohibition in America or the war against drugs. The subject may be unsavoury but I think it is dangerous to simply try and . . .*

I stood up. I couldn't watch any more of this. I was already starting to tremble slightly.

"Excuse me," I murmured, putting the empty bowl down with a bump. "Nature calls. I will wash that up in a moment." I hurried out of the room and into the corridor, feeling an acute relief at the cessation of both company and news. My heart was racing and I felt a leaden sensation in my stomach, the taste of flesh from the previous night all too vivid in my mouth again. I leaned against the wall for a moment, breathing heavily and staring at nothing, then fled to the bathroom, urgently needing to hide away.

Shut securely in the peace of a toilet stall—a place probably more private than my own room when you get down to it—I found myself sitting there, head in my hands. The walls, with their dense texture of scribbled writing and crude sketches, stickers and scratch marks, were spinning round me. What had I done? Even my insides were punishing me now as the urgency that had driven me from my bed in the first place suddenly accelerated into something more dramatic. Cramps gripped my bowels as my shocked and guilty system sought to expel the alien and forbidden substance in a miserable explosion. Oh well—never again, I thought. Never again. Humans had the right to go off the rails occasionally, provided they learned from the experience.

Didn't they?

They'd fucking better.

With a huge sigh I looked up and found myself reading some of the daubing on the walls—crudities, anatomically unlikely sketches, slogans, miserable gender-based sniping, grumbles and complaints. Almost hidden under the chaos, I could even see yet more of the old *meat is murder* stickers from before the law was changed—which only proves how long it was since this place was decorated. I don't remember much about that, of course—I was at college at the time and everything seemed a bit withdrawn and distant. But I remember a lot of petitions and protests, a lot of shouting and violence as the last few specialist restaurants were clobbered. Of course, it hadn't made much difference to me—I had never eaten meat in my entire life. That was the way things were.

That toilet door and cubicle walls, more than any strange goings on of the people that made them, brought a crashing sense of stiflement and gloom. What the fuck was I doing here? Most of the time, I didn't care much about this place I lived in, provided people, government and culture would leave me the fuck alone—but now it suddenly seemed unendurable. How had history and human life and my own existence progressed to the point where I was in this situation? London was a vast sea of these places—one-time houses or industrial spaces subdivided into apartments, then subdivided again into rooms—and sometimes even those split in half with dividing walls until it was a warren of small cupboards. And most of those were supposed to have a double bed in them because, of course, anything other than a family was incomplete. Down by the river, those parts not 'Soaked' anyway, millionaires lived spaciously on the new Sea Wall or the old river views, or overlooked the parks or other swanky areas, but that was the minority. By a long way. London was a hive—the perfect term for it.

Looking up at the gloomy mess of the walls, externalisations of everybody's paranoia and yearnings, I found the call of the train and the thrumming of the tracks loud in my mind again. And suddenly I was furious. Maybe I was simply trying to find some subconscious justification for my carnivorism the night before but fuck the animals, I thought. Why did nobody seem to care what conditions humans lived in? Nobody. Ever. Throughout fucking history, the same problems over and over, and the same utter resistance to ever defeating the greed and selfishness that caused them. Why was I still living here in this place, in a single tiny room and pissing out of the window so I wouldn't have to venture out into public? Yes—hate me for it if you must, and it probably is rather unfair, but that's what I thought. At that moment, I honestly couldn't see much difference between myself sitting here on this stinking toilet and the cut-up pink flesh on the bloody table in Hackney Wick. I was especially furious with Star Girl and the rest from yesterday. If it wasn't for them, I might already have escaped all this. Well it didn't matter. Fuck it all—fuck my jobs, fuck people trying to help, fuck roommates and neighbours, fuck animal rights and associated guilt, fuck everything. I knew what I had to do . . .

☼

Back in the corridor, having washed my face to get rid of any lingering moisture around my eyes, I finally saw the dramatic sight that I had completely failed to notice earlier—the massive burned patch marring the floor a little way down the corridor. I must have been in a state to blank this out. It was a couple of metres long—bike-sized, basically. A volcanic lake of melted plastic flooring and charred wood, roughly fenced off with some ancient orange witches' hats and nylon tape. Scorch marks and blacking writhed up the wall and onto the ceiling. I approached curiously. Sometimes the scent of destruction can be very satisfying. Even profound.

Then click and clunk and the door opened. I flinched rather more than I should have. "Hello," Tea said—or Tea-Cup as some people persisted in calling her. It's pronounced TE-ah, just so you know—derived from Dorothea, I think, and thence related to Dorothy, but Tea somehow managed to sound much more exotic. Her Slovenian accent was sharp-edged and harsh yet very musical—something I always liked. Her face with its prominent cheek-bones, and the flurry of pale brown hair that framed it, always spoke of something faintly exotic as well. Whatever diffuse and seemingly random meaning that word has. I was puzzled, though, because this time she was wearing an eyepatch like a cartoon pirate. I would have assumed it was costume but that didn't sit right, either with the rest of her clothes or her personality.

"Hi," I said, looking at her—a friendly smile plastered on my face.

"I have not seen you since I got back," she said. "How are you doing? Is everything good here?"

"Everything is . . . pretty much as good as ever," I said, unsure whether that was a yes or a no. In some small way, it was as though she was a light filter that had been placed over the world, subtly changing its colour. I don't know if you have ever used digital graphics software, but there is always a control in there where you can tweak the colours—add just a little more red to the overall image maybe. Yes, even now, after all this time, Tea still had that kind of effect. I can't paint a beautiful or idyllic picture though—not even close. This was what you might call the tail-end of an unrequited attachment, when everything has started to turn stale. Have you ever been there? When love is dying after years but with nothing specific to replace it? Those are strange days. The threads snapping and fluttering around loose. Maybe this is a time when logic is starting to win the war against the deeper places. Or maybe it is just rot, pure and simple—proof that no love can sustain itself forever with nothing to feed it. If anything, it is even bleaker and more depressing than the early days when it all burned like magnesium. Sometimes the magnesium is still there, of course. There are still those nights when it all ignites again—a blazing need for connection that is far more than just erotic, no matter what some people say. Then maybe you lie there wanting to claw some physical part out of your body, anything to shut it down. There is a feeling as of some chemical or drug oozing into the brain—a physical cloud that starts as some point deep in the frontal lobes, then slowly floods outwards towards the eyes like food dye in water. I don't believe that is the source of love though—I believe that is where grief lies. As though grief has an actual gland in there. On the other hand, sometimes the whole thing seems dead—sunken and withered by pointlessness. Death becoming a Pavlovian reaction to pain that can rot even human love and sexuality.

And no—I had never told her about any of this. What would be the point? Seriously. Sometimes you have to go along with what your logical mind tells you. Even if there was a miniscule chance of success, which was doubtful, there would be nothing worse than blindly falling into relationships that would never work—the benighted pair running headlong at each other while everyone else can clearly see what a sham it is. I sometimes wondered if she knew anyway, but she never gave any sign.

But what's wrong with your eye? I wanted to ask.

"I am glad to see you," she said. "I was going to invite you to join me tomorrow for a little—gathering. A bite to eat and a chat. Now that I am back. At last."

"That sounds nice," I said, and right then it did. This wasn't something that happened very often around here. Not something I did very often anywhere.

But are you okay? I mean—that eye is . . . ?

"Bring a bottle of something if you care to," she said.

"Yes, sure."

I was about to move the conversation into slightly edgier territory, possibly touching on the bike-shaped ruination, but I never got the chance. The door of my apartment—or rather the girls'—or whatever—opened and we both turned. Our voices must have carried and attracted Kate and Aceline to join us.

"Tea-Cup," Kate cried, her voice suddenly very eager and girly. "You look great. What the fuck happened to your eye?"

Dammit.

"Oh it's nothing," Tea said, looking a little uncomfortable—then grinned again. "Well—the holidays you know. I spent a month walking in the Bohinj mountains—good food, good Medica. That is, a booze we have. A brandy made with honey. It was really nice. Good against the high places."

"Wow," Aceline said. "You must be fit. You only just got back?"

Tea shrugged, and I noticed Kate giving her a slightly unhappy look. "I don't know about that. But hey, you must also join me tomorrow for my little gathering. A bite to eat and a chat."

"Thank you," Aceline said. "Do you mind if I bring a friend? There's someone I . . ." She blushed. "Well—I'd rather like to ask over if . . . that's alright."

"Of course," Tea said.

"Thank you!"

"So how was it?" Kate asked.

"Home? It was great. The mountains there, they are not so high, but . . . there is dense woodland everywhere—and meadows filled with insects and flowers. It is very sweet. The sort of place where you can lie down and half a day goes by without . . . and you barely notice."

"Wow. What did you eat?"

And that was when things changed abruptly.

"Just about everything," Tea said. "Best food in the world down there, where three great cuisines come together. You have the Italian coming in from the south—pizza and pasta—and the Slavic and Turkish from the east. Ćevapčići and burek. In the mountains though, you get a lot of Austrian influences . . . it was so nice to eat klobása—and sarma—and jota stew."

"I don't recognise a single one of those," Kate said. "Chi-what?"

"Ćevapčići," she said. "It's great. It's a—meatball, stick thing with mixed meat. Beef and lamb. With seasoning. You grill it and serve it in a roll or . . ."

My brain, already traumatised once today, did another backflip at that. "Really?" I demanded stupidly. Tea nodded with a wry look. There was a brief silence and I glanced round with some interest at the expressions on everyone's faces.

"Beef . . . and lamb?" Kate asked at last.

"Yeah," Tea said. "My father has a small farm—pigs as well. He sells meat and makes klobása—that is, makes the dry-cured mountain sausages. Just beautiful to eat. And to . . . to live with as well."

"Oh my god," Aceline said with a nervous laugh. "You actually ate meat?"

"Wow . . ." Kate managed.

"Oh fuck off," Tea said with a friendly grin. "Things are different round the world. I miss it . . . the fatty cuts of pork that you can buy hot in the shops. Or the pršut ham dried in the burja wind . . ."

"Really?" Kate demanded.

"You ever tried pršut ham, Kate?"

"Um—noooo," she said indignantly.

Tea shrugged, her grin widening, looking far less sweet now and more predatory and mischievous. "Or sometimes in the mountains we serve sliced sausage in minced crackling . . . I mean . . ." She sought for the words. "Minced pork fat . . ."

"Um . . ."

She laughed. "It's heavy . . . but you know, you need heavy in the mountains. You need the fuel."

Kate and Aceline exchanged glances. "Right . . . okay . . ."

I have to admit, I was watching the expressions on their faces, Kate's in particular, with utter fascination. Both of them had fallen silent—neither seeming to have a clue what to say next. Horror and politeness were waging violent war. And I could sympathise. It was weird to have Tea inadvertently weigh right into my spiral of guilt at precisely that moment—taking eating meat as the most normal thing in the world. It derailed something in my head.

With neither Kate nor Aceline showing any signs of rescuing the conversation, I remember blathering some crap about how it sounded a beautiful place and hey, one day I would have to get up there and pay it a visit, ride the trains down through the Alps maybe—knowing full well that I probably wouldn't. To which she responded with the expected polite enthusiasm. It all felt agonisingly artificial, and soon I quietly made my escape back into the flat and the safety of my room. It was time to get ready for my second job, anyway. Or was it my third? Whichever. Makes no difference here.

TUESDAY

BE READY! That's what it said, scrawled in rough spray paint on the crumbling brick of the sea wall railway.

Actually, there was something familiar about this. I had seen that same scrawl elsewhere—street artists often have rather one-track minds and maybe you need that if you are going to carve any sort of identity for yourself on the bleak walls of this city. But ready for what? In this city, there wasn't much one needed to be ready for. Unexpected letters from the council or the HMRC? Some new polity or tweak from those elitist clots in government that just makes your life that little bit harder? In my case, though, it rang with a much more sombre triumph. Was I ready? I really hoped I was. Ready to die. Oh yes. I even had a replacement black sheet and bottle in my bag. Yes, gin again . . .

However—there was one call to make first. Something I owed, right at a time when I had never wanted to owe anyone anything ever again. That was the reason why I was back here at the sea wall rather than at the old cemetery further north. I wouldn't need to stay—certainly wouldn't need to eat anything . . . but they had been kind to me. More than kind.

Then I could head on, back to the railway line.

There was something else, though—even then I was aware of it. Something that I hardly understood and that nagged at me. That was the gleam of sheer rage in Star Girl's eyes. For some reason that rage haunted me. That rage was the spanner dropped in the works of all thoughts concerning this or anything else. Why was she so angry?

Was that not maybe a bloody stupid question?

It seemed so long since I had been truly angry about anything.

But as I stood uncertainly, studying that dark urban environment and its scrawled graffiti, I must confess to a feeling of interest. A feeling that her rage might just contain a buried treasure. Something I wanted to know about in spite of the planned finitude of my life.

I slowly walked along the path below the sea wall, looking for the one awkward way up that I remembered from before. This rearing concrete, brick and metal monster looked the least inviting thing in the world as I passed—old brick invaded by rough, almost brutal engineering with the forest of railway infrastructure high overhead. Razor wire and mesh fences. Warning notices about trespassing and electric death. It wasn't giving me a good feeling. For all that I loved London and devoted so much time to knowing every street of it, I had never broken in anywhere forbidden before. But at least the claustrophobic nature of the place meant I was well hidden.

The journey took me to the point where the ruins of the old Limehouse Curve once branched off. The accumulator tower. The structures came together into an ever-narrowing wedge of hazy night sky and here were the footholds up that I remembered. The image of Star Girl just *drifting* upwards over the bricks like a monkey was large in my mind. She could get up here in a few seconds, it seemed. Me—this was when I came very close to giving up, the physical reality of trying to get up that wall able to crush any dreams. I could make the climb, I just didn't want to be reminded of that loathsome physicality, which only seemed to make the fantastical quintet of people I was aiming for retreat and fade away into the mists. Maybe I was merely trying to put off the inevitable, here. Not quite as ready for death as I thought? Nobody wants to die—it is forced upon you by external pressures. So maybe this last visit of mine was just another form of weakness.

Fortunately, though, before all these thoughts could reach their obvious conclusion, I found my footing and made it up there, ending up puffing and blowing on the ballast at the side of the sea wall railway line. I had about eleven minutes before another train would be along, so I hurried down the dark tracks, stepping from sleeper to sleeper, towards where my memory told me I would find the route down again on the far side. It felt exposed up here as the wall barged through the city. I could see lighted windows on the landward side on a level with me. They were brief glimpses into people's lives in a place that had been so coveted until the wall came through, until the Soak happened—and I hoped they weren't also a brief glimpse out at my life. I hoped nobody would look out and see the dark figure lumbering past. It was a relief to get over the wall and onto the ledge, then through the old window and the black curtain to where it was even darker—so dark that it looked unoccupied, and I tugged the curtain back to let in as much night illumination as possible. This was a relief, actually—it would give me a chance to collect my breath before facing other people. So I settled down comfortably in one of the chairs to wait and watch the scene outside.

This particular Soak was only flooded at high tide, and then shallowly. Sometimes you could get in here among the buildings using a canoe or shallow-draughted boat, sometimes even that was impossible. It all depended on the spring/neap tide cycle. You could walk there when the tide was out, as it was now. I could see a wide stretch of concrete covered with mud and marshy areas that faded down towards the river, which was just visible through the buildings. The occasional light that gleamed in that urban wilderness looked extremely isolated against the black silhouettes of what had once been a most desirable area of the city: Limehouse Basin. Once upon a time they must have been some of the East End's finest buildings—I could see the remains of swish architecture and luxury, now crumbling and boarded up, black with mud and green with algae. It was in marked contrast to Canary Wharf Island, which loomed over it from the middle distance, or the new cable-stayed bridge that arched across the old black slithering Thames, scuttling and roaring with traffic. Above me the occasional train came past, booming and echoing round this bizarre space.

Sitting here, in this long-dead arch, it seemed as though London had had its heart ripped out. That was hardly a new though, though possibly of a certain profundity nonetheless—but this was the first time it occurred to me that the city's rotten heart that was its river somehow perfectly matched its rotten heart on a more metaphysical and spiritual level. As I sat there, in this city of decay and despair, it almost seemed as though I was staring at the cause. I couldn't run with that too far, though. The proliferation of art all over these crumbling walls gave it an air that was almost beautiful—a sense of life that was, if anything, more vibrant than the sterile glass facades of some areas. Again I was staring at those eerie figures—stick-like with blank faces in which one white orb was placed at random. Up, down, sides—never corresponding to any kind of human anatomy. These weren't white eyes—just a single glaring white spot. I was sure I had seen this before somewhere. No surprise if so, since street artists often seem to run with the same theme. It was a reminder that the despair of London, a city filled with suicide and the post-modern death of hope and life, had been around for vastly longer than this wall. It was a city on the waning end of civilization, fading and decaying into a sickly mush as capitalism and politics sagged and unravelled with rot—as human stupidity and greed held dominion over all. That was the cause, not the sea. But hey—it is human nature to appreciate patterns that reinforce or mirror each other.

 Before I could think myself any deeper into that murky area, there was a clatter and a scuffle at the entrance—and Clay Man stepped in, dressed in what looked like the exact same grey suit that he had been wearing last time and laden down with bags. He gave me a slightly awkward smile . . . and a dead rabbit landed on the table with an un-dramatic clunk. I stared at both it and him rather warily and there was a hint of embarrassment in his body language. In spite of his somewhat threatening words right at the beginning, I was starting to realise that he was a quiet character—one who hovered in the background, obscure and silent. Maybe, like me, he was also not so at ease using his voice. I empathised, of course, but it did make conversations somewhat awkward.

 A heave landed a second, much heavier, cargo on the table—a bag containing six large bottles filled with water.

"It's all rather primitive here," he said. "No electric lights. We've got an extractor fan on the stove, running off car batteries, but that's all. There's candles if you want them, though. Lighter over there."

"Oh," I said stupidly, remembering the warm glow of my last visit. "Right. But that's okay. Actually I was sitting here looking at the view."

He nodded and stared out, following my eyes. For a brief moment I wondered whether to try and put my thoughts of rotten hearts and rotten souls into words but quickly decided against it. They were probably thoughts thought a thousand times by anyone here for any length of time.

"Yeah," Clay Man said. "It's nice. The fading city speaks to the fading soul. And—umm—good to see you here again anyway. I was wondering if you would turn up."

He sounded so exactly like a slightly uncertain host politely welcoming me to some tea party or community event that I couldn't help smiling.

"Thanks," I said. "I can't stay long—but I wanted to pop in as . . . as, well, to prove that I am still here. And . . ."

Now I was sounding even worse than he was.

"And . . . to thank you for looking after me . . ."

"Don't mention it," he said. He offloaded yet another bag, and this one was filled with art supplies—spray cans and other things. I focussed on them with interest, then glanced at the huge scribbled sketch just visible on the wall. Oh yes—he had been introduced as a street artist, though in his quiet grey suit he certainly didn't look the part. And no doubt this wall was a work in progress.

He tugged the curtain closed again, then flicked a lighter and began to light the nearest candles. Glow finally invaded the arch, lighting up the old brickwork. "And . . . look . . . sorry if I sounded a bit unfriendly last time. It is just that I worry about . . . Well, you have to. Star has the most bizarre fantasies sometimes—of whipping up some sort of army and precipitating revolution. The power of the people—kicking the political system to pieces somehow. But it doesn't work like that. This isn't some nice fashionable protest meeting—it's not fucking gay rights or some environmental issue. It's illegal and people can get quite hysterical about it. So . . . we have to be cautious."

It always felt discomforting to be apologised to, but at the same time, it was a bit of a relief, I won't deny. "Don't worry about it," I mumbled.

I remembered the frozen awkwardness that had descended on the conversation the moment Tea had mentioned her Slovenian ćevapčići—a sort of shock held in restraint by a very British politeness. And it was true. Some things one could take pride in fighting for and yelling about, but it was hard to imagine anyone, even Star Girl, standing up and declaiming in favour of death.

Wasn't it?

I had no idea, I realised.

Fortunately, it didn't matter now.

But still I glanced at the rabbit that Clay Man had tossed on the table. He followed my eyes. There was no blood on it anywhere—almost no sign that it was even dead except for its complete lack of movement.

"Hungry?" he asked with a grin.

"I dunno . . . as I said, I can't stay long. I have to . . ."

"Maybe we can tempt you again—we have a great chef with us, after all."

"The Butcher?"

"Yes—we are all here for our own various reasons, and his was a very simple one. He loves cooking."

I nodded and glanced again at his bag of art supplies. So what were his own reasons? He was a curious, quiet character, seemingly fading into the background but also giving the impression that there was a lot going on, in some very unexpected places where we couldn't see. I was going to ask more questions, but at that moment there was a new slither outside—a new intrusion of legs. Four this time. Star Girl and the Butcher stepped in and joined us, both with bags slung over their shoulders.

"Well well," Star said. "Look who's here. You're still alive?"

"I think so," I said with a smile. "I can't stay long but I wanted to . . . drop in." She nodded and glanced at the table.

"One small rabbit," Clay Man said.

A second thud and Star Girl had dumped another by its side—and this one was far less clean—soaked in red in fact. Gruesome. I flinched slightly, hoping my feelings weren't showing on my face.

"Two small rabbits," she said. "Still not much for six of us—we will have to go out again, I think. But that's all good. A night of exercise and then a morning feast."

There was another thud as she unloaded the rest of her cargo. Several more litres of water in bottles. This must be their water supply in the absence of taps—water for cooking, drinking, washing . . .

Another scuffle then and the Philosopher and the Beggar joined us—and yet more water was unloaded. It was a lot—but hey, humans can get through a lot of water.

"Were they farmed?" I asked cautiously, returning to the rabbits.

The Butcher glanced at me. "You saw the news from Hackney, I take it," he threw straight back at me.

"Oh yes," Clay Man said with a frown. "I remember that place. I even did a mural on the wall there once. I don't trust those places much, though. Some are okay, some really look after their animals, but . . . well, in an unregulated underground it's all on the conscience of the farmer, so . . ." He shrugged expressively. "No, these weren't farmed."

"Where did you get it?" I asked uneasily. "Was it a . . ."

"Yeah," Star Girl said with a laugh. "I caught it."

"Caught?"

"That one, yes. Out in the city wilds . . ."

She held up a kitchen knife, still in its blister packet, and made a dramatic thrusting gesture. I winced.

"You mean you caught it yourself?" I asked.

"Of course," she said. "What did you think I was doing on the railway tracks when I fell over you? I was on the hunt." She brandished the blade. "And you cost me my dinner."

"Blood and thunder," the Butcher growled, standing up with a grin.

"Yeah," she cried, also jumping to her feet. "Chew the bones and rend the flesh. We aren't just a den of scrounging meat-eaters you know—we are the City Hunters." Her still-packaged knife flashed in a playful gesture at the Butcher, who gave a grim chuckle and produced his own blade, which was conspicuously unpackaged and huge—as big a kitchen knife as you could expect to find. The two blades clashed in the air with a muffled clang of steel against plastic, and for a few moments they engaged in a lively sword-fight, Star Girl blocking the Butcher's terrifying weapon in the air with playful skill. Then she danced away with a whoop.

"Hunted with full cunning and sneaks and virtuosity, in the shadows of London," she said with a grin. "It makes me feel alive—oh boy."

"Star," Clay Man said gravely, "is a vicious predator, don't be fooled."

"You bet."

"And angry too."

"You bet I'm fucking angry," she said with a big grin. "Having a good rant and rage makes my pussy tingle."

The Butcher gave a languorous smile. "So long as it's not the only thing that makes your pussy tingle," he said. "Then you have a problem." She flipped a finger at him.

"Gawd, there's no way I could do this," I said with a slightly embarrassed smile, and feeling a weird stab of admiration that I didn't analyse at the time. "I am not nearly . . ."

"Aah of course you fucking could," the Beggar said simply. "Tell me who you would like to go with tonight and we'll soon sort that out."

"Not me," Clay Man said. "I'll stay here and work on the wall this time, I think. Otherwise it will never be finished."

"Well, come with me," the Beggar said. "I will show you what it's all about."

I stared at her blankly. Shocked. I wasn't going anywhere tonight—except the railway line. I had a train to catch.

"You mean—you want me to . . ."

"Sure," Star Girl said. "Why not? This isn't a restaurant, you know. You are a part of this now. You can't leave, or Clay Man might just come after you."

Clay Man gave a mock-scary laugh, which sounded all the stranger and actually creepier coming from one so quiet. "Yeah," he said. "And of all of us, I am by far the most efficient."

"Like hell you are," Star Girl howled.

"You are the cheetah," he said. "I am the spider. Spiders are more effective than cheetahs—cheetahs just look good. This stupid respectable suit I wear may seem drab and boring—but that's just my city camouflage. Don't let that fool you, Train Man."

"Fuck you," Star Girl said with a grin.

I stared round at them, feeling terrified for a moment. Of course I was leaving. All I had wanted was to pop by and reassure them with a white lie. No way was I going to get involved in any of this. The Beggar must have caught something of that because she held up her hand.

"Okay okay, no pressure. But still—I gotta say, you look as though the familiar has never done you much good . . . right?"

I didn't know what to say to that. It was as true as anything could be and I stared round at them in the dim candlelight, feeling my skin prickling all over. The perfectly athletic Star Girl, the good-looking and boyish Butcher in his waistcoat, the ordinary-looking but apparently cunning and spidery Clay Man, the quiet grey-eyed Beggar and the thoughtful and rigorous Philosopher. And even as I panicked, even as I floundered around trying to find an excuse to escape, some part of my mind was already making a choice. Star Girl—no way. There was no way I could keep up with her or would even want to. And the Philosopher, weirdly enough, seemed too alpha, too dominating and lecturesome. Remembering quiet conversations with the Beggar and her remarks about isolation from the world, it was her I found myself focusing on.

But no—that was crazy. I wasn't going to let myself get diverted a second time.

On the other hand, though, some wild part of my mind came up with right then, if you are going to die, then what does it matter? You can do whatever you damn like.

In the end I gawped at them in blank silence for almost a minute, while they looked back at me with a range of expressions. And I couldn't refuse. Maybe because I was hopeless at saying no to people—but just maybe there was something else going on down beneath all that.

"Um," I said at last, "I . . ."

"Well, Train Man?" Star said.

"I suppose . . ." I said at last, "if you really don't mind me inflicting myself on you . . ." I nodded to the Beggar. "I guess I will come with you. Though I fear I will hold you back."

She gave a pleased nod. And somehow that was that.

"Good," she said. "We will bring back a dinner fit for a king."

"Of anywhere except this country," Star Girl put in with a frown.

"Oh bugger that," Clay Man said, reaching down and unpacking his spray paints. "I bet anything you like, *they* don't go short of anything they want. You hear stories."

"True that," Star said with a sigh.

Will you be surprised or shocked, reader, if I admit to thrilling with a strange, deep excitement right then? For the first time in my life, I was actually going to do something. A crazy, stupid, even dangerous something—but something nonetheless. And it didn't matter—because on the path to your own death, nothing matters. Suicide is a place where suddenly anything becomes possible—where anything kept in place by the repression of the world can be overcome. This is a place where 'they' have no further power over you. Fuck the world—I owed it nothing at all, so why not go out with a bang?

✪

After a bustle of departing, the Beggar and I dropped down from the railway line, hurried back to the Regent's Canal Watergate and made our way quickly along the towpath. The presence of another had rather calmed my usual nerves about the dark city around us and I found myself looking at it in a new way—even appreciating the mix of colours that the night brought—street lights, housing lights, ornamental lights, and all reflected in the still water. This mysterious 'underclass' that was supposed to be swarming all over the city seemed conspicuous by its absence—I couldn't see a single human being. On the horizon though—one single glowing red light again. As before, I couldn't see what it was attached to. Maybe it was indeed a crane or some such construction, but I couldn't shake off the feeling that it was actually suspended there. Something floating.

"So," I asked my unexpected teacher, "where do we go? Where is there food here?"

"First, we take the bus," she said with a smile, hustling me up onto Commercial Road. The wait wasn't long, and we were soon sitting together in the best seat—upstairs front right—watching the city go past. I was not used to having company while travelling and I wondered for a while whether I was supposed to be talking. But the silence seemed quite comfortable. Our legs touched in the narrow seats while a dream of the city passed by outside. Having a companion painted a different colour over the streets and buildings—a touch brighter and darker, better defined. You sit there in the knowledge that other eyes, grey eyes, are seeing the same view, so you scan it with more attention as you pass. Throngs of traffic, swarming pedestrians, restaurants and fast food joints—mostly stuff with chips, but still a few Chinese and Turkish places. London still had its tinges of multiculturalism in the air, for all that it had been waning over the years. Grilled halloumi cheese and Kofte made of soya, sweet and sour tofu and curried vegetables—for the first time in my life I found myself wondering what these foods tasted like with their original ingredients. Ancient recipes that must have travelled some long and strange journeys to end up in the last lingering foreign takeaways on the London streets. What did they taste like in the hot Turkish backstreets where lamb sizzled on the grills—or from flaring woks in cluttered Chinese markets? The scents were still appetising, though, as they wafted in through the bus windows. The smells of frying would never change, no matter what happened to the ingredients.

The Beggar glanced sideways at me with a grin. "You are a strange one," she said. "I have never met such a silent type. I hope you are strong to match it?"

I felt myself blushing. That stung slightly, though I knew she didn't mean anything other than a slight tease.

"Yeah," I said awkwardly and laughed. "Give me a few hours and maybe I will have figured out some small talk."

She gave me a wry grin.

"I'm not being deliberately silent or aloof—it's just . . ."

"I know, I know. It's okay. I have spent a lot of my life pretty much without talking—or people to talk to. It makes a change sometimes, I must say. Look at Star. Try getting her to shut up sometimes. She does keep going on and on—everything anyone believes is wrong and everyone is an idiot. Yes, we know, Star. It's as if her life is one continual argument with the outside world. It must be exhausting."

It was at that point, that slightly longer speech, that I first focussed on her accent—or rather the lack of it. Unlike Star Girl's slightly rough East End voice, the Beggar seemed to speak with perfect BBC English—low-pitched and refined. You might almost say there was a hint of the posh about it, as though she would be more at home in a snooty Kent village than in the wild east of London. It struck me as curious, even though the intelligent part of me knew very well that it was a totally pointless thing to find curious given the eternal blur of life and the eternal falsehood of stereotypical expectations. I wondered what sort of life story could have brought this character first into beggardom, and then here. In London of course, there is indeed one great equality—the fact that doom can fall regardless of your class or circumstances. The circumstances you are born into do of course spread their influence throughout the rest of your life and that is a long long way from equality—but doom can still fall. It is nothing more than one or two glitches away in an uncaring world. It's an equality that people tend to forget about, maybe deliberately, but it is an equality nonetheless.

Outside, the bus was moving through residential streets now—ranks of houses, some bright and cheerful with decoration, some dour and depressing. Rubbish bins and recycle bins standing to attention outside the gates. The occasional abandoned toy or item of litter in the grass. In my head, of course, I was mapping out the journey—though I will not be too specific here.

"Here we are," she murmured at last, as the city gave way to one of its innumerable open spaces and we jumped off the bus. London has a lot of green areas, but this was one of those few places where things were a little wilder than usual. Rough marshland fringed with canal boats—patches of trees, long grass, short grass, sports fields, reeds and wild waterside. We left the road almost immediately and began walking, leaving the more populous areas behind. For some reason, this place was unnerving me more than Regents Canal had been, and I caught myself studying the darkness carefully for any sign of human activity—but it was clear that away from the waterside, the place was pretty much deserted. It was very dark here indeed. Massive plants clustered around—the tall, slightly sinister shapes of Giant Hogweed haunting the hedges. Ancient concrete from an old facility or structure patched the grass occasionally. Unusually, I wasn't sure what it was—maybe old railway land or some other long-abandoned loading yard, now totally overgrown.

I was also surprised to realise that I wasn't feeling any pain. Usually my feet hurt and my body protested—but that seemed absent now. We were walking unhurriedly and I was relaxing more and more—maybe that was why. Normally there is a battle going on between me, my flesh and the hard pavement.

"Do you like the dark?" I asked at last.

"Love it," she said with a smile. "The dark feels like home. I'm like some small animal that avoids the day because that's when it can be seen by everything."

"You feel safe?"

"Oh yes, safe enough—you don't want to pay too much attention to the newspapers. What do they know?"

"You mean . . ."

"Them and their fucking 'underclass'—what planet are they living on? We're the underclass, mate."

Yes, I had to admit, that was probably true, even though I at least had a home.

She popped one finger in her mouth, then reached up and tested the wind. "I know every inch of this place," she said. "I grew up not far from here—back in the happy days when I lived with my mother and everything was fine . . ."

She gave a sigh, then refocused her attention.

"Look," she said, switching on a torch and gently indicating the grass. I could just make out a faint trail there—not a path as such, more a sequence of small indents in the leaves. "That's a rabbit run," she said. "Hop, hop, hop along. And the snare should go just in-between those marks.

"Okay," I said. She held up a length of wire.

"Star would probably wait here with a knife. Clay Man might festoon this whole field with dozens of hidden death-traps linked up to some jangly alert thing. Then spend half an hour photographing it and scaring everything away. Everything is art to him. But me—just a normal snare is quite enough."

I studied the wire and swallowed, something of the reality of it getting through to me. I—or we—were about to kill something. No two ways about it.

"Star Girl can catch a rabbit with her bare hands?" I asked in amazement. I found it hard to imagine how that was even possible, though I suppose this must be something we humans had all done back in our more primitive past.

"Either that or by throwing a stick and then running in and grabbing," she said. "She is lethal with some rough old stick. More dangerous than most people are with a fucking flick-knife."

The Beggar shut off the torch, bent over and began adjusting the snare with the help of a few plant stems.

"Star," she said, "between you and me, there's something slightly creepy about her. Much as I love her. I suspect—I think she takes a lot of pleasure in this hunting and killing because it lets out a bit of her anger. Because it is an act of rebellion and . . . I suppose a visceral satisfaction. I find that rather . . . bizarre. She can be brutal sometimes, you know. Not cruel as such—just . . . wild. For me—well—it was simple necessity that started me doing this. Either that or starve. I was broke—no proper home, nobody who could or would help me, so what choice did I have? It was either hunt and shoplift or starve." She gave me a sudden sharp upward glance. "Are you shocked?" she demanded a little suspiciously. I shook my head in silence.

"Well," she continued, straightening up and moving on a few metres, and producing another snare, "I learned how to make these—I somehow found out all I could, though most of the websites on the subject are blocked. And there was something rather . . ." she sought for words, "pure about it. Your strength and cunning and thought against it's—and you win and win yourself sustenance and live a few more days. The Philosopher says that's what life is about, whatever modern gloss we put on things—and I guess he's right there. Compared to struggling to make money or fit in to this mess of a city, that seems the most beautiful thing in the world to me now."

Her talk was giving me a strange tingly feeling that I couldn't remember ever feeling before with its suggestions of worlds beyond the basic one I knew. I was still uneasy but at the same time, I could relate to what she was saying far more than Star Girl's wild aggression.

"Maybe I am being defensive because, you know, it's not very nice seeing the shock and dislike in your eyes. It feels like a judgement, Train Man."

That froze me. "I didn't mean . . ."

She waved that away. "Just—let me explain," she said with a smile, then bent to her snares again. I followed, still feeling a little shaken at that 'judgement' bit—but could I really disagree? I suppose the uneasiness I felt was a judgement—of course it bloody was.

She produced another wire and tossed it to me. I caught it clumsily.

"You set it up," she ordered. "I'll show you where." I studied it. It was little more than a running loop firmly attached to a long peg of rough wood that looked as though it had been shaped with a knife. I glanced at the ground, at the rabbit runs that traversed the long grass. A quick analysis of recent memories and a careful look and I had focussed on a possible place.

"Here maybe?" I asked, pointing into the grass.

"Yeah," she said, looking faintly surprised. "That's perfect."

I quickly set it up, ramming the peg deep into the soil and arranging the loop among the stems. The Beggar nodded approvingly.

"You ain't as stupid as you look," she said with a smile.

"I look stupid?" I asked—stupidly. The Beggar gave an awkward cough.

"Um—that was a joke," she said. "I didn't mean . . ."

I gave an uncomfortable giggle, wishing I could rewind the conversation by about two sentences. "Gimme another one," I said. "Maybe over here?"

She nodded. A few minutes later, we had set up all the snares—a dozen or so—and we straightened up in some relief. I brushed at my forehead, which was starting to slime with sweat.

"Okay, great," she said. "I don't know about you—we could go and come back later—but I usually just stay not far away and relax. Maybe get some sleep."

"You mean sit here all night?" I asked, slightly surprised.

She gave a grin.

"There speaks one who has never lived on the streets," she said and I flinched slightly, even though there was a smile on her face. "When you have lived without a home, you start to develop a somewhat different attitude to time. All the usual stimulations you have—TV, internet, whatever—those are gone, so you inevitably have to refocus yourself. Any place in the quiet where you can keep out of the way is a good place—and you learn to watch simply because there is nothing else. Nature and passers-by are your movie."

We stepped out of the long grass and back towards the more populated areas of the parkland by the river.

"You're . . . not like that now are you?"

"No," she said with a smile. "I was lucky. I have a small place . . . somewhere. I'm not supposed to say." She gave an uncomfortable shrug. "No emails, no texts, no personal details—you can't trust any of them. It's all supposed to be anonymous. But I'm one of the elite now. But once you've been out there, fallen through the cracks of the world, you are never really the same again and you always look at the world a bit differently."

There was a long silence. Ahead in the darkness, the waterside and its paths were approaching again—people were moving—and I glanced round suspiciously.

"Does it matter if anyone sees us?" I asked.

She gave a grin. "Not really," she said. "They'll just think we've been in the bushes for a quick late-night screw or something."

I didn't know what to say to that outlandish thought. We sat in the grass near the canal and watched the world around us, time slowly passing. The water, wide and faintly menacing in the dark—moon and clouds overhead. Actually, the Beggar was wrong in one way. This quiet observation of the world was something I was also quite familiar with, albeit during the day. It was part of my travelling- and London-obsession, after all. But even beyond that, I have spent a lot of time watching the world and, even on a smaller scale, the little performances people put on are intriguing. To me, this night was like an alien land and the performances were only more so.

People occasionally bustled around the boats in the distance—a strange blend of the rich wanting a bit of idleness on the water and people who couldn't afford anywhere else to live. The occasional scuffle of conversation, hunched figures moving along the paths, a distant glow of an open fire, a kiss between two lovers, a distant shouted row cut silent by a sharp scream, a cyclist passing along the towpath in a skritch of gravel. Overhead, the MPS police helicopter droned by, heading to who knows what reported problem. And in the end, an hour or so later, it was she who tired first and stood up.

"Shall we walk a bit?" she said, lowering her voice to a whisper to avoid disturbing the evening.

We approached the waterside, as human beings always seem to be drawn towards water. In this part of the city, canals and rivers twined like lovers through the marshes and it took all my mental mapping skills to know which was which. This was the canal, dotted with elegant and scrappy canal boats. From one, faint music came drifting, cut down to little more than the monotonous pulsing bass—and I imagined that boat to be a train. The inside a sleek cab covered with levers and switches and a big picture window staring ahead at the speeding world. *Good evening ladies and gentlemen, in about ten minutes we will be pulling into old London town, if the water doesn't get to us first. If you look to your left you will see the sad sunken remains of our once-great riverside, where only the meat-eaters and drug addicts now fester in their holes of iniquity...*

From another boat, two voices were raised in sex behind a lighted curtained window, and I found myself imagining the rustic interior of the boat hanging festooned with sweets and candy, lollypops and sugar. Crinkly discarded wrappers and a sickly sweet taste in my mouth. The Beggar glanced at me, her lips twitching in a grin as we passed.

Then an open fire crackled at the side of the path—tended by a few young guys and girls dressed in the edgy arty style of certain parts of East London—and I found myself unexpectedly remembering some of the images plastered around when I was a kid. Blood-soaked cartoon murder and the caption *Does your mummy kill animals? Ask her!* Seared, scorched eviscerated bodies impaled on spikes and licked by flames. No, I remember thinking with some pride and satisfaction, mine didn't and nor did I. Message received and understood. All was right with the world. And as I stared at the flickering flames of the little campfire, I felt a chill again. Those simple, glorious days of propaganda and my own sense of purity seemed a long way away now. A long long way indeed. And everywhere I looked, the world seemed to drip blood in spite of its vegetarianism. Mine, others'—victims'. The whole world was wounded and even the animals were still bleeding.

I glanced surreptitiously at the Beggar, strolling beside me and looking very relaxed. Like a cat, I thought.

"Say something, Train Man," she said suddenly with a laugh, and my increasingly complex thoughts suddenly unravelled.

"Hmm?"

She touched my arm. "Sorry," she said softly. "Sometimes silence can be good. But the expression on your face looked rather bleak."

I shifted uncomfortably. "Yeah," I said. "I was . . . thinking."

"About?"

I shrugged. "Old history."

She looked at me for a moment with a curious eyebrow up, then shrugged it off.

"Let's go and check," she said. "It's been a few hours."

We strolled back into the grasslands. Part of me was hoping that the traps would be empty, so that in my confusion and fear, I wouldn't have to deal with what was coming. And indeed, the first five snares were as quiet as dodder stems. At snare six, though, there was a flicker of movement and I cringed. Something grey and white jumped and floundered in the gloom—its brain seemingly not quite able to register the fact that it was attached to something and still trying to run, even though it was dragged in circles.

"Yes," the Beggar said quietly, instantly transforming into something filled with purpose as she paced forward to claim her victim. As she did so, though, the rabbit gave a panicked wrench—and the snare was uprooted out of the ground. The rabbit staggered away.

The Beggar gave an actual hiss of shock, then moved faster than I think I have ever seen a human being move before. She darted forward and landed on the rabbit in a flurry of legs and there was a high-pitched squeal—also unlike anything I had ever heard before. Then she was up again, holding the struggling animal in one hand. Her eyes were glowing—her face ferocious. I stepped back a pace. Then she had thrust it at me.

"Kill it," she ordered. I fumbled and almost dropped it, my hands sinking into warm fur. "Careful," she yelled.

"How?"

She gestured a savage twisting gesture with her hand. "Grab its head and its hind legs, then yank hard and twist. Quick and clean."

The rabbit was squealing again as I struggled for its feet, sounding like a terrified oboe reed without the oboe—a wavering high-pitched useless sound. It was a sound that shocked through me, causing a clench deep inside—but in a rather unexpected way. My face screwed up and I shut my eyes, but right then, I wanted to kill it—to stamp it out of life, just so I could shut that ludicrous noise up, which seemed to be ringing across the whole marshes. In this chaos, there was no time for analysis though—my brain had shut down and there was nothing but utterly vestigial and withered instincts pushing me. I flailed with my hand, trying to do as I was instructed. I pulled sharply, but it didn't work. The squealing changed pitch, becoming a high-pitched wheezing sound. It slipped through my fingers and lay kicking in the grass.

"Again," the Beggar snapped. "You are causing massive pain."
I gave a desperate yell and tried again.

This time I got it right, and it was as though I had hit an off switch. There was a faint snap of its neck and instantly sound and motion stopped. I dropped it again. The furry body lay still and the Beggar touched it with her foot.

I turned away and leaned against a tree. Now it was over, my entire body was trembling. There were tears in my eyes and for a moment I even thought I would be sick. Then her hand was rubbing between my shoulder blades.

"Baptism of fire, Train Man?" she asked with a twist of humour around her eyes.

"Yeah," I muttered. "I didn't expect—I mean . . ."

She stepped away, then made a very quick check of the remaining snares, plucking them out of the ground and making them vanish. Meanwhile, I stood and stared at the rabbit in the grass, trying to work it all out. It had been alive and moving—and now it wasn't. What exactly had changed? Some fine and delicate machine that I had broken? Something else? I didn't know. No one does.

"Come on," she said, returning quickly. "That was a bit noisy. We should go."

"Sorry," I muttered. She waved that away. "Is it dead?" I asked, unsure if that was a stupid question or not.

"You bet," she said, grabbing the rabbit from me and stuffing it into a plastic bag, then into a second, and then into her rucksack. "That'll do—it's enough, and maybe the others will have some more as well and make it a feast."

She set off quickly through the grass back towards the busier areas, still walking easily and relaxed. I followed more anxiously. It suddenly seemed to me as though anyone and everyone wandering through these nighted trees could clearly see what we had done—could see the guilt written clearly on both of us—and it made my skin crawl.

"Snap out of it," she said at last, trying to sound humorous but not quite masking a serious exasperation. "If you don't, we're travelling back separately. You look too guilty—you'll get us nicked."

I could see why. Her with the rabbit, me with the panic—at a safe distance. But I knew that if I did that, I would never see her again. I would go straight to the railway line and that would be that. Indeed, maybe that would be the best thing. I think she also had a vague awareness of that, for she gave an impatient sigh and grabbed me by the hand.

"Gawd," she growled and dragged me into the bushes. For some reason, she took off her rucksack and tossed it a short distance away, then turned to me and grabbed me firmly by the shoulders.

"What's the matter with you?" she demanded. "Have you never killed anything before?"

"Of course not."

"Wrong," she said. "Have you never swatted a fly or poisoned a mouse? Yes, I know we're not supposed to—but just about everyone does."

". . ."

"You've killed millions of things," she said. "From your disinfectant, insect killer and pesticide . . ."

"I don't use . . ."

". . . to the small things you kill when you roll over in your sleep or walk down the street—to the millions of lives snuffed out by your very existence in this concrete jungle, the food you eat—the poison that everything you do generates, the natural world obliterated to keep you going. And us—we have caught one rabbit, that lived a pretty much natural and normal life and we are going to eat it. Your loaf of bread for breakfast did more damage to the world and caused more pain. So get a grip. It's okay, dammit."

She let me go and I leaned against a tree trunk staring at nothing. I wanted to say something about intent and deliberation but the words stuck in my throat feeling completely hollow.

She was watching me carefully—and I wished she wasn't. I didn't want to be looked at—I didn't want my face seen in all its nakedness, in terms of skin and emotion and general feelings of uselessness. She drew a deep breath, the atmosphere relaxing a bit as she did so.

"Okay," I said shortly. She nodded.

"Shall we go?"

"Okay," I said again. I stepped out onto the path and waited while she went to look for her rucksack. She joined me after a moment with a slightly artificial smile, and we hurried on towards the road and the bus stop.

Several more red lights seemed to have appeared on the horizon now and I focussed on them, trying to analyse their origin. It was hard though. Some seemed to be among the distant buildings, others in the sky. More tower cranes? Nothing surprises in London. Nothing whatsoever.

Once on the bus, she leaned over to me. "You sit back there," she said. "I'm sorry—but I need to be cautious." I stared at her blankly as she slipped into a seat, then without a word I retreated a few rows back. I settled into a window seat there, vaguely aware of her giving me a worried look over her shoulder. Then I settled my head against the glass to watch the world go by. A monstrous cloud of gloom had settled on my shoulders. I felt a fool. I felt inadequate. I felt as though I had failed at something and been banished to sit alone in disgrace. And yes, by then I was more worried about that than about the fact that I had just murdered a rabbit with my own hands. The events of the evening went round and round in my head—things I should have done. Or not done. Things I should have done better.

I glanced up again, but could only see the back of the Beggar's head. It seemed farcical to me that I was even in this situation. What was to stop me from getting off at the next stop and drawing a line under this whole thing? Why should I care if I had let her down in some way? What did it matter? What did anything matter?

Every time the computer-voice of the bus read out an approaching stop, I felt a tingling in my hand—the urge to reach out and press the button, then slip off, ignoring any following stares from the Beggar . . . every fucking stop.

But I didn't. Like some stupid loon in an entrancement, I sat there until I saw her rise to her feet, give me an anxious look over her shoulder and make for the stairs. And yes, I followed.

"Okay," she said and hustled me off Commercial Road and down the steps onto the familiar towpath. And once in the darkness, she finally paused. Her eyes looked huge in the dark—and without a word she slid her arms around me and squeezed. I flinched in surprise.

"I'm sorry, Train Man," she whispered, leaning her head on my shoulder. "Really—for all that. Are you okay?"

"Yeah," I said awkwardly.

"Hug me back, for fuck's sake," she said giving me a hard squeeze—and I did so, rather shakily allowing my arms to encircle her, feeling her body firm and soft and warm. Alive. Her long nose pressing into my skin. She drew a rather wavering breath. "Okay," she said. "Let's get back."

✣

Arriving back at the hideaway, the mural had taken shape considerably under Clay Man's hands, adding a vivid and somewhat dominating splash of strangeness to this rather drab arched space. Colours were bringing it to life now and some areas were laid out in great detail. Clay Man stood there wrapped in some kind of protective black smock, a small smile on his face as we studied it. The art was aggressive—startlingly so. Hints of spider web and blood, earth and city—even a few actual objects fastened to the wall—knives, a dinner plate, burned wood. Cartoonish creatures stalked the skeleton of a real small animal among urban bricks and plant stems.

"Nice," the Beggar said at last. Clay Man nodded and dragged off his smock.

There was a clatter as Star Girl stepped in. She was wearing a frown, and it seemed that I wasn't the only one to have had a somewhat dramatic evening.

"Fucking pigs everywhere," she growled, "and not the kind we can eat. I actually had to dump my catch, which was a fucking waste."

"What were they after?" Clay Man demanded. "Did they hassle you?"

"I don't know what they wanted," Star said crossly. "They were just watching the passers-by. Maybe protests of some kind—or, maybe not. Everyone is a bit tense and fiery these days so maybe they are watching to make sure none of us lose it and overthrow the government. I saw them browbeating a young photographer and a woman on a bike. Maybe they had criticised the King's hat or made a bad joke on the internet or something."

She slung her bag across the room. "So nothing from me. Sorry darlings."

"We got one," the Beggar said with a smile.

The Butcher nodded. "Good work."

Then Clay Man gave an awkward gesture.

"Star?" he said softly.

"Mm?"

"You, er—your trousers are covered in blood."

She glanced down at herself sharply with a frown.

"I am? Where?"

"Back of your leg, where you can't see."

"Oh for fuck's sake," she said angrily.

"That could have been very dangerous," Clay Man said, a touch of reproof in his voice that even I found a little irritating. Star shot him a dark look.

The Butcher chuckled. "That knife of yours," he said, "tends to make a lot of holes. Maybe you should wear a waterproof?"

Star grabbed at the back of her leg and studied the faint smear on her hand.

"Knock it off," she said crossly. "It's bad enough that it even matters."

She examined the pile of rabbits with an angry frown.

"As with any instance of going against the norms," The Philosopher murmured, "it is usually best politics to keep quiet about it."

"Ach," she said, looking even angrier, "they live in a fucking fantasy land and we have to keep quiet so they don't get offended?"

"That is usually the way," the Philosopher said with a smile.

"What about offending me?" she demanded. "Why does nobody care about offending me if they are so fucking considerate?"

Star Girl's angry hands descended on the rabbit she had caught earlier, already cut severely, and her fingers clawed into its entrails. "There are times . . . when I'd like to rub those fucking vegetarian morons, those prudish squeamish wankers . . . rub their faces right in it," she said, holding the bloody mess up. "Right there on prime-time TV—take their smug opinionated judgemental faces and shove them right in, in, in the blood and the shit—because . . . because—because, because it's the fucking truth, right?"

"Calm down, Star," Clay Man said with a smile.

Not the right thing to say, as even I was dimly aware, because that was when Star Girl blew up completely.

"Don't tell me to fucking calm down," she yelled, while Clay Man leaned back slightly, eyebrows up. "Since when has this fucking world ever deserved calm? I'd like to sit on their faces and take a huge crap, right all over them. Again, on fucking prime-time TV. I'd like to make them drink my period blood . . ."

Everyone was staring at her now. She glared round, then slung the intestine-trailing rabbit back on the table with a grunt. "You blame me?" she snapped with a shrill tinge to her voice, grabbing a startled Beggar by the shoulder, leaving a red smear. "They don't have the fucking first clue about what humanity is and yet they sit there telling us what to think. How am I supposed not to be fucking angry?"

She stormed away and collapsed face-first on the mattress with a grunt, her body shaking.

The Philosopher gave a gentle cough. "I can't help thinking, my dear Star, that no matter how understandable your rage, all that blood and guts won't actually convince many people."

Star Girl gave a grating yell and buried her face in the pillow. There was a dull silence. Then the Butcher stood up. "I will see to the cooking," he said. "We will all feel better with a bit of food inside us. Will you help me, Beggar?"

I suppose this was called 'giving her a little time to collect herself'. The Butcher took the rabbits, including the half-eviscerated one that Star had abandoned, and stepped through into the other room, swinging his huge knife in a gleaming pendulum. But for some reason I still don't understand, I found myself sitting down by her side and briefly placing a hand on her shoulder. Rage tends to shut me down completely—it's something I just don't know how to deal with and I knew I wouldn't be able to say much useful, but I just didn't want to leave her alone. I suppose it was up to her whether she accepted that tiny comfort or not. She shifted and turned to look at me, her face damp with tears that gleamed in the candlelight.

"I'm sorry, Train Man," she said with deep weariness. "Sometimes it all becomes too much to bear, it really does. I get so angry and there's nothing I can do about it and I just want to tear my own flesh to pieces to try and get it out."

"Yeah," I murmured—just the word.

"What do you do with anger?" she asked.

"Nothing really," I said. "It seems such a long time since I was truly angry."

She shifted and looked at me with gleaming eyes.

"You're not?"

I shrugged.

"How do you look at . . . at all that *falseness*, and not get angry?" She sounded genuinely mystified.

"I—I . . . Maybe I just gave up, that's all. It all feels dead."

She gave me a curious look that I didn't altogether like—not critical, just very very alien to me.

"I suppose my hatred of some of these people may be going a little beyond the rational," she said with a hint of reluctance. "I don't really know what to do about that."

"But what is it that annoys you so much?" It was a blunt question—maybe even a naïve one at that moment. But I had to ask it—humbly, hopefully. "I mean . . . you're talking about me, right? That's what I have been all my life. So . . . ?"

Fortunately, she responded with a sad laugh. "Oh, I'm talking fuck loads worse than you," she said. "Not one issue either. Prudes, religious nuts, repressive politics—anyone who tries to tell me what to think, or what to be." She sat up with a long, whistling breath. "I suppose I don't like the vegan brigade much, it's true. It's none of my business what they do with their own bodies. It's when they start getting opinions about what I should do with mine that I go wild."

"But . . . why?" I pressed uneasily—and again somewhat innocently, it has to be said, in the face of the frown that immediately settled on her face. However, this was a rage against something I pretty much took for granted, after all, and there is no rage more confusing. "It always seemed a good cause to me."

"What cause? The veggie brigade?"

"Well—animal welfare, I suppose."

"Not the same thing," she said. "They pretend it is, but it isn't. You can care about animals and about . . . I dunno, a healthy relationship with the world without going absolutist and telling me the human diet is somehow evil. I'm not even convinced some of them care about the environment or health or whatever deep down—I think it's just some kind of visceral psychological need that they are trying to find excuses for."

She smiled rather bitterly. "Sure it's a good cause. I remember joining the marches against factory farming, I remember shouting and attacking and protesting—I even kicked in a couple of windows early on. I enjoyed it. I enjoyed taking on horrors and trying to make them better. I remember the rush of it—the warm feeling when we actually succeeded."

I nodded.

"But yes—I suppose I've seen too many things." She hesitated. "I don't like what people become when they get too involved in those ideas—and I don't like what the ideas become when people get too obsessed with them. Basically . . . it scares me. It took me years to admit it, but that kind of crap really really scares me, whatever the subject. When I see that, I see everything that's bad about people. I see sexual prudery. I see stoning people to death for using the wrong fucking name for god or for asking some minor question about life. It's hideous . . ."

". . ."

"And there's no way, no fucking way that such an attitude doesn't get transmitted outwards to other people as well. It's instant pre-packaged judgementalism—how can it not be? I don't care if it's silent judgement or, or . . . calling me a whore or a cannibal in the streets or whatever. I mean, have you even seen some of the things they do? I've watched them pushing disabled people out of wheelchairs because they used medicine tested on animals. I . . . I've watched them lying and manipulating the emotions to destroy ancient traditions that are perfectly in tune with nature—while they tuck into their nice monoculture sandwich. Talking like serial killers, gloating over human torture and murder—even fucking genocide. It just goes on and on. I have even heard of them murdering pets because . . . actually I've no idea. Maybe they think it's better to be dead than domesticated."

Her voice had risen again throughout that tirade until it was some kind of wild free-flow of fury. And I stared in silence, deeply shocked.

"It's not just them," she muttered, winding down again a little, "but whatever the fucking subject, just don't tell me such things. You think you have a fucking monopoly on right just because your visceral clutch has been tickled? Because your dick is erect from righteousness? You think you know enough about the way the world works to pass judgment on an entire species? And when people are forming opinions about me based on that monumental ego, or trying to manipulate my life with it, or tell me something about me is morally repugnant . . . I just see red. Who the fuck wouldn't? It's exactly the same as those prudish wankers trying to tell me I shouldn't show my arse in yoga pants."

"I . . . don't think I ever formed opinions about your life," I stammered, wishing I had never started this conversation.

"Oh I think you did," she growled. "Don't pretend. You're a nice guy but I think you thought things. I could see them in your eyes. I crash right through your world-view, therefore something's wrong with me, huh? You seriously telling me that wasn't in your head at some point? Seriously?"

I stared at her, my mind swimming. It sounded like nonsense, but it still pricked at me. After all, the Beggar had said something similar, though far less aggressively.

She leaned forwards. "I am sick and tired," she said, suddenly crescendoing again, "of people telling me what I should be. As a woman. As a . . . as someone who lives in this stupid bit of the planet instead of that stupid bit of the planet. What I should wear. What I should think. What I should feel guilty about. What I should eat. Fucking anything. I am sick and tired of other people's opinions—other people's ideals, when they haven't a fucking clue how the world works. Just . . . don't, okay?"

"But I'm not telling you anything," I cried. It was rare for me to actually raise my voice, but here I felt pushed far enough for the familiar ice to collapse into a pained shout. "When have I ever had the power to do that?" I drew a deep breath. "When have I had the *luxury* to do that to anyone?"

There was a frozen silence. I was aware of the others watching us in surprise now. The row, if such it was, had grown dramatic enough to attract attention even from the other room. I drew a deep breath. Somewhere I had a train to catch—why the heck was I wasting my time on this?

"Train Man," she said intensely, "I am not talking about you."

I gave her a dubious look, because I was fairly sure she had been.

"Oh fuck it," she snarled. "It just hurts, that's all. They live in a fantasy land—and every fucking thing I do is somehow stifled by that. Every fucking thing."

She punched the chair viciously and her wineglass fell off the adjacent box with a dismal smash. She swore again, staring at it with more desolation than a wine glass should ever command. I also was feeling somewhat desolate. This whole exchange was getting worse and worse—and it was my fault.

"All I know," Star said, softer but still intense, "is that somehow these people have lost something. They've been . . . dehumanised by some force that I still don't really understand. I am not going to go along with it and fuck you if you think that is somehow wrong—if that offends your pathetic little sensibilities."

There was a shocked silence and I stared at her, mouth open like an idiot. In fact, it was more than shock. Almost a horror. Any loquaciousness I may have found for a moment had utterly vanished. And the eyes of the others were all on us now, watching with expressions I couldn't read.

Then the Philosopher raised his arms soothingly. "Please," he said with a hint of sharpness. "What exactly are you arguing about? All I heard was a question."

She growled wordlessly and jumped to her feet. The Philosopher gave her a piercing look, but she stormed out, pushing past the startled Butcher in the passage and into the next archway.

The silence continued.

"Well, that's a bloody good end to the evening," Clay Man said heavily.

For a moment there, I felt almost ready to burst into tears but I repressed it harshly. "All I meant was . . . I mean I just wanted to know what . . ."

"Star is a bit obsessed," he said. "She always has been."

"I'll go after her," the Butcher said and hurried off.

Overhead, the boom of a passing train echoed through the bricks and I stared at the ceiling, the sound pricking at me.

"I think I had better go," I whispered, also making to stand up. In the flickering light of the candles, this room suddenly seemed very dark and unfriendly.

"No . . . no," the Beggar said urgently, sliding into the seat beside me and grabbing my arm. "Don't you dare. Don't . . . look, Star can be a bit wild sometimes, but . . ."

"What the hell was all that even about?" I said, staring at nothing. "I don't understand . . ."

The Butcher stepped in again, looking forlorn.

"She's gone," he said. "Out."

"Oh dear," the Beggar muttered.

The Philosopher sighed. "There is indeed a lot of obsession in her," he said. "There is almost a desperation—a deep fragility. The world in general drives her wild and sometimes she can't keep control of it. It becomes a matter of visceral reactions rather than any kind of rational thought."

"And we've all been there, I think," Clay Man said.

"True enough."

"Everything seems to annoy her," the Philosopher continued sadly. "And you know, I don't really blame her."

"I suppose not," I said. "She—takes refuge in rage, I took refuge on the railway line . . ."

I felt the Beggar's hand tighten its grip. The silence dragged on and could have become awkward, but this time I didn't think it was my responsibility to break it. It stretched out—until it was interrupted by a twitch at the curtain.

"Um," Star Girl said with an awkward smile that didn't get anywhere near her slightly moist eyes, "if I come back in, are you going to hit me with anything?"

Everyone looked round.

"Get your dumb arse in here," Clay Man growled, obviously relieved.

Star Girl stole in sheepishly.

"Gawd," she muttered. "I've—done it again, haven't I?"

"You've done something," Clay Man said with a smile. "Champion debater, you are."

"I sounded like everything I hate, didn't I?" She rubbed her face. "Gawd sake . . ."

Then she grabbed me. I almost yelled in shock, but it was only a hug. I was still sitting in the chair, which meant she had to scramble on top of me and the whole thing was very strange. I could feel her face pressing into my neck with a desperate warmth and I hesitantly returned the squeeze.

"Sorry, Train Man—I am such a messed up bitch sometimes. It seems no matter what side I end up on, I am too fucking used to yelling at people. Are you okay? Or are you hating my guts? Please don't hate my guts."

"Your guts seem okay to me," I said, giving her a poke under the ribs, trying to lighten the atmosphere. She gave a wan smile, squirmed over and sat up, actually sitting in my lap and still holding my arms around her, which was an intimacy I wasn't used to by any means.

"You want to know where this came from?" she said with an obvious effort.

"Where?" the Philosopher asked.

"There was one time when . . . I really lost it. I mean, really really lost it. People tried to stop me, but . . . I just exploded. I attacked a group of them who were yelling at me—I was evil, I was disgusting, etc. etc. Shoving me around, calling me a whore and a slag. Pulling at my clothes. I was totally—well, you have seen me when I lose my temper, right? The main guy ended up in hospital having his eye repaired and various screwdriver holes stitched up—and I . . . was dragged off to the police holding cells." She swallowed again. "That was the end of my protesting. And . . . my involvement in any of those issues. I suppose I shouldn't hate, but it was just a continual drip drip drip . . ."

"I didn't know that," the Philosopher said with interest—and I actually found myself squeezing her a little bit tighter. In spite of all, it was quite nice to hold her there, feeling her weight, her arse straddling my thigh.

"It wasn't so bad. Back then, they still cared a bit about rehabilitation and doing the best thing—so they went pretty easy on me. Better than now, you can bet your arse . . . Diminished responsibility or something. I ended up on heavy medication and in some . . . government paid . . . therapy kind of thing. It was okay—didn't do much, and most of the time I couldn't really say what I thought, only what they wanted to hear. But still—okay. Now though . . ."

She gave a particularly nasty laugh.

"Now I suppose I would be in the London Labs. The animals are safe at last so all these fucking wankers can feel good taking medicine tested on poor people instead."

"And what does that prove?" the Philosopher asked.

"That evil takes all sides?"

He gave a chuckle at that. "Possibly. It certainly leads us quite a dance."

"But you know, I stand by my thoughts, in spite of . . . all that rage," Star said. "I know what I believe in, even if I sometimes lose it."

The Philosopher chuckled again.

"What are you laughing at?" she asked with a slight frown.

"Nothing, Star, nothing," he said soothingly. "I agree with you—really." He gave a cough. "Broadly anyway."

"Oh good," she said, a little fierce. "So tell me which parts you agree with. What do you believe in?"

"I don't like the word 'believe' for a start," he said reprovingly. "It smells of having to form opinions without data. But I do agree that there is nothing more terrifying than a human being with an idea or a nice generalised, over-simplified enemy lodged in their head." He paused a moment. "Any enemy," he said pointedly.

Star looked at him, eyebrows up with suspicion, maybe trying to work out just who that was aimed at.

"And the worst idea of all might be a beleaguered idea," he continued, his voice getting a little grander. "One that is open to attack. One that may in part be true but in part also wrong. Nearly all ideas are wholly or partially wrong unless they contain within an awareness of their own incompletion. But often that plurality, that blur if you like, is only seen as a defeat and defeat is unthinkable. So you then have to position yourself as a fighter. You have to find the aggression—find your warrior soul. And anyone who disagrees becomes a heretic, as I believe you were saying."

"Are you having a go at me?" Star said uncertainly.

He suddenly rose to his feet. "Get up," he barked, waving at her with a theatrical gesture. She did so, scrambling off me and staring at him in surprise. For a moment I wondered what he taught in his normal life. Whoever they were, those students might just be very lucky. He was a real performer.

"And then," he yelled spectacularly, arms spread, "when the idea is lodged, the pantomime starts. It's all *bow down to its majesty*."

The Philosopher did exactly that, bending over in an extravagant formal bow accompanied by a few graceful looping hand movements—only slightly spoiled as his top hat fell off with a thud and rolled away across the concrete floor. The Beggar giggled briefly. If nothing else, this completely over-the-top show was helping to clear the intense atmosphere out of the room better than any miserable discussion could have.

"*Bow down,*" he yelled again. "*To its majesty.*" He waved at Star. "Do it—now."

Star Girl gave a nervous laugh and obeyed, trying awkwardly to imitate his movements.

"Does it smell worse here as I get nearer the floor?" she asked with a small grin.

"That's what you get when you kowtow," the Philosopher said dryly. "It's also what you get when you brown-nose."

"Uggg," Star said, straightening up again and rubbing at her face.

The Philosopher clapped his top hat back on his head. "Yes," he said grandly, standing tall like a grim black column in the candlelight. "It is a terrifying thing. The age-old fight between good and evil, even though neither ever actually existed, as though the dualism of life wasn't a complete illusion. The age-old desperation for a simple solution—something nicely black or white that we can all comfortably blame—even though that never existed either. Or conversely something we can imagine is perfect, when it's actually meaningless. And, I repeat, *bow down, arse in the air, to its majesty. Worship its blackness and its whiteness. And swear allegiance to defend it unto death, to never criticise, and to dedicate yourself body and soul to its perpetuation.* And please, for the sake of demonstration, would you care to pantomime this for me again?"

Star Girl did as he asked—another awkward attempt at the hand gestures and folding herself in half, her face wry. "And you will observe," he said with a smile and a wide gesture that encompassed her with both hands, "that this obeisance has a few interesting characteristics of its own. The worshipper is de-elevating the head, the organ of thought, while a certain other part of the anatomy takes centre stage."

"Oi," Star said with a laugh, not straightening up though.

"This can be interpreted in two ways," the Philosopher continued. "A) as a symbol and critique of ideas metamorphosing into gut instincts and staging an invasion of replacement while the head itself is retired, and B) a reveal of the basically masochistic relationship that exists between humans and ideas. There is no question in my mind that ideas wear leather and big boots, and maybe carry a few implements . . ."

"Ahem," Star said. "I should just like to interject at this point, that if you spank my arse, I am going to jump on your top hat." She straightened up, looking rather red in the face.

"In conclusion," the Philosopher said, ignoring that, "I think it's fair to postulate that one of the crucial goals for the human race should be to maintain a balance between the head, the heart and the arse and to make sure they are all playing their correct role. Thinking with your heart is not good. And thinking with your arse—even worse. After all, if you are thinking with your arse then the role of the arse must be played by your head . . . and common though this is, it really ain't pretty."

"Oh gawd," Star said with a grin. "Okay okay—I take your point. But . . . fuck it, you'd better be using me as the model for this because I have the best head, heart and arse here—that's all I can say."

"Actually I think the Philosopher has the best head," Clay Man murmured.

"And I would suspect the Beggar has the best heart," the Butcher put in with a teasing grin, while the Beggar went crimson.

"Fuck you all," Star Girl yelled. "Get your clowns' arses over here and join in if you are so clever."

"Alright," the Philosopher said happily. "*Bow down,*" he yelled again. "*To its majesty.*"

And this time, to my bemusement, we all ended up playing along, a ragged circle of obeisance and bad hand gestures around the Philosopher, all with subdued giggling. And by this time, in spite of the seeming ridiculous nature of his performance, the atmosphere had become energised and filled with fun and relief.

"I am liking this," he said dryly. "Behold the great adversary. This is why we must question everything—especially the things that people believe most intensely. Especially the things that get a hysterical reaction. Especially the things *we* believe in. Because maybe everything is wrong. Every side of the argument. Every moral, every custom, everything we believe, every way the world works—every aspect of our lives, from our work, to our money, to our morality and values, to our identity. Every single thing we have built up around ourselves. And this is why we must arise. Arise, my children," he yelled, raising his arms in a dramatic gesture. "Arise my lords and ladies. And go forth."

Star Girl didn't arise though, she dropped down onto her hands and knees, threw back her head and gave a shrill howl—vaguely wolf-like—before scampering away across the floor with surprising speed, then back again. The Butcher was still bowed and she jumped on him, sinking her teeth into that most elevated part of him.

"Ow," he yelled, straightening up rather precipitously. "What's got into you today?"

"I'm just having a wild evening," she cried.

"You don't say. Okay, okay, I guess there are worse things to do to people who bow."

Star Girl went bounding away, then crashed face first onto one of the largest beanbags, a moment later rolling over onto her back in an inelegant sprawl.

"Now . . . may I finally get on with the cooking?" the Butcher asked. "If you've made me burn the dinner, I'll . . ."

"You'll what?" Star asked with a thin smile.

"I'll . . . think of something both embarrassing and mildly painful," the Butcher said, his eyebrows flicking up.

"Promises, promises. Yes, go on. I guess rage gives me an appetite because I am famished."

"Will do," he said, making for the passage through to the next room, where the stove waited.

"Hurry, hurry," Star cried cheekily.

The Butcher just gave an expansive shrug. "You, sort out the damn tableware," he growled as he left the room, the Beggar and Clay Man following. Only the Philosopher remained, also lying back in his comfortable chair and seeming to dismiss both of us from his thoughts.

Star made no move to sort out anything at all, though—and with nothing else to do, I stood looking down on her sprawled out, arms and legs both spread wide and dangling in a floppy and, it has to be said, rather sexy human X. Her head was dangling backwards as well, staring up at the wall behind her before closing her eyes with a sigh.

And now, peace seemed to descend on the room for the first time in a long while. A long drawn-out silence of slow breaths—indeed, for a while it seemed as though she was trying to meditate. Then, to my mild surprise, her hands came up and she began unbuttoning her blouse. Under it was more of her curious angular colour patterns, green and brown—a loose but body-hugging top.

"Did you . . . make that?" I asked shyly. I wasn't sure—but there was something about the clothes that looked handmade.

"Yeah," she said. Her eyes opened and she chucked the blouse on the floor. "That's what I do—I make clothes, I sell them. I have a place in Hackney Wick; I go round the alt fashion shows and sell them online. It's a life, I guess."

The Philosopher's eyes flicked open again, but he said nothing.

"Nice," I said. "I love the Wick."

"It's almost a ruin," she said. "My place. I need to put plastic over the windows in the winter because there's no seal and I sometimes have to defrost my toothpaste in the morning—but hey, that's London, right?"

"Right," I said. "And those clothes you are wearing . . . some kind of camouflage?"

She gave me a look with a hint of respect. "Spot on. Not everyone gets that, even when I tell them. I designed them for these meetings, though I sell some of them in the shop as well. I originally wore black, but you know, it's a funny thing, in nature there's very little black—and when you are trained, you can pick out black as an unnatural zone in the world, even at night. That's why I went for these greens and browns. It fades away much better. I didn't want to go for a standard camouflage pattern either because that sends out messages when they *can* see you—so I ended up with this. The shapes are there to break up my outline in the dark but in the daylight it just looks like an outlandish art print."

I studied her unselfconsciously. This was the first time I had really let myself take a close look at these clothes. I could see that the pattern wasn't actually a print at all—the different colours looked to be stitched together minutely. No doubt there was a lot of planning involved, a lot of work going on to find the best way to break up the shape of the body as effectively as possible, and then to somehow project that into pieces of fabric that would hang correctly on a human body as it moved and changed.

"Feel it," she invited. "I am actually quite proud of this stuff."

I ran my hand over her leg appreciatively, and yes, under my fingers, I could feel the stitched seams where the colours were attached together—precisely how, I wasn't sure. It created a patchwork feeling—just a hint of ragdoll about it, but the darker colours giving it a good dose of glamour.

"And that's a lot of seams to split in some very funny places if you get something wrong," she added with a laugh.

"They actually look really beautiful."

She looked up at me with a flattered grin. Then, with a lazy movement, she rolled over onto her front, then onto her back again. Standing up, it would have been a twirl, and as it was it was still a full three-hundred-and-sixty-degree turn for me in the candlelight.

"Behold," she said with a grin, "the latest fashions for discerning and effective city hunters."

"Very nice," I murmured.

"Soft loose trousers," she said brushing them, "complete with cords on both ankles. And an equally soft long-sleeved

T-shirt thing, cut shortish at the hips—I don't want it grabbing me round the arse when I am trying to move. Both loose and comfortable enough so I can do whatever I want, but without it flapping around everywhere—and without making a sound. You've no idea how much work it took to get these things as silent as possible. I must have tried a dozen different fabrics."

She closed her eyes again.

"I wanted to be a dancer when I was young," she said, "but they told me I had the wrong body. Guess what I studied?"

"I wouldn't dare," I said, sitting down again.

"Performance art," she said, the grin expanding, still moving gently. "Would you believe it?"

"I would, actually."

She hummed softly to herself, moving gently on the beanbag like a snake, like gently swirling water.

"I was the girl getting up to all the weird stuff in the background," she said, her voice singsong—and the Philosopher chuckled quietly. "The stuff that nobody really understood. The sort of thing everyone mocks. 'Oh she's just an art student—don't pay any attention.' But you know, studying something with an experimental touch like my . . . like performance art, it gives you a bit of an edge with other things as well. It also taught me all about how the world worked, how the mind worked, how humanity worked, how creativity worked. All the real stuff."

"True that," the Philosopher said.

"I just wish they'd taught me a few other things as well—like how to sell my soul. How to stop feeling—and stop caring. How to flaunt my arse for gold coins. I miss that place—the old college. You find a weird bunch of people on a performance art course, but it was a place where you could think properly without being stifled by the constant presence of . . . what are they?"

"Who?"

"The sort of pathetic souls TV censorship was created for . . . or the squeamish morons who get things banned because of their own psychological issues?"

The frown flashed in her eyes again for a moment—a stab of energy into this quiet. Then she shrugged it off and relaxed again.

Of course, on one level, she was being simplistic with much of that and I think she knew it. But on the other, maybe it didn't matter. It was rage porn—the blunt expression of frustration that went beyond more reasoned and complex debate. Something I was still not used to hearing. But maybe it's not a bad thing provided you are also capable of thinking your way through it all.

"You're a good listener," she said with a brittle laugh. "Better than I deserve. You are the worst talker in the entire history of the world—but maybe one of the best listeners. I like that."

I felt a glow of rather odd warmth and glanced round in embarrassment. In the next room, the Butcher was standing over his stove and pans like a young wizard in a fantasy novel—especially given the phantasmagorical art on the wall behind him.

"Shouldn't we be laying the table?" I asked with a smile.

"Oh why thank you," Star said with a huge grin. "So kind of you to volunteer."

I glared down at her.

"They're in there," she said, pointing to a basket. "Spoons this time, I fancy. And some glasses."

With a sigh, I opened it up and rummaged until I found a box of them and then returned.

Actually there wasn't a table as such in here—only small occasional tables or wooden boxes draped with cloth accompanying the comfortable chairs. But I laid out cutlery and wine glasses, while Star lounged there and watched. Then, a short while later, bowls of stew appeared—a creamy stew with a hint of wine and lots of vegetables. Looking at the bowl I held, I couldn't help wondering which chunks of meat had come from the rabbit I had switched off myself. No way of knowing, of course. I glanced round furtively at the others. The Butcher smiled thinly as he tasted a sip of gravy. The Beggar actually had her eyes closed as she chewed. The Philosopher looked emotionless, as always. Star Girl still looked drained and rather unhappy, I realised, but she was trying to derive warmth from the food.

Then the Beggar's grey eyes flicked open again and glanced at me, so I hastily dipped in a spoon and tasted.

It tasted good. Very good. After a fraught and tense night, a bowl of good stew calmed the nerves very nicely—lingering guilt fading yet further in the mellow atmosphere. Following the Beggar's earlier words, I could sense something basic and natural in all this—maybe good flavours and the feeling of warmth were finally making me admit that she was right in her earlier rant. Maybe everyone was right and it really didn't matter—law, paranoia, fear, disgust—who's to say any of these are absolute and not manufactured?

And later still, when we had made it vanish, Star Girl settled beside me on the sofa. The others sipped wine and relaxed, also sprawled out with a glorious sense of candlelit comfort.

"Feeling better, Star?" Clay Man asked, rubbing at her shoulders. She gave a weary and appreciative smile.

"I just—lose it sometimes," she said quietly. "I don't think it is entirely unjustified."

"No—I guess not," the Beggar said.

"I think we can agree, though," the Philosopher said, "that whatever trials and tribulations may beset us, there is something precious about being here, being together. That is the talisman we can raise against whatever the world can throw."

I gave a frown, that shadowy area at the back of my mind suddenly filled with turning wheels and wondering where the railway line lay in all this. Being here, with Star Girl's weight against me, just felt so infinitely comfortable.

"Yeah," I murmured. "This . . . is true." And it was. I was reminded of nature documentaries—the great old documentaries by Sir David Attenborough and others, the ones that contained less propaganda—where animals would pile together in a comfortable heap to keep warm, too 'stupid' for paranoia or self-consciousness. Too real. Okay, so it is hard these days to see those programs in their original forms, without uncomfortable jump cuts and suspicious breaks in the narrative—but what I am referring to here was of no interest to the censors anyway. Just animals in a heap. But maybe that was what we were doing. Snuggling together to keep alive the warmth of companionship against all the forces ranged against it.

And, like a cat scratching at a metaphorical door, I wanted in.

"Are you coming back next time, Train Man?" the Beggar asked as though reading my mind. The light of the candles glowed warmly, casting shadows that only made her face seem sharper. For a moment, she looked unreal—like a painting.

"Yes—please do," Star Girl murmured, her face nuzzling my shoulder hopefully.

I looked round at them all. Was I coming back? Was that the way things were going here? Screw the train, I thought at last. Maybe that could always remain there as a comforting presence—always ready to take me on its journey, if I needed it. But maybe, well, maybe I could catch the next one. Or the one after that. Or some other future train, as yet un-timetabled.

"Train Man?"

Lingering uncertainty and discomfort notwithstanding, how could I possibly say no?

WEDNESDAY

There's one thing I will say about home. There is a sense of community—scrappy and sometimes borderline insane community, but community nonetheless. Community that is rather forced upon us since we are all in such close proximity and it doesn't make up for a lot of other things . . . but it is there.

"How do I look?" Kate asked, turning round for me. She was wearing intense, almost savage-looking makeup and costuming that was very alien to her usual rather scruffy house-clothes. A short skirt over black leggings and a frilly black top. Large metal earrings tugged at her ears. Her eyes were marked out darkly, accentuating the corners in black and green, her hair styled roughly and streaked with blue streamers of some non-permanent colour by one of our haircutting neighbours.

"You look great," Aceline said. "Really. What about me?"

But Kate wasn't paying any attention. By contrast, Aceline was dressed simply in jeans and a blouse with dark stripes—a simplicity that I rather preferred. Might even say was sexier.

"My arse is too big," Kate grumbled. "Gawd, you men are so lucky. Your arses behave themselves far better."

I gave a dry smile. "Do they?"

"You're fine," Aceline said. "The days of the scrawny non-existent rear are gone. Now it's all about a nice proud round . . ."

"Okay, okay," Kate cried with a high-pitched giggle. "I don't know—I eat hardly anything—I go for hours without meals . . ."

She leaned over the laptop and clicked a bookmark, then went back to gazing into the mirror. On the screen, though, flames were now licking through a wrecked shop daubed with slogans in

German—while furious men and women were dragged away by the police. The sort of scene that demands at least some attention, even though it was just the familiar bedraggled chaos of urban unrest. A woman screamed in the gutter while florescent uniforms bent over her. Were they helping or hindering? It was hard to ever be sure anymore. I watched curiously, wondering what it meant. I couldn't remember much news from Germany lately, but nowhere seemed immune from troubles these days. The world seemed to be threatening to boil over everywhere you looked—the news was continually permeated by economic troubles, cruel austerity legislation, increasing inequality, hate everywhere, elitist politicians—all of these bred ill feeling and resentment, protests and scuffles. None of which seemed likely to fade away any time soon.

"What about me?" I asked at last, brushing at my jacket. "Am I okay?" Nobody answered my question. I was never at my best round mirrors, but right now it didn't look too bad. It was a loose blazer-type jacket, chosen to hide my pudgy body as much as possible—the black fabric revealing gleams of red silk from my shirt below. Yes—this was me in smart mode.

A man yelled into the camera, with a heavy German accent. *"We will not be—be bullied into badly thought-out nutritional regimes or legislated eating disorders. Our children will not be malnourished and not isolated from the animal kingdom... and every—person, everyone knows this has nothing to do with—with looking after animals' welfare, none of this is anything to do with saving the world or making things better. It is just... just pure self-loathing, hateful masturbation over our nasty failed... umm, culture and failed relationship with the environment—pure ignorance to just blot out something we can't be bothered to address properly. A sort of puritanical... what is the word? Scarification..."*

The view cut out, back to stock footage of the burning restaurant.

High drama in Berlin, the presenter said. *Maybe stirring up all-too-painful memories of our own country not so long ago. For those that just joined us, a protest has turned violent in Germany as pressure mounts for the country to sign the Amsterdam Animal Welfare Reform Plan, which...*

"I didn't know the Germans hadn't joined us yet," Aceline said with mild interest.

"No," Kate said, "but they will. It's all over Europe now."

"What about Slovenia?" I asked, thinking of Tea.

"Not yet either. Austria has—and Finland. Wasn't there a load of fuss in Lapland quite early on? Denmark has. Not Norway or Iceland. But I am sure they will. I hope so—it would serve Tea right."

I wondered briefly what Tea and her family would do if meat farming was suddenly outlawed. Funnily enough, that had never occurred to me before. It's not as if you could switch to growing wheat on a high mountain pasture at the drop of a law, after all. I tried to remember the UK's recent past, but aside from a vague mush of half-ignored protest, it was all a blank.

Kate gave a prim twitch of her dyed hair, then clicked a link again impatiently—but there was no escape.

"Eugenics in other words. And can you state definitively that the UK government is not considering such a path?" "I . . . afraid I am not able to comment on future medical policy . . ." "You will not even deny something as grave and unacceptable as that?" "I—I cannot comment, simply because there is nothing to comment on and . . ."

"Gawd," she grated, and closed the page completely. Then she grinned and posed one last time in front of the mirror. "You sure I am okay?" she cried. "Come on, would you contract this?"

I pulled a face, unsure how to reply. A negative probably wouldn't have gone down very well, but I've never been a good liar. Fortunately the conversation was interrupted when Aceline's phone rang.

"Hey," she yelled into it. "Yes—come on up. You remember the combination? Oh great. See you in a mo . . ."

"That was . . . ?"

"Yes. Okay okay," Aceline cried. "He's here. Are we ready? And hey, if I get lucky tonight . . . a little privacy, please?"

"What if we all get lucky?" Kate asked with a grin.

I shrugged with a comical grimace. "We'll have to draw up some kind of rota."

"Either that or work together," Kate said happily.

"No. Fucking. Way," Aceline said with emphasis. "This one's mine."

"Hey," I said, "you've got separate beds. What more do you want?"

Before anyone could respond to that, there was a bang on the door and she went to open it at top speed. There was a squeal of greeting and she dragged in . . .

Oh, I knew him vaguely. Fairly new in the landscape, and with Aceline all over him. I try to ignore the politics going on among my neighbours but tend to pay rather more attention when it's politics taking place directly outside my only route to freedom. I can barely remember his name now—I think something like Jayden, and I guess that will do here. I might come across as mean, but there seemed very little for me to latch onto. A sense of ordinariness dominated. If he had been an insect, his Latin name would have been *vulgaris*. Clothes so normal I can't even remember them. Body pretty normal as well. Short cropped hair. No doubt Aceline saw something more in there.

"Talk of the devil," Aceline said cheekily, and Kate gave a loud laugh.

"What devil?" he asked.

"Nothing, nothing," Aceline cried, hanging onto his arm. "I'm so glad you made it."

I watched warily, in high alert mode. The smell of sex was nothing new here, but now it seemed very immediate. I don't mean a literal smell, of course, but a smell in the brain. An awareness. It was in her body language—the way you move when you are already, consciously or subconsciously, imagining his dick inside you. My dismay might confuse some of you—but think about our living circumstances for a moment. Maybe, I remember thinking, I could invest in a rope ladder of some kind and never have to open that damn door of mine ever again.

"Sure," Jayden said. "I brought something . . ."

It turned out to be a six-pack. Not the most imaginative offering—but then, nor was my wine bottle waiting by the door.

Aceline still hadn't let go of his arm. "Shall we go?" she asked. "Or do you want to chill for a few minutes?"

"Nah—I'm good."

He hadn't even acknowledged my existence yet—and that made a weird kind of sense. From where I was standing, he seemed on another world entirely—no overlap with mine whatsoever. He might as well have been a holographic projection and I just stood there with a frozen smile on my face, ready to be agreeable but probably looking like a complete lunatic. It was a relief when Kate gave one last tug of her skirt, which barely covered her arse, and we hurried out and down the corridor.

☼

I could hear the sound from Tea's room long before we reached her door—a depressing presence of music, little more than a pulsating noise that came booming through the walls as though this old building was a musical instrument itself. It's the sort of thing that makes me want to go in the opposite direction quite fast, but in this case, among the complex conflicting forces at work here, there was only one winner. Facing Tea was always a blend of being drawn inexorably and wanting to keep her as far away as possible. It's a battle of inner and outer—hungry and rational. But there was no changing plans now. I would just have to deal with it.

There seemed little point knocking at that door so Aceline pushed it open, releasing a cloud of noise that I could almost see in the air. Beyond was Tea's home—a small den like all the others here, complete with a shower cubicle in the corner and all the usual scraps of furniture. And also like the others here, it was as individual as you can get. It was an extension of herself like the shed skin of a spider. A room filled with that shocking poignancy that you get when staring at the rather desolate environment of one you want to connect to. The sort of poignancy that wants to take every single one of those objects, those hints and clues about another existence, and enshrine them in a museum because the message they convey is so powerful.

The room was crowded, though in a place this size, it doesn't take many people to achieve that. Various neighbours and outsiders, some known, some not, all looking sweaty and rather swamped. Everyone was trying to make themselves heard over the music and over everyone else, and the net result was that the entire proceedings dissolved into a wall of sound, none of which could be heard. It might as well have been a ship's engine room.

Tea herself came to the door with a crow of greeting and swept us all inside. We exchanged rather formulaic greetings and handed over the cheap booze we had contributed. She looked quite striking now, her face also touched with some quite extravagant make-up—including some sharply angled patches of colour around her eyes, all set off with washes of blue in her hair. It was handy having a neighbour who is a hairdresser, though she did end up stamping her style on the whole building as though she was marking her territory. I understand she also specialised in hair and makeup designed to confuse facial recognition software. Such is the world we live in.

Tea's clothes were also striking—ragged tight jeans with holes revealing pale skin. Theoretically that was a simple enough attempt at being grungy, but in reality those jeans were not cut for someone who walks in mountains. The tight fabric was causing the muscular flesh of her thighs to bulge out of the holes as though her legs were home to four or five small arse-cheeks. It didn't look very comfortable and I found myself furtively studying those mounds with interest—the sort of weird phenomenon that, once seen, is hard to look away from. She was also wearing a light jacket in black velvet over a very low-cut top with dazzling coloured stripes and a large necklace of black stones in silver hanging over her skin.

In short, she looked great on several levels. I liked the fact that she was trying to show herself off and also that she was somehow bursting out beyond that.

However, she was still wearing that eye-patch and I stared at it uneasily.

"Come and get a drink," she yelled, grabbing my arm. "We can go up on the roof later if you like."

That was heartening—mostly because it would presumably be quieter. What was this racket? A quest for a place where the voice and all its shallow layers of civilization is just irrelevant? If so, it didn't work for me. When I can't hear myself think, when the music is so loud that you can't actually hear it, there is one image that always seems to come back into my mind: a single violin in a vast space . . . and that violin was playing in my head now. Imagine long quiet notes that go and go—as long and as wide as the space itself—a space hard to imagine in London. A beautiful image. Somehow sound and silence can become confused—sound you can't hear and silence that you can, silence represented by sound and sound coming across as silence . . .

She waved at the table and said . . . something.

"What?" I screamed.

Her finger darted round the various bottles, which ranged from wine and beer to some less familiar things that I could only presume she had brought back with her from Slovenia. I recognised the word Medica among them (pronounced med-eet-sa). Each poke was a question—an offer. I was curious about the Medica, but in the absence of speech, I went for the easy option and pointed to a large bottle of cloudy cider. And a moment later I was holding a glass, mercifully filled with ice. I mouthed the word *thanks*—not even bothering to make the sounds.

". . . ay so h . . . you?" Tea said companionably. "Haven't s . . . ch . . . ly. Should . . . ore of . . . in, right?"

I stared at her, eyebrows up, again wondering how I was supposed to deal with this. I have enough trouble with words at the best of times, but now, even that limited medium was stripped away from me. It really was quite comical. In the end, I opened my mouth a few times, earnestly pretending to talk.

She leaned forward. ". . . ?"

I gave up with a huge shrug, backed away a few steps with a small bow—then drew a quick zipping gesture across my lips and shrugged.

Sorry—but my lips are bound.

She gave a giggle and circled both ears with her fingers, rolling her eyes slightly—waved at the people around the room, then made an expanding circle with her arms.

Yeah—it is rather loud, but it has to be done, you know. I think.

I responded by leaning over sideways and punching myself on one ear, as though cartoonishly trying to dislodge something from the other. I mimed a 'failure' shrug and cupped my hands to the side of my head with a pulsing gesture.

Nope.

And hey—I was communicating! Certainly the only kind of communication I was going to get around here. I sipped my drink, made a bow, pointed at her, drew a vertical line straight down across my heart and spread my arms.

She grinned wider, slapped at her ragged and bulging thigh, pointed at me, drew a circle in the air, tapped at her wrist where a watch would have been if she had had one, and made a quick three-fingered eating gesture.

Then a new figure entered the room—and something about her caught my eye. I think it was because she stepped in like a cat entering an unfamiliar space. Cautiously, as though smelling the air for any hints of threat. People who moved like that gave me a small flash of fellow feeling, for good or ill. She looked ordinary enough at first glance, dressed in simple jeans and a brown jacket. It was quite a contrast to some of the other costumes here, but it wasn't as simple as it looked. That could be seen in the details . . . oddly coloured buttons and the flash of almost hidden jewellery. Subtle but there.

Her name, I knew, was Feather. And she didn't live here.

That was pretty much all I knew.

I watched Tea greet her—something in her body language revealing that this newcomer was not an acquaintance of hers either. Nevertheless, she was quickly drawn in. We ended up together at the table in a little knot and I watched with some amusement as they went through the familiar ritual of trying to talk—and failing. In the end, I couldn't resist butting in with another comical mime. I traced my finger from my nose, to Tea's eyes, then in a graceful arc towards the computer that was blaring out all this racket and mimed a sharp explosion. *The remedy to all your problems,* the translation might have gone, *is within your hands.*

Tea responded with a laugh and Feather with raised eyebrows—then she leaned forward, tapped Tea pointedly in the chest and drew a question mark in the air.

How are you? I mentally translated, feeling strangely pleased that my little game was spreading.

Tea gave a wide shrug, raised her eyebrows, placed two hands against her face in the universal gesture of sleep, brushed one hand over her eye, pointed to the room and the general world around her and gave a happy and celebratory jump.

Not bad—rather tired and . . . this eye thing. But it's great to be back here.

I stared at that eyepatch—and then found myself reaching out to it. From an inch away I circled it with one finger, then spread my arms in a questioning gesture, eyebrows up. And hmm—it seemed I had finally asked the question I had been so shy about putting into actual words.

Tea traced a circle in the air with a rather complicated look—embarrassed, melancholy—then she seemed to give up. She reversed out of the door, a flick of her chin inviting us both to follow. I obeyed—and found Feather by my side as well. Out here, the sound was cut at least to a level where voices could be clearly heard again, which was a huge relief.

"Oh wow," Tea said in that rich and rather sharp-edged voice of hers. "And hello."

"Hello," I said with a laugh. "Good to see you again and how are you and all that?"

Tea looked hesitant for a moment, then seemed to shrug.

"Yes, it's real," she said sadly. "It's very kind of everyone to be asking about it. It's a medical eyepatch—sort of."

"What happened?"

Again that slightly uncomfortable look.

"I mean . . . sorry, maybe none of my business, but . . ."

"That," she said, her remaining eye narrowing slightly, "is quite a story. I will tell you sometime—when there are a few minutes. It's . . . fine though. Nothing to worry about."

"Isn't there?" Feather asked. These were the first words of hers that I had heard, and her voice came across as surprisingly strong. Quiet, serious, almost meek—but strong. The kind of voice that might get confused at a convoluted joke, but could maybe tell you the secrets of life . . .

Again, Tea looked embarrassed. "It will be fine . . . hmm . . ."

The two looked at each other, and I got the feeling that I was missing part of this conversation—as though levels of information were being exchanged that were going straight over my head.

"I'm sorry," Tea said at last. "But I don't actually know who you are."

"I am Feather," the newcomer said. "The mudlark."

"The what?"

"That just means . . . I collect stuff," Feather said with a grin.

That word was ringing faint bells. It basically meant a scavenger—specifically one who lives off the bits and bobs lost in the river. Once it had been the domain of the poorest, who would grub for coal on the Thames banks. Now it was more a matter of collectors and amateur treasure hunters. I presumed that Feather was the latter, since there is no way on earth that anyone could earn the London rents out of detritus these days. The times had changed—and changed—and changed. Now I could look at her more closely, I realised that the details of her clothes bore out her statement—a disparate mix of colourful buttons holding it all together, a necklace of odd stones, the occasional brooch that looked close to an antique. And around her waist, threaded through the loops of her jeans, a black belt with a buckle that had the rough ornate and slightly battered appearance of old gold. I stared at it in surprise, wondering if it could possibly be real.

"You are a warrior," Feather said at last with a small smile.

"I . . . what?" Tea smiled with a hint of discomfort. "How do you know about . . . ?"

Feather just shrugged. "A warrior's scars always have a story to tell."

Tea actually blushed slightly. And I was getting a creeping feeling down my back. Had Tea been in a fight?

"Sadly, in the war against the Measuring Men, there are a lot of scars," Feather said—that same quiet and serious voice.

"Uhhh . . . ?"

"Who?" I asked with a nervous laugh. This was all getting decidedly strange.

Feather spread her arms with a rather bizarre smile.

"The Measuring Men and the World Polyhedron. The World Polyhedron that binds you tight in servitude. And the Measuring Men that watch you all the time—they make notes on their little clipboard and tut disapprovingly. They measure you with strange implements and, once you grow above a certain length, tut tut . . ." She whipped a finger across her throat, eyes flashing wide for a moment.

Both of us were staring at her blankly. I didn't remember ever speaking to her before this—she was nothing more than an occasional presence in the corridors. And to hear such words coming out of the mouth of a stranger, in such a quiet tone, left me with no idea how I should respond. I was feeling somewhat uneasy, confused—and a bit intrigued as well. I wondered whether she had been taking anything stronger than esoteric booze on this potentially wild evening, but she didn't look like it. She seemed quiet and normal.

"But something has to give way soon," she continued. "The Polyhedron must die. And when war comes, I only hope people don't forget the important things. We will not forgive, but we must also be wise, otherwise what's the point?"

"Right," Tea said with a bemused smile. "Okay."

I knew what a polyhedron was—a solid form with flat polygonal faces, straight edges and sharp vertices. The cube, the dodecahedron, truncated forms, the star-shaped stellations and a million other mathematical constructs. They are beautiful, elegant mathematical things, sometimes extremely complicated—but how the heck could a polyhedron die? Or be an enemy for that matter?

It was maybe fortunate that we were interrupted then for the conversation could have become very awkward. The door burst open and Aceline appeared, landing on my shoulder with a yell. Her face was red and I stared at her curiously.

"Um—you don't have any contracts printed, do you?"

"What?" I managed, trying to refocus, while Feather gave a quiet chuckle.

If possible, Aceline went even redder. "You know—contracts. BIAs? I thought I had one—but I don't."

I gave her a dry look, eyebrows up. I couldn't help feeling that expecting such things from me was somewhat optimistic. "You got lucky already?" I asked, glancing in at the doorway, where Jayden sat quietly with a glass of beer. She gave a crimson-faced giggle in response.

"I—dunno," she said. "I have my op cert of course—but no contract. So . . ."

"Well—I haven't got one."

"Nor have I," Feather murmured.

For a moment, I wondered whether to offer to run to my room and switch my computer on. I had a small printer in there and printing contracts so people could get laid was no great chore. Somehow it spelled out the story of my life though. Always the printer, never the signatory.

It wasn't needed though.

"Hang on," Tea said. "I might have something. She hurried in, leaving the rest of us staring at each other in silence. Sex, Measuring Men, wounded eyes, romance, World Polyhedra . . . yes, I think the others would have to carry this conversation for a little while now because I was in shut-down mode. They didn't though—and the silence was rather frozen.

Wait—wait . . . Tea has contracts?

It seemed so, for she came back in just a moment, waving a few pieces of paper. "I found some."

Aceline spun round with relief, still crimson in the face. "Thanks," she said. "Just in case, you know. Today might be the day."

"Standard or fun fun fun?" Tea asked, holding up two pieces of paper.

"Oh gawd . . ."

"Try this one," Tea said with a laugh, handing it over. I leaned over her shoulder and studied the paper, feeling a massive and not altogether pleasant chill somewhere in my stomach. This was a side of Tea that I had never really known about and I was curious in a sickly kind of way just what kind of 'fun' she was talking about. Those contracts were still quite new at the time—or at least quite new in the mainstream. They always made me feel a little weird in ways I won't analyse here, but hey, one from Tea's files was only going to do that times a hundred. It caused a bloom of that weird heavy sensation in the middle of my brain.

Bilateral Intercourse Agreement

The hereinbelow named signatories declare that sexual intercourse taking place on the following date . . . . and at the following location . . . . is fully in accordance with the wishes of both parties and that it involves no coercion of any kind. Both parties agree to respect the wishes and limits of the other, especially where any below-mentioned restrictions are concerned. Such consensual acts may only encompass acts that may be considered regular and usual acts, unless specifically defined in Article 2. below.

Sexy isn't it. Print it on pink paper for the proper effect.

"What have you got in the additionals?" Aceline asked, studying the paper. "Licking your . . . oh boy. Spanking top/bottom? No way! I'm crossing that out. And that."

"I just listed everything I could think of," Tea said, her grin widening—that exact same mischievous look she had worn while teasing us all about sausages in 'crackling' the other day.

"You're nuts."

"Why not? It is good to be open to whatever sensations come your way, don't you think?" An innocent smile.

"Come on Tea-Cup," Aceline wailed. "Gimme the other paper . . ."

"No, no—you should try it. Try everything twice, that is the key to life."

"I never knew you were so bloody kinky."

Tea just shrugged and grinned again. "Well—good against depression, you know. Very relaxing. Numerous health benefits."

No doubt, no doubt.

The whole exchange was giving me a thunderously weird feeling. Again that blend of responses that the confused pendulum generated—as though some part of me was pleading with me to flip out in a jealous and frustrated storm but instead I was mostly numb and ready to laugh. Before I could read any more details, though, Aceline grabbed the other, presumably more innocent paper, folded it up and pocketed it, then she went scampering back into the room. I watched her sit down about as close as she could get to the object of her affections without actually sitting on him and I sighed. Communications communications—messages sent and received—body languages—dance—things you could never catch in a contract, or even in words. And now more communication of some kind must be going on in that noiseless space.

I took a long drink of cider and glanced round. Somewhere in the middle of all that, Feather had vanished as mysteriously as she had come, so my eyes rested on Tea with a wry smile. It was all a farce, of course—any dreams of connection to this person. She had never seemed more alien than she did now, rattling away in this particular life like a pea in a shaker.

"I'm heading to the roof," I said.

"I'll be up soon as well," Tea said. "Then we can talk."

I nodded with a smile that I hoped would feel genuine.

✿

The roof of our building was a special place—one of the few things that really stood out about living here. It was a wide, flat expanse surrounded by a low brick parapet. Like everything else, it was a bit of a mess, but it was a striking and very urban mess. A couple of sheds had been erected there, fastened to the hard floor, and even a small greenhouse filled with plants. Graffiti art covered everything, including the low walls, in a storm of uneasy colour and hidden meaning. It was hardly a garden, but it was our equivalent. A popular place to relax when the weather was right—to lounge around and socialise, or sunbathe, or moonbathe, or get on with things that needed doing.

As I climbed the stairs and emerged into the light, I was greeted by a blast of warmth. The sun was setting and the warmth was mostly radiating up from the surface now. It was countered by the wind, which was quite brisk at this height. A few people sat sprawled out in deckchairs—not many that I recognised. I strolled over to the parapet and leaned against it, downing the last of my drink and staring out at the city. It was a good view, not obstructed by too many other buildings. I could see London stretching away in a carpet of trees and roofs, occasionally pierced by some taller building. In the far distance, I could even see the Orbit tower in the Olympic Park and the glittery skyscrapers of Stratford. The railway line passed nearby, which was always a comforting presence. Passenger trains ran every few minutes, interspersed with the occasional freight train. I am not really a trainspotter—I don't care much about the train numbers or types of rolling stock—but there was something about watching a smoothly functioning railway that said at least something was right with the world. When they are late, I can feel it from up here and it is as though a minor sickness has taken hold of the city. Kind of like a stuffed-up sinus.

True to her word, Tea soon appeared, though she wasn't alone. There was an eruption of arrival as a whole group of them came spilling out onto the roof. I watched the excitement for a while but was happy enough to remain on the fringe of things. Soon though, she came hurrying over.

"Something I want you to try," she said, waving a bottle.

"Oh?"

"Or should I say . . ."

She reached out to me and circled her fingers around my face, then drew a quick line to the bottle in her hand and circled that vigorously, before performing a formal bow.

With a mischievous and rather pleased grin, I returned her bow, then patted my heart gratefully. There was absolutely no need for this now as the only sound was chattering voices in the middle distance, but it was a fun game to play nonetheless. How much could we actually communicate without using words? Probably quite a lot, if we let ourselves. In my case at least, it might even be an improvement.

She quickly poured a small glassful and handed it to me. I took it and sniffed. Honey. And then . . .

"Wwwhhhhhhheeeeuuuuuu." One of the most beautiful, heady, intense and almost dreamlike flavours I could ever remember. Honey, yet a million times more than honey. This was honey as might be produced by the bees in a fantasy world or religious afterlife.

"Is that Medica?" I asked in awe, so impressed that I forgot to gesture the question.

"Yes," she said with happy satisfaction. "Honey brandy. Now tell me we don't have good eats up there in the mountains."

Putting the glass down on the wall, I tried to find some gestures that would work in response to this—no harder than finding words, I suppose—and ended up tracing tears down my cheek followed by a massive dizzy circle—then spreading my arms in a huge dancey flourish.

To my surprise, she responded by engaging, taking my hands, and we danced a few musicless steps around the roof. For a moment I felt shockingly alive. Powerful, almost predatory—the human animal, glorious in its warmth and hunger. This, I realised, was how the Beggar felt when she made a kill, yet this wasn't aggression in the sense we humans are used to it, this was something else. The pure ecstasy of functionality? Life force? I'm not sure how, but the two forces were the same. The same hunger. And definitely the same reality. A hunger for experience and sensation—for fulfilment. Tea's body crackling with energy under my hands, her eyes glittering with exhilaration, the weight of her arms on my shoulders, the brush of her blue-streaked hair, tight denim against my severe black trousers . . .

For a brief moment, things were perfect. I was alive—I was hungry . . . but of course it soon broke again. She stepped away and leaned against the wall with a bump, breathing heavily. And I was left feeling strangely shaken. No, no, no. I didn't want this—I had never wanted this. Let us not reawaken the bonds of yearning. That would be bad. It was nothing more than a moment of fooling around, but I felt as though I had touched a live wire. Almost the same feeling as when I had dispatched the rabbit . . .

I mentally shrugged and watched her—eyes following her every small movement, every curve of her body. *Calm down,* I mentally ordered myself. *Remember reality.*

"Is that Feather?" she asked and I glanced round. In a more secluded area of the roof, rather hidden from the rest of the party, a figure sat cross-legged and with her back to us. In front of her, on one of the larger areas of wall, was a huge text. It was scrawled in what looked like black and white brush strokes, obliterating layers of earlier art: *BE READY!* That phrase again.

"Who is she?"

"I . . . really don't know," I said. "I never spoke to her properly before today."

Tea nodded, then stepped in her direction. "Hey," she cried. "Try some honey brandy."

Feather looked round with a quiet hello. In her hand, a spray can. Not a brush. There was more text clustered around the main one, I realised as I drifted over to join them—all in different hands. It was among these that she was working, as though adding her own commentary to some already existing game.

Remember justice.
Remember equality.
Remember the homeless.
Remember the Measuring Men.
Remember freedom.
Remember diversity.
Remember the fugitives.

And the last one, still being penned: *Remember the true enemies.*

"Be ready for what?" I asked, and she looked up at me with a smile.

"Have you ever seen the Measuring Men?"

Tea and I exchanged glances, then I sat down heavily with my back to one of the walls. The ghosts of my two drinks were leaving me relaxed enough to cope with this a bit better and, you know, maybe it was good to be talking to someone right now. Someone else.

"I don't know," Tea said. "How would I know? What the . . . what are you talking about, Feather?"

"I think you have."

"Okay . . ."

"I mean—we have all been measured, right? All the time. Every day. Even now, someone somewhere is measuring us . . ."

"That is . . . true enough."

"The question is . . . are they real or are they metaphor? Just basic human judgementalism or some kind of . . . entity?"

"Judgementalism?" Tea said with a frown. "Measuring? I guess so. I don't know how everyone knows what has happened to me, but . . ."

"I don't," I said. "I don't have a clue what either of you are talking about."

Tea hesitated, then also sat down, leaning back against the wall with a sigh. "Alright—I'll tell you. It's not a secret as such, it's just . . ."

Her voice trailed off. I watched her, feeling a creepy sense of seriousness now as she flipped the eye-patch up. There was an eye underneath it—but not a human eye and I flinched, tipsily unsure what on earth I was seeing. Strange and alien—lopsided . . . Then I got it and laughed aloud. It was a plaster, on which she or someone had mischievously filled in the blank with coloured pens. Quite realistically.

"What happened?" I repeated.

Tea grinned, not a very nice grin, then lifted up the plaster as well—and I cringed again, this time for real, any relaxed party atmosphere going to another place. It was hard to even look at what she had been concealing—her eyeball vivid red and misshapen like a squashed fruit, her pupil wonky. I stared closer, my skin crawling, and saw something even stranger. Her cornea looked as though it had been split revealing blackness behind it, then clumsily drawn together—like a broken lace curtain in a poor woman's flat. There even seemed to be infinitesimally fine black threads in her eyeball. Stitches?

"Nice, isn't it."

"No," I said. "No it isn't. What the fuck happened?"

"Measuring Men," Feather whispered.

Tea heaved a huge sigh.

"Measuring is maybe a good term. I was arrested a few days ago for taking part in some protest. That was after I came back here. I just walked right into it and . . . well, I suppose I shouldn't have got involved, but sometimes you have to, right? Even someone like me who minds their own business and keeps my beautiful secrets—we have to lose our tempers occasionally, right?"

Beautiful secrets?

"I . . . suppose so," I said.

"It was all rather—nasty. The mood was furious—things got smashed. The police broke us up. Water canon—truncheons . . ." She sighed. "And—yes, they got me. Dragged me away, beat me up a bit—locked me up. They slapped a criminal damage charge on me—though I don't recall damaging anything particularly. Of course, I couldn't find the money to pay that off so you know what happens then."

I cringed some more. Yes I did know what happens then.

"A nice little volunteering appointment with the doctors at the London Labs," Tea said, drawing the words out ironically.

She was silent for a very long time—as was I, with very little idea what to say.

"Maybe I should have just . . . not gone. I could have gone home, maybe."

"Or just vanished," Feather said. "I . . . know a place you could have gone to where they would never have found you."

"Where?"

She gave an enigmatic smile and said nothing—and eventually Tea grunted and carried on.

"But—I didn't want to go home. *This* is my home. And it seemed simpler to get it over with. Most of the time it's fine after all. They try their little experiments and tests, maybe learn something—and nothing much happens. So I went. And it wasn't fucking fine. I don't know what they were testing that day, but they put something in there that they probably won't be prescribing or selling any time soon. It was so bad that they kept me in there for surgery to try and put it right again . . . but well, you can see the result."

She stared at the worn floor with a frown.

"Dragged off for mandatory medical testing because I was broke and pissed off with the world," she said, her voice icy. "When things like that happen, you end up taking sides big time, even if you never did before. I hate those fuckers and I hope they get torn to pieces by the raging mob."

I stared at her in horror. She stared back, her one functioning eye narrow.

"It's no mystery why people are so angry," Feather said. "It's an anger supermarket these days." Tea shrugged, then gave a wry smile and replaced the bandage.

"It's time for war," Feather said. "War with the Measuring Men, and with the World Polyhedron. And we must all be ready."

She looked deadly serious, whatever she meant by it all. The insanity of her words, the cold and curling reality of Tea's wrecked eye and the story of how she got it was causing a roiling in my mind. There was a familiarity about it as well—a tone of voice very similar to Star Girl's glittering rage. Had I really been living in some little self-absorbed bubble while revolution rumbled and festered out in the streets? Aside from vague and half-dismissed news reports—strings of odd incidents, fights, protests, clashes with the police, minor terrorist attacks—I had never noticed this degree of seething rage before. But in all fairness, I hadn't noticed much of anything before the past few days. I had assumed people were mostly like me—pretty much dead and apathetic. It had never occurred to me just how many people must be sitting in their microscopic shared homes, or no homes at all, subsumed and screaming in frustration and rage—and instead of catching trains like me, they were yearning to kick back against the world. To kick and to hurt . . .

"I'd better go back," Tea said, looking melancholy and confused. "I want everyone to try my Medica."

She scrambled to her feet. Her back and her backside were colourfully marked with the crumbling and paint-laden plaster and dirt. This was one of those deeply sexy moments that can come like a white-hot bar of bronze straight between the eyes, even though no one else could ever be aware of them. Oh the complicated emotions an arse is capable of generating—even in just a split second before I dragged my eyes away harshly, a voice in my head yelling warnings.

I watched her as she hurried back. In spite of her wound, she looked quite happy again now—and I wondered just how much of that was an act. One curiosity about Tea was that no matter how good her mood, I always seemed to detect a massive sea of melancholy underneath it. It was something that drew me to her. I did hear that her home country of Slovenia, seemingly pragmatic and beautiful though it is, also had one of the highest suicide rates in Europe. That suggests something is going on in the national psyche that is not so much the sunny side of the Alps.

On the other hand, of course, maybe it was true. Maybe she really was happy to be back here. If so it was quite heart-warming. I wouldn't have valued this home very much compared to what she had left behind—or at least what I imagined she had left behind. But what did I know about her life back home save for the legendary farm in the wooded hills that she had grown up on? I watched with a mix of appreciation and sadness as she swirled round the roof, making sure nobody failed to try a sip from that bottle of heady dreams.

It would have been nice . . . you know, some bastard part of my mind said for the millionth time. *You could have tried harder.*

"No point," I muttered aloud—and Feather looked at me eyebrows up.

Chasing that away, I took a sip of my Medica, my mind floating again to the graffiti on the wall beside us. Was I ready? What would I do if London really did boil over as Feather was predicting? As Star seemed to yearn for? Just stay home and remain glued to the computer? Probably. I could imagine Star Girl raging through the world, but not me. I would be sitting there hoping that people had actually worked out who the true enemy was. I wasn't sure, myself. The government? The police? The dominating corporations? The financial system? What did I know about any of this?

Be ready!

No doubt following my eyes, Feather pushed the spray can into my hand. "Anything you would like people to remember?" she asked. I thought for a moment, but there was only one thing I could find in my head to write. Hardly an original thought though.

Remember reality.

"Nice one," she murmured.

"Ready for what?" I asked again. She looked at me with a thin smile that I couldn't quite read.

"I wish I knew," she said. Her gaze seemed remarkably perceptive—as though she could read me in ways I couldn't even manage myself. It was a little unnerving. But in a way, I liked it. I liked her. Feather the Mudlark. I liked that I had found a maverick here in my own home complex. And I was serenely content to let her expound her fantasies.

But then an interruption.

"There you are," Kate said, standing over me and blotting out the sun. "Can I have a word?"

I gave a comical groan and scrambled to my feet. Feather watched me with a smile, then turned back to the wall, staring up at it as though it contained the solution to all the world's problems. And maybe it did.

Kate and I ended up leaning against the parapet a short distance away.

"We are banned from our room," she said.

"Huh?"

"A great big fucking reserved sign on the door."

I gave a sigh that might have been humorous or impatient or both or neither. "Aceline got lucky," I murmured.

"Sure did," she said. "She's out of her tree. Came bundling out giggling herself silly, Jayden waving that bloody contract after her, trying to get her to sign it. She threatened to hit me with something if I went anywhere near that room for a few hours, then made me promise to say the same thing to you. Then they both went running off."

"Sound like she's going to need the additionals part of that contract after all."

"Oh bloody hell—I'd like to see her try."

"Who is this guy exactly?"

"Don't you remember?"

"I try not to pay too much attention," I said dryly.

Kate laughed. "Well, you know that girl who lives . . ."

And she launched into a dreary explanation. I suppose I shouldn't complain, any more than I should complain about those damn contracts. People are people. People interact—always have done, always will, within the realms of possibility. And who am I to accuse things of being dull and dreary? Me, gripped in the tail-end of a fading lust for an inaccessible Slovenian from the comfortable funk of my own little world. At any rate, I couldn't bring myself to care much about Aceline, except for the potential horror of having to deal with yet another human being outside my door.

Down below, a freight train came crawling past—a long line of hopper cars, dirty, gruff-looking and emitting an unearthly howl across the city. It rolled west through its long thin world of the rails and I watched it until it was out of sight. I suppose it's no mystery why people like trains. It's the romance of the distant—the feeling that, if one wanted, one could ride those trains to somewhere else. Anywhere else. Some new life, some new world entirely. The rails that run through your town are the same rails that pull into Vladivostok—or Tokyo—or Alice Springs—or Fairbanks. Or Bohinj, Slovenia. You ride the train and suddenly the season has changed—the world has turned—the grey has pulled aside like curtains replaced by the clean rain of the unfamiliar. Even the freight trains somehow convey that, though there is hardly a train-hopping culture in the UK.

"Now Tea-Cup's at it," Kate said with massive weariness.

"Hmm?" The words didn't get through to me for a moment.

"You'd think there's something in the air. Is today one of those wild nights when the whole world loses it?"

I glanced round—and Kate was right. One of the last sights I particularly wanted to see was taking place on the roof, Tea's Medica dance transformed into something else as she snogged an oily-looking guy with a beard—hands questing flesh with therapeutic intensity. I stared at them, feeling that weird bottomless feeling that one gets at such times. You learn it and learn it hard in your teens, but it never truly goes away.

"Oh great," I murmured—that feeling in my brain again. The grief gland springing into action.

So which will be the top and which the bottom?

"Alright for some, isn't it?" Kate was saying gloomily. "Some people—all they have to do is snap their fucking fingers."

"Do they?"

She gave me a melancholy look. "What the fuck has she got that I haven't? I mean—she's not *that* good looking."

"Reality," I murmured without thinking.

"Huh?"

"I mean . . . that's the mountains, right? The cold wild air, good food . . ."

"Good food?" she grumbled. "Sausages in minced fatty tissue? You can't be healthy if you do that . . . she must be riddled with cancers. I don't understand . . ."

She gave me a challenging look, which I met feeling slightly bemused. I was watching a pair of hands conspicuously massaging the arse of one I still found far too attractive, yet it was Kate who seemed to need the comforting.

"I've been alone too long," she said.

"Yeah?"

"I mean—I know I'm not perfect—but jeez. You'd think I had some horrible disease."

"You seem normal enough to me," I said awkwardly.

"Is normal good enough? Or . . ."

"Maybe you can't quest and yearn—only relax and be ready for whatever comes." It was a pointless thing to say, but she looked a little mollified.

"Look at her," Kate muttered. "I dunno—she could have the entire party if she wanted. They'd form a queue."

I looked. There were even a few paint stains still visible.

"Could she?"

"Admit it," she growled. "You'd love to get your dick inside that, wouldn't you?"

That was a bit too close for comfort. I couldn't disagree but right then my mind felt very weird. Some part of me was literally singing with great clarity: *accept it, swallow it, forget it. Let it go.*

Over and over. Infinite weariness. *It doesn't matter.* It's all a fantasy—all a construct. I didn't even know this person really. Force yourself to step back a pace and there was something very comical about it all. What the heck was I doing getting even slightly jealous about her? Love, lust, companionship—it all seemed fake, and these days I could hardly tell them apart in their alienness. None actually existed, I was sure. My dick, as Kate put it, was subsumed in a safe fantasy universe with no connection at all to this reality anymore.

These were dull grey thoughts.

And the pair separated. Tea disengaged from the unknown oily man with obvious reluctance, one hand unconsciously brushing herself down, straightening her clothes, then briefly rubbing her own arse. He headed for the stairs and vanished. For a while, Tea stared after him, her body language still anticipatory, then she hurried on, back in host mode as though nothing had happened.

I forced myself to turn away, leaning back over the wall and staring out at the city. From up here one gets the feeling that London is an orchestra, playing together guided by some imaginary conductor. A somewhat bloody-minded and stroppy conductor, playing us all like the world's biggest puppet show. Maybe another train would pass. Right now I felt as though I really needed one—a train that could take me to some other life entirely.

"I'm going to crash," Kate said. "I imagine she who must be obeyed will be at it for an hour or so yet. At least it's a nice evening."

I nodded and watched her collapse into one of the deck chairs nearby with a sigh, putting on a pair of headphones and lying back comfortably. Then I turned away. Even if my room was out of reach, I could at least re-join Feather and put the shed between me and that damned Slovenian. And hopefully any other eyes as well. A bit of peace would be very welcome.

I never made it though.

"I said murderer," came ringing across the roof, accompanied by a sound of something breaking. I jerked round. What looked like a diorama had formed on the main roof—a frozen theatrical tableau. Tea was standing there, arms out in wary shock, facing off against someone I had never seen before. A guy with long scraggly hair. A stranger—no doubt another of those friends of friends from outside. "Don't give me that," he said—surreally enough, with a surprisingly posh British accent. The voice wasn't loud but it somehow manged to cut through the atmosphere of the roof like a knife.

"You should not waste my Pršut," Tea said, her voice shrill.

On the floor was a smashed plate—and scattered around it several slices of something—paper thin, and a rich, deep pink-brown in colour. And my heart sank.

Meat.

No doubt Tea had been playing waitress again, only this time . . .

I saw something else as well. Quite a few people held a slice in their hand or were chewing on it. It seemed enough were prepared to at least try it. I had been thinking of it as something deep and deadly and underground, but here, to these people at least, it was nothing more than an exotic curiosity.

To some anyway.

"Trash," he said, leaning forward with a horrible expression on his face, eyes as predatory as any animal I had ever seen in a wildlife documentary. Like an intense and staring hawk. Then there was a gleam of metal in his hand and the temperature of the roof dropped even further.

"Oh fuck," Kate muttered, suddenly at my side again. People were half rising to their feet, or sitting there goggling as though it was a scene from a film. The guy leaned in close, obviously trying to intimidate—trying to make the shocked Tea back away. His voice was low and intense, but I clearly heard what he said next. "People like you should be raped," he said. "Right now. We'll all do it—it's a fitting punishment. How would you like it if I was to cut those slices out of you? I should, you know—you fucking deserve it. I'll cut out your liver. I'll slice your skin to strips and—and rape you till you bleed, you fucking murderer."

It was an utterly ridiculous speech, and in that posh accent, it was nothing short of surreal. However, the reality of it—the simple fact that it was being said in spite of its stupidity—came with a creeping horror. Suddenly the Medica seemed a long way away.

The movement continued. Him stepping forward, her stepping backwards. They had covered several feet, but every step ratchetted up a tension. I could see it in Tea's body, in the muscles beneath those tight jeans. And when it suddenly released, it was hardly a surprise. I have no idea whether she was responding to some sign of a more direct attack or whether she just reached snapping point but her leg lashed out. Maybe she got him in the nuts—at any rate, it was enough to end the exchange almost farcically as he folded up with a yell and sagged to the ground. Then her foot lashed out again in several deliberate kicks that made my stomach tense up. I had long been aware of the melancholy that sat at her centre, but here was a glimpse of a ferocity that also seemed to reveal a flash of the alien. I guess yelling threats like that means that you deserve pretty much whatever response you bring down on yourself, but the look in her eyes was terrifying nonetheless, as though channelling centuries of history and years of personal demons down into one very sharp point.

"You're mad," she yelled. "You motherfucking . . . Kúrc. You all are." She stared round at the shocked group. "Drek," she yelled at last. She hesitated a moment, then swooped down and grabbed the scattered meat off the floor before storming away to the stairs.

"Holy fuck," Kate muttered again.

I watched as a few people gathered around the fallen man and helped him up, body language very uncertain and confused, then I glanced round at Feather, who was still sitting against the wall nearby. "Ah well," she said with a smile. "Yes . . . be ready."

✧

Dark now. The roof almost empty. My head swimming. By this time, I had undertaken a rather dedicated exploration of the bottles Tea and others had provided—from cheap American whiskey to blueberry borovničevec. I loved all of it, though I will concede that my sense of subtlety had dulled fairly quickly. But who cares. This may have been dangerous, of course. The last thing I needed under the circumstances was being put in touch with my emotions, but I went for it anyway.

I hadn't seen Tea since the bust up, though. Part of me wanted to go and find her—but I didn't. *Not my job,* another part of me said childishly. *Let her elected representative handle it.* The party had continued, though, rather dispiritedly and fading as people trailed away.

And now, only Kate was still on the roof, and she seemed to have fallen asleep. Returning to the wall, I could see a red glow somewhere off in the distance—a glow of fire. Something in London was burning. After Feather's strange talk, it hardly seemed surprising and my eyes wandered back to the scrawled lettering. It seemed to have expanded to fill most of the wall now. Various hands had been working on it in recent hours—and suddenly it seemed much creepier . . .

Remember hope.
Remember the sun.
Remember your warmest day.
Remember my dick.
Remember midnight.
Remember the bombs.
Remember I love you.
Remember your dreams.
Remember to kill the bastards.

Then another slogan occurred to me, the Philosopher's voice again ringing out in my head with all the trumpets of drunkenness.

Remember you're human.

Unfortunately I couldn't find the spray can to record that vital instruction, so I had to shrug it off and leaned over the wall, staring out at the scene below.

In the city around me, several more red lights were gleaming, alongside that fire-glow—and, even as I watched, one or two more appeared. They just winked on, first not there, then there and unmoving. I registered them vaguely—just a faint sense of redness in the universe, that's all. Yet somehow familiar. I had seen these red gleams around the city before, though never as many as this. I think I must have already been aware that there was something wrong here, but even so, all I could do was stare as more and more of them flashed into being. And then, turning sharply, I realised that they were picking out the shape of my own roof as well, glowing on and, in some impossible way, within the building.

After a few moments staring in mystification, I leaned over the wall again and looked to the north, but the lights were there as well, picking out other buildings and still winking on. The whole city, as far as I could see it, seemed to be decked and festooned in them, like the world's biggest Christmas tree.

In London, nothing ordinarily surprises. It's a place where, even now, artists and designers can still occasionally play around and have fun and create crazy projects. But this seemed beyond possible. I studied the lights, but, stare though I might, turning around and around trying to focus on them, I could not make out any details. I couldn't see if they were on poles, attached to something, hanging from something . . .

I hurried across the roof for a closer look at one of them.

Okay, this is where you will no doubt start questioning my sanity and wearily tossing this book into the nearest recycling bin . . . but hey, all I can do is tell you what I saw to the best of my ability. The red was pricking at me now and I wanted to see for myself that it was a light bulb hanging on the wall or something. But the closer I got, the more confused I became because there was nothing supporting that light. No bollard, no wire, no little electrical device, no solar panel . . . I couldn't even see a bulb. It was a spherical orb about the size of a grapefruit that gleamed a deep red, but with a powerful core of white shining through. When I approached it, I walked right round it, even bent down and peered under it—but there was nothing. The light was just . . . there. I could feel no heat from it. It made no sound—no electrical hum. There was no visible movement at all.

I didn't dare touch.

There was one other thing, though, something so faint that I only noticed after a moment. Stretching out from that orb were three glowing streamers, seemingly as insubstantial as the orb itself. Indeed, barely there at all. Following a streamer simply led me to a brick wall, which likewise provided no reason for its existence. No devices there either. And now I realised that this whole world of red lights was held together by these streamers as a triangular mesh. It was a web of lines and angles—a luminous map of the city—an undulating, jagged surface of ups and downs.

So . . . the glowing point was what happened when these streamers met? Maybe it was a laser—or, or, or some weird new technology that I had never heard of. Government up to something. Strange electrical phenomenon. Humanity's urban despair affecting the earth's energy grid, which I didn't even fucking believe in . . .

My skin was prickling all over by now. This didn't make any sense at all—a kind of impossibility I had never had to deal with before in my life. Had there been more than just booze in those drinks I had downed half a lifetime ago? Again, I was staring round at the nearby buildings, turning round and round as though dancing, trying to find a key to it.

And then suddenly it was gone. As though my mind had gone 'oh yeah' and remembered reality. I was back on normal mundane roofing material under the normal mundane orange city glow, staring out at the normal mundane constellation of lighted windows while Kate still snoozed in the deckchair.

I ended up standing there for quite some time, slowly collecting myself, my tension fading, watching the view—watching the lights of London.

THURSDAY

Good morning good morning good morning the alarm clock on my phone bawled and I came up with a jolt, feeling like a snail must feel when it is yanked out of its shell. Gawd—you have no idea how much I hate alarm clocks. The destructive power they possess ought to be some kind of human rights violation, especially given how many less harmful things are illegal. Every time that beep sounds and drags me up out of vital and health-giving sleep, it grabs my wizened, sickly little happy gland and rapes it with the most aggressive buggery, its barbed dick ejaculating massive doses of adrenalin and miserablin deep into it. The adrenalin makes the heart race so you can't go to sleep again even if you are rebellious enough to try, while the miserablin inevitably takes more than a day to clear out of your system, so if you have that thing going off every day you embark on a steady downward series of steps until you are a jittering, shivering brain-dead wreck. And eventually your happy gland ends up permanently traumatised and dies alone, forgotten, uncared for and unavenged, while that evil clock just keeps raping its corpse for all eternity.

And when you are working utterly irregular hours like I am, starting at anything from six in the morning to midnight . . . well, it fucks you up, that's all.

What do I actually do to earn my existence? Or rather, what three things, since I have three jobs? You know, I really can't be bothered to go into that here. The one thing I will say is that whatever relationship I have with this, it doesn't involve regular hours—or indeed much definition. I find out or argue over my schedule not so many days before it happens—some weeks I am busy every day, morning to night, sixty-seventy hours. Others I have plenty of time at home to think and panic about the rent. Maybe I need an alternative and personal source of income to supplement this zero-hours crap—make it four jobs, maybe. Or six. Why not? That's what most people do. I think the most I ever saw a guy working was eighteen. Eighteen scattered fucking jobs. And no surprise the haunted look in his eyes. People hold down one or more main 'jobs' that *almost* cover the rent, topped up with a bit of government welfare to take us up to mere 'poverty', and then comes a muddle of separate little threads of extra undeclared income that feels vaguely schizophrenic but at least means you occasionally have a slight buffer against problems—even a bit of spending money occasionally. Aceline teaches a fitness class in the evenings and sometimes other stuff—I suppose she qualifies as fit, for London. Some sell or attempt to sell home-made trinkets and oddments—some cut hair—some design websites or proofread—some sell themselves as independent prostitutes. I am vaguely aware of one woman upstairs who offers up her arse for a spanking porn video every few months—something the Great British Public never seems to tire of, and at least she is putting her theatre studies degree to good use, unlike most. Some even try to make music or art or writing because the arts are indefatigable, though if they earn the price of a cheap dinner a month then they are lucky.

That morning I groaned and curled over, staring into my pillow, wondering again why I was doing this when I could be waiting quietly for that last train. Sometimes thoughts of suicide can be very comforting, reminding you that there is an escape if you want it—that you don't have to do what you are doing. There are times, and this was one of them, when it feels next to impossible to force myself to open that door between me and the outside world—or more specifically between me and the other flat that stood between me and the outside world. It's not that I minded Kate or Aceline—or even Jayden. In my own way I really quite liked them. It's just that sometimes . . . do I even need to explain this? I know it is taken for granted these days, but having a cloud of privacy to barge through every time you leave your room is just one more thing that fucks you up. Just as it no doubt fucks you up having someone barging through *your* cloud of privacy to get to theirs. Sometimes I even wondered what would happen if I was to bust a hole in the wall connecting me directly to the corridor. Was there any way I could remake my world to that extent? Had I any power in this universe?

One friend of an acquaintance moved into a little place a bit like mine not so long ago—some place with two or three 'residences' shoehorned into what had once been one—and she was also not so happy to have to go steeling through her room-mate's bedroom whenever she wanted to go anywhere. In her case, though, one wall of her room was up against the shared kitchen. So what to do here? In the end, she unofficially bust a hole in the wall and then—I am not kidding here—she cut the back out of an old fridge and installed it over the opening. That fridge sat there against the kitchen wall like any other fridge, covered with stickers. It was only if you opened the door, hoping for a beer or a slice of cheese, that it might finally dawn on you that something was wrong. But as for that friend of an acquaintance—from that day forth her life had new meaning, because she could enter her bedroom by opening the fridge and climbing in. Welcome to London, folks!

☼

Kate was also in a foul mood when I finally stepped out of my door—just possibly having something to do with Aceline sitting there glowing with satiated warmth from her exploits of the night before. She was in front of the fan dressed in the lightest lounge pants she had and a tiny vest that clung to her skin in a way that would have been sexy if my shirt wasn't also clinging to me in exactly the same way. Trust me—it wasn't sexy. It was like wearing a lascivious octopus.

This heat was getting seriously draining.

Somewhat to my surprise, there was a third figure there as well. No, not Jayden, thank goodness, but Tea, looking at me with friendly greeting. That pulled me up in a complete mental reformat and I squirmed inwardly, suddenly very conscious of the state of my hair and general sweaty appearance. I wish the world would give me fair warning before confronting me with things like this.

She seemed cheerful enough, in spite of what had happened the night before.

"I didn't keep you guys out all night, did I?" Aceline asked rather absently, swallowing the last of her supplement pills. I sat down cautiously—as close to her as I dared so I could get some of the fan but be far enough away that I wouldn't inflict myself on her. She took a long drink of water and gave me a wry look.

"I crashed out on the roof," Kate said.

"And I slipped through after you were asleep," I added.

"We were at it for hours," Aceline informed us cheerfully.

"Too much info, Ace," Kate growled.

"Only because you didn't get any," Aceline said with a slight barb.

Kate made an exasperated noise, then looked at me.

"Maybe we need to come to an agreement that every time someone lands a contract, you let her have your room for the night?"

I refocused my attention rather quickly.

"You mean every time one of you drags some guy home, I have to move out?" I asked, rather sharply. "Are you crazy?"

"Well—yeah, no, you have a little privacy, you know. That's rare enough. We don't have any privacy whatsoever." She gave Aceline an even more barbed glance.

"Can't you go back to their place?" I said, still sharp.

"Most of them probably still live with their parents," Tea said.

"Yeah—we are the elite, remember," Aceline put in with a nasty smile. "We're the top dogs. Places of our own and fuck the world."

Kate paused, a very odd expression dawning on her face. "Elite," she muttered, staring at the corner of the room with great interest. "Oh fuck that."

"Uhuh—all you will ever get, darling," Aceline continued, rubbing it in. "Short of a revolution. Have fun still sharing with me at fifty."

That seemed to have struck home as intended, for Kate had gone silent, still staring heavily at nothing. I could feel the cogs of gloom turning in her head and I sighed, not without sympathy. Nevertheless, I couldn't resist applying a slight boot now she was down.

"I believe the rent here is about forty to fifty pounds a night," I said mildly. "I would have to work it out. You are very welcome to use my room as your fuck pod for that. I'm not interested in making a profit. I will even give you clean sheets."

"Fuck you both," she said heavily.

"Sure, would that be one night or two?" Aceline asked with a cheeky grin.

Kate gave her a dirty look and stamped off to the kitchen.

Aceline and I exchanged smiles. Well—she was trying to smile anyway, but I could see she had managed to depress herself as well. The magic of sex only went so far, it seemed—it was no match for the housing crisis. Indeed, a small pall of gloom seemed to have settled over the whole room now, up to and including the news burbling from her laptop. Aceline poured herself a morning glass of wine, then shoved the bottle in my direction before refocusing on the screen. I helped myself. I like to go to work on a glass of wine if I can, it acts as a lubrication, helping the world slide past just that little easier. It's not an unheard of tradition in some parts of the world, you know—like many things we in the 'West' think are weird.

. . . the democratic process. That's what we are losing here. If they take away our right to peaceful protest, then what do we have left? Certainly not democracy. They hassled us all evening, arrested us for erecting a tent, even for spreading a tarpaulin on the grass to sit on. They have even declared pizza boxes an 'illegal structure' and dragged people off for having one. I guess I now have a criminal record for carrying a pizza box. It seems I have been wrong all this time. I always thought the main threat to everything we hold dear came from government mishandling or corporate greed—cruel austerity, lack of housing, cost of living, whatever. But now I can see. The real threat to our world comes from pizza boxes and tarpaulins. How stupid of me . . .

Tea, who had been watching the exchange so far with a bemused smile, leaned over to me then. "How are you feeling?" she asked. "After last night. Or maybe I should say . . ." She waved her hands eloquently, pointing from her own chest to me with an enquiring look.

I turned to her with some relief and gave her a precise thumbs up—which then morphed into a circling of said thumb around my right ear. Loopy! Oh yes just fucking great, don't you know!

Aceline stared at us in surprise.

"I agree," Tea said and nodded thoughtfully. "It was a . . . a wild night. And hangovers in this weather . . . oh boy," she wailed, lying back on Aceline's bed. "I wish I was at home. Last winter, in the mountains, it reached minus twenty-two. It got so cold I thought I would have to set my boyfriend on fire to keep me warm." She hesitated. "I miss it. Such blissful, blissful cold . . ."

"Shut up," Aceline growled, tugging at her lounge pants.

"It was so cold, I thought . . . I thought it was heading for absolute zero."

"Set him on fire?" I asked, not entirely disliking the idea.

"Only in an emergency—it was close. But . . . he would probably just have been moaning."

"Not very gentlemanly of him. I am not an expert but surely it's one's duty to make oneself available for any service? Or am I that out of touch with boyfriend politics? It's been a while."

"Such self-sacrifice is unfashionable these days," Tea said with mournful seriousness.

"I wonder," I said, half-consciously imitating the Philosopher's quiet but blood-and-thunder lecturing style. "Is nobility dead? Might there not still be certain circumstances when one could be driven to such sacrifice, even now."

"Well, hmm . . ."

"In fact," I said, leaning back and lying down in her parallel and turning up the drama in my voice yet another notch, "one might argue that no matter what principles one has, what expectations, there are always going to be exceptions. Right? That's one of the great inevitabilities."

Tea shrugged expansively and I glanced at her, wondering where the hell these words were coming from. They were both looking at me as though I was growing a second head before their eyes or something—but right then I really didn't care.

"And I suppose," I continued, "if the methane and carbon dioxide are crystallizing then that may be one of them."

Tea gave a snort of laughter.

"It would be a heroic self-sacrifice," I continued. "Dying about thirty seconds before your friends . . ."

"Have you been drinking?" Aceline asked, her lips twitching.

"No," I said with a mock-frown, glancing at my barely touched glass of wine.

"Then maybe you should. Maybe you need it."

"I suppose it's as good a therapy as any," I said with an innocent smile.

"Sod therapy," Tea said. "It's just like talking to a mirror. And a mirror is cheaper."

"And if I end up having a punch-up with a mirror, it can't sue me . . ."

"Might cut you if you are not careful," Tea said.

"If it's nearing absolute zero," I said, "so can a therapist if she gets broken." Tea gave a gratifying squirm of laughter at that and punched me on the shoulder.

Aceline stared at me, eyebrows up, a curious smile on her face. "I am getting the feeling I hardly know you," she said with a smile.

"No?"

"You seem very relaxed, that's all. You seem more relaxed these days than I can ever remember."

"That's good, I guess," I said thoughtfully. I didn't feel relaxed. I felt sharp and sad and fed up—and this dumb exchange felt more like a friendly wrestling match.

"Yeah," she said. "What's changed? Seriously? Are you in love?"

I stared at the ceiling, wondering what on earth I could say to that. *Oh, I tried to kill myself the other day—then I joined a band of city carnivores who hunt rabbits and talk weirdly into the night and group hug—then I realised that London is haunted by red lights and this nutter of a mudlark says that an apocalyptic war might just be coming towards us like an express train—I guess these things change a person . . .*

"Maybe I am just getting out more," I said. "Maybe I just realised a few things that are important—and a few things that aren't."

Maybe I am just learning to talk again . . .

Fortunately—or maybe unfortunately—I never got the chance to expand on any of that, for with all the timing of a TV drama, the main door opened and someone else stepped into the room. Tea glanced up.

"Aaaah," she said. "Did you ever meet Tad, my ljubimec? My . . . boyfriend? Not, I must say, the one to be set on fire." I flinched—of course—but I swallowed it as I focused on the oily man, preparing a desperate attempt at that particular kind of frozen politeness that one has to call upon when confronted by people's other halves. And yes, he was just as I remembered—a rather rake-like young man with a thinly clipped beard and sideburns.

"Set who on fire?" he asked with a puzzled grin.

"Nothing," Tea said. "Just joking—but you know, strange things happen in the lonely green hills of my homeland."

"So I hear," he said, sitting down beside her.

"Drowning salamanders in brandy and having sex with trees, that's one of my favourites."

The expression on his face was almost cartoonish at that one.

"You never heard of salamander brandy? Thank goodness. I never tried it but you hear rumours."

She lazily rolled over onto her front to get closer to him, and I watched thoughtfully. To me, it was all a performance—a presentation of claims staked and fences erected—worlds forged and worlds excluded. In response, I found myself infinitesimally putting more space between me and her—a sickly dance in a room full of strands of desire that we all so carefully pretend aren't there. We are not supposed to react negatively to public displays of affection. And fair enough, I wouldn't like it if it was directed at me. But at the same time, seeing them can cause almost monumental agony sometimes—even to the extent of making people want to hurt themselves. Or worse. Not much I can do about that though.

"I wonder if you know what you have let yourself in for," Aceline said with a teasing grin.

He rubbed Tea's back with a laugh, hand floating over the curve of her spine, then settling on one buttock for a moment, before withdrawing. There was an awkwardness between them—obviously they were still in the stage of trying to mould themselves to each other, to work out what shape they each needed to be. No doubt they had come together with a bang at some prior point, and were now trying to pick up the pieces and sort out the paperwork, as it were.

Then he seemed to remember my presence and gave me a nod. "Hello," he said with a rather uninterested glance.

"Hi," I managed, desperately. "Pleased to meet you."

"You live here, right?" he asked mildly.

"Yes. Right here. Right there." I waved at my own personal private door.

"Ah yes, I thought I remembered you from somewhere. You are one of the lucky sods who has his own room," he said with a thin smile.

"That's right," I said noncommittally.

"I remember seeing you last night. Not a bad evening, though I did hear that a few . . . illicit substances were involved."

"There's always illicit substances," Tea said with a laugh. "People do what people do."

"I don't like it," he said with a frown. "I'm all for a good time—but not illegal stuff. I dunno though. Did you see anything," he asked me. "Any . . . incidents?"

That got my attention. Incidents? In my mind, thoughts were turning over very quickly indeed. The only incident I knew of involved Tea, lying right there beside him—and the look on his face at the talk of illicit substances was not very sympathetic. Maybe he knew nothing at all about the pršut Tea had handed round. *Was I being pumped for info?*

"What sort of thing?" I asked.

"I dunno—hard drugs. Meat . . ."

There was a silence. Tea was staring at him, and I could almost hear the sudden sharpening of her attention. I winced. The thin and tenuous thread of lust and connection that stretched between them had quivered and twanged. There was a look of distaste on his face that I could read without trouble.

"No," I said. "I didn't see anything. Though I spent most of the time up on the roof."

I caught Tea's almost non-existent glance in my direction.

"I am aware that some . . . meat may have been shared around," he said. "I fear this building has some rather undesirable activity. Meat—illegal drugs—even a few unlicensed pets."

Tea gave a lazy laugh. "If you don't like meat, you'd better not cross the Alps," she said.

The frown on his face increased slightly. "With any luck, they will catch up with the rest of us soon."

"Uh-uh," Tea said with a frown. "No."

"Do you know what I found this morning?" he asked me. "On the roof?"

"What?" I asked cautiously.

He leaned closer, and I leaned back a fraction to compensate. There was an intensity in his eyes now that I didn't like at all.

"A bag," he said. "A bag . . . of bones."

"Bones?"

"Bones," he said, leaning closer still with a glimmer of revolted intensity. "On the roof of our own home. In the shed up there. I would very much like to find out who did that."

"Well I never heard about it before," I said a little sharply, feeling somewhat shocked, and also getting angry at the apparent cross-questioning.

"I reported it to the police but of course, with all the undesirable activity going on in the city at the moment, they never really responded. I will have to chase it up, I can see. I'm fairly sure you shouldn't have to 'chase up' a crime . . ."

"At the moment, nothing surprises."

He nodded wearily. "Too right. Well—hopefully it can be . . . resolved soon enough. The last thing we need is a bag of bones on the roof. The last thing we need is a cannibal in our building."

I stared at him with a jolt.

"Human bones?" I managed, my skin crawling.

"No—animal."

I sighed, irritated but not in the mood to start arguing over the definition of words.

"I don't know what kind." He shook his head, an incomprehensible expression on his face for a moment. Tea was also watching him curiously. There was a silence—a complex silence, invisible swords clashing. Then Tad shrugged awkwardly and appeared to drop the subject.

I stared at the two of them, and suddenly I was feeling a totally different sort of discomfort. What I was watching was a dead end—a complete horrorshow. Already. The threads between them had barely even formed and they were already dying. And here I was feeling upset and jealous? I took a sip of my wine, which had rather lost its flavour.

If anything, it was a relief when a massive crash from the kitchen interrupted everything.

"Oh for fuck's sake," Kate's voice came yelling.

"Now what?" Aceline called.

"I'll kill those fucking mice," Kate said furiously, stamping back in, while the rest of us stared in surprise. "I will—I'll cut their legs off with the kitchen scissors and put their eyes out with a toothpick."

"And then cook them over a charcoal grill?" I asked dryly before I could stop myself.

Kate ignored me. She was shaking with rage—with a rage that had finally found something to aim at, which is the most dangerous kind.

"What was that crash?" I asked.

"I threw a saucepan at it," she said. She held up the sonic repeller. "And this thing isn't worth the paper of its fucking health and safety notice," she yelled.

"Hey wait a mo . . ." That was Aceline—but too late. Kate had hurled the device across the room. It hit the wall, leaving a pronounced dent.

"Oh great," Aceline said angrily, scrambling to her feet. "That thing cost seventy five pounds."

"Then you were had, darling," Kate said. "You were right. Get that fucking poison."

"Yeah," Aceline growled, "I was had. Just like this whole fucking city has been fucking had." She opened the door. "I'm going to work—and you can mend the wall this time."

Kate glanced restively after her as she stamped off—then at the dent in the wall. Then she dropped down on her bed with a grunt. Tea and Tad also stared in discomforted silence.

Kate reached over and switched to a different stream on the laptop. But as usual there was no escape.

. . . in Parliament Square today erupted into violence that left several people injured. Police have arrested seventy-four protestors on public order offences. Already nicknamed the pizza box wars, the incident was quickly contained but resentment is still simmering on the streets of Camden and the City. The events have been called a mark of shame in the history of London and a strong police reaction has been called for—but others have warned that heavy-handed tactics against what was initially a peaceful protest may only increase the tension leading to . . .

I had had enough. "Anyway," I said, stumbling, "I will let you get on with whatever it was you were doing. I need to get to work too."

Tea laughed. "Joj, we're just lazing around and scratching ourselves. Hardly doing anything. But I hope you will be there next time we go wild."

"Yes—I need to practice my . . ." I fluttered my hands vaguely in a spiralling gesture, then tapped my ears, secretly delighted at the bewildered look on Tad's face. "Not to mention my . . ." Still seated, I danced a few comical swaying steps, and Tea gave a chuckle, circled a finger round her chest again, then fluttered it in my direction, finishing it with a tiny seated bow.

"You guys are nuts," Kate said dryly. I retrieved my bag from my room, then escaped into the corridor, closed the door behind me and leaned against it, still feeling discomforted. However, it only made me look forward with greater urgency to my third visit to the hideaway in the New Sea Wall this evening. It might seem a bit of a turnaround, given my rather dramatic last encounter—

but you might say there was a touch of desperation in me now. Everything around me seemed to be filled with an emptiness so massive that it burned.

✿

I went to work. I did work. Hours passed. I stopped doing work. And depression was coming three by three as I walked to the station—like some kind of excited child-demon sitting in my mind and keeping up a continual stream of piss into it. I just wanted to be at home, staring into a bed sheet from about a millimetre away, and possibly drunk. The air was like a blanket—a solid presence, with all the smells of the city amplified, which is rarely a good thing. Whether it's smog or the leftovers of Kate's pasta dying alone and unavenged in the kitchen, it's rarely good to be reminded of smells around my London world. As you may have gathered, I don't like the heat much—it is debilitating and damp, it makes me feel dirty and repulsive. My temper frays and my self-esteem drops from merely 'low' to 'through the floor'. I rode the train, which only didn't resemble a sauna because nobody was naked. Then my second job. I sat around all day collecting gold coins while my shirt got wetter and wetter—whatever feeble defences against the heat I may have possessed rendered useless by these annoying things called clothes.

Oh, don't worry, reader. I won't start moaning about work here. It's not important. If I ask you what you do, I don't want to hear some crap about where you waste your time earning money—I want to hear about your passions, about what makes your world go round, and how you follow those passions in a culture that regards them as not unlike some minor form of terrorism. If your passions coincide with what brings in the cash then great, but don't get full of yourself because if they don't, then that doesn't invalidate the passion. For me, work is nothing more than this vaguely inconvenient force in my life that channels money from the company to my vampire landlord. The flow of cash like a kind of perverted lifeblood. "I got paid"—what a beautiful modern balm those words convey. That comfortable fuzzy feeling down the back, kind of like a kiss on the neck, as one is permitted to survive a few more weeks. O sweet, sweet poison teat that drools its ichor into our ever-desperate and ever-more-desperate mouths—the tingle of acid that splashes and stings the eyes and mercifully blinds us to that which crouches over us, a monster so universal that we call it the sky . . .

Or, yeah—money in the bank again. Nice.

But really, who needs to moan about it since that seems to be one of the few great things humanity can really get together on? If, and I repeat, if there is any kind of group consciousness to us all on this bizarre planet then I am reasonably sure it arose entirely due to the mystical communion of an entire species hating working for others, yet still being forced to do it, for reasons that I can't quite grasp right now. In my hate, I embrace you all—a damp, slippery embrace that expresses one of the few bonds we possess.

Instead of heading straight to my room as I probably should have done, I found myself climbing up the stairs towards the roof. It seemed weird to think of anyone in this building involved in illicit food. Maybe it really was more common than one might think. The flat expanse radiated heat like the cracked surface of a desert and I was soon even more sweaty and uncomfortable. It hadn't changed much since yesterday—the same chairs laid out in various places, even some abandoned glasses and plates on the rough floor. I approached the shed—a small one that some residents had erected to store chairs and other stuff—and I cautiously opened the door and fumbled for the light switch, igniting a rather dim bulb. I couldn't see anything at first, but I could smell something—very clearly. A sickly scent of rot that made my skin crawl. It was not a smell I had ever smelt before in my life and I didn't like it.

A poke around and I eventually found the bag, shoved well back among some boxes—a normal bin liner that had once been sealed, now opened again. I have to say—the contents were hard to look at. A pile of stripped bones, jumbled together and covered with smears and strands of flesh in an advanced stage of decay in the heat. A few maggots moved purposefully. It was hard to tell from the bones, but something about the size suggested cat. And just to be clear—this was not a corpse. There was no doubt that these had been stripped. With a knife.

I found myself thinking over the residents of this place, running face after face through my mind trying to analyse who could possibly be behind it but coming to no conclusions at all. An absolute blank. It must have been in there while we were up on the roof yesterday. Somehow this was more disturbing than anything the City Hunters had ever done, though I wasn't really sure why. Maybe it was purely the matter of the unknown leading my imagination to run wild with aggression and cruelty. What could it be? Madness? Desperation? Curiosity? The desire for atrocity for its own sake? Cats seem to have struck a weird deal with human beings—grabbed us by the heart-strings with their baby-like cries and cute faces. In my darker moments, I even find myself wondering if there is something slightly chilling about the hold they have over us—after all, they themselves would not hesitate to reduce almost anything to the state of the contents of that bag if they could.

As I stared, it almost seemed as though red light was flickering again at the corner of my eyes. A faint smell of burning in the air—though that could have been from anywhere. It was enough to catch my attention, though—and finally drag me away from that bag.

I emerged into the harsh sunlight again, feeling slightly unsteady on my feet—as though the strange sensations had affected my muscle control. To my dismay, there was a figure in the middle distance now, leaning against the parapet. Under the circumstances, the last thing I wanted was to be seen coming out of that shed and I stared at her, my skin prickling. She had her back to me—her arms up, holding something to her face, studying the city skyline. Binoculars. And I somehow wasn't really surprised to see that it was Feather.

She looked quite a spectacle, I have to say. In spite of the heat, she had a black waterproof coat slung over her shoulder. A wide-brimmed hat tied on with a ribbon and a dirty bag by her side. There were traces of dried mud on her from top to toe. No doubt this was her mudlarking gear—the sort of get-up that spoke of 'doing something', which I rather liked.

But why was she wearing it now? Here on this baking roof?

I spent far too much time standing there wondering whether I should try and slip away or go and speak to her in some attempt to legitimise my presence there, before it dawned on me that the passing time was killing any chance I had of the former.

Idiot.

With a hopefully inaudible sigh, I approached her. She looked round and I flinched. As well as the binoculars, she had a second device strapped to her face, over one eye. It looked like some kind of night-vision, image-enhancement thing . . . actually I have no idea what it was beyond the fact that a lens was staring at me with a sci-fi glint in the sun.

I could smell her, I realised. A tang of mud and river and sweat hanging in the air.

"Hi," I said. "I was just . . . sorting something out and . . ."

I'd better not ever commit a crime if this is how good I am at lying. She looked utterly uninterested, however.

"What are you doing?"

She shoved the eyepiece up onto her forehead. "Over there," she said, pointing. "Between the square apartment block and the glass tower. Can you see anything?"

I took the binoculars and looked. But honestly, I couldn't see much. Just a jumble of verticals and horizontals in various shades of brown. Buildings. Nearly all flat-topped. Cladding, glass, concrete—some of it gleaming bright in the sunlight. It was all very geometric, but beyond that, what could I say?

"What am I looking at?"

"I'm not really sure. I just suspect . . . something wrong."

I was silent.

"You," she said, "hold the city of London in your head—am I right?"

I glanced at her sharply, wondering how on earth she had heard that. Some people knew of my little talent, but I didn't think it was the kind of info that would get spread around.

"Kind of," I said slowly.

"What am I looking at there? Between those buildings?"

"You mean what part of the city?"

"Yes."

I studied it again, working it out in my mind, following the landmarks . . . then I delivered my results, explaining that what looked like one knot of buildings were the high parts of several city blocks that happened to be in alignment with us, with several roads passing through them invisibly. I listed them—and Feather even wrote the names down on her smartphone. Then she nodded quietly.

"I should look closer," she said, "now I know. Thank you."

"Any time," I said. "But—what are you looking for again?"

"The Measuring Men," she said, simply enough.

I put the binoculars to my eyes again and studied that scrap of city—but still there seemed nothing at all that set it apart from any other. Nothing had changed. It looked totally mundane.

"So—what are these Measuring Men?" I asked at last, finally getting into the open a question that had been bothering me since yesterday. "What is the World Polyhedron?"

"I've clashed with them once or twice," she said, a matter of fact tone to her voice, "and that was twice too much. You can tell them by their eyes. Not human. The antithesis of human. They do inhuman things. Have you ever seen a person—when you look into their eyes, they seem like a different species? Somehow so utterly alien that you can't recognise them at all?"

And I won't deny that sent a small prickle over my skin.

"They exist behind the life we know, looking down into it from above and up from below. They haunt the cities—and London being the centre of the world, they haunt this place especially. And when the war comes, this shall be the nexus of it."

She hesitated—then continued. "I don't know much about all this, but . . . In the early days," she said, her voice changing subtly to a storytelling tone, "when the Measuring Man first appeared, he looked at the world and looked in the face of his first enemy. The Measuring Man was the Polyhedron—the people he surveyed were curved and infinite. The Measuring Man was a thing of lines and angles and he knew that curves were an obscenity. Curves should not exist in this new race of humans. And so he set about eliminating them from the minds of men. The curves were replaced by the mathematical formulae—the lines that intersect—the angles that define. The obtuse—the acute—the truncated—the stellated—the rigid vertex—the regular-sided polygon. The World Polyhedron. And this new human progressed into the world and the Measuring Man and his progeny followed behind them.

"The fight continued for many years—many centuries. But it was a fight with only one outcome. Now curves may no longer exist. Curves are illegal. Frowned upon. You can run and run through the human world but nevermore will you find a curve acknowledged. In even the deepest places, the angle rules. The Polyhedron rules. And they say that to deny the angles means to deny human life itself. And those who do deny the angles become the running men and the running women—the fugitives. We who run through the world with our heads down, trying to keep from the eyes of the Measuring Men and below the continuous angular nets they have created. Trying to keep away from the billion faces and billion angles of the Polyhedron."

Feather gave me a melancholy look, taking the binoculars and hanging them around her neck. "These stories make me feel very sad," she said, "and I never quite know why. The angle and the line together make up an absolute—and I suppose that is what the Polyhedron is. The irony is that the Measuring Men hated the infinity of the curve, but in so doing they only managed to replace it with another far more destructive infinity. That of the absolute."

There was a silence. As I have made abundantly clear in this text, I am not much of a talker, but what would YOU say to that? I didn't even know where to begin—save that the use of the word 'absolute' took me straight back to the sea wall and Star Girl raging at me . . .

In the end, Feather gave a weary sigh.

"Now you just think I'm nuts," she said. "Maybe I shouldn't talk about such things. You are trying to work out whether I mean any of that literally, aren't you?"

"Well . . ."

She looked at me thoughtfully for a moment.

"I know you hold the city of London in your head," she continued. "Have you ever seen a place where the Polyhedron breaks down? They are not so unusual these days."

"How would I know?"

"Any places where there is something—not quite right with the world? Where something seems skewed? Or out of place?"

"I don't . . . think so," I said. "In what way?"

Another nod. "Maybe I should show you." She said. "If you like. A certain . . . thing . . . place that I know of."

"Yeah?"

"My instincts are usually good," she said with a smile, "and I think I trust you. And besides—the more who know the better. What do you think?"

I still couldn't find a reply, so I shrugged expansively, which I suppose was an assent.

"Good," she said crisply.

"Okay . . . but—where . . . ?"

"You'll see." She gave another grin.

"Where?" I demanded, a little crossly. There are enough problems in the world without deliberate mysteries.

"My home, that's all," she said with a shrug. "Where I live. I live right on top of a polyhedral anomaly. Maybe not so surprising, huh?"

"Okay," I said with a half-smile.

"You doing anything now?" she asked.

I was startled. For some reason, the thought of doing something *right now* without the usual formalities of appointment or preparation felt a bit strange. But I pushed that away. There was such a quietly eager expression on her face that I had to go along with her. Maybe actually doing something was not such a bad idea. At least it would mean I didn't have to lie in my room festering in the heat. Thinking. Maybe that would help get the child-demon off my shoulders for a while at least.

"Okay, I guess not," I said. "I have to be somewhere after, after dark but . . . not for a while."

"Where?" she asked. "More maps?"

I gave her an uncomfortable look. For some reason I didn't want to lie to her.

"Well—no, I . . . can't really say," I mumbled.

There was a gleam of curiosity in her eyes.

"No?"

"I'm not supposed to."

"That in itself is a confession," she said with a smile. "You need to lie better if you are going to survive in this world."

"Well," I said, "I am not that used to secrets."

"Gawd blimey you ought to be," she said with a laugh. "Everyone has them. If it wasn't for keeping these beautiful secrets, our world wouldn't work. Shall we go?"

Beautiful secrets?

"I suppose," I said with a smile.

☼

"Do you know where we are?" she asked, coming to a stop.

We had ridden two trains and then a bus and I was feeling a bit more cheerful by this point. Travelling does that to me. And yes—I did know where we were, though it was somewhere as obscure and narrow as my own little appendix. We were surrounded by vague London buildings of no definable purpose, mostly businesses but many also no doubt converted into residences of some kind or another as part of people's increasingly desperate efforts to squeeze into this ever-hungry city.

"Good," she said. "This is where I used to live."

I looked around politely.

"This is also a point where the Polyhedron breaks down," she said. "Some of the angles are a bit bust and a few curves and blurs have crept in. There are several around the city, but so obscure that nobody really knows about them. I think it's pure coincidence that I ended up living on top of one."

"Okay," I managed.

"Come on—let's go in and I'll show you."

She crossed to an anonymous-looking gate, about as ordinary a gate as any in the city—set in a high wall painted in crumbling white. She dragged out a key and opened it with an aged scrape. There was a sign on it that looked as though it had been there through a lot of rainstorms:

Mail Service and Basic Facilities
<u>Helping the Homeless</u>
Registered charity #28475588

Feather hurried me through into a small courtyard that contained little more than paving slabs—a block of empty space surrounded by high walls and overlooked by blank windows. Ahead was a door, the only other way out of here, also painted in ancient white, and Feather was already taking out another key. It looked like the kind of door no longer intended to be opened—an abandoned portal, long forgotten. But Feather soon disproved that and we stepped through into the building.

"Come on," she said. "We have a little way to go yet."

With a mental shrug I followed her. I won't deny that I was intrigued by now. I liked these forgotten places in the city; I liked venturing into the private places on the other sides of gates—it was one area my travels didn't usually cover. Whatever strange mythology Feather was living in, I had to agree that places like this stood as a symbol of the inability of humanity to ever really control their world, which was always comforting in the face of the surveillance state and paperwork sea that is life.

Feather closed the door behind us, causing a small shower of debris and dust and paint chips, and locked it carefully. We were in a drab dark corridor that stretched a few meters into the building. Several more doors led off, as forgotten-looking and tatty as the one we had come through. Signs were mounted on some of them—*Shower, Shower, Toilet, Mail Store 1, Mail Store 2, Safe Room, Internet*—and then, rather stranger, *Crying Room* followed by an 'open' sign. We made for one of them at the far end, marked *Office* and Feather banged on it and loudly called a cheerful hello.

"I hear movement," she said at last. There was a scuffle, bump and scrape—then it opened and what I can only describe as a grizzled young man peered out. He was a scruff-bag, something I say without any massively negative connotations—short and dusty and with untidy hair, looking as though he had recently woken up. He gave us a startled look, then greeted Feather as one might greet an old friend. I could feel him unobtrusively studying me at the same time.

"Come in," the young man said, then looked at me. "And this is?"

"A friend of mine," Feather said with a grin.

"Yeah," I murmured awkwardly.

He nodded and stepped back to let us in. The room behind him looked more like a storeroom than an office. It was small and filled to the brim with filing cabinets and pigeonholes, most of them bursting with letters. We picked our way through, barely able to prevent strews of paper and packets from collapsing all around us. Dust left a thin layer on Feather's hair and clothes. I was vaguely aware of places like this around the city—places set up to receive mail on behalf of the city's vast army of homeless, so that their employers, family, loved ones, the council or whatever could still keep in touch—keep up a pretence of control and functionality. But I had never actually seen one before. Some of these letters looked as though they had been here for years and I found myself with a sudden dizzying sense of what might be contained in this room—in terms of human chaos and strange stories.

"Yes," the guy said. "I see it in your eyes that you accept this place on some level, even though you have only been here a moment."

I gave him a rather blank look.

"You have seen this room, and yet you are still eager. I like that."

I looked around the overloaded store cupboard in confusion. Was I? Eager seemed an alien term for me, but intrigued, certainly.

"And I certainly don't need to tell you not to tell anyone about it either, do I—that is also nice."

"No," I said on autopilot. "You don't."

This had a ring of familiarity about it and no mistake—the City Hunters all over again. But what was so secret about a mail dump?

"You don't," Feather echoed.

"Who would I talk to?" I said in a deliberate repetition of another similar assurance not so long ago. "I'm not even sure anyone else out there is even real."

We laughed awkwardly, and the nameless young man with the chaotic hair quickly unlocked yet another door that I hadn't even noticed among the stacked boxes and Feather and I passed through. Beyond was a stairwell—a spiral staircase leading both up and down. It was dark, with only a faint glimmer of light coming up from somewhere. It was grimy, adding yet more stains to my shirt. And, above all, it was steep. We tramped down carefully, Feather leading the way, and my eyes open for whatever secrets were coming. But all it led to was another room one storey below, containing nothing but more filing cabinets filled with what looked like even older letters. But Feather simply reached out and slid one out of the way easily as though it was on oiled casters, as indeed it probably was. And behind it was another door. A very solid one—a door that looked as though it wouldn't yield up its secrets easily.

Feather produced yet more keys and unlocked it in four places, opening it inwards and away from us. "This way," she called cheerfully, stepping into what looked like a small hollow space or cave of crumbling brick. "It should be clean enough, but watch your clothes."

I nodded quietly. "What is this place?" I demanded.

She gave a smile over her shoulder.

"This," she said as she tugged the cabinet back into place behind us as best she could, then slammed the door with a heavy thud, "is where I live."

"In here?" I asked in amazement. It seemed hard to equate any of this building with a residence, let alone this little hidden crevice. This hole in the wall. But then, should I be surprised at that? Did my own place up there on the surface look much like a home? London was a swarming hive where people lived or failed to live in any way they possibly could—I knew that. People lived in sheds, in attics, in converted hallways barely wide enough to take a single bed, in old warehouses or factories with ancient, long-dead machinery still in place, in shipping containers, in repurposed train carriages—all that was familiar enough. So what was the surprise about living underground?

"Yes—hey, you haven't seen anything yet. Come on—I'll show you. And introduce you to the others."

Others?

She hustled me into motion and I followed her further in—and instantly I realised that this crevice went back a lot deeper than I had thought. This wasn't a crevice at all . . .

It was a tunnel—a rough passageway plunging into the ground and into another world entirely. It was not earth or old brick, but smooth concrete. Smooth but irregular—sprayed shotcrete maybe. An organic-seeming grey tube—but after a metre or so, the grey gave way to a spectacular tangle of sprayed or painted art. This was considerably more than normal graffiti—these were works that had been executed over a considerable time and by many hands—a startling contrast with the drab world the other side of the door. It was safe to say that this art would never be seen in a posh trendy gallery on the surface, for there was a satirical aggression about it that sometimes pushed into extreme territories. There was a serious sense of violent and bloody anarchy and outrage—even revolutionary in tone and considerably harder and more vicious than anything the above-ground protest movements or political cartoonists would dare produce. I remember people that might just be recognised as real-world politicians in suits with bank notes oozing from cracks in their skin being executed by firing squad while various icons of the UK burned or were destroyed. The Gherkin building. The Shard. Westminster. And of course, the Union Jack. It looked like a classic London souvenir shop that had been utterly subverted in some violent revolutionary performance art.

We walked on. It wasn't that long a walk really—only about twenty metres or so—but it felt huge as we drifted through that tube. It was narrow and low and sometimes we had to scramble along half bent over. It was dimly lit by the occasional lamp, attached to wires that snaked along with us—presumably tapping into the electricity supply somewhere up above. As well as the art, you could also get hints of the substrate. It looked as though the passage had been carved out of the earth and city itself, then reinforced with whatever could be found—bricks, stone, paving slabs, concrete blocks, wood, road signs, parts of fences, then sealed in a thick coat of grey. I stared round in complete amazement. Occasionally we'd bust right through a brick-jagged hole in an ancient wall, or some other part of an existing structure would be incorporated—massive metal pilings or concrete foundations. It was like a surrealist painting itself, even leaving aside the artwork on the walls. The amount of work that must have gone into this was staggering—but it still didn't look remotely like a home yet. It was not until the tunnel opened up on one side that things began to change.

There was a curtain strung across the opening and Feather twitched it aside to reveal a huge, rounded cave, brightly but softly lit by several ceiling lights within paper globes. It had been carved out leaving four equally rounded pillars supporting the ceiling, then reinforced like the tunnel and smoothed off with the familiar grey shotcrete. The art continued here as well, though less aggressively, acknowledging that a more homely atmosphere was needed. The effect was beautifully rounded and organic. Desks and chairs, beanbags and what looked like sofa beds were dotted around. There was a computer against one wall, and what looked like a projector and a sound system. A bookcase, struggling slightly against the rounded walls but packed to capacity with books of many kinds. At the far end, some machinery or equipment that I didn't recognise for the moment. Several large metal tanks, as well as smaller containers on stands, a cabinet and what looked like a fridge.

There were also three or four people there—I can't remember precisely. They looked round at us.

"Hey, Feather!" someone said, greeting her with a hug. "How's it going?"

"Not bad. This is my friend from up above," she said, introducing me by name. "I am just showing him around."

"Well, hi," someone said. "Welcome to our wonderland."

Instant acceptance, I thought. No suspicion. As though they were all happy to trust Feather's vetting and instincts. Everyone seemed very friendly, surrounding me with greetings and small talk. I was hardly used to such friendliness, far removed from the calculating and rather stiff politeness of most residential complexes that I had known. This was closer to what I remembered of college and in spite of my surprise, I was liking it a lot.

"Would you like some apple wine?" someone asked, and I accepted gratefully—fluid was always welcome in this heat. He took an unlabelled bottle from that small fridge among the tanks, filled a glass generously and handed it to me. The word 'homebrew' floated into my mind and I tasted the cloudy liquid with interest. It was crisp and cold and refreshing—stronger than cider, still and heady.

"Shall we go to my room for a moment?" Feather said. "Then I'll show you."

"Sure," I said with a smile. "I'm just following."

After giving thanks again for the drink, we stepped back into the corridor, glass in hand.

"So," I asked with a weirdly lyrical tone, "how many people are there here?"

"About thirty," she said. "We all have our own little spaces. That was the common room, of course."

"Of course," I muttered, looking around. Every so often now, more rooms were opening out on either side of the tunnel, leading into more excavated chambers, or occasionally even underground parts of buildings, though the official doorways were long since bricked over. Most were screened off with curtains, but a couple were open and I paused, staring in at what was basically a small home. Furniture, personal belongings, clothes . . . and other things like artwork, art materials, books and computers, all set against that smooth concrete. I was utterly astonished.

"Here we are," she said at last, pulling aside a curtain and stepping into one of the rooms. I followed her—and stared round in even more amazement. Like the others, it was rounded, with a flat floor. A large hemisphere, basically, with a tunnel leading off deeper, also shut off by a curtain. The space was cluttered from floor to ceiling. I don't think I had ever in my life seen a room with so much—I can only call it 'stuff'—in it. Aside from mundane things like a wardrobe rail hanging with clothes and several wicker storage baskets, there were racks and racks of trays all filled with a jumble of odds and ends that I couldn't begin to recognise—no doubt from her mudlarking and scavenging. Bags and boxes were piled up, filled with unknown . . . 'stuff'. Bowls of water in which things were soaking. Tools and machines for repair. A tang in the air of mysterious cleaning fluids and river water. Boxes and padded envelopes labelled for posting. Perhaps even more bizarrely, there was a lot of technology on display as well. There was a small computer with several peripherals I didn't recognise—and also what looked like a ham radio set with an aerial trailing off to parts unknown. There was a telephone-type thing with a lot more buttons and displays than you'd normally see on a phone. There were other things as well that seemed more at home in a laboratory or technical control centre than a tiny London room. On one device, a small digital screen was building a list of numbers, a new one every several seconds or so—clearly map co-ordinates. My memory of London's co-ordinates was definitely not as clear as the streets, but I knew enough to place a rough curved line tracing its way across London—Kentish Town, Camden, Islington, Hackney—with no clue what it could mean. On another device, a second stream of numbers was spewing out, these less identifiable but I think they were eleven digits each. Phone numbers? All in all, it was quite impenetrable and gave me an odd feeling.

Feather saw me looking around and grinned. "Yes," she said. "I know—but hey, I do my own measuring as well—you have to measure the Measurers after all, right? I should probably have hidden a few of these things, but I guess I will trust you."

"Thanks," I said stupidly.

"Besides—I know where you live." She gave a dark laugh.

"Measurers . . . ?" I murmured. The Measuring Men. I gave her a slightly worried look.

"I listen in on the police and the MPS helicopter radio," she said, "as well as several illegal broadcasters around London, digital surveillance systems and a few others. It's all good fun."

"And this place is . . . secret?"

"Yeah," she said, waving me to a chair. "Well, it's something we dug out and expanded on over the years. It's just . . . well, what choice did we have? Most of us could never live on the surface, with the prices and the red tape."

"That's . . . pretty amazing."

"Yeah. Oh and there's a mushroom farm down one of the tunnels. Some hydroponics as well. Every little helps."

I had to laugh.

"It's secret, but I really think the government just doesn't care anymore. They've given up—on housing in general. Down here we don't pay them any taxes, but we don't cost them any benefits or services either. It's complete madness—and one day it's all going to crash this city. And then maybe we can all move back to the surface again. But until then—this really ain't a bad place to be."

"And—how many . . . places like this are there in the city?" I asked, my voice almost failing I was so amazed.

"Well—I don't know, do I," Feather said with a lopsided grin, "'cos they're secret. Right?"

"Okay . . ."

"I know of at least seven," she said—"but there must be many, many more. Everywhere you can squeeze a crack into the city, there is someone there to take it. Maybe there's thousands. Through the cracks, hidden under the stones?"

"Thousands," I echoed, leaning back in the chair and taking a long drink of apple wine.

"In a way, this is the real London now," she said sadly. "Just as the eccentric and arty communities and bustling markets used to be the real London compared to all the posh, gentrified development. Now the markets are all trendy and rich, and the arty types are down here—there's nowhere for them on the surface anymore."

I shivered at that. Then the curtain twitched and something else came in—a small black cat, who immediately went sniffing around Feather's legs, rubbing up against her affectionately. It seemed a long, long time since I had last seen a cat, except maybe as a brief glimpse of a stray in the night—no surprise since it was harder and harder to get a licence, and feeding them was getting increasingly controversial. You certainly cannot feed cats vegetarian food, so the problem was obvious and rather an embarrassing one for some.

"Hey, Fitzroy," Feather said, reaching out a hand and rubbing his head. Then she dragged a grey plastic tub from somewhere and emptied the contents of her muddy bag into it. I couldn't make out much—a substantial pile of odd jewellery, stones, devices and objects, mostly unrecognisable to me. She dragged the tub over to a tap on the wall, filled it with water and swirled it around.

"Look at this," she said, fishing out a small bottle, opening it and tipping out a tiny thing that gleamed red. I leaned in and studied it—just a rough red stone, or so I thought.

"It's a garnet—probably lost by some jeweller around the old London Bridge years ago." She waved at her machines. "I can give this a simple faceting and sell it—not bad at all. And coins—a little legal tender and some old ones—might sell them for a bit as well when they are cleaned. Edwardian clothes pins—hair grips. An old brooch that I will have to study a bit . . ."

She rummaged for a moment, washing them clean and examining them with interest. Meanwhile, Fitzroy was surprising me by turning his attention to me—approaching and sniffing at my shoes, no doubt reading a lot of my past history in them.

"Reach out your hand," Feather said. "Let him sniff your fingers." I did so cautiously—half afraid he would sink his teeth in. But it was like a formal greeting, as he sniffed me over. Then Feather slipped a little something into my hand—a scrap of meat. "Try him with this." I gingerly held it out and the cat immediately plucked it from me. I flinched back, but for no reason. I scratched his head, feeling a distinct prickle down my spine now—I was interacting with another creature here. An actual non-human entity, and we were sharing some kind of communication. It says a lot about the disconnect of the world, how utterly alien that felt to me.

The cat purred quietly. "There you go," she said. "You've got him—you've said hi. The mighty hunter has a new friend." She shoved the bowl of oddments out of the way. "Anyway—just give me a few moments to get this gear off and I will show you what we came for."

As though I wasn't there, Feather stripped off her outer clothes, shoving the waterproofs into her kitchen sink, then found and scrambled into a new pair of non-muddy trousers. This mysterious process of making herself acceptable for the outside world was not a performance I had seen very often and, since she didn't seem to care even slightly about having company, I found myself watching her appreciatively as she dressed and washed and dabbed and brushed. Then she hustled me back into the corridor.

☼

Walking down the tunnel, my mind was wordlessly singing in awe. I had devoted my life to exploring this city and mapping it out, but now I was wondering whether I had ever known anything about it—anything at all. Initially, I had been horrified at the thought of people having to live like this—illegally and deep in the earth. Had the city really degenerated to this state? But then I remembered my own place, no different in any way save for a hint of daylight and rent and bills that vampire-sucked about 95% of my entire income if I was lucky—about 130% if I wasn't. Rents that just kept on climbing, heedless of who they spat out at the bottom. Thinking back, I remembered articles about lost generations—entire generations of people on the streets or sleeping three or six to a room, with no hope of freeing themselves—before even that was largely forgotten. That was a failure if anything was—a complete breakdown of society at a very fundamental level. And when the world you live in has failed you to that extent, I suppose you have no choice but to find or make your own world—or at least to try. Just as my City Hunters had done in their own way.

And this place—well, even on this first glimpse it seemed to feel more like a home than anything on the surface.

No—I wasn't horrified, I was fucking jealous.

The tunnel went on for quite a distance, changing direction several times but keeping reasonably level, presumably following the structures and foundations among which it had been cut. Sometimes other tunnels branched off, but Feather led me onwards determinedly. Once it broke into a short section of arched brick that looked like the remains of a Victorian sewer. Sometimes other smaller metal pipes would cross our path and we would have to scramble over or under them. Sometimes it would be wider, with the artefacts of human life stored in boxes, then it would narrow again. At one point, it even dropped down to a few feet high and Feather gave me an apologetic look. "Yeah—we still need to expand this bit," she said. "It's all rather complicated." I dropped onto all fours and followed her arse towards the next open space up ahead—and the next little inhabited side-chamber. In my head, of course, I was trying to map it. I knew we were heading vaguely north, but that was all I can say. It was as if the tunnel led off perpendicular to the familiar three dimensions that I knew.

At last, after quite a few tens of metres, Feather stopped and we stepped into one of the little spaces—another rounded cave-room like all the rest, save that this one was empty of any trappings of home. It was eerily bare, but the walls were decorated from floor to ceiling with some of the most complex art yet—some of it immensely detailed, some just crude scribbles, but all combining to cast a bizarre atmosphere over the place. It was like a shrine. A central mural dominated the whole rear side of the room—a group of blank grey figures without faces. Familiar figures now. Stick-like, rudimentary suits and hats represented by little more than a couple of rounded shapes of paint. But their faces were black circles, in which one single white spot resided like a single eye. Never at the centre but always offset—floating somewhere up, down, left, right. And they stood against an urban backdrop of tall buildings, among which were a few recognisable London icons. The Gherkin—the O2 Arena—the Shard—the Post Office Tower . . .

And here, so far removed from the normal, the creepiness of those figures really hit home. Such a simple artistic concept—yet so utterly terrifying.

In the place of an altar, there was a large metal pipe set into the ground, stretching right across the floor. It looked ancient and corroded—almost three feet across, I think, and if this space had been inhabited then it might even have served as something to sit on. An area of the metal had flaked away leaving a rusty hole, so whatever it had been designed to carry, certainly wasn't being carried now.

"Take a look," Feather said, waving at it, her pointing hand directing me straight to the hole. I stepped over and looked in, but still couldn't see much—a hollow dark tube leading to places unknown in both directions. I studied it briefly, looking for something to justify what the fuck I was doing—then gave her an uncomprehending stare.

She pushed in beside me, then bent over and shoved her head right inside, half kneeling on the metal. If this was indeed an altar, if I may continue with that potentially annoying simile, then this must be the posture of obeisance and worship.

"Yes—look properly. That way," she said, waving vaguely down the pipe in a certain direction.

Wincing at the awkward posture, and still wondering if I was being made a fool of somehow, I tried to imitate her—tried to get my head right into the hole and look . . . at . . .

No, I am still not sure quite what it was, even now. But it wasn't darkness as it ought to be. It looked as though the pipe ended in the middle distance, giving a glimpse of bright points of light. And yes, the light was red. Connected by a web of glowing red threads like a laser maze or a luminous spider's web.

I stared at it, my heart sinking—every inch of skin prickling with chills.

"That's it," Feather whispered, somewhere behind me.

I withdrew my head from the pipe in a shower of rust, to find that she had settled down comfortably astride it. I brushed the red off my jacket, trying to calm down my raging brain.

"Okay," I whispered. "So—what exactly am I looking at?"

"That's the London Polyhedron," she said. "Or I should say the World Polyhedron. A glimpse of it, anyway."

I looked at her in silence.

"I wouldn't crawl through," she added. "I did once—it wasn't very nice."

"Right," I said slowly.

I sat down, staring at that black hole again, wondering whether to put anything of what I had seen before into words. But I didn't know how. This . . . this luminous web, this haunting phantasm of red . . . was Feather's Polyhedron? The mere thought came with a confusion that was almost unendurable. No, seriously—what was this thing? Some technology for the underground trains? Some security laser guarding a mysterious underground facility? Step through it and the entire city would erupt in a clamour of alarms? Or was I just going mad?

The World Polyhedron?

Feather was watching me quietly—probably giving me time for my thought processes to sort themselves out.

"That's the enemy," she said at last. "Think of it as like the spokes of an umbrella—holding us all rigid and chained rather than allowing us to flutter free. And one day, we shall destroy it. Or . . ."

"Or?"

"Or—we shall become extinct as a species," she said simply.

Silence.

I glanced round the room, trying to earth my mind—again focussing on the art on the walls. And this time I noticed that some of the grey one-eyed figures were carrying rulers—long rulers. And if there was a way for a simple ruler to be unnerving then this artist had found it. There was little doubt who they represented anyway—not after listening to Feather's talk.

And, with that realisation, something that was small within me suddenly grew a lot larger.

Feather gave a quiet grin, a faint hint of satisfaction in her eyes.

✡

I was spooked. I will admit it—I was spooked. It would be easy to dismiss everything that I had seen, every weird fantasy Feather had related, as some bizarre construct of her own. In fact every sensible part of me strained hard to do so. But as I walked home later that evening, I found myself staring round at the city I was flowing through, expecting to see mysterious stick figures with glowing white orbs for faces everywhere I looked. Or glowing angles. Red lights. Gossamer threads of light. Faces. Vertices. And indeed, sometimes I did see them—glimpsed out of the corner of the eye. Maybe they were car brake-lights or traffic signals, but no matter how much I tried to bring logic to bear on it, I couldn't shake off the feeling that something was not right with the world. It followed me down the streets like a blanket of static electricity and everything I saw, even the road I was walking along, seemed insubstantial. Every road surface, whether cracked tarmac, paving slabs, concrete, earth, cobbles, gravel, all seemed as though I was walking over a sheet of glass, with some utter mystery visible below it. And somehow—don't ask me how—that mystery was sentient, and maybe watching me. Maybe watching me just as it was watching everyone—or maybe it was watching me especially now. After all, I seemed to be in the process of falling through the cracks in the world. I had seen things, done things, thought things . . . and the result was that every angle in the city was the unbending Polyhedron. Every building was a face—every window a staring eye, through which the Measuring Men could watch.

I thought I must be going mad.

Or maybe the whole city was.

Arriving home, I didn't even go inside, just came to a halt in the little appendix, unsure what to do. The obvious course of action would be to run to my room, where it at least pretended to be safe and private—but no. This was a particular dreamlike kind of spooked that had me almost helpless. The night air came with a glow of energy—almost euphoria in some twisted and frightened way. I stood there, taking in the constellation of lighted windows. Every one of those represented a life. Sometimes, one might have been able to say that metaphorically, but here it was close to literal. Now, as far as I could work out, each and every one of us was responsible for just one illuminated square. That's two lightbulbs at the most—maybe one. Maybe a half if you shared a room. How's that for energy efficiency? I could gaze up at the front of that building in which I lived and I could know that every gleam, and every dark hole in the brickwork, represented one human life. In that gleam, someone lived and worked, fretted and struggled, fucked and cried. It was all very philosophical, but these dark and lighted windows didn't convey that much information really. Little more than an anonymous 'I am here' on the constellation of the city. From here, I could make out which window belonged to Kate and Aceline. Tea's was out of sight on the other side of the building and I wished I could see it. Would it be lit? Would it be dark? What would either mean? No bloody idea!

What did it matter?

One of the lights on the top floor flashed red, as though someone had slapped a filter over the bulb. I flinched in shock. Then another a couple of rooms down. Red light was haunting me, but to see it happening in my own building made my stomach tighten. The red even seemed to propagate into the sky itself, into the dull red haze that hung over the city eternally. And with that sky, the weird frightened euphoria continued. Maybe there was indeed a storm coming—some invisible blanket hanging over London that would only descend lower and lower, heavier and heavier. I don't normally feel much energy, but I did now. Now I almost wanted to dance. I wanted to move. I wanted to run through this city screaming, feeling the warm wind on my skin.

And besides, the Sea Wall was calling.

However, I didn't head for the station. Something about this night seemed to demand independence, not sitting in a train and watching the world drift past. Somewhere in the hefty loading area from the days when my building had been anything but a residence, there was a rough storage space shut away behind an apocalyptic-looking gate. And in there somewhere was my bike. It had been a while since I had used it and no doubt I was going to be out of shape—but could there ever be a more perfect vehicle for the haunted city night? Silent, fast—it could go anywhere, flitting like a ghost, like a moth through the trees. Even the fact that I could outstrip anyone on foot and theoretically slip away from any car through some narrow gap or other contributed to the feeling. It was not 'green transport'—it was not 'exercise' . . . it was stealth travel.

I unlocked the ancient gate and dragged it open with an unpleasant noise, then plunged into the chaos within. Bikes, boxes, crates, old machines of various kinds—even something that looked like a cinema popcorn maker lurking at the back. Stuff that people used regularly was at the top or outside of the pile—stuff that people hardly ever used was on the inside, and looked as though it ought to be forming new states of matter under the pressure. Fortunately, I found what I was looking for eventually and, after a few minutes checking it over and dealing with anything that needed dealing with, I was spinning off down the appendix and out into the slightly less little street beyond. They say you never forget how to ride these things—stored in your brain as a learned coordination skill or something—and I found I was really enjoying myself. It was the first physical activity I could remember in a long time that was in any way a pleasure. At least at first.

I passed from street to street, all almost empty at the moment in spite of or because of the unease the flowed over the city. Very quickly my body began to give way—pain in my legs, my chest howling for more air than it could physically get. I am embarrassed to say so, but it was the slight elevation of a railway bridge that brought me to a halt at last, leaving me leaning against the parapet—ironically up against some very familiar words: *BE READY!* Recently, wherever I went in London, I would see at least one or two of these scrawled. They never came with any explanation though. I was starting to wonder whether one was even needed.

When my lungs had stopped bellowing, I pushed off again and continued. And it was now that I began to see other people for the first time. It felt as though performances were being put on all around with every action fractionally unreal. The first performance I passed was a girl tramping along, head down, while one who was presumably her boyfriend followed awkwardly behind, trying to talk but getting no response. I then saw a group of women together, skirts short and hair crazy, but also unusually quiet and downcast as they progressed down the street—hurrying, but whether away from or towards something I am not sure.

The drama became more overt as I arrived at a main road. There was a clamour of voices and I saw a woman standing in the middle of the traffic, shouting as loud as she could in seeming despair, as though screaming abuse at the gods and heedless of the people staring at her with open mouths. Another, possibly an accompanying boyfriend, was urgently trying to quiet her down.

"Shh," he murmured awkwardly. "Don't shout about it in public—please."

"Can't you see what a fucking sham this is?" she shrieked as I passed. "And every single fucking relationship I see—just a complete fucking sham . . ."

There was a gleam in the eyes of the audience though—haunted and agreeing. Some pale and drawn, some embarrassed or annoyed—or even obscurely satisfied. And yes, she was probably right. The fact that our lives themselves are all so false means that most relationships are equivalently false. And when that realisation finally hits . . .

I cycled on through the streets. These were all classic dramas of the city night and ones I certainly wouldn't have seen on the train—but it felt like a year's worth crammed into one evening. At one point, the urban unrest that was the norm now began to come to the fore, with the flicker of fire in the distance—and shouting voices. I simply turned into a side street and kept my distance. Here though, I noticed a couple of doors standing open, letting into dark apartments or empty shops—even an entire street's worth in one area, one after another. I couldn't tell if they had been forgotten or, chillingly, invaded, though I could see no sign of violence anywhere. There were also what looked like a couple of abandoned market stalls, still with wares naked on the shelves or food cold on the stoves. This was getting significantly strange, as though there was some major event happening that I knew nothing about—yet should. Really, really should.

Something more, wider and deeper than mere protests. Feather's words were large in my mind. *Be prepared to fight?* But what war is fought with open doors?

Alongside all this, amid the usual plethora of racist scrawls and anti-political protests, every other wall I passed seemed to be decked with that one same phrase—BE READY. Other versions intermingled—READY alone or I'M READY or WE'RE READY—a general muddle of readiness plastering just about every surface of the city. All colours, all shapes. As I watched them, the creeping feeling within me crept harder and faster. An impending feeling. The volcano was shaking the ground—even the heat was tangible.

THEY SHALL LIGHT THE FIRE, someone had written under one of them.

It was a real relief to arrive at the sea wall, lock the bike to something and scramble up onto the railway line. Normally it was the other way round, with the illegal side of the viaduct always seeding a slight restlessness. But this time, the empty and isolated Limehouse Soak and the prospect of good company in the arched hideaway seemed much more appealing than the edgy city. I came to a stop for a while, though, staring out at the artwork dimly visible in the ruined gloom. The stick figures. Were those white things eyes, I wondered. A nucleus in a single cell. A planet drifting across the face of the sun. Or was the whole thing beyond my comprehension? As I stared, the figures almost seemed to move—to dance maybe.

It was an effort to get into motion again but eventually I managed it and made my way along the tracks, my railway timetables ticking gently in my head, then down to the ledge that was the top of the wall and along it to the hole. The long exhaust tube of the extractor was poking out through the curtain and I realised it was on—a steady flow of fumy air making a bubble of gassy cooking smell. There was something homely about that—some very very faint ghost of what it might have felt like in the past, when one could still approach an actual home and smell dinner being prepared. Maybe it's your family, or friends inviting you round for socialising. I suppose this nefarious subterranean alternative was pretty much all we had left now. It's hard to imagine feeling house-proud or food-proud when your guests have to sit in the corner of your one room while you awkwardly cook on your little tabletop hob. Hard to imagine it in people's heads either, so subsumed are we all in suspicion, analysis and paranoia. Simply accepting what is generously offered seems a lost art in some ways, being replaced by a strange balancing act of politeness and wariness . . .

Dismissing a brief feeling of melancholy, I slid feet-first through the curtain and onto the wooden platform, into that world of delicious cooking smells and darkness. There was also a noticeable blast of heat, which I was less happy about—the still air within the arch several degrees hotter than the outside. I shuddered and flapped my damp shirt, then made for the ladder.

Down below, one single candle illuminated the stove, on which some stew was simmering gently over a very low heat. Clay Man's huge mural dominated the wall. Maybe he had been working on it since, for it looked even more substantial than I remembered—and quite disturbing in the low light. Powerful, elaborate and surreal art. And to my relief, no Measuring Men. Among the plant stems, several eyes had opened and almost seemed to glow, while the hunting creatures had developed a curious flowing sense of motion. And a human figure, as yet undefined stood behind it all, hand raised as though holding something . . .

The room was empty, but more light was trickling in through the passage to the next arch, along with a faint murmur of voices. I hurried through to join them, looking forward to a touch of sanity . . .

Um—yeah.

After a few seconds, I decided that the two almost naked figures had to be Star Girl and the Butcher. Had to be. It still felt like a dream though—maybe many times more so. It's very hard in this world to recognise people from their bodies alone, and I came to a shocked halt, frozen in a way that really was quite ridiculous. No—the wavering glow hadn't deceived me.

Both their faces were concealed by two rather dramatic animal masks, and they were stripped down to their underwear. He was wearing a pair of loose shorts in grey, sitting comfortably in the armchair, cross-legged and consciously elegant—somehow as handsome as ever, even with his clothes missing. She was sprawled out on a beanbag, legs dangling and looking very relaxed, divided into the classic three portions of body by black knickers and bra. Above those bodies, the masks painted a very strange picture indeed. Star was some creature that looked like a weasel or marten, and the Butcher was what I decided had to be a cockerel.

I felt as though the world was drifting sideways for a moment. Dreams within dreams within dreams . . .

"Train Man," Star Girl yelled welcomingly, giving me a wave with both hands.

"Um," I said.

The Butcher gave a snort of laughter. "Gawd, the expression on your face," he said.

The humour brought me back down to earth a bit. "Would you two prefer to be alone?" I asked, blinking heavily.

"No," Star Girl said, "we would fucking prefer not to be alone. Get in here and sit down."

"Okay," I said with a bewildered giggle, dropping heavily into a chair, still studying them with several loud questions in my head. Neither of them looked even remotely concerned, unless a slight sense of theatricality in their posture could be seen as a symptom of 'concern'.

"The Butcher has been cooking," she said happily, shoving the mask up onto her forehead. I knew that—I could smell it. If I hadn't been so startled, I would have been going wild over it like a hungry cat. As it was I nodded absently.

"Um," I tried again, "you're going to have to explain, you know. Dare I even ask what's going on?"

"Oh come on, Train Man," she protested. "How can anyone not be naked on a night like this? It's so fucking hot."

The Butcher gave a chuckle. "We were just trying to cool off after all that cooking. These arches are like a crock pot tonight."

"Clothes are such a drag," Star Girl said, for some reason affecting a posh accent.

I tugged at my wet shirt, and I had to admit I could see their point.

"And the masks?"

"Who needs a reason?" he said. "It's a wild night—a night of midsummer madness. Haven't you noticed?"

I frowned—and the sense of dream dissolved somewhat. It was indeed a night of madness—madness that had chilled me on some level, half in my head, half from without. These two sounded remarkably happy about it though.

"Join us, Train Man," she said. "Gawd—you looked soaked. Get those stupid clothes off for fuck's sake."

I was tempted—it would have been bliss to dry off a bit. But naaah. My ugly body would not look well alongside those two, even in candlelight. Before I could find a response though, there was a scuffle outside—the sound of more feet landing on the platform.

"Here we go again," Star said with a grin, meeting the Butcher's masked eyes and quietly replacing her marten face. "Perhaps we should hide by the door and jump out on them?"

The Butcher gave a cackle, but nobody moved.

"Something smells divine," Clay Man called from the other room. Then he and the Beggar stepped in and, like me, came to a surprised halt.

"Is this a private party," the Beggar asked after a moment, "or . . . ?"

"Put the following words into the correct order," Star said with a hint of sourness. "'Fucking'. 'It's'. 'Hot'. And 'too'."

"I ain't disagreeing," the Beggar said with a weary sigh, while Clay Man gave a laugh, dumped his bag on the ground and began unloading his cargo of water bottles.

Almost immediately, though, there was a third scuffle and scramble, the creak of the ladder, then the Philosopher stepped in. He took it better than the others, I have to say.

"Aha," he murmured, eyebrows up. "Okay, we have wise people. Good evening, everyone." He dragged off his coat, which seemed to accompany him no matter what, and sat down with a grunt. He looked even more clobbered by the heat than I was. He also dragged a water bottle out of his bag and splashed some over his face.

"Hello Philosopher," Star said politely. "Thank you. You are just in time to tell us all about nakedness. Please enlighten?"

"Ummm . . . you're not naked," he murmured, pouring water into a cup and downing it in one.

"Yes, I am aware of that," she said, snapping the elastic of her knickers.

"For gawd sake, sit down," the Butcher said with a frown. "You are almost as bad as those clots outside. Don't make me self-conscious. You'll make me get dressed again if you are not careful."

"No they bloody won't," Star said flatly.

The Beggar and Clay Man exchanged a comical look and obeyed.

"Right, right," the Beggar said brightly. "Okay then—nice to, um, see you again. What's the agenda for today? Are we going out, or . . . ?"

"Like that?" Clay Man asked with a grin. "You want to go out and do it like the ancient hunters did—bare arsed?"

"Oh, if only," the Butcher said.

The Philosopher grinned. "You know, the main reason we have no fur is apparently because we needed an efficient cooling system to hunt in the wild grasslands. Sweat," he said. "It's all about sweat."

"Really? That's kind of interesting," Star Girl said. "I've always hated getting sweaty in the hot weather. Clammy clothes . . ." She paused. "Did you just say that it was the fact that we were meat eaters that made us naked?"

"I . . ." The Philosopher hesitated. "I wouldn't like to make a definitive statement based only on some vaguely remembered scientific theories but . . . it's possible."

Star gave a quiet laugh, savouring the thought for a moment.

"Oh screw that," the Butcher said. "We've got food, whenever you want it. Let's all just go and dance on the railway line."

"Naked on the railway line would be part of a true reality," Clay Man said, "but maybe a rather visible part. Do the night trains deserve such sights?"

"Okay then," Star said with a comical shrug, "we'll go and roll in the mud."

"I second this motion," said the Butcher.

"Still rather visible," the Philosopher demurred.

"Nonsense darling," she said. "On this night anything is possible."

Again, I felt a slight cringe somewhere inside. They seemed far too happy about things, while the strangeness that seemed to have settled over the city had done nothing but seed a knot of ultimate unease in me. I looked round at them, not at all sure I liked the way things were going. I didn't care even slightly if Star and the Butcher—or indeed anyone—wanted to prance around in their underwear. Make no mistake, I have always admired people who are able to do that without fear. From where I am standing, bodily confidence seems one of the most amazing things, up there with watching someone do a magic trick. But my instincts were ticking. Somewhere, I knew with great clarity, something was wrong.

Star jumped to her feet and replaced her mask again. "Let's get outside. Maybe leave your shoes on," she called, shoving her feet into them again and bounding through into the next room, the Butcher right behind her. "And bring the masks," she yelled back.

I glanced round and, for the first time, I noticed the box full of other masks in one corner. Clay Man grabbed it and hurried after them, also looking fired up with excitement now. The rest of us were left exchanging glances.

"It's not just me, is it?" I asked softly, after a moment. The Beggar looked at me, eyebrows up. "There's something . . . not quite right?"

"Maybe," she murmured.

"I don't mean them," I mumbled, no idea how to put what was in my head into words. "I mean . . . over . . . everything . . ." I rubbed at my eyes—again, the world was moving sideways ever so slightly. And for some reason four more words came out of my mouth, somewhat ironic, deliberately obscure, and with no direct, simple or even known meaning. "Death to the Polyhedron . . ."

"Huh?"

"Nothing."

"I suppose we had better go with them?" the Beggar asked, a puzzled smile on her face. "It would be nice to be in the fresh air. This place is cooking me." She flapped her clothes, which were soaked with sweat. The Philosopher nodded and stood up. No more words were exchanged. We extinguished the candles, made our way to the ladder and up it. Then out through the curtain into the night air and onto the ledge. It was a relief to get back into the relative cool.

"Come on," Star bawled. The three of them were already down below on the muddy concrete, I saw—Star and the Butcher standing out startlingly white in the darkness, and Clay Man had also removed his shirt now. There was no sea in evidence anywhere—the tide was out, showing plenty of mud throughout the Soak.

"How do we get down?" I asked.

"There's a way along here," the Beggar said, pointing east—the other direction to usual. "It's a quite nice—interesting place down there. I go out there sometimes . . ."

We headed that way. I soon saw that there was more half-demolished masonry adjacent to the metal wall just before the Limehouse Cut Watergate—it must once have been a building—and a portion of ruined brickwork jutting over, a short step from the railway viaduct. The Beggar picked her way carefully across and the Philosopher and myself followed in her footsteps. And then it was an awkward scramble down, brick wall to brick wall, rather like the familiar way up on the other side. And my feet landed on the muddy concrete with a splash.

The almost-naked pine marten gave us an eager wave. "Come on, you lot," she yelled.

Down here at the foot of the wall, there was what might be called an apron—a flat shelf of poured concrete, looking even more geological than I remembered. It was like a lava flow, engulfing whatever had been here before—bollards, paving slabs, pieces of masonry. It was another demonstration that when they had built this wall, aesthetics hadn't really been a priority. It sloped gently down to the original ground level, before giving out into a world of mud and ruined car park. Water and construction together had left it very uneven, though, with patches of deep mud and rough areas of shingle. And beyond it, a little way into the Soak and among the ruins, was the old Limehouse Basin, the small enclosed harbour where once ships and narrowboats had moored, now a deep tidal pool of brine connecting the canals to the Thames beyond.

Star Girl was still bubbling with excitement—seeming unable to keep still. "Come on guys," she called again. "Don't be shy. Pick an animal and taste the liberation. Beggar?"

The Beggar gave an awkward squirm. "Oh—I don't . . . you know I'm a bit . . . beat up under here . . ." She tugged at her clothes shyly.

Beat up? I gave her a sharp look.

"Oh fuck that," Star said. "You know nobody cares about that."

"And Train Man? Philosopher?" the Butcher yelled.

I gave an uncomfortable cough. No matter what measurements you use, no matter how nice and accepting you are, I was the ugliest one here. That wasn't an emotive moan, simply a basic empirical fact. I was still the unfit blob and I wasn't sure I could cope with anything like this. It's one thing for a beauty like Star Girl or the Butcher to run round in their underwear, quite another thing for me—and no matter how much people may try to be accepting, that is a basic physicality that is not easy to escape from. "No no," I said with an awkward laugh. "I . . . think not."

I sat down on the rough concrete and the Philosopher joined me. I thought I detected a brief moment of disquiet in his face as well, but he was silent, just doing what he always did—watching with interest. Not for the first time, it occurred to me that he was slightly out of place here, older, quieter, less involved, watching the interesting things his little flock got up to. Had he ever actually hunted anything? He didn't seem to have brought anything back since I had been involved.

"Give me a mask," Clay Man said, unbuckling his trousers. "I want cool air."

Star gave a triumphant whoop. "What animal speaks to you?" she said.

"Eh? Ohhh—give me the grey owl this time," Clay Man said with a smile.

"Welcome, Grey Owl," she said, tossing a beautiful owl mask in his direction. He put it on—and his face vanished into the general strangeness of the evening. "No one else?" Star said dryly.

The Philosopher and myself gave her a stubborn look. "Well never mind this lot," she teased. "Let's go and dance." She grabbed the Butcher by the arm. Then the two were running off and scrambling up the broken masonry again to the ledge, and then further up to the top of the viaduct itself. They went bounding away, literally running along the parapet, bodies white in the darkness, and looking rather perilous. Laughter and calling voices came drifting back.

"They are not exactly being secure," Clay Man said.

"I wonder why those two are finding it so easy," the Beggar muttered. "I must admit—I am rather jealous." There was a silence, then she seemed to give a mental shrug and began peeling off her T-shirt. That gave me a prickle. I have to say, I found myself watching her much more keenly than any of the others—and the moment she slid off her top and tossed it away onto a dry patch of that concrete lava, I felt that prickle increase massively. Even in this quite low light, I could now get a look at what she meant by 'beat up'. Her skin was covered with scars—nothing overt, just a faint tracery of white and corrugation on her skin. As I looked at them, I felt something very dark turn over inside me.

Clay Man, though, only grinned. "Nice," he said. The Beggar gave an embarrassed smile in return and slid off her trousers as well. She stood there, pure white—basic white underwear on white skin. "Give me . . ." She hesitated. "Oh—give me the rat. I guess that's what I have been all my life."

He tossed it to her and she put it on—a sharp and cleverlooking rat face that went strangely well with her scarred skin and muscular body.

She stood and looked around at us for a moment, then sat down gingerly on the edge of the concrete, her feet trailing in a small muddy pool. "Oh boy, it feels weird," she said. "Kind of nice though . . ."

Clay Man joined her with a smile, settling back comfortably on the rough surface—and yes, it did look comfortable.

"Yeah," she said. "I mean—well, I know I am a bit messed up but . . . I mean, this doesn't bother anyone, does it?" she demanded, brushing at the scars on her body.

"Of course not," Clay Man said from behind his owl mask, reaching out and touching her arm. "All a scar does is tell a story. Well—all anything on the body does, I suppose."

I wondered if I was telling any stories. I suspected so—but not stories anyone wanted to hear.

"The only thing that bothers me," I said, trying to be funny, "is that you look as though you are going to bite me."

The Beggar turned to me briefly, and the concealed look behind her mask could have been anything. I gave a micro-sigh and looked away, focussing instead on the city—the artwork—the Measuring Men staring down at us. I was trying to drift away into a little world of my own while the occasional whoop from Star and the Butcher faded into a background haze. The blocky shapes of the empty buildings certainly did not look much like the vertices of a polyhedron—not like the glorious star-points of the mathematical forms I could remember anyway. Yet somehow I could clearly imagine it there now—an over-arching structure simultaneously supporting and binding this world we live in, on some level fictitious, on some level not at all. Lines and angles filled with tension and glowing an impossible red beneath the cityscape. Permitting it to exist . . .

Gawd, what the fuck was it with Feather and her fantasies?

I was starting to feel rather sad here. Maybe the term is self-pity. It was depressing to watch the others fooling around so easily—with such liberation. Especially the Butcher. He looked good naked—assured and confident, as though it was the most normal thing. His body was not particularly muscular, but slim and elegant. Very pale, not much body hair. It was next to impossible to prevent comparisons buzzing in my brain, however much I tried to shut them up.

Fortunately, I was brought back to earth by a thrumming in the tracks up above—a sound I am particularly attuned to. In the excitement I had forgotten the time—and the timetable. I was about to yell after the two dancing runaways, but there was no need. They had also heard it, quickly scrambled over the parapet and crouched down on the ledge. In the distance, towards Canary Wharf Island, moving lights gleamed—the familiar majestic crawling worm making its way through its city lair. An old 125, unusually enough, and what it was doing out here in commuter land I am not sure. Maybe it was a charter or tour train returning home. Probably not something the readers will care about much, save that it was big, dramatic and heavy. I stood up and scrambled onto a chunk of broken house so I could see it better. It rolled by towards city centre very slowly—its massive engine passing with a roar, then a procession of lighted carriages. There is something truly awe-inspiring about a long, slow-moving train—perhaps even more so than one going flat out. The sheer weight and presence of it really hits home. I stared up, wondering if they could possibly see us in the shadows. I doubted it, given the darkness that lurks outside a train window. We would be nothing but faint white or dark ghosts.

But Star Girl was irrepressible. A yell and she had jumped up again. She leapt up onto the parapet and started waving at the train, whooping with excitement. The Butcher followed her. They danced again on the parapet itself, light bathing them now, just metres from the passing windows—and I could clearly see startled faces looking out. I could imagine their shock—quietly travelling home after a long long day, minds on little more than journey's end now, only to be confronted by a capering marten and cockerel outside their safe little windows. And if anyone had had a camera . . .

The Beggar shook her head, a stifled laugh from behind her mask.

"Gawd fucking blimey," Clay May said. "Is everybody insane tonight?"

"I am wondering," the Philosopher said—and again that faint hint of disquiet in his face.

The two danced, showing off with stylised absurdity. Star Girl even shoved down her knickers and mooned the train. My memory turns up a tradition of mooning the Amtrak trains in America in a certain place and on a certain day—exactly why I have no idea. But the image of it in the London night, with added animal masks, seemed very strange indeed. Then the rear locomotive had passed with a second roar and Star was left waving after it happily.

"Oh boy," the Beggar groaned, kicking up a splash of water. "Is this the way the world is going?" She scrambled to her feet again. "I can't match those two beautiful idiots, but at least these two things don't bloody matter."

To my amazement, she stripped completely, laying her underwear carefully on a dryer part of the concrete. Now the white was interrupted more, if anything, by a substantial tuft of dark hair between her legs—the feral-looking rat-faced woman. I was left gawping at her like a virgin in a very bad comedy show—in actuality with a powerful blend of admiration, lingering shock and inevitable erotic fascination.

She picked her way down off the concrete and sat down with a squelch in one of the deeper mud pools there, hiding her hips again with an embarrassed hunch.

"Nice one, Beggar," the Butcher yelled as the two came scrambling down to join us again. "Shall we join her?"

"You two are absolutely nuts," Clay Man cried.

"Yeah," Star said. "But in the best possible way. Fuck them all."

The Butcher flung his shorts away and landed heavily in the mud in an impressive splash—drops flying everywhere.

"You clumsy wanker," Star called and he slung a handful of mud at her, spattering her white skin. She gave a whoop, then, in one scramble, had dragged off her own last few garments and launched herself at him in vengeance, heedless of her mask. They both went over into the mud and shingle, rolling and wrestling, turning themselves black in the gloom and kicking up a tremendous noise.

Then the Butcher bent down. "Alright, alright—slap my arse," he called and Star Girl obliged with a shrill giggle.

"Fuck that," he cried, sticking his tongue out. "That the best you can do? Harder."

"Don't provoke me, darling," she said, brandishing her hand. "This thing here is a lethal weapon."

"Prove it," he called, while the rest of us watched in bemusement. Star Girl whacked again, with a blow that could be heard half way across the Soak, then danced away, flapping her hand.

"Ow," she giggled. The Butcher gave a cackle.

"Your turn," he cried, jumping up. Star Girl screwed her face up in a grin and grabbed her submerged ankles, bending herself over for a hefty series of whacks that made her shriek and almost go headfirst into the mud again, still laughing to the point of hyperventilation.

"Should we applaud or something?" Clay Man asked dryly.

"Oh boy," Star Girl said, hauling herself back up onto the concrete, black with mud. What little I could see of their faces looked flushed and excited—what little I could see of their arses was heading towards pink. She squirmed against the rough surface in a futile attempt to rub some of the Thames dirt off, then stretched herself out on her face. The Butcher also extricated himself and sat down with a squelch. The Beggar watched us for a moment then hauled herself out of the mud into a deeper pool of actual water and rolled over a few times, rubbing herself down, carefully protecting the mask. Washing herself clean. Then she stepped out onto the concrete and sat down beside me. She still looked slightly uncomfortable, but had relaxed enough to stop trying to hide her skin or keep her legs together. And . . . something was going on here. Star Girl looked sexy yet her nakedness had only demystified her—the games we end up playing with ourselves and our sexualities fading. The Beggar, though—she was hitting me hard. Acknowledging sexual attraction is an awkward thing to write about, given the hostility and awkwardness that surrounds it on all sides, but naked skin inevitably remains powerful. And I have to be honest—an honesty that the world also needs. I can't say that there was anything new in this, no massive realisations—

instead her skin acted as a lens, focussing my attention very sharply indeed. She looked so pale in the dark that she almost seemed to glow—and her proximity and the general surrealism of the scene was making me prickle again. *Dammit all,* I thought, depression washing harder. *Is there no escape from the flesh?* There was a sense of peace here now, yet it was a peace I felt removed from—filled with tension, unease and bitterness.

This uneasy yet peaceful atmosphere was cut though a few minutes later when, like a manifestation of my own storming feelings, a faint rumble came cutting through the London air—a deep deep thunderous sound that seemed to come from no definable direction. London is full of sounds of one kind or another, but this one was sufficiently odd to get my attention. It plugged itself into my already somewhat edgy and nervous mood enough to make me want to jump up and go bolting for the hidden safety of the sea wall again.

"What the fuck was that?" the Beggar demanded suspiciously. Everyone glanced round at her, then at the surrounding cityscape. There was nothing unusual to be seen, though. Nothing more than the normal backdrop against the orange sky. The far bank of the Thames, just visible between the ruined buildings, the dominating glowing mass of Canary Warf and the illuminated pillars of the big road bridge next to it.

"Anyone got their phone?" Clay Man asked, casually enough. "Anything on the networks?"

The Philosopher took his phone out of a pocket—a small smartphone with computer features, unlike my simple old thing. He studied it a moment, then shrugged. Nothing.

"Shall we go back in?" I asked. I felt uneasy at the question, wondering whether I was overreacting—but the moment I asked it, I could see it mirrored in everyone's faces.

"Yeah—let's," Clay Man said.

"Gawd." The Butcher hauled himself upright and brushed at the semi-dried smears of mud. "Now what? We need to get clean somehow. I ain't going on the bus like this. It stinks as well."

"Just wash it off," the Beggar said, waving at the water below. "Then let's get in. Then we can relax and take our time." She

189

rubbed at herself—even though she was nowhere near as muddy, she was still wet and she collected up her clothes and threaded them onto one arm for transportation.

Before anyone could wash anything, though, things were interrupted a second time by a distant approaching drone of engines. Helicopter. And more than that, a helicopter whose sound I recognised immediately.

"Metropolitan police," I said softly.

"Damn," Clay Man said, the last of the party atmosphere evaporating in a second. "Okay, enough's enough. Let's get back inside—right now."

Nobody disagreed with that—indeed we pretty much ran for it. Everyone grabbed whatever clothes they had left scattered about, Clay Man took the box of masks and we scrambled awkwardly back up onto the wall, then quickly along it to our space in a perilous race. I don't know how the others felt, but they looked very naked and conspicuous now. It made little difference to the old MPS since I knew they carried infrared cameras—but still, the mind works in certain ways and it was a great relief when we got through the curtain and inside onto the wooden platform. However, the helicopter wasn't interested in us. It roared past high overhead in the direction of Canary Wharf and quickly vanished.

We could hear sirens in the distance as well. On the face of it, nothing unusual—there always seem to be sirens somewhere in London—but even so, it was quite a clamour.

"Something's going on," the Beggar said as someone fumbled for a candle to cast illumination into this dark place. The Philosopher looked at his phone again, running a few searches. Then he shrugged. I still felt a slight chill, though, somewhere at the back of my brain. And as the others made their way down the ladder and into the next room, spreading the light to more candles as they went, I lingered behind at the hole in the wall staring out, curtain round my shoulders to keep the light in. Over London, something was swirling. It might have been a surreal cloud system, or a dark aurora. And the words 'death to the Polyhedron' were in my mind again, not because of any meaning but half as a joke, half as a mantra, as though the words themselves had power.

"Train Man?" the Beggar said softly, glancing round at me and returning to my side.

I drew back onto the wooden platform and looked round at her, her candlelit masked nakedness giving me an even greater jolt in that mundane environment. Stuck between her and the city nerves, I was feeling as awkward as I had ever been and I shrugged with a tiny smile. "I feel weird."

"Hm?"

"Something in the air. Something moving. Something angular . . ."

She stared at me in silence, expression invisible. "Let's go down," she said at last. "I'm hungry."

"Yeah okay."

I scrambled down the ladder, leaving her to follow me, then stepped into the other room feeling hunched and miserable. Partly, I wanted to blank her out of my world, but that was a futile undertaking. When she joined me, she stood out even clearer in the glow of the candlelight—her scars included. Her nervousness seemed to have evaporated now, I noticed. She seemed to have accepted that nobody here thought any the worse of her for the traces on her skin. And I admired her for it, as far as that means anything.

For the others at least, though, the unease seemed to have dissolved again into giggling relief.

"Okay, we must be crazy," Star Girl said, "but that was fun, right?"

"Definitely fun," the Beggar said, rubbing at her damp skin. "And we can't even get dressed again yet—I'm soaked."

"So does that mean we get to eat in the nude?" the Butcher asked, taking off his mask and setting it aside. It looked muddy and bedraggled.

"Great idea," Star said.

"Oi," Clay Man barked. "You two—you are not, I repeat *not* sitting on the furniture like that."

She glanced down at herself, at the mud that still liberally smeared her.

"Oh fuck—well I'm not standing here all evening."

"Hang on," the Beggar said with a wry sigh, dragging off her own mask, her sharp face causing an even greater shock of reality. "There's some newspaper somewhere."

She went rummaging, then returned with a stack of it, which she proceeded to lay liberally over the seats of two of the chairs.

"Okay," she said, "now get your muddy arses on there and don't move."

The two muddy ones sat down with sheepish grins.

"How about me?" she asked, turning round. "I am a bit wet still but . . ."

"Not so bad," Clay Man said. "But you know—a little muddy."

"Okay okay," she said wryly, putting down some more paper for herself and sitting down gingerly—then pointedly handed a sheet to Clay Man.

"Cool," Star Girl said. "And as the only two who didn't get their kit off, you can get us the dinner. I don't dare move."

I gave them a wan look, not quite ready to share their high spirits. The Philosopher shrugged comically and we both withdrew. It was actually a relief to retreat to the other room, where the stew was simmering, the stove's extraction fan whirring noisily. I wondered for a moment whether to try and ask him about what was going on. The high spirits that seemed just a little too high, the strange moods in the air, the feeling of something weird marching through London.

But as it turned out, I didn't have to.

"What do you think?" he asked in a low voice. "Should we have gone along with their liberation?"

"Naah. I think there may be some sights for which the world is not yet ready."

"You are self-conscious? Very interesting."

"Is it?"

"About what, though?"

I was silent for a moment—then words came. "When you are defective, you probably have some kind of duty not to inflict yourself on others." I don't normally come out with things quite that blunt—but I was still feeling far from happy. The Beggar was sitting somewhere in my stomach like a prickly sea urchin that I had swallowed whole and was trying to digest. And there was a realisation connected to this that I wasn't happy about at all.

The Philosopher did not react, though—didn't jump on me for moaning or try and comfort, for both of which I was rather grateful.

"I feel older than the rest of you," he said at last. "Wearing out, losing the bloom. I fear I am a bit of an odd one out in this group."

"I'm not sure that counts as defective."

"Also, the removal of clothes feels like losing something of yourself. Maybe something that should be lost, or at least that one should be able to lose if needed—I don't know. Like the peacock's tail, our clothes have become a part of our identity. But then, maybe it's like daring to reveal your innermost thoughts, even though they lay you open to possible criticism or wounding . . . something that should come with a sigh of relief, as though you have relaxed some muscle that you weren't even aware was tense."

"I suppose . . ."

"I came here because I am interested," he said. "I want to know what the human being is—and the normal world can never show you that in its entirety. You won't find it in any comfortable professor's study or intellectual pondering. You need to look below the surface—including what is perceived as negative. You need to find those kinky sex communities . . . the drug houses, the underground meat farms or wild hunters—if you want any real idea what we are. And yet—maybe that's all I am. Just a spectator."

I nodded and we began dishing the stew out into bowls.

"Very—very interesting," he said softly. "People can come out with all the high-sounding intellectualisms they like, they can circle-jerk over Jung and Nietzsche all they like—but I am coming to think that we will never truly get much beyond a diffuse cloud of 'humans are weird'."

We didn't say any more as we ferried the bowls through to the others.

"And would sir, madam, like wine with that?" he asked gravely.

"Yes, please," the Beggar said. And I quietly retreated to get it, then served it, trying to play along with the Philosopher's teasing formality.

"For gawd sake sit down you two," Clay Man said with a laugh. "This is tasty—relax and enjoy it."

The Philosopher sat—and that meant the only free seat was next to the Beggar—and I took it. I was sure that the strange feelings in my head were radiating out into the world like a radio signal that could be picked up by anyone who bothered to listen. However, the stew had a nice richness, unlike anything I had tasted before. It was the flavour of the deep earth—the pulsing, straining fire of life itself. And when it was gone, I was feeling rather better.

"I feel strangely relaxed," the Beggar said. "Maybe—more relaxed than I have for many many years."

Her grey eyes were fixed on me, giving me the feeling that she was addressing me personally. "I guess I trust you—all."

Trust us to do what?

Star Girl stood up, taking most of the newspaper with her. "Gawd," she muttered, awkwardly peeling it off her backside. Scraps of dried and half-dried mud flaked off onto the floor. The Beggar gave her a thoughtful look, then also tried standing up, plucking the paper away with a sigh.

"Don't take this the wrong way," Clay Man said cheekily, "but I think I can read your arse. And I am rather liking the experience."

The Beggar actually blushed.

"I can't read those mucky bastards," she said, looking at Star Girl. "All I can see is mud."

"Is anyone dry yet?" Star asked with a grin.

"No—this fucking heat is making me sweat as fast as it's evaporating away."

"Drat," Star said with a laugh. "We got any towels?"

"Of course not," Clay Man said. "That would be far too easy."

"Anyway—I vote we eat all our dinners like this in the future," Star said. "It shall be our new formal dress."

I glanced at the Philosopher, expecting a response to that—some thought from the only other coward who had lacked the nerve to strip off. But he wasn't listening. He had his smartphone out again, I realised, and was earnestly studying the screen, his eyebrows twitching uneasily. There was something about it that I didn't like.

"What is it?" I asked, and the others glanced round as well.

"Well . . ." he said, hesitating. "I'm not sure but . . ." He looked up at us. "I think something's happening," he said simply. And somehow I knew what he meant without any doubt whatsoever.

"What?" the Butcher demanded.

"That rumble we heard . . . I was just . . . checking the networks again. And it seems . . ."

We all gathered round. "Hmm?" Star Girl demanded.

"It says here . . ."

"What?"

He shrugged. "Well, it says a bomb has exploded . . . in the Canary Wharf area." He looked up at us, his face uneasy. "A big one. And riots have significantly increased there, and in south London—and Camden—and Tottenham . . ."

I felt a chill of shock. We stood in silence looking at each other, then as one we rushed back into the next room and traffic-jammed our way up to the entranceway, staring out at the city, heedless of escaping light. For the moment we could still see nothing. Nothing seemed different. Nothing missing or altered from this angle.

Or was there?

Was that cloud and city haze over Canary Wharf—or smoke? Was that a lively London sky or a column of faintly glowing black against faintly glowing black that seemed to divide the sky in half? Yes. It looked more like a volcanic eruption than any kind of smoke I was used to—it was vast. And still the distant sirens were sounding from all around us.

We stared at it in dark awe. There was no sign of its source from here, save that this weird tree of smoke was growing right among the tallest buildings of Canary Wharf. Was there an orange glow at its base or was it the reflection of street lights? At night, cities always look as though they are burning, so I wasn't sure. Until . . .

"Look at the bridge," I said at last.

We stared at the Isle of Dogs Bridge, which was empty of cars—something I had never seen before in my life.

The Philosopher returned to his phone. "Says here . . . more rioting. Dalston this time."

"Fuck," Star Girl said. "On this night I am hardly surprised. I said it was midsummer madness."

"And why do I have the feeling that it's only going to get worse?" Clay Man said.

We slowly drifted away from the window and settled down again, around the little table on the platform, huddling round the Philosopher's smartphone like some weird travesty of that comfortable image of a family around a TV. After all, let us not forget here that four of us were still naked or almost naked—and filthy—and with Clay Man's artwork staring down at us from the wall in bloody surreal glory. None of it mattered, though. We were trying to digest the news—trying to get some idea of what was going on. Rather than a 'story', the news website had launched a live update page where the latest snippets of info would appear automatically in one long continuous feed, so it was quite hard to find a beginning or any progression. *Unrest in the Capital,* it was called. The bomb blast dominated the news, of course—indeed it only seemed to increase in scale with every new snippet, including some first startling images of one of the iconic and vaguely chilling towers of Canary Wharf with much of the lower part of its façade blown away into ruin, lit up by street lights and floodlights and the flashing blue of the emergency services—but there seemed to be more and more other stuff as well. Violence here, scuffles there, vandalism here, arson there—much of it not unusual for the city at the moment, but maybe that blast was the spark that had ignited the London volcano. Bigger—wilder . . . a deeper plunge into chaos than before. No, it wasn't surprising.

That plume of smoke over Canary Wharf was the kind that changed things in the human consciousness, even if the human condition itself never really changed.

We are urging the public to stay home tonight, save for essential journeys . . .

Be ready to fight.

After a long few minutes of reading, Clay Man glanced round at us all. "We have to clean up and get out of here I think."

"I . . . suppose so," Star Girl said.

"I think we had better," he said. "Go home—scatter and go home. If this is as bad as it seems to be getting, then the city is going to go mad."

"Yeah," Star Girl said. "And—if the city is finally letting rip a bit then I want to see what's going on."

"Hm?"

"Who knows—maybe I can help rip it a little more."

"You serious?" Clay Man demanded.

"Of course I'm fucking serious," she said.

"Rather you than me," Clay Man muttered. "I would like to be home right now, I think. Not trespassing beneath a railway line."

"Ach, you are no revolutionary," Star Girl said without malice.

"Whatever," he snapped. "I don't trust London. If things have got wild enough to be significant, then suddenly every surveillance camera is going to be pored over—every member of the public is going to be goggling out for anything unusual . . . something even slightly out of the ordinary could be enough to cause serious trouble."

"Yeah—maybe."

"Come on, let's get our stuff and get the fuck out of here. For gawd sake don't leave anything important behind. Just in case."

We quickly made our way back down the ladder to the concrete floor.

"We have to get cleaned up first, though," the Beggar said. "Are any of us dry? I think I am."

"I'm not dry at all," Star complained, rubbing at the mud that smeared her skin. "What fun."

"Now what?" the Butcher demanded.

Clay Man gave a mischievous grin. "I guess it's newspaper time," he said, grabbing the bundle of papers.

"Oh boy," Star said, hands on hips. "Okay, hand it over. I'll try."

Clay handed out sheets of the stuff and she dabbed at herself unenthusiastically.

"I can't reach," the Butcher complained.

"Oh bloody hell," Clay growled. "Here, everyone. Grab some of this and let's get these mucky bastards cleaned up."

"Now wait a minute . . ."

I stood back and watched as, after a few humorous exchanged glances, Clay Man, the Philosopher and the Beggar descended on the two of them and began scrubbing them down in a flurry of rough newsprint.

"Ow, steady on," Star Girl yelled. "Mind where you're . . ."

"Stand still," Clay Man ordered. "Bloody hell, just like a pair of kids. Look at yourselves."

The Butcher gave a laugh. "You're right, sir. We're dirty sods." It seemed to be working though. The flurry of hands was clearing their skin of the smelly mud, leaving them standing there breathlessly, pink and relatively clean—clean enough to make it home without too many odd looks anyway.

The Beggar stepped back and examined herself. "Am I okay?" she asked me, turning round.

"A few streaks," I said. "Looks dry to me."

"Um," she said shyly, "is there still any . . . newsprint on my . . . my um . . ."

"Very little," I said.

She looked quite red in the face. "Thanks," she murmured—then burst out laughing. "I think."

And again I found myself studying her scars—a close look under candlelight now, brighter by far than the city glow of earlier. I don't mean to give the impression that she was a mass of scar tissue, but her beautiful skin was covered with that fine scattering of marks—little white streaks, places where the natural texture was missing or skewed, even a few small corrugations and raised ridges. They were all obviously old but they still sent a very nasty sensation through me. They were signs and traces of something that didn't quite make sense in my world—of some sort of horror. If all that we did was about finding reality then the scars jarred unpleasantly with that because they spoke of a different kind of reality. A reality not so good. A reminder that maybe not all realities are ideals. She looked at me with a curious expression on her face, probably having a very clear idea what was going through my mind—but she didn't say anything. I sensed that on some level she didn't mind me examining her—didn't mind me trying to read the stories etched on her skin. It was a curious moment.

While we were communing in this quiet little place of our own, the others were bustling around. Those who needed to were dragging on their clothes and starting to pack up—personal possessions left scattered around were retrieved, last items of clothes dragged on.

"Come on, Beggar," Clay Man growled impatiently.

"Oh—yeah," she said. "Where's my clothes?"

She grabbed up her knickers and pulled them on, then glanced at me again, a tinge of red in her face. I realised I was still watching her and I forced myself to attend to my own stuff—not that I had much other than an empty bag. But even so, my eyes kept finding her as she sorted herself out, disappearing inside her clothes again.

Dammit . . .

Clay Man glanced round the room urgently. "Get the gas cylinder, someone," he ordered.

"What—why?" Star Girl demanded.

"It has a serial number. Chuck it in the canal or something if you have to—just don't leave it behind."

"Oh fuck . . ."

"Aren't we being a bit paranoid here?" the Butcher demanded.

"No," Clay Man said impatiently. "You know damn well what this city can be like . . . they'll lock it down. There'll be eyes everywhere."

The Butcher hesitated a moment, then nodded and ran to disconnect the cylinder.

"When shall we meet again?" Star asked.

"Oh yeah. How about two days' time?" Clay Man said. "But only if it seems safe. If not, we'll have to find our own ways together again. Ach, I really need to set up some kind of online dead drop to co-ordinate things in an emergency."

"Okay," she said. "Right—let's go. Someone get the candles. Train Man—what about the trains? Anything coming or can we cross the tracks?"

I hesitated and checked the clock on my phone. In the chaos I hadn't been thinking about the trains—but now another point came hammering into my brain very clearly. "There should have been three in the past quarter of an hour—but there haven't. I don't think they are running."

Star Girl's eyes glittered and a thin smile twisted her lips—unlike anything I had seen from her before.

"Cool," she said. "This just gets bigger and bigger. Any last reports?"

The Philosopher glanced at his smartphone again. "No—well, nothing seriously different. It's the same feed. Something about a shop on fire up in Hackney. A guy with a knife arrested somewhere. A fight broken out in Tottenham . . ."

The candles were out now so we shoved the curtain aside, scrambled out onto the sea wall and stared round uneasily at the city. Aside from the smoke still rising over Canary Wharf, everything looked totally normal—but big cities don't give up their secrets easily. Especially at night.

☼

On the towpath, the Beggar stared round at the sky, at that still looming eruption of smoke, then shook her head. The others had gone now, leaving the two of us standing in the dark. "What a night," she said with a frown.

"Yes," I said. The air over London almost seemed to crackle. The Beggar looked at me with a perceptive stare. "It feels . . . strange," I said. "I . . . I'm probably just being stupid."

"No. I don't think so . . ." She gave a groan and tugged at her clothes. "Fuck, it's hot," she said. "Is this the hottest night of the year so far?"

"It feels like it. And tomorrow could be even hotter."

"Gawd—okay," she said, "what do you think? Shall we walk together? At least as far as my bus stop?"

"Yeah," I said. "It's early yet, anyway. Let me get my bike." We walked a few dozen yards to where I had left it and I quickly unlocked it. It was going to be a pain to wheel it, but worth it for company. Even in this heat.

"Which way?"

"The other canal," she said. "Limehouse Cut. Is that okay?"

"Of course," I said, even though that was substantially further east than my route, and we paced back down the path again. We made our way through the buildings that clustered up against the sea wall and then onto the Limehouse Cut towpath. Here it felt tranquil—a long long way from the drama taking place only a few blocks southeast. Dark shapes of boats on the one side and imminent buildings on the other.

We walked on, and the familiarity of the London darkness enveloped us. There was something eternal and unchanging about this place, this waterway, even as the city itself swarmed and grew and sweated and evolved and decayed. The London towpaths are unique—at once very ordinary and totally bizarre. They are canyons through the city that are somehow isolated from the familiar streets, rather like the railways. They flow behind and below, hemmed in by tall buildings or scraps of park—down here you can almost forget that you are passing through a world of eternal streets and bustling cars. The route was a straight line on a level beneath the city, passing under low claustrophobic bridges and with the black, shimmering water always just a few feet away on our left. Every so often bodies were fished out of this water—it was in the news regularly. Human remains or body parts. Murders, suicides—and it was easy to see why. It was such a self-contained world. Yet at the same time, I found these canals a fairly friendly place—the quiet and lonely foundation to the ever-bustling and depressingly practical streets overhead. The towpath itself always seemed to be squeezed in as best it could, as though resented by both the black water and the buildings that struggled to overrun it—even by the plants that grew out hopefully to conquer this tiny space. In places the path was squeezed out of existence entirely and then some newer construction would take over. The point where the canal passed under the Blackwall Tunnel Northern Approach road was one of these and an echoing walkway struck out above the water under the massive bridge. Here the floor was of metal that clanged lightly under our feet and the way was illuminated with green lights set in two gleaming strips, shining upwards like something in a cyberpunk movie. A fusty, hot, dark place—a concrete box basically, low flat ceiling overhead, black water below. Us suspended in the middle—between heaven and earth—between grey and black, the whole thing gleaming green, the walls painted equally with graffiti and cast shadows.

We passed into this curious green world, and as we did so we spotted the first other human figure we had seen since the watergate. Nothing but a green silhouette at first, though even that was enough to give me a tiny flicker of the odd. It approached . . . and it looked very pale. Strangely pale. Shadows flashed around this space from his moving feet and I tried to make out what it was about him that was not right. The figure was unornamented and very uniform in colour . . . almost like a ghost.

The Beggar gave a murmur as it dawned on us both more or less simultaneously. He was naked from top to toe—even barefoot. We waited, too startled to do anything but politely fumble the bike out of the way as he approached. I felt a throb of real fear. It was one thing to play around together in the Thames mud, arses exposed to the air—quite another to come across a spectre like this out of the blue in the city. We tried not to look at him—tried to keep up some level of politeness—staring blankly at the concrete box beyond him as he drew level.

He paid no attention to us, though, just walked by as casually and easily as any other passer-by.

We stood there for a moment, still facing forward, but casting furtive glances over our shoulders.

"Um," the Beggar managed at last, "you did see that as well, right?" It was a joke—but maybe not entirely.

"I guess so," I whispered.

We turned round at last, just in time to watch the green-bathed figure pass out of the concrete box and abruptly change from green to orange . . .

"Someone else got a bit too hot?" she asked, sounding by no means certain. "High as a kite?"

I shrugged in silence, and we slowly continued walking.

"Well—why not?" she said with a sudden smile. "When the heat kicks in . . ."

I watched her green face curiously, not disagreeing. But then we emerged from that strange green light into the normal world again, and such thoughts seemed to retreat. We passed a row of deceptively ordinary-looking houses and then there was more water and water technology joining us to our right. The River Lea and the huge Soak area stretched as far as the point where it flowed into the Thames. I realised that we had walked quite a way along the dark towpath—far off my usual route. We came to a stop on the high footbridge across Bow Locks and looked back towards the Lea watergate and the massive new containment reservoir. From here, the towers of Canary Wharf had become visible again as a familiar constellation of gleaming lights and we stood for a while in silence. It had never really occurred to me before how much the isle of Canary Wharf resembles some old medieval castle—normally the place is bustling with cars and pedestrians and metro trains running in and out, but now in the eerie silence the impression seemed very strong. The huge towers rise up behind massive sea defences and deep moats, windows studded with light and smoke still wafting from the earlier conflagration. There are no Soaks there, except of course for the chaos of the Isle of Dogs to the south. Canary Wharf was affluent enough and supposedly important enough to develop itself properly with navigable waterways and maximum security—indeed, I think it quite enjoyed the process. I don't really know, in fact I think not many really know, what systems might be built into the glittering towers. I wouldn't be entirely surprised if they could drop boiling oil from the tops of the skyscrapers or catapult massive rocks at invading terrorists. Though more realistically, it's probably all sound weapons and incapacitating gas these days. Some of the conspiracy theorists are as likely to be correct as the official sources.

All that security hadn't saved it today, though.

The plume of smoke looked diffuse now, spreading out and fading into the air. The colour of the sky itself seemed weird—red and orange glows in various places all the way round the horizon. More intense than usual. The light of other fires? Was London burning? Or was it the normal luminous clouds that hang over any city? As usual, I wasn't sure.

It seemed, though, that, from the far far distance, heard momentarily as though carried by faint changes of the wind, the sound of shouting voices was drifting.

The Beggar looked around, a slight frown on her face.

"Not far now," she murmured, making no move to start walking again. "My bus stop is just up ahead."

"Where do you need to go?" I asked, forgetting the prohibition on personal information and immediately wishing I had kept my mouth shut.

"Well . . ." She paused, giving me a thoughtful glance. Then she shrugged. "Camden."

Almost on instinct, the route mapped itself out in my head. "205 to Angel from Bow Road and then the 214?"

"Uh-huh."

I also mapped out the one or two other shorter routes she could have taken if we hadn't gone on this walk, but I said nothing about that—merely saved the thought for due consideration later on. There seemed no hurry for this to end, even though we had now walked almost one and a half miles.

"You know what I like about you," she said out of the blue.

". . . what?"

"You seem extremely authentic. Even when you are going off into dark places, it just feels totally honest. Are you even aware how rare that is?"

I stared in silence. This was the kind of talk that froze me completely—no idea how to respond.

"Even when you piss me off, you are just totally being yourself," she said with a grin. "Not performing. Not hiding things. And I just love that."

"I . . . never could perform," I said. "I think that's one of my problems in life. If I could perform—so much might have been different. But—I guess I never learned how."

"Please don't," she said. "If the world needs fake facades in order to function, then screw it. Seriously—fuck them all. All I ever see is wasted lives. Some total corruption of what we are. People living lies from top to bottom. Entrapment in a totally ridiculous system. Until I almost want to smash something myself." She glanced back at the plume of smoke and I felt a chill. The silence dragged out for a moment.

"Have you ever wanted to hit back at this place?" she asked.

That was an intense question, especially given the circumstances, and I gave her a brief suspicious look.

"I love London," I said.

"But?"

"Sometimes," I whispered at last. "I suppose . . . I might love a person, but if there is a sickness in them then—I guess I want to attack the sickness. I don't particularly want to hurt people, no matter how horrible they are, but . . ."

"But sometimes it feels as though the only way out of the mess is through violence?"

"Yeah."

"I . . . don't actually believe that's true," she said. "I don't think it works . . ."

"I'm sure it doesn't. But the instinct . . . one feels it. Fight or flight—and I guess I chose flight."

We stared for a while at the smoke again, then she shook her head.

"So strange," she murmured, turning away from that view and leaning her back against the bridge parapet. "I wonder who did it."

I shrugged. "This world is like a . . . supermarket for rage. Could be almost anyone."

We finally started walking again, continued along the narrow strip of land that separates the River Lea and the Canal, passing under the monstrous low-slung shape of the bridge that carried the District Line overhead, then arriving at Three Mills where a cobbled and grassy area opens out and where picturesque oast houses lingered in the cityscape looking slightly surreal. I remember reading once that during World War II, the entire river here lit up and burned with an eerie blue flame after a bomb hit a gin factory—a sight so bizarre it was remembered for a long, long time. Now in the dark it gleamed with reflected lights in all colours, and with a similar sense of eeriness, for here we again encountered human life and, even though she was clothed, she stared at us unselfconsciously as we passed—that simple act alone enough to render her alien. Her eyes were huge and she was turning to watch us as long as she remained in sight.

"I wonder what Star Girl is doing now," the Beggar said softly, coming to a stop on the cobbles.

"Probably raining thunder down on those who annoy her," I said with a smile. "I wish her luck."

"Yeah—Star wouldn't blow up a building, but she'd sure beat up anyone who said anything nasty. For her it would be direct and personal." The Beggar turned to me, with a thin grin on her face, the likes of which I had not seen her use before. Her grey eyes gleamed orange in the reflected light from the city. "This is a strange night," she said. "Maybe she is right. I really do think . . . I dunno, but there is an appeal in going slightly mad, right? Or . . . crazy?"

"Oh yes," I said softly.

"Maybe this is a night when we can all walk naked through the highways and byways, and bust this city down to size . . ." She tugged at her top, still grinning, then unselfconsciously rubbed at her crotch. "That thought is actually making me feel rather . . . hot."

That prickle of energy again—and I remember I gave her a very piercing sideways look. I felt completely unqualified to analyse what she was thinking at the moment. Or wanting. In some areas I can be quite perceptive—in others I am almost blind.

Then the quiet night was torn completely in half. There was a clamour of shouting voices that made both of us flinch violently. Two voices. Both genders. Sounding shrill.

We both stared as two figures came barrelling past out of the streets of Three Mills and across the small bridge, narrowly missing my bike and still yelling. I barely got a chance to see them in the dark. I had no idea what was happening—there was no obvious pursuit and this explosion seemed self-contained. As they ran they swung and grabbed at each other, scuffling and fighting and stumbling.

"What the fuck was that?" the Beggar demanded, her voice sounding much more normal in tone now and filled with real shock. I had no answer, but my heart had also plummeted a bit. The night had become a notch stranger still. And yet—even now there was nothing completely alien here, I rationalised to myself. London is filled with strange happenings all the time—odd clashes and eruptions and eccentricities and madnesses. If you are out at night, you occasionally encounter them. But it still felt as though someone had taken the volume knob and was slowly turning it up.

Eventually we started walking again. We crossed the canal and stepped out into a city that was totally silent. At first I was relieved to get back into the more lighted and familiar world of streets and shops and houses, but that silence was heavy. The streets stretched away, baked to motionlessness. Nobody walking, no car moving—something subtly removed from anything I had seen before in my explorations of the city. As we walked, we passed a house, dark and equally still, but with the door wide open. A black cave in the night. The sight stopped us in our tracks for a moment, but there was nothing to be gathered from an open door beyond its own mystery. I suppose we could have knocked—maybe should have. We could have been responsible citizens and checked that nothing was amiss—called into that darkness a questioning hello. But this wasn't a night for questioning hellos and we walked on. The sense of something fundamentally wrong was so intense that we actually ended up holding hands as we walked—though I can't remember who initiated it. It was a comfort.

Eventually we reached the bus stop on Bow Road and studied the route information. Yup—this was the bus to Angel. According to the digital display, it would be arriving in three minutes.

"Are you going to be okay?" I asked.

She nodded. "Are you? What are you doing now? Going home?"

"Yes," I said. "A last cycle ride—see if that place I live in is as wild as the rest of the city tonight."

The Beggar nodded. "Give me a hug," she whispered. "I think I need it."

I held her tight for a while, and she actually closed her eyes and dropped her face onto my collarbone. It was a long hug that didn't seem to have any impetus to end. And as I held her, I was remembering her earlier, naked and muddy—and remembering her scars. And with that I suddenly felt a blast of emotion—a massive poignancy that was agonising in its intensity—and I squeezed her tighter still, as though sheer pressure could tuck her away somewhere from the world that must have assailed her. Though even as that thought came, there also came the reminder that she was probably far more worldly and aware than I was—far tougher and more clued up about herself and the world around her. It didn't matter though. A hug was a hug, and beyond such thoughts as these.

I could still smell the Thames mud on her. Not to mention the heat of the night.

Finally she slipped out of my arms as the familiar red form of the bus appeared in the distance—such a mundane and familiar sight that it changed the world for me on some level. If the old red bricks were still running round London then it couldn't be the end. Yet. Also, I guess that timed our hug at pretty much all of three minutes, which seems quite exceptional looking back on it. At the time, though, it didn't feel long. "Thanks, Train Man," she murmured as the bus pulled in—though I wasn't sure what she was thanking me for. "Yeah—time to go home."

She gave me a rather awkward smile and stepped aboard.

It turned out that she had caught one of the last buses to run that night.

And London burned . . .

FRIDAY

It was a nightmare morning—though morning is probably the wrong word, because when I finally woke up, the sky was actually beginning to darken. I had slept through most of the day and through two summonses to work before I surfaced. Sometimes any human being needs to crash and burn—to shut out the world and sleep until the clouds lift again. At least, that's the theory. In reality maybe the clouds never lift—and no sleep seems long enough, except maybe that sleep you never wake up from . . .

Online, there was a sense of complete shock. How could this have happened? Everyone talking seemed totally mystified, whether it was on social media, blogs or any of the news sites. This was one of the Canary Wharf towers, those domineering gleaming obelisks of glass and metal standing like nails in the coffin of humanity. One of London's financial centres—a place that was bound tight in a web of paranoia and security, defences and watching eyes. The ornamental planters, flower beds and bollards that dotted the area were actually a carefully planned and hyper-strong fence that could keep out anything big enough to cause damage. Those flower pots would have stopped a tank. So how on earth had they managed to penetrate that? Later, we would look back on it and realise that this was one of the most extraordinary stories to come out of London in these troubled times.

You will probably remember the details, but in case you don't, or in case this book reaches places far removed, I will tell it again here. If no car-bomb could get through, the only way was to build the bomb on the other side. And that's what they did. Astonished police and security soon pieced the story together with the help of the surveillance cameras—an image of twenty-three cyclists making their way across the city on heavily laden bikes. Rear panniers, front panniers, backpacks, saddle bags—a bike can carry an lot of cargo if needed and the combined weight of those bikes was many hundreds of kilos. Not enough to take down the tower completely, but enough to draw an exclamation mark on the island that would never be forgotten. And, of course, nobody paid them any attention whatsoever in a city filled with every kind of cyclist you can imagine. Even when they came together in the streets of Canary Wharf itself, they looked like little more than riders on a long-distance cycling tour, loaded down with supplies. Their clothes were ordinary—their faces even more so. Even when they passed through the bollards and security planters and came to a halt in a tight group up against the glass, staring in at the puzzled security guards and suited bankers, no one realised anything was wrong. Like a performance, they even stared down the surveillance cameras for a moment, revealing a line of very British faces—young men and women that were already hopelessly confusing the politicians, who wanted nothing beyond odd-coloured terrorists in their world. Then everything went simultaneously white and black and several storeys of the building ceased to exist.

That was one story. There were others. The rest of London seethed as well, dominating whatever news space wasn't taken up by Canary Wharf. A bank on fire, wrecked vehicles, columns of smoke, ruined buildings, debris everywhere, doorways barricaded with whatever could be found in the panic of nocturnal uprising. As the hazy sun rose, the rage seemed to fade—a night of madness that ought to have blown itself out like a storm. But come this next evening and the graph was climbing back into the red. Fights and attacks, fires and arson, clashes with police and the same devastated streets . . . more and more stories everywhere that came with a terrible sense of seriousness. Certain parts of the city especially were being yelled far and wide—do not go there. Here be monsters. Here be death and pestilence. Here be the Underclass. The Square Mile, the City, Parliament Square, Tottenham, Stoke Newington, Camden . . . From the clamour of the news, it looked as though London was tearing itself to pieces, in spite of the eerie silence that seemed to fill the world outside your own windows. This was big, it said. This was huge, in fact.

The London holding cells were full—police were coming into the city from miles around and crawling through the streets making arrest after arrest. One had to read through the social networks and the feeds of info directly from the police themselves to get a sense of the details. Apparently these feeds were supposed to be reassuring, but there were some strange goings-on listed here. Arson, theft, assault of various kinds etc., a number of cases of public indecency and sexual assault. Animal cruelty was mentioned a few times, oddly enough. But beyond these, there were a million more little regulations busted. That's the thing about legality, as it stands. It no longer seems to be about bad things that you shouldn't do, now it's about making sure the police have a tool for any job. Making sure that if you annoy the powers that be, no matter how, there is always some way to get you. Like the pizza box wars of a few days ago, which left people with criminal records for carrying a pizza through the streets of London. Such a state of affairs means two things—one can never ever feel safe again, and any record or feed of crimes committed is basically meaningless. Illegal gathering, photographing the police at work, open container of alcohol, disturbing wildlife, trespass, illegal waste disposal, illegal use of fireworks, illegal flying of a kite (seriously), interfering with an aircraft, a long strew of driving offences—whatever you could think of on the vast and unending list of things you can't do was probably in that feed somewhere, and none of it actually said a single fucking thing. I was getting the impression that anyone displaying any sort of unusual behaviour was at risk of being dragged off for examination. However, it did suggest that something much darker was going on than merely a battle between police and protesters and I had to wonder what they were doing with all these people since the holding cells were apparently full. Maybe they had a concentration camp somewhere?

I wish I was joking—but in the weeks that would follow, there was no shortage of rumours of people vanishing, never to be heard from again, in spite of frantic searching and enquiries.

There was one other thing I could gather very clearly from all this: that no matter what posturing and pontificating there was from the politicians and no matter what aggression from the police, the London Madness seemed to be getting worse, not better.

☼

"Why can we never manage to keep things tidy?" Kate was grumbling almost the moment I stepped through the door, her voice an ugly piercing tone. "It's you," she said, pointing at me—and I raised my eyebrows. "You barely set a foot outside your room—never lift a finger to help with the housework."

I just stared at her. After all the suppressed madness in the city, all the violence now flooding the news and all my own weird experiences, Kate's voice sounded like the broken chalk of stupidity on the blackboard of my brain. For a brief moment I wondered what would happen if I lost it completely—started trashing the room, dragged her off and vigorously inserted her head into the rubbish bin, then kicked her backside . . .

Nothing good, that was for sure.

Given that keeping animals in captivity is a breach of their basic rights, and given the amount of suffering caused by these vicious hunters, I don't think there is much we can or should do in terms of saving the species. It may sound heretical to some, but maybe specific species should not be considered sacred if they stand in the way of potentially making a better world, and now that the last of the UK's tigers have been sold to China . . .

I gave a weary sigh. I think it was safe to say that I despised both of them right then. Even Aceline, who was sitting there very quietly staring at the TV streams on her laptop. It wasn't a hot enough emotion to call hate, I just felt a weary exhausted contempt. One fat, one thin, neither healthy. Two opinionated judgemental poisoned bitches, no different to everyone else. The pathetic result of egomassaging and paranoia—fear of anything that wasn't unreal mixed with the continued legitimising of hate and blame. Not that I was elevating myself here—they had reacted to the world by setting themselves in this shallow tepid concrete and ceasing mental processes, I by hiding away and lying on a railway line. I was every bit as pathetic a creature.

"I haven't used the kitchen in four weeks," I said mildly. "I wouldn't dare, because no matter what I do, you will be whinging about something. You made the mess, you clean it up."

Aceline gave a bark of laughter and Kate gawped at me for a moment. Then she lost it. "Fuck," she yelled—then a sudden movement, a fist coming at me at high speed. Somehow I managed to block it in spite of my surprise. I caught her wrist and held it for a moment as we stood there frozen, Aceline staring at us blankly. Then Kate wrenched away.

Oh bloody marvellous.

"Well," she grumbled, as though the last few seconds hadn't happened at all, "at least you could help out once in a while."

"Yes I could," I said with nasty sarcasm, "and you make it sooooo appealing."

. . . as the number of European countries still to sign up for the Amsterdam animal welfare treaty is now reduced to seven, with Germany likely the next signatory. Norway and Iceland still remain independent, insisting that it is doubtful what farming families could do as high mountain pastures and tundra are useless for much other than animal rearing. Eastern Europe likewise. However, massive pressure is being applied. It is believed that unless we work together, unless we achieve some form of unity, no environmental reform will be possible. There is an increasing sense of desperation and therefore . . .

Kate stamped away into the kitchen in a sulk but in the frozen silence that followed, I realised that we weren't the only ones having a row in this stinking old building. Drifting in from somewhere else, I could hear other voices raised and sounding stupid with fury. One of each gender, I was not so surprised to realise, but when voices are raised like that, they become almost impossible to recognise. I couldn't hear what they were arguing about either—only the swear words seemed to come punching through the distance with any clarity. Fucking cunts and stupid bastards. Even leaving aside the general atmosphere at the moment, it merited little more than a shrug. Live squeezed together and of course you will have shouting and temper tantrums and worse. The increasing enforced intimacy of life coincided in an almost perfect inverse correlation with the increasing suspicion and isolation inherent in the population, the fear of opening yourself up to others and the fear of human relationships/interactions. And maybe that was the key to what was going on more than Star Girl's revolutionary mutterings and ideals—a pressure cooker of frustration and inhumanity that had probably been searching for release for a long, long time. I could feel it, now that I was bothering to pay attention to the world beyond my two ears. I could feel something muttering and roiling above the city like a black cloud. Was that the source of the unease and restlessness that seemed to pervade last night? I was reminded of something volcanic, festering, seething, muttering, giving out the occasional tremor . . . and now maybe finally erupting.

. . . to 'Buy Me a House'! The gameshow where we give one of you the house of your dreams. Yes—no more landladies who can throw you out and leave all your precious belongings in the gutter. No more unpredictable mortgages taking all your money until you are ninety-seven. No more blushing as you scrounge for benefit claims—an actual house of your very own. All you have to do is . . .

Aceline gave a weird shrug and emphatically jabbed at her laptop, closing whichever browser tab was broadcasting this background TV babble.

"I dunno what's with everyone tonight," she muttered, handing me a bowl of salad with cubes of cheese and croutons. I took it gratefully, then sat down by her side. Her screen now showed an online image gallery—one of the many comedy / weird stuff websites out there trying to keep us all from killing ourselves or each other with the help of stupid internet memes and joke images. It was currently showing a video of a woman in a bikini equipped with LED lights in those places the eye is automatically drawn to in bikinis. They twinkled and flashed as she pranced across the stage, then bent over showily to grab a light silk robe, which she slung round her shoulders. Aceline had her eyebrows up, and I wondered whether she rather liked the idea of strutting around with a luminous pussy. No reason why not. Some people love to show off and emphasise what they are. But I couldn't focus on it. The dichotomy between that spritely performance and the bickering reality all around me almost hurt my head.

Then she clicked again and we moved on to another image—a woman in a miniskirt who had turned her hair into a plastic explosion of blue tassels. Then again to an immensely fat guy in the worst pair of multi-coloured sweatpants I had seen in a long time . . .

The site seemed solely designed to mock—which seems to be the noble aim of 90% of the internet. As she clicked through page after page, though—ridiculous T-shirt slogans or crazily bad-taste prints, the guy wearing a skin suit decorated with dozens of cat images, the woman with glitzy shoes decked with doll heads—I have to say I found myself rather warming to these people. All of them, even the scruffbags. Either they had developed a seriously original sense of aesthetics or they didn't care—or both. And both of the above seemed thoroughly admirable to me. Far more admirable than sitting there subsumed in boredom sniggering at anyone who attempted to be different.

And anyway—what was so good about the normal? It was the normal that had left me on the railway line, not the unusual. And, I was fairly sure, it was the normal that was still arguing somewhere down the corridor . . .

"I even had a fight break out at my exercise class today," Aceline said. "Two girls lost it and tried to remove each other's faces. That was fun."

I stared at her, eyebrows up.

"Oh yes—lots of suppressed frustration, loathing and envy at your friendly local exercise class." She gave a sad grin. "Everyone is on edge. Everyone is scared and enraged . . . I dunno what is going to happen next."

"Yeah," I murmured.

"You ever wonder whether it's time to leave?" she asked. "I mean—London? Give up and get out?"

I looked at her sharply, twanged by the thought like a harp string.

"And then what?" I said. "Unemployed again? The unemployed don't have to worry about fucking privacy. Only about what to do when it rains."

"Well . . . yeah. But . . ."

"Or the slave camp, of course—didn't you end up there for a while?"

"Yeah," she muttered. "Until I set up my little yoga class and got the stigma of 'unemployed' off my forehead. No—I'm not talking about going back to that fucking shelter. I still have joint pains to this day from the crap they made me do to pay for my bed. There's still a few exercise moves I just can't manage . . ."

I sighed bleakly.

. . . for those who have just joined us, the government has announced new emergency legislation to protect public order banning unlicensed gatherings in several more locations across London and designed to prevent the increasing tide of political protest that is . . .

"It's maddening," she continued. "No matter what we do, you can never really . . . do anything. The amount of money we get would make us ridiculously rich in some places—but we never fucking see any of it. I'm still here—you're still in my cupboard—no real way out . . . It's all a trap really, isn't it?" she muttered. "Once this city gets its claws into you . . ."

I nodded, somewhat on autopilot. This was just a fragment of the old formulaic outrage, reiterated every day for the rest of your lives.

"But you know—I do wonder if there aren't . . . other ways."

"Other?"

"You hear stories. Hidden homes. Illegal homes. Squatting in the Soaks . . ."

I pulled a face at that, thinking of Feather's underground complex. Yes you did indeed hear stories . . .

"Everyone always sounds so outraged about it," Aceline said. "But you know—fuck it all, it's the only affordable housing I have ever heard of in my entire life. Okay, so the lower floor might be underwater . . . but all you have to do is live upstairs and keep a boat to hand . . ."

I sometimes wonder to myself what intrinsic value a home has—including the materials and work involved but stripping out the entirely artificial values that we seem to put on them for no other reason than that some people made them up. I'm not sure where to begin with this, or to end—but I did once work out that if I could leave out the land values and location, location, location and build it myself, instead of this cupboard I squeeze into, I could be relaxing somewhere approximately thirty-two times the size for the same wodge of cash. That is probably one of the most pointless calculations ever carried out in the history of humanity and all it succeeded in doing was making me miserable again—but it does make a small point I suppose, and the point is this: if I ever meet the hypothetical person responsible for commodifying housing, what happens next will be reported on the news worldwide in hushed and awestruck tones.

Fortunately, such musings were interrupted when Kate came back in, her face still stormy.

"Is that real?" she asked, staring at the computer screen and the images Aceline was still clicking through. I followed her gaze and saw a photo of a Japanese woman in a sumptuous fur coat. It was here because it had just been drenched with paint—red paint—and the expression on her face, frozen by the camera, was priceless—a sort of bewildered squeamish fury.

"Probably," Aceline said. "Looks like a Japan fashion show."

"Ug," Kate said darkly. "Gawd, look at her. You know what they say? People like that should be raped—so hard it scars them for life."

Aceline glanced round with a sharp look in her eyes. "Really?" she asked sardonically.

For some reason I looked closer—long enough to see the expected torrent of abuse, death threats and obscenity on the screen—*Fuck you bi-atch just fuck you, Its just cos shes retarded that's all just a guess, Is this for real/fur real? Absolutely vile and looks ghastly!, Sleepwalking into a nightmare, um, like most, I wish she'd die should do that to her see how she likes it, Id like to take her skin off with my bare hands*—it was somewhat a relief when Aceline clicked 'next' again. "Suppose it's a guy?" she asked sarcastically.

"Then fuck him up the arse with a wine bottle till he bleeds. That ought to do it."

I rubbed at my face. *One kick. One kick—that's all. Why, world, am I not allowed to hand out just one little kick up the backside?*

"For gawd sake, shut up talking like that," I said. Somewhere, very close, total rage was trying to break through now. It was too hot for this—I was too fed up for this—the city was too insane for this. I don't often find things people say getting to me to this extent but it was such a perfect progression from Star Girl's rage, from the roof the night before last, from this insane city and from the general chaos of my own thoughts that I found myself dangerously close to losing it. My tone of voice was horrible, to put it bluntly.

"What's with you?" she demanded.

"Correct me if I am wrong, but didn't you spend half an hour the other day slagging off just about everything from the entire continent of Africa to the entire male sex after seeing that petition to crack down on corrective rape in Uganda? Why the fuck do you want it in Japan?"

"Yeah, but look at her," she snapped. "It's not the same thing. Those African lesbians didn't do anything to deserve it."

"Ach—you don't have a fucking clue what you are talking about, do you?" I said, trying to keep a grip on myself, reminding myself over and over that it would not be wise to lose control of what I was saying. Was this how Star Girl felt when she let rip? Was I on the edge of rage porn? It seemed downright scary, to be honest.

"Are you trying to defend the fur trade?" Kate asked, a fierce tone to her voice.

"Knock it off, Kate," Aceline said wearily.

"Knock what off?" she yelled. "Dogs and cats and rare animals clobbered with clubs or strangled with wire just so some bitch can wear an expensive coat? You can't be defending that?"

"I'm not defending anything," I said. And that was true.

"It's evil," Kate continued. "It's . . . it's just pure bloody . . ."

"Oh shut up for fuck's sake," Aceline said impatiently. "You put down mouse poison, didn't you? You were the one threatening to cut off their legs with kitchen scissors. You swat flies or moths without a second thought. Maybe you'd better bend over right now and atone for all that. You agreeable?" She brandished a wine bottle in a quasi-comical gesture that made me wince.

"Oh fuck you," Kate snapped bitterly. "You really think that . . ."

"Wait a minute," Aceline said, her voice suddenly changing.

"Huh? Look, you can't be . . ."

"Shut up a minute."

I looked at her in confusion. This conversation was trying to change gears, I knew it.

"Fuck off, Ace," Kate snapped. "This is too stupid to . . ."

"*Shut up!*" Aceline yelled, so loudly that Kate actually obeyed in shock.

There was silence and Aceline ran to the door and opened it.

"What is it?" I asked. She was listening carefully. I listened too—but could hear nothing. Yes—nothing. The row had stopped as well, I realised—and for some reason that made me uneasy.

"I thought I heard . . ." she muttered.

"What are you on about?" Kate demanded.

The silence stretched out—and then, somewhere in the building, there was a bump. Then more silence.

"What did you hear?" I asked.

"I thought I heard some sort of . . ."

A door opened abruptly. Aceline and I exchanged glances as we waited—and my heart sank rather when the figure that stepped into the corridor turned out to be Tad. The open door was to Tea's room—which suggested who the other performer in that row must have been.

And a perverse part of me silently asked *already?*

"What the heck was that noise?" Aceline demanded.

Tad stared at us both, eyes more gleaming and predatory than ever. "Fucking meat-eating bitch," he said under his breath. Then he hurried to the stairs and down them, picking up speed and vanishing.

"Come on," she said.

"What did you hear?" I asked for the third time, following her down the corridor, Kate in turn following me looking confused.

"I thought I heard some kind of scream," she said, as though not wanting to confess to something so crazy. But it gave me a chill. I had been so focussed on Kate at the time that anything might have happened.

The door to Tea's apartment was still ajar and inside was an icy silence. Aceline kicked it open and we barged in—and part of me froze completely when I caught a flash of blue hair.

She was lying on the floor in an untidy and inelegant heap. Yes, one tends to be inelegant under such circumstances, but I use those words deliberately because all most of us are ever familiar with is the stylised and overdramatic portrayal by actors. In reality though, when a human being is smashed to the floor, the result is a mess that cares nothing about human vanity, aesthetics or modesty. Tea lay face down, one arm under her, the other by her side, her body twisted so her hips were sideways, one leg as though taking a massive stride forward. And a pool of blood was smeared around her head and soaking into her hair, clashing horribly with the blue.

Beside her was what had done the damage—her own rickety, battered and stained wooden chair. Still intact. Generally speaking, things like furniture and bottles don't break that easily. Instead it had been a bludgeon—and I could clearly see the small smear of blood and strands of hair on the edge of the flat seat—a few of them blue. Aceline gave a groan and hurried over to the wrecked figure—and after a few complex seconds, I followed. Yes—I wasn't just a spectator in life. It wasn't all just some movie. As Aceline was fumbling ineffectually around her head, trying to find out what was wrong, Tea gave a long, high-pitched wail and half-turned over, staring up at us out of dizzy eyes. At least she was still alive—for a moment there, I had wondered. Her face revealed the damage though—the long gash across her forehead where the chair had hit. Her nose was bleeding as well—marked with a nasty red bruise.

"Fuck sake," Aceline babbled. "Are you okay? I mean . . . I mean . . ."

Tea gave a sobbing groan and tried to sit up.

Kate was standing in the doorway now, looking stunned. A few more faces were starting to gather there as well.

Aceline waved to me urgently. "Call the police now please," she yelled. "I mean—ambulance. I mean . . ."

I grabbed my phone and prepared to dial the dreaded three digits.

"Ne," Tea said with surprising urgency. "No."

She was leaning over and trying to clear the blood out of her nose. Aceline gave her an uncomprehending look.

"What do you mean, 'no'?" she demanded.

"Don't," Tea begged, beginning to sob, her face an extraordinary mix of blood, bruises and tears that I won't forget for a very long time. "I do not—I . . . cannot have police in. He thought . . ."

Aceline gave a harried shrug and then turned furiously on the assembled audience. "Will you lot just get out of here," she said harshly. "Now."

Such was the look on her face that they began to melt away again, looking quite shocked, while I attempted to help Tea to her feet and to somewhere more comfortable than the floor. She reached up plaintively and locked her hands round my neck—a childish gesture that really sent a chill through me. Then she was up and we helped her across to her bed.

"Well—that didn't last long did it," she said, settling down with a shaky laugh. "I guess this means I am single again?" She gave me a tragically comical look and circled her finger round her ear in the familiar gesture of insanity—then circled it outward to include the entire world. "Oh jojojoj. Know anyone else who might be up for paying that part of the rent in exchange for a . . . a sex or two every weekend? I had the op."

I stared at her, probably with an odd expression on my face—one that she was fortunately in too much of a state notice. Not so long ago, stupid thoughts might have jumped up in my brain at a remark like that . . . but now, nothing.

She gave a shrill giggle, then exhaled sharply, blowing a mass of blood and snot out of her nose, splashing all down her front, the bed and all over my shirt. I ran off to get some tissues and water, while Aceline got her back into a sitting position.

"Sorry," she muttered.

"It's okay," Aceline soothed as I returned. She clutched a pad of tissue to her nose while I began cautiously dabbing at the gash on her forehead.

"Where the fuck's Kate gone?" Aceline demanded. I glanced round—and she had indeed melted away with the other watchers. "Oh that useless wanker," she said heavily.

Tea suddenly shifted, a panicked look in her eyes. "Oh god," she said, "he still has his keys—to this place . . ."

"Don't worry about that," I said. "We can get the lock changed."

"But," she said, "how much will that cost? I don't think I can afford . . ."

"Don't worry," Aceline soothed. "It will be fine. We'll all chip in if needed. But you really should let me phone the police. You can't let people do things like that."

"I have to," she said. "No police. He was right. I let a friend sell me a little chicken meat. Just a few slices. What the fuck is wrong with you people?"

She gave me a strange look, while my heart plummeted even further.

"But I didn't kill that cat," she wailed. "We don't eat fucking cat in Bohinj."

"Cat?" I asked in mystification.

"On the roof," she said miserably. "Nothing to do with me. I don't fucking know who . . ."

She stumbled to a halt and we stared at her in silence. I remembered that reeking bag of bones I had found in the shed.

"Maybe it's good that he did this," she said.

"Huh?"

"Maybe—well, maybe after doing that he won't report me. I don't wish to be thrown out of the country. I'll be fine—I just need to . . . recover a little . . ."

She tried to sit up again, but immediately keeled over and ended up back where she started, breathing heavily. "Jébem ti máter," she wailed, tears beginning to stream down her face again.

Aceline and I exchanged glances. "What are we going to do?" she asked. "I don't like it. You really should have someone look at you. I mean, what the fuck do any of us know about . . . ?"

"Please don't," she whispered, sitting up again. The bed was also liberally splashed with blood now, I realised with a yet further increase of that leaden feeling inside. "I'm not brain damaged—my head isn't broken. I'm just a bit beaten up . . ."

"Okay," she said dubiously. "But if you show the slightest sign of getting worse, I'm phoning immediately. And that's final."

Tea lay back on the damp sheets. "Okay," she said with a tiny smile. "Thanks, both of you."

At that point there was a tap at the open door and Kate looked in again.

"Is she okay?" she asked in a small voice.

"Sort of," Aceline said shortly. "I think she'll be alright after some rest."

"And . . . he did this because . . . ?"

"Yes," Aceline grunted. "Because."

"It was only a few slices," Tea said mournfully.

There was a silence. "Anything—you need me to do?" Kate asked at last.

"No."

"Oh. Right," she said, looking even more forlorn. "Well—call me if you need me."

She wandered away again. I stared after her curiously, trying to work out what was going through her head. Something was storming there. I had never seen her looking quite like this before.

No time to wonder about that for long, however. I settled down beside Tea again, carefully peeled off her bloody eyepatch and dressing, then helped to clean her face. Her nose didn't seem to be broken and that particular fountain soon began to slow. The wound on her forehead was still oozing though, sending a regular curtain down over her eyes and generating quite a mound of gruesome tissues beside the bed as I fought to staunch it.

"Oh what a mess," she murmured, brushing at the bloody bed.

"Is there a first aid kit around here?" I asked—something we should probably have got to much sooner.

"I think . . . in that cupboard over there . . ."

I gestured to Aceline and she shook herself. "Oh—yes, of course." She hurried to get it. "What are we going to do?" she said, handing it to me. "I . . . I have to go soon, that's the thing. Yoga class to teach. But . . . I mean . . ."

"I'll stay here," I said, rummaging in the box. "Nothing else to do this evening. I missed all my work today for some stupid reason."

"Awwww, guys . . ." Tea murmured.

Aceline gave a relieved smile. "Okay then—I'll be back in an hour or so. I'll put her to bed—you look after her for a bit, then I'll be back."

"I'm sure I can put myself to bed," Tea said with a smile. "Going to have to change this quilt cover though. Look at it . . ."

She rose to her feet—then wobbled sharply, leaning against me with a giggle, before settling back down again, using her backside to shove the red splashed quilt out of the way.

"Just sit still," Aceline ordered, and she subsided meekly as we worked on her, cleaning her up as well as we could, then finishing off with a rather more effective bandage. Then she was changed into her pyjamas and settled down comfortably in a newly made bed while Aceline hurried off with an armful of bedding . . . and before I knew it, I was left alone with her, wondering what to say. I sat down there with what I hoped was a sympathetic look. I desperately wanted to find something to say, some perfect words that would make it all better—but I knew I might as well forget about that. I fluttered my fingers from the area of my heart down to her face, which I encircled quickly. She gave a smile and made a very simple gesture that seemed to collect all that, and all of me, and gather it close to the area of her heart—a gesture that actually left me a little choked up.

"Is there . . . anything else you need me to do?" I asked shyly.

"No—except exist. I will just try and rest for a bit."

She reached for her book and settled down comfortably—as comfortably as she could. Almost immediately, though, she gave up again and put it down with a grunt and a swear word.

"You okay?" I asked.

"Yeah," she said. "It's just, the reading is not very good—I can't lie comfortably . . . 'm a bit sore."

"Hey, I'll read it to you," I said eagerly, jumping on the chance of doing something helpful that didn't involve conversation. "Unless it's in Slovenian?"

To my surprise, she gave another small sob and a trickle of tears.

"Oh dear," she said. "You guys are so nice I don't know what to . . ."

"I'm not nice," I said with a grin. "Just a normal fat London bastard. Heaven help us all if someone nice comes along."

She gave a faint smile and handed me the book.

"Where were you up to?" I asked.

"Top of the page—there . . ."

I studied it a moment, then began. And you know what? Reading other people's words seemed so much easier than formulating my own that it was as though a new world had opened out before me right then. I don't remember much of what the book was about, save that it was slightly intellectual and fairly realist in tone—but the words came out of my mouth maybe easier than any words had ever managed to before. I was enjoying this. And more—I was actually quite good at this. I think she must have picked up on my delight, for she watched me for a while with a small smile, before shutting her eyes. And I just read and read . . .

And that was the scene that greeted Aceline when she returned. It was one of those events that sweetly massaged my ego—the feeling that one is actually doing something of value, which seemed rare enough. And as I read, I felt as though just a few more ice crystals around my heart had shattered and flaked off. The latest in a long series. Aceline also settled down to listen for a while, before the whole event faded down to an end as naturally as a musical composition.

"Shift change?" she asked with a grin. "How is she?"

"I'm okay," Tea said opening her eyes. "Feel a bit better."

"Right, good," Aceline said. I closed the book with a slight feeling of regret.

"Call me any time of course," I said as I left. We all needed to fuss over her a bit now so she would remember that only some humans are messed up monsters. Something we all need reminding of, I think, because there is no life left if you forget that.

✥

Kate found me in the corridor as I made for my room. She caught my arm, her body hunched, staring at the floor. I could smell a whiff of wine.

"Is Tea-Cup okay?" she asked.

"Yes—she will be, I think."

Kate nodded and stared off at nothing.

"What a horrible thing to do," she said at last.

"Him?" I asked, just making sure.

"Yes—I mean . . . why?"

I shrugged wearily. What could I say to that? *Obsession, ideas, polyhedra, dogma, unreal duality . . .*

"Tell me," she asked after a moment, and I was surprised to see some tears moistening her eyes, "do I owe you an apology for anything? Seriously?"

"I don't think so," I stammered. "What sort of thing?"

"I dunno—existing, maybe?"

"No." I frowned. "Of course not."

"You're a good neighbour," she managed. "You put up with me outside your door all the time and never complain . . ."

"Well—hardly ever," I said with a smile, but she only gave an even deeper sigh. "What is it?" I asked anxiously, brushing at her arm. "It's okay—I didn't mean there was anything wrong. You are a good neighbour as well, you know. I mean gawd—I am one of the lucky ones . . ."

I guess it was time to quietly forget about that attempted punch in the face. Such individual moments are maybe not as important as we sometimes think.

She gave a wan smile. "Are you coming in?"

"I . . . no, I'm just going upstairs. You going to be okay?"

"Yes—maybe I will have an early night."

She gave my arm a squeeze, then stepped inside.

A few minutes later, I was where I least wanted to be. The last of the day's heat radiated from the rough surface of the roof and the shed was like a sauna. Fortunately, the place was deserted. There was nobody to see me unlatch the shed door, slip inside and flick on the torch built into my phone. The stench instantly announced that the bag of bones was still there. As Tad had said, the police probably had far too much to deal with at the moment to worry about this—for now, anyway. And nobody had stepped in to clean up the mess either.

Don't ask me why I was doing this. I actually felt lightheaded as I opened up the bag a second time and studied the contents. It was revolting, yet I was forcing myself because it seemed to me that there was a truth in it somewhere. This was what I would be, the moment I gave up stewardship of this meat-bag I lived in. If the train had indeed taken my head off—or if I finally muddled my way through this world to some sickly end of life. Our instincts are very clear about this. It rings a huge warning bell, telling us to keep away because here be pestilence, here be sickness and contagion. Yet at the same time, what do we know about this? Nothing wants to die—very few things, anyway (remembering a few devoted mothers who feed their own flesh to their babies or males who offer themselves as food to their mates)—yet this is still the great substrate to it all. We live in a world that floats on top of an ocean of shit and rotting corpses like a raft—a huge enigma for all of us, and one we tend to run a mile from rather than consider. We prefer to imagine sweetness and light—a world where lions lie down with lambs or whatever, simply because we can't cope with the world's brutality and stench when judged in our human terms.

After a moment, I picked up one of the bones, feeling the slime under my fingers. A few maggots fell away back into the bag but I ignored them and studied it more closely. This had been what? Some stray? A beloved pet that had seduced us all with its baby-like cries? The thought seeded a massive pain inside. But I could also imagine Star Girl working the knife with gruesome pragmatism, hands soaked in blood. And before the knife existed, it would have been teeth, like the teeth of the lion tearing flesh, or of the cat itself for that matter, chewing its prey, tiny bones crunching, guts trailing. The red running down human cheeks or staining fur like a carnival mask. There was a confusion in this that only made the pain pulse stronger.

For some reason, I touched the bone to my cheek, feeling a spot of moisture like a kiss . . . then I suddenly cracked. Dropped it again with a grunt and recoiled out of that shed shivering from head to toe. I ended up hanging over the wall, staring down at the city below for several minutes, at least three passing trains, while I got myself under control again.

I seemed to be living in a city filled with edgy eyes—always watching you to make sure you didn't transgress any boundary of behaviour, etiquette, thought or opinion. Eyes sharp and angry and self-righteous and mostly regardless of political allegiance—faces filled with a supressed rage, or maybe with a crippling and stifling fear, as though one movement out of place, one muscle relaxed, one freely expressed word would doom them. Sickly faces—eyes dull and flesh soft, allergic to the world. Gender terror. Paranoia. Jealousy. Fear of the self—and of others. Pain translated into sarcasm and contempt. Anything, so long as the brain could be shut down to some realm where thought could be muffled and the harsh reality of the world's wrongness and complexity hidden.

As I leaned there, my whole body was overcome with a prickling sensation—'the creeps' you might call it. It was a sensation that some might feel if insects were crawling over them if they happened to be afraid of insects. As if all these old yet strangely beautiful buildings of East London had sprouted fingers and were plucking at me with strengthless pinches, trying to pull me this way or that. It occurred to me then with greater clarity than ever before that no way—no effing way—was this world I lived in any kind of reality. Not me. Not the city. Not that bag of bones. Not anything. The Philosopher was right. There had to be a past. A fundamental. And lessons from that fundamental. Somewhere, underneath everything we had built for ourselves and all the chains we had willingly shackled ourselves in, there had to be a fundamental human. The primeval, naturally evolved human. It may not be the answer to all our problems, since times change—evolution continues. But surely to crush it out of existence with barely an acknowledgement was little short of an ultimate betrayal. And also, it had never seemed clearer that there were no simple right answers to any of the questions that surrounded us. Simplicity was nothing more than a fucking lie.

✧

To the UK government: Close Down the London Research Laboratories Immediately!

The holding cells were absolute bedlam. I'm sure they were intended for one person but I was shoved in a room with I think six other girls. I suppose we had all been involved in the London Madness. The London Madness is everything, right now. It was just an irregular white box, totally sterile with a few surveillance cameras up in the corners, a bed thing and a little metal toilet sink unit in one corner that stank a bit. Some of us were enraged rioters, some other things. There was one girl sitting hunched in the corner who I gathered had been dragged in for running around with no clothes on. She seemed to be on another planet—bruises on her face that I didn't like at all. We all sat around, not talking much. There might have been microphones—I don't know. I certainly didn't tell them anything about what I was in for—I was in enough of a mess already.

It was all quite quick. I suppose in the chaos they wanted to process as many people as possible. Every few minutes, they'd come and hustle off one girl or other from my cell. And we didn't see them again. And even from the cell we could sense the strained atmosphere out-

side. *The whole thing was stretched to bursting point. Tempers were fraying—the whole fucking system was fraying. Just a dreary fraught mess. Then I was dragged out, talked at for a few minutes, then shoved in another cell with another bunch of people—dragged out again, talked at for a few more minutes, questioned—I had clammed up by the way; never tell 'em anything except your most basic details. I remember one nice man telling me that if it was up to him, I would be publically flogged in the street outside. Then they threatened a body cavity search if I wasn't more cooperative—and oh boy, having my arse probed would have been the cherry on top. They never found any weapons, stolen goods or anything actually incriminating on me—so maybe they hoped I had a treasure trove up there.*

I just shrugged, and that annoyed them even more—their attempts to shame me or freak me out with bodily violation weren't working. They never did anything, though. There probably wasn't time—or I wasn't sexy enough or something. In the end, a few hours later, I was chucked out into the street and wandered home, with no idea where any of my friends were. No need to lock me up. They know where to find you if they need to. Once they get their claws into you they never let go and are all-seeing. All-seeing eyes staring down on the city from on high.

They fined me, of course. But you know—I am hardly rich. Not when the rent has been paid. So we all know what happens next. And now stitches trail across my skin like a surreal centipede. Only a few centimetres long, but two on my neck, two more in front of both armpits, and two more right where I least want them, in my groin—spidery threads binding the skin into puckered ridges. I've no idea what they were about.

It must have been some fucking strong stuff they gave me, though. They could make a fortune with that on the recreational market. It really numbs you and I can still feel it. Hopefully I just need to sleep it off for a while. Then maybe I won't feel so slow in the head. Then maybe I will be able to work again. But this is one of many many reasons why people are pissed off. Would you seriously expect people not to be, given the circumstances? That is why I prophesy that there will only be more riots—worse ones—until something in the world changes. We've all had our humanity stolen, if some only knew it. You can't go through life being vampire-sucked dry, under constant pressure merely to survive, treated like dirt, your future constantly uncertain, filled with fear. You just can't. Watching this current snap is the least surprising thing in the world and it amazes me it didn't happen years ago.

In my fever dreams I was imagining all the surveillance cameras of London piled up and welded together into a tower higher than the Shard—a monument to an age of history every bit as dark as any other. And I would live at the top of that tower in a house made of glass and fabric. And I would have a spotlight that I can aim down anywhere in the city. Anywhere that is murky—I would bring light. Anything hidden I would expose. I suppose I should at least thank them for giving me some great dreams.

I don't think these labs can last much longer, however. It's just too much—a few stages too controversial and too incendiary, even for this appallingly cruel government. It was a wild-card in modern politics—an insane idea. A festering mess where our extremist right-wing government meets a messed-up left-wing insanity, not in the centre but at that point where the extremes curve around and come back together again in pools of blood. They call it voluntary—one option in place of a fine—but the government knows as well as I do that if you take a person who has nothing and threaten them with a judicial fine of hundreds or thousands of pounds then there is very little 'volunteering' involved anywhere. It's preying on the most vulnerable to achieve an end that was made considerably harder by the Amsterdam Welfare Reforms. That simple. Some say that the worst excesses of the labs are a backdoor death penalty. They assure us that patient welfare is paramount, yet there are still twenty-eight known 'executions'. You hear worse stories, as well—proposals from certain activists to expand the testing to cover other 'volunteers'—specifically severely disabled infants, something I very much hope would be impossible to implement—ever.

We've gone off the rails somehow. Our attempts to eliminate cruelty and implement environmental reforms have flipped over into the obscene. Almost into farce. And no question that both the more twisted and out of control ideologies of the left and the innate cruelty of the right are responsible. The protest is constant outside the London Labs now, sometimes close to pitched battles. Smoke bombs, sticks, stones and worse. Exactly what will happen when it inevitably closes, I am not sure. We can but hope that there is some way to function as a progressive and effective society while still embracing kindness—and rejecting cruelty. But I have to confess that a part of me, when I am feeling at my darkest, has little hope of that.

Prove me wrong.

SATURDAY

That night, I dreamed that there were four moons. On a city skyline that might have been London—or might not. Different coloured moons. Blood moon—blue moon—earth moon—white moon. Moons that came like a foreboding, a portent. They hung over that city like a sign of doom. Somehow I was sure I was seeing double—yes, double. Or maybe some kind of weird refraction was taking place in my eyes. I tried to take a photograph, hoping that it would be clearer than my own sight. But with the rather familiar malevolence of dream-technology, I couldn't. You ever get those dreams when you are trying to do something fairly basic, but just can't? Those futility dreams—where you try and try to achieve some end but it never happens? It always fades away—winds down—is just out of reach. It was as though the world was embedded in butter and one flounders through it with some ghastly entropy dooming all attempted actions to just . . . not happen. Two of those moons were definitely unreal, though, which was a relief because there definitely should not be four moons in the sky. Yet something was still not quite right here . . .

There were traces of laser light in the sky as well—moving red beams cutting through the air or flashing off the clouds. And yes, these were lasers, not the incomprehensible red cobweb. They were of the type you might see lighting up the sky from some event or other. Including one that was emanating from a nearby building. Security system? Somehow, it was associated with searching. The city caught in a web that was supposed to be protective, yet definitely wasn't. Flitting round left and right—then reduced to a dot. That meant it had focussed directly on me. Watching me.

I pointed the camera at it in some weird notion of self-defence, only to have a smoking hole burned through the lens with an insignificant blip of energy. I stared at the camera in shock.

"They don't like being looked at," the Beggar said.

"But . . . they're looking at me?"

She shrugged. And I suppose she was right. When had that ever mattered? She was standing on a rooftop very near—naked again as she had been in the mud below the sea wall. With a glance at me that flashed with blue light, she put her rat mask on—and now she looked like a figure in a surrealist painting. Glimmering red with reflected laser light and with the four moons behind her. She dropped down on all fours, the rat's mouth opening in a sharp screech.

And that was it. I woke up with a jolt. Actually I had been half awake for a while—on the edge of lucid dreaming as the dreams gave way to the dreary grey of morning. But that image of the Beggar-Rat crouched down, arse thrust back and hips tight with beautiful brashness, dragged me out of there in a rush. Dreams often come with flesh, of course. We all know that. At one point or other, pretty much everyone I knew had turned up in one sexual dream or other—that's just the way life works. Sometimes it was Tea, though she didn't dominate things as much as one might expect. This was the first time the Beggar had put in an appearance, though—and the massive blast of feeling that she generated shocked me. The thoughts that had been lurking at the back of my mind had now been nailed straight through my forehead. I remembered the sharp angles of her face, the feel of her in my arms, the strength of her muscles as she hugged me. I wanted more. I wanted that hug to never end. And it came with a feeling of terror, as at the first symptoms of a relapse into some major sickness. In my mind, Tea was in descendancy—a thing of rot and pain and pointlessness. The Beggar was in ascendancy—heated and buzzing with fresh energy. This was a time of transition, of replacement. I had to acknowledge that fact.

It would have been easy to carry on dreaming—easy to lose myself in a masturbatory fantasy right then. Take any one of those images plucking at me, mix it with some delusions of connection and whisk well. But no. It might sound strange, even edging towards some kind of dreary chastity, but the simple fact was that I knew from experience the pain that could result from allowing myself to fantasise about connecting with real people. I knew it far too well and no fucking way was I going down that road again. If the Beggar was starting to insinuate her thorns into my heart, my stomach and my dick, and if I let it happen, then there was only one possible outcome. I would have to withdraw like a salted snail. And then what?

I don't need to spell it out again. There's only so many euphemisms I can find for being mangled by trains.

After a few moments waking up still further, I scrambled out of bed and pushed myself through the morning routine as quickly as I could. It was better to be moving, however early, than to lie there thinking about this, so I washed myself down and packed my work bag for the day. Bustling mundane actions—just go go go. Run, in fact. Run away from this murky future *and for fuck's sake get over this, you complete fucking idiot!*

The momentum of it propelled me outside past the sleeping Kate. There was no sign of Aceline—maybe she was still with Tea—and I slipped into the corridor . . .

And stopped.

I came to a halt on the stairs like a broken-down train that has finally run out of forward motion. The bag sank to the floor with a bump and I slumped against the windowsill—and swore under my breath. I stared out at the familiar straight-shot down this city appendix, just in case anything had changed, just in case the world had melted or transformed in the night. Overhead, the sky roiled in its eternal grey burning haze. It is as though something hangs over London that you never see anywhere else—something more than the city smog and the old marsh clouds of the river swamp this city is rooted in. It is like a personality—a great revolving disk, so universal overhead that we call it the sky.

That sky was normal enough, but the sound of the city wasn't. There is always noise here—distant moving cars, a murmur of voices, sirens—but now it seemed reduced. A quiet hung over the grubby brown bricks, flowing like treacle down the streets and alleyways. It seemed as though it even affected the colour. London always seemed partly desaturated—but now it was downright colourless, in spite of the heat. A blend of greys relieved by nothing more than a few dull browns. And the city was mirrored in my own soul. I found myself swirling with loneliness and paranoia—as though my isolation from the city had crystallised into outright enmity. As though the city I did love on one level was now trying to squeeze me out of itself like pus out of some unfortunate pimple. I was indeed the underclass that the newspapers keep blathering on about. I was the outcast—the misfit—the scrounger—the parasite. I would be better off hidden . . .

A light touch on my arm almost made me shriek. But it was only Feather. Unusually for me, I had not even heard her approach.

"Sorry," she murmured. "I had no intention of startling you."

I looked at her. Yes, I thought. Hidden somewhere underground and non-existent.

"Yeah," I said. "Never mind. I . . . was just thinking."

"That is good, right? Or not good?"

"I dunno."

She gave me a look that I couldn't read—some blend of curiosity and resignation. She was in full mudlarking gear, clean waders over her shoulder, and I smiled—at least I hoped it was a smile. It felt weird on my face. Presumably 'Feather' was a nickname—I had never bothered to think about that before and I had certainly never heard her called anything else. She did indeed look a bit feathery . . .

"You okay?"

I wanted to ask her why she singled me out for that question when I couldn't think of a single person in the entire building who was 'okay', including her—but my eyes felt hot and gleaming, and maybe that was the answer. I felt as though something inside my head was actually glowing with a physical light.

"Yes," I assured her. "I'm fine." There was no way I could reveal or 'confess' what was still roiling in my mind then. Some things just cannot be released from the prison of your thoughts. I gave a grin—probably even weirder than my smile. Like everyone, she looked like a skeleton on which bags of water hung. She was made of string and bone and water balloons, all bundled in slush and pale skin—her limbs stick-like, her arse and belly protruding. That's how she seemed then—how anyone would have seemed, walking around in these weird meat-bags we call home.

"Right. Good," she said, still looking a little uncertain.

"Tell me," I said, feeling an urgent need to talk about something other than the Beggar.

"What?"

"This . . . Polyhedron that is everywhere?"

"Yes?" Her face developed a wary look.

"By that, you mean . . . the mathematical forms, right? Cube? Dodecahedon?"

She shrugged. "Sort of—though I suspect they come with a purity that this World Polyhedron is lacking. In the universe of geometrical polyhedra, they are all there is. Beautiful, yes—the product of a simple law or system. But try imagining making a human being look like that? Imagine our sensual flesh frozen and formed into that star. It doesn't work, does it? That is what they are trying to do to all our souls . . ."

She leaned against the windowsill beside me.

"And the disturbing thing is—they seem to be succeeding. I really don't know if we ever have any chance of escaping this thing. Or whether we are doomed to live bound by these unreal angles forever—or rather, until they destroy us."

She looked even more depressed. However loopy her talk sometimes, there was no denying that the images she conjured up resonated on some level. Measurement seemed pretty constant in life—everything from your income to your beliefs to your dick size is constantly graded by forces somewhere . . . so why not resent it?

"Tell me more," I said at last. She gave a sigh, her eyes flickering with an uneasy emotion that I couldn't identify. But then she seemed to shrug it off and leaned back comfortably against the windowsill.

"The strange thing is," she said, after marshalling her thoughts for a moment, "the Measuring Men strive to create some form of order—what they see as order—but their path inevitably points towards chaos. In these days, the running men and the running women fill the world, more and more of us. And that is scary because we fear the Measuring Men will end up noticing us one day. Or maybe they already have. Always have. But it is not just us. There is a fundamental falsehood in society—and that will one day tear it apart. There will be war that the Measuring Men don't expect. A new kind of war. War at the most fundamental levels. Not the trite matters of country against country. Countries are meaningless. Not even civil war. Instead the Measuring Men will finally be destroyed as the impatience of the people reaches a certain critical mass. That is inevitable." She paused. "So they say, anyway."

There was a silence.

"Who's 'they'?" I asked.

"There are many many running men and running women now—more every day. Haven't you noticed?"

I was silent again.

"The war is approaching," she said with a smile. "Maybe I will soon be avenged and the Measuring Men will soon feel the wrath of those tired of measurement. Are you going out tonight?"

"Maybe," I said.

"Then please be prepared to fight," she said.

"Fight," I murmured. It wasn't even a question.

"I will be listening," she said. "If the world needs help." She leaned against the window beside me with a sigh, looking so gloomy now that I gave her a worried stare. "You going to work now?" she asked.

"I suppose so."

"Mind if I come with you?"

I stumbled slightly in surprise. "Well—I mean sure, but it's just a short bus ride to . . ."

"That's okay," she said with a smile. "I also like to travel around the city. Though I suspect we are looking for different things. And I am hungry . . ."

With a mental shrug, I accompanied her down the stairs and out into the street. She was not one to easily betray emotions—

happiness, sadness, anger. I suspect that she normally kept them hidden in some strange crisp little box inside her. But this time I would have to be blind to miss the radar signals.

"What's wrong?" I asked as we reached the bus stop.

She glanced at me. "I am feeling depressed," she said with a tiny smile.

"Why?"

"The sense of chaos in the air—around the entire planet . . . it is simultaneously terrifying and deliriously beautiful. Sometimes I go one way, sometimes I go the other."

I frowned.

"You mean . . . ?"

"Yes—humanity always makes my heart bleed and burn at the same time."

There was a silence, as far is the outdoors is ever silent.

"I guess I know what you mean," I said. "Though . . . your life underground seems safer than some. Or am I wrong?"

She shrugged. "Possibly. That is a good place. I am lucky."

"Can I join you?" I murmured, starting to feel gloomy myself. It was a half joke—but only half. Her eyes swivelled and gave me a piercing glance—though with a distinct lack of surprise, I noticed.

"Maybe," she said. "We would have to go back, speak to everybody—see if you would fit in . . ."

Fit in? That was the sort of term I didn't like since even now I didn't feel as though fitting in ever really happened. I still felt too cut off, too damaged, to really connect to others. The instinctive response was that I was surely not going to function as a valid part of any community—and my tiny flicker of a dream began to flicker out again.

At that point, the correct numbered bus arrived and I flagged it down. We climbed aboard with the familiar beep of electronic cards being read. The beep of a few quid more extracted from one's life. If such a beep was applied to rent, it would sound like a siren. The bus was almost entirely empty so we aimed for the best seat—upstairs front right. Feather slid into the window seat and immediately leaned forward, pressing her face against the glass, staring out at the world as though her hunger was literal and every passing sight might or might not offer sustenance.

"What's it cost to live down there?" I asked at last, and with a certain reluctance.

Her eyebrows contracted in another thoughtful look. "Hard to say. Maybe about fifty pounds."

I winced. "A day?"

"Month."

Month. I stared at her for a long moment. She might as well have told me it cost three goldfish, or six spanks with a table-tennis bat, or two jellybeans, or one paragraph of H. G. Wells for all that made any sense to me.

"A bit for the utilities we all share," she added before I could ask her to repeat herself. "And the usual home improvements."

"You did say fifty—a month?" I asked, still not able to compute. If I was a calculator, I would be displaying an E. If I was a computer, it would be the blue screen of death.

"Maybe seventy, unless we decide to upgrade the electrics or something. They're working to improve the ventilation system at the moment as well, so—there's always some little thing."

"That's . . ."

I couldn't remember being this tongue-tied for years. I had been sucking at the poisoned teat of the London housing market for so long that such a thing sounded downright impossible. Feather gave me a look, a glimmer of humour on her face.

"This is why we don't tell that many people about it," she said.

I nodded, still feeling stunned. "What's the catch?" I asked. "There has to be some fucking catch for seventy a month?"

Feather shrugged and smiled.

"Well—the catch is that you are technically homeless and need to be a bit self-sufficient. You can't rely on the council or police or anything—if anything goes wrong."

I nodded.

"Essentially," she explained, "we are all renting the one small crap apartment where the tunnel starts—the little charity mail-drop thing. So instead of seven people squeezed into three rooms, there's about thirty of us. The apartment is registered as another of those set-ups to receive mail for London's forty thousand or so homeless—and it really is. The world just doesn't know that some of the homeless it serves live right underneath it. London has no idea where everybody who fell through the cracks of this city is. That is one thing it has completely lost control of—and that is a massive advantage."

"Okay . . ."

"We all share the little showers and bathrooms upstairs. We just have to take turns and chill out and love one another, even their mess. Prissy people or misanthropes tend to run away pretty quickly. We might plumb something more sophisticated in, but at the moment there is a tap and drain in the common room. The bathroom is way upstairs on the surface so . . . people make their own arrangements as best they can. There's a few emergency exits at the other end of the tunnels—just in case. They've never been used. There's also room twenty-eight, which you saw before. No one lives there, of course."

"Right," I said, very quietly. She was sounding like a house agent now, which only added to the surreal feeling.

"Aside from that, it's all homes. Electricity and internet in all of them—do what we like with that, it's all wired into the upstairs. No gas down there, obviously. The walls of the rooms are very thoroughly grouted and double-layered—there's drainage and a pump to keep things dry—you need that in London. We did a good job. And hey, if we need more room, we can always dig . . ."

"Dig?" I echoed faintly.

"Sure, why not? We are all pretty good at making a working tunnel now. I told you, we have engineers, architects, bricklayers, carpenters, computer technicians, electricians, artists, even a few ex-military with survival training. One guy is a fairly experienced vintner. None of them can afford to live on the surface so the world's loss is our gain."

"Okay," I said, a little louder than I intended. I stared out of the window again at the passing world, clutching the edge of the seat with a painful grip. I had to end this topic of conversation right now, otherwise my smooth, cool, collected exterior was going to shatter like a dropped lightbulb. Feather seemed to read my mind.

"That's what it's like," she said with a smile, leaning back against the glass and staring out with that same hungry or questing expression. "And remember—I did tell you about it, so ..."

I stared at her, feeling numb. That place—that hole in the ground—that community—it was like a dream. What seemed a fairly decent quality of life—for seventy fucking quid? Was that really the result of finding a way to do the impossible and take control of your environment? It didn't seem fair. In fact, you might say it really stung. Not that I resented Feather for it—I was not that dumb—but I had never before resented the city of London and the artificial, greedy, soul-sucking housing market quite as much as I did then. It burned so hard for a moment that I ground my teeth and muttered a few things under my breath that I won't repeat here. I am not kidding—for a while there I really thought I was going to be sick. And of course, there was the inevitable question in my head. It had been a half joke but *could I possibly join her?* Was it possible that there was a way out of this life, after all? I had always known there was no hope whatsoever of escaping upwards to any kind of increased comfort—everything that vampire-sucked your money and time and strength was too perfectly engineered to prevent that. It had never occurred to me that it might be possible to escape downwards, though. To tell the world and all its insane demands to fuck off and to become as the rats and the mice—just living. Was that maybe a rose-tinted fantasy? My head was swimming trying to find a catch to it all, but finding nothing that was in any way worse than my current circumstances.

"What are you looking for now?" I countered, desperate to change the subject.

"Places where the Polyhedron is broken," she explained. "There's a lot of them at the moment. More and more. Look over there."

I followed her finger—pointing down a small side street. I knew that it just led through to the next road—contained a few minor shops and side entrances, as well as some hidden residences lurking as always among the buildings. I couldn't see anything even slightly unusual about it, except for a few orange traffic cones with tape between them surrounding something or other on the pavement. Just a broken paving slab maybe.

"And there," she said again, a moment later.

This was a brief, tree-lined crescent that arced away from the main road for a few yards, overlooked by tall, narrow houses. Just blank windows and parked cars—again totally ordinary and normal.

"There's a lot of them," she said. "They are increasing, which I suppose isn't surprising."

I watched her with a slight smile, feeling oddly content with her bizarre fantasies. Why not? That was what humans were about, after all. Aren't we all just a little bit mad? Aren't we all just telling our own stories on the substrate of an unknowable world? A world that still appears to glow occasionally with red light . . .

"Yeah," I said. I looked out of the window again, and realised we were within moments of the bus stop near my work. I had been getting so absorbed that I had almost missed it entirely. I flinched and jabbed at the button.

Feather looked round.

"This is my stop."

"Okay—I will stay here and keep looking. I also am drawing maps."

"Right," I murmured, then stood up. "But . . . but tell me . . ."

"What?"

"Do you have any idea what is going on out there at the moment?" I asked at last, waving at the world in general.

"No—not really," she said, very quietly. And this time I did believe her. "It's not exactly the war I was expecting. I was expecting violence—civil unrest . . . but there is the feeling of something very strange out there in the city. Who knows—we may be witnessing the death of the Polyhedron."

We remained for a moment in silence, staring out at the hazy burning sky as the bus pulled into the side of the road.

Then I felt a touch on my shoulder.

"We shall talk later, right?" she said with a smile.

I nodded and ran for the stairs.

☼

After another day of work that I won't go into—save that it was more like being beaten for eight hours with sock puppets than eaten alive by ravening vampires, by which I mean tolerable in a certain very specific definition of the word—I found myself back in the gated loading area below the building I called home. The place stank—a subtle bouquet of mould, bike oil and piss—but I shrugged that off. I was trying to extract my bike, of course, which was always harder than it should be. Even though I'd only put it there two days ago, it was lost in a tangle of its fellows.

No wonder Tea preferred to keep hers up in the corridor.

It was dark now—the hazy sunset faded to black and a pallid moon in the sky. Another moon of dirt. This told me that I should be making my way down to the sea wall again. I wasn't rushing though. It was too hot for rushing anywhere. That was no doubt why I noticed . . .

Okay. As I am writing this, after a certain time, all of this next part feels totally scrambled in my mind. I can't say for sure any of what happened next is real. I saw a glimmer of white in the depths of the storage area—just small and barely visible. A white spot. But it was moving. Slowly. Following a curve. And around it was a circle of black—a black that I could clearly see against its surroundings. It floated against the dark rather like the helium balloons I remember from when I was a kid, back in the days when you could still get them. As though a balloon of utter lightlessness was floating in mid-air, the white circle orbiting within it gently.

I just stared at it transfixed. Frightened out of my wits, though for reasons I couldn't pin down, either then or now. A black blob with a white circle in it was a familiar image of course—associated with graffiti—with rulers and angles. Stationary artwork—not moving phantasms. But no. Even then, even standing there in that cluttered space, I couldn't allow myself to follow that thought to its conclusion. This was nonsense. Complete nonsense.

After a moment, I dragged my bike free and switched the headlight on—and instantly the whole world lit up with a blaze. I screwed up my eyes. Now I could see nothing at all and that was more disturbing than the darkness. For long moments, my eyes struggled to adapt, but eventually they brought me enough of the space to reveal that it was empty. Nothing there. No Measuring Men with their rulers. Not even any scrawled drawings of them. I snapped the light off again, replacing the glare with a mass of squirming after-images. It seemed I had blown it completely now. My eyes were useless. I blinked hard for a few moments, then a swell of panic sent me stumbling back, dragging my bike out into the appendix outside. I was deeply disturbed, breathing hard and tense all over—not so much in paranormal terror as in shattering confusion and a complete inability to determine how much of what had happened in the last five minutes had been real and how much hallucinatory.

The main reason why I was and am so confused is actually the colour of that black shape. It might sound strange, but there was something about that black that just didn't fit. If you have done any design or printing work, you will know that there are indeed different colours of black. Or more accurately, different blends of colours so dark that to our perception they are basically black. Yet they are distinguishable. Some indeed, like Rich Black, look darker than actual digitally defined black does. This proves that what we call 'black' is another of those unattainable concepts, like silence. We can approach it, yet never quite get there. Scientists have worked hard to make the blackest possible blacks, substances that drink nearly all the photons that hit them. A while ago, there was Vantablack—then more recently Hyper-Black, I think—yet even these were nothing more than very, very dark. I had never seen these materials in the flesh, and by definition you cannot image them, because you will only achieve the blackness of your paper or of the darkened pixels on your screen.

The point I am trying to make here is that the black shape I had seen stood out against the almost-black world around me surprisingly clearly—so clearly that it was more like a hole in my perception than an object. It was a black that shouldn't have been—a dream of black. A black that rendered the whole deep, dark storage area nothing more than a dull grey in comparison. It was the closest I have ever come to the otherworldly, and yet it was nothing more than a colour.

✥

As I cycled through the evening towards the sea wall, the fear and confusion lingered in my mind. The performances of the London citizens also continued against a backdrop of scattered violence and distant fire. A musical crescendo might be an appropriate simile for these few days. If London was indeed an orchestra, then we were slowly building up from an eerie quiet with the occasional sharp phrases from the woodwind through to some serious brass eruptions—demonic fanfares and dissonant trombones. And in spite of the explosion at Canary Wharf, it still felt as though the true climax was to come.

I was keeping to the back streets and though the occasional violence and burning seemed at a distance here, the performances and odd encounters still came in a continual stream. One after the other, now there, now gone again into the depths of the city, like a year's worth of London eccentricity condensed into one evening. It was as though some of the shackles of civilization and normality had been lifted. The silent streets were like a musical score of details as I rolled by—things, debris, detritus, signs and symbols. The whole thing could be played in my mind if I wanted—a concerto for urban landscape, continually building.

A short distance into my ride, I came close to colliding with a woman with a blooded face, walking barefoot, black hair trailing—gone before I could react, but not before I had glimpsed the shard of glass in her hand. And soon there were other figures, sitting or standing around as though slightly stunned, some with dishevelled clothes—a few even naked again, sitting amid the city like a dream, as though whatever clockwork powered their souls had wound down. As before, there were open doors—residences letting straight onto the street, revealing nothing but darkness and a shadowy hint of mundane furniture. One or two fires had been lit in the middle of the road—bonfires rather than arson—and the occasional figure stood watching them or sitting in the flickering shadows.

I rolled onwards, feeling electrified from head to foot, as though the air itself was energy. I keep banging on about the performative feeling of all this, that sensation that it was all unreal and staged. I suppose that is just an extension of the alien nature of it all, and the fact that people seem to be acting out something from deep in their souls. I remember once, long before, I was sitting quietly by the Thames in the South Bank area when, all of a sudden, two girls appeared out of nowhere—no doubt two dance students engaged in some performance or flash event. They landed on the bench beside me, and seemed to flow over it, squirming past me as though I wasn't there in a series of performance-arty movements. No, I don't know what that was about, but it was a performance taken from its stage context and consciously shoved into the public space. London had been a stage then and it was a stage now—a graffiti-scrawled, dark and deranged stage, and we were all performing, though to whom I wasn't sure.

My bike struck something in the dark—something that bumped dully. I looked down and saw my first dead cat of the evening. It had been torn to pieces. I stared at it for a moment, registering the mess on my wheel with a horrified chill, then cycled onwards again. A dead pigeon soon followed—also ripped open gruesomely. Whatever had done this was making even Star Girl look delicate. It was a mystery at first, and I was half expecting to cycle directly into an urban version of a *Memento mori* or *Vanitas*—but several streets later it was solved when I almost collided with a figure in a suit. A grey figure with his face buried in a shapeless mass of feathers, red smearing across his cheeks and chin. A figure of anthropomorphised death? After all, what use was a scythe and robe in modern times? A grey suit might be quite a good modern-times update for the ultimate destroyer. But no. My headlights picked him out clearly and he flinched with a feral movement. Death would not flinch. He was just a person like any other—a predatory yet eternally vulnerable animal.

And of course, as the dark closed around me again, I was back on my roof and whatever unimaginable horror had taken place there. What was going through the air of London to cause all this? Could madness be contagious? Could this even be called madness? For the first time I was starting to feel afraid for my own safety. After all, if history teaches anything it's that humanity is not a calm and tranquil species at heart. Whatever modern environment we live in, humans themselves still seem every bit as territorial and aggressive as they have always been. If London was becoming soaked with blood and filled with naked figures cavorting against the fire-glow, then what else might be unearthed from the depths of the human soul?

And yet, fear notwithstanding, there was something enthralling about this city invaded by the surreal. Familiar old London, peopled with quiet bodies like a Delvaux painting.

I had been increasing speed as the minutes passed—whirling through the almost empty streets faster and faster, as though trying to outrun a storm front. It nearly wrecked me, though, when I swept round a corner and rode smack into another tableaux. A circle of standing bodies. All colours and all naked. I was in among them before I had any time to react. I nearly smashed right into the back of one, a woman with black hair. She barely flinched, even though I careened past close enough to see every hair standing up on her arm. I stumbled to a stop, right in the centre of the circle—right at the focal point of all their eyes. And then there was complete frozen silence. Looking at their faces, they could have been anyone. Their bodies were skinny or a little chubby—either one or the other, flesh slightly pale and sagging. The somewhat adventurous hairstyles and occasional tattoos marked them out as from the more alternative and arty side of the city, but that was all I could say about them. Most of the women were shaven at the crotch, while a few had shaped it into arrows or landing strips. Only one seemed to have a full natural bush. I have no idea what they were doing there—whether it was some new-age communing with the night, trying to raise the devil through orgiastic ritual, or on the hunt for postmodern blood. For a long moment I was frozen, totally terrified—then I pushed at the pedals again, getting into motion, half expecting them to close ranks and prevent me escaping, hands grasping and tearing. But I passed between them without incident, then drove the pedals hard, my heart racing and my skin crawling. I am sure I heard some quiet laughter drifting after me.

I hurtled onwards, scanning the occasional passing figure for any further performances. And they were there . . . even at the level of body posture or darting eyes—little gestures or dishevelled hair. There wasn't much further to go, fortunately—all that was left was the stretch of towpath leading to the watergate. This stretch was dark, though. Dark and rather isolated. Under normal circumstances, it wasn't a place where many liked to walk at night, but on a night like this, anything might be possible. The darkness could have hidden figures doing anything as far as I knew—and any number of traps or ambushes for passers-by. But fortunately the last few hundred metres to the sea wall passed without incident . . . until I rolled to a stop, ready to park the bike, and became aware of a noise.

Some noises catch your attention—there is something odd about them that pricks you on a primal level. There was a scuffle somewhere further down the towpath in the shadows—a sort of growl, and a hiss of breath.

I could feel my skin freezing. These were instincts that had evolved when those sounds from beyond the firelight might have come from entities able to tear us limb from limb, but they were still maybe useful now.

And then, out of nowhere, a horrific figure exploded into being, leaping on me with arms spread and emitting a deafening screech.

I gave a kind of whoop of shock and scrambled back, trying to climb off the bike and almost falling right into the canal in the process. I tangled in it and landed heavily, arms up in frantic defence.

"Boo," the figure screamed—and shoved its face, no, shoved her mask up onto her forehead.

Star Girl.

I stared at her for a moment, then put my head in my hands. "For fuck's sake," I said, trying not to scream the words.

She gave a wild laugh and dropped onto her heels beside me. "Did I make you jump?"

For a moment, I was absolutely livid—the London madness whispering in my ears. I was ready to grab her and chuck her in the canal or worse. But I never got the chance, because she quickly replaced the mask, which I recognised now as the same marten one she had worn before, then gave a wild screech and whirled away. "Can't catch me," she yelled, before scampering off down the towpath, actually on all fours. It was pretty high up among the weirdest things I had ever seen and I was astonished at the speed she managed. She was not on hands and knees but hands and feet, arse in the air, and she looked like a monkey in night camouflage. I wasn't sure I could keep up with her, even on two legs.

Then there was a crash as another figure barged past. This one looked like an old-time plague doctor—long black coat and a huge black-beaked bird mask. Utterly terrifying. The coat might have been the philosopher's, but the mask could have hidden anyone or anything. The masked eyes fixed on me for a moment but whoever it was didn't slow, just melted into the dark of the towpath.

I stared after them, hearing the occasional whoop drifting back, trying to get myself under some kind of control.

Then a cat was bending over me. A cat in scruffy jeans and a black top.

"Come on Train Man," the Beggar cried. "Get up. Let's go—let's go."

"What the hell are you doing?" I demanded, still furious. "Are you out of your tree? You nearly had me in the canal." It was rare indeed for me to be this angry, and even rarer for me to respond by yelling—but I did then. Maybe it was the London madness, or maybe it was actually a measure of my trust in these people.

The Beggar shoved the mask up with a grin, while a familiar cockerel also appeared staring down at me like the last thing a mouse ever sees. Then a hand hauled me unceremoniously out from the tangle of bicycle and to my feet again.

"Are you okay, Train Man?" the Beggar asked.

"Yeah," I said crossly. "Just about. Thanks for that, though. Maybe in a couple of years my adrenalin levels will have returned to normal again."

She rubbed my shoulder with an apologetic giggle. "Sorry, Train Man," she said. "It's one of those nights. And you looked quite fierce there for a moment. Catch her and I am sure you can get your revenge."

"Catch her?"

"Yeah—come on, let's get after them. Clay Man is out there somewhere as well."

"What are you blathering about?" I demanded, with a sudden wash of impatience again. "What the heck are you guys doing running around in those things?"

"This is the wild hunt," the Butcher cried, spreading his arms with a cackle. "We shall play games," he cried. "We shall hunt and kill, carnivore against carnivore. The cat shall take down the silver fox, the silver fox shall take down the pine marten—and the cockerel shall take down all of them, of course."

"Take your pick," the Beggar said. "The masks are just here. What would you like to be?"

"Be? Oh boy—I don't bloody know."

"Maybe I do," she said. "Just a moment." She went running off into the dark again and momentarily returned with something white. "You can be the white bear, you're a big strong guy," she said with a smile. It was a dramatic white mask—a hugely stylised polar bear I suppose, though with painted fur almost long enough to be a lion's mane.

"Oh—thanks," I said. "That sounds dramatic. Maybe I am fattening up for the winter."

I put the mask on, feeling ridiculous at first. I was not dressed for masks—even this mask. But I have to say, disappearing behind it gave me a thrill of satisfaction.

"Rowr," I said crossly, still wondering whether I was being made a fool of.

"Come on, Train Man," the Butcher cried. "You can do better than that."

"Well, what sound does a polar bear make?" I demanded.

"A dull growl that sends shivers down the spine of anyone who hears it out in the dark," the Beggar said.

I tried again—something like a dog's growl but deeper.

"Better," the Beggar said. "Try again—feel the terror and the power."

I growled again—as deep as I could. And I felt a prickle. Okay, so I doubt it sounded anything like a bear—I doubt human vocal chords can even produce such a noise—but maybe some of the spirit of the thing was there. Behind that massive stylised mask, maybe there was a little enjoyment now. Masks were good. The only way it could have been better would have been if it was a full bodysuit—then I might have been completely invisible. A non-Train-Man polar bear . . .

"Still not terrifying," the Butcher teased. "If you're a white bear, you have a lot to live up to."

"Oh yeah?" I shot back. "Is that why you are dressed as a chicken?"

"Cockerel, if you please," he said, hands on hips. "And I can tell you now, this thing here is bloody ferocious. Hens too. If you're a mouse, don't venture anywhere near the chicken coop." He threw back his head and gave a surprisingly accurate cockadoodledo that made my skin freeze.

"Terrifying," the Beggar said.

"This cockerel is moving up in the world though," the Butcher said with a grin. "This cockerel wants a nice bit of marten for dinner."

"Well, good luck with that," the Beggar said with a grin. "I bet Star Girl is shaking."

I stared at them in bemusement. In this bleak but mundane bit of London concrete and brick, the sight was seriously weird—like something out of a very surreal movie. That strangeness had begun to take root in me as well, though at first I hardly acknowledged it. Maybe there was a spark of something here—some excitement that was very alien to my life. I glanced uneasily round the towpath, wondering if there was anyone else out there in the dark. I didn't envy any late-night wanderers who came upon us out of nowhere.

I shoved the mask up onto my forehead again.

"So . . . what do I . . . ?"

"You know what to do," the Beggar said with a grin. "And if you get your revenge—if you give her a bit of a rumple in the grass, give her some for me too."

I gave a wordless grunt.

"Oi," the Butcher said. "Don't even think about it. That's my dinner, not yours."

"Then you'd better be prepared for a scrap, Butcher darling," the Beggar said. "Four hunters, two quarries—at least two of us of us will go hungry."

I gave a weary sigh, fairly sure who one of them would be. Was that the way this was going? Some pathetic competitive playground antics? I tugged at the bear mask restively. Maybe there was somewhere I could sit and collect my thoughts while the rest of them fooled around . . .

"Kiss my arse, Train Man," the Butcher yelled and charged off into the night.

"Rather not," I muttered. "Wrong gender."

The Beggar gave a tiny giggle. "You are okay, aren't you?" she asked. "I mean, aside from that idiot jumping on you . . ."

"Yeah—fine," I said evasively. "Just responding to this crazy city, I suppose."

To my complete amazement, she gave me a quick kiss on the lips. It was an astonishing tiny touch of moisture, then she pulled away and slipped the mask down over her face. "Go on after Star before that blasted Butcher gets her. Find her, catch her, spank her arse or something . . ."

I just stood there, still blindsided and feeling very strange, but somewhat to my surprise I was agreeing. I was still cross and grim, but I could feel a darkness flickering inside that probably wasn't darkness in any gothic sense but something old and deep and dangerous. Flickers of myself buried and hidden—and yes, it *would* be nice to hunt down and catch and kill . . . well, to maul a little bit. Maybe there were indeed games to play here. The bear mask demanded it—but so did something else. Something that was very much my own.

I nodded.

"And I," she said, "wanted to bag me some silver fox. I dunno, though—they could be anywhere. We've let them run off. The Butcher's going to beat us both at this rate, since the Philosopher will probably just stand there and watch."

"Want an unfair advantage?" I asked with a smile, replacing my mask.

"Huh?"

I picked up my bike again. It looked none the worse for the tumble. "Climb up behind," I said and the Beggar laughed.

"Does that work?"

"Well enough," I said. "I've done it before. At the very least we can beat walking pace. Or even a running pace."

Leaving my mask in place, I mounted the machine and she scrambled up, her arms slipping round my ribs. That contact gave me a nervous thrill but I tried to ignore it. "Okay," she said in my ear, "you ride and I will try some tracking."

I hadn't a clue what that meant but I pushed off anyway, wobbling along the towpath. The Beggar gave a worried gasp as the water loomed very close beside us and I hastily steered us away. We passed along beneath the vertiginous walls of the buildings and soon arrived at one of the many ways up into the streets—a paved ramp. The Beggar gave me a squeeze. "Off here," she said.

"How do you know?" I said, swinging my bike in that direction.

"That stick—that looks like one of Star Girl's clues. It's pointing up here, see."

I toiled up the steep path away from the canal and then came to a stop again.

"That way," the Beggar cried excitedly.

I was beginning to allow myself to enjoy the feeling of the Beggar hanging onto me, though part of me was trying to insist I shouldn't. The general feeling of wildness in the air was also adding its note to things. I was joining in with the London Madness, and even this came with an odd sense of community, as if I was becoming part of the city in ways I had never been before. We raced down the road, picking up a bit of speed, the Beggar holding on tighter. "That way," she said in my ear, reading some sign I certainly hadn't picked up. We passed from road to road, then the Beggar poked me in the ribs. "I know where they've gone," she said with a laugh.

"Hmm?"

"Right back to Mile End Park. If I know my Star, that's where they'll be."

"Okay then," I said and spun onwards directly towards it, picking up speed.

Mile End Park was actually on the canal we had left behind us—I had already been through it this evening. It was a long thin strip of modern landscaping filled with sweeping undulations and moored narrowboats—even a garden bridge across Mile End Road. Star had obviously been leading us a dance. But the speed we were going we must have caught up with anyone on foot. We couldn't have been that far behind them.

When we got there, it was substantially darker—a few lamps supplemented by an invading glow of the city beyond. As we slowly cruised through that darkness, the game suddenly seemed more real. Then the Beggar gave me a sharp squeeze.

"Woah," she said. "Stop, stop."

I stopped.

"I think this is where we should enter stealth mode," she said, scrambling off and rubbing her arse.

"This is stealth mode," I said with a grin.

"You know what I mean. Time for the wild hunt proper."

I nodded and quickly locked the bike to something.

"I will go that way," she said. "Sure I saw something. Good luck finding your fallen Star." She snapped into cat again then, brandishing her hands at me like claws with a growl and hiss—then a shrill giggle. I mentally shrugged. If I could communicate with Tea in gestures, I could communicate with the Beggar in cat. Or do I mean bear? Whatever. I gave a small purring growl of assent. She nodded and dropped down into a momentary crouch, then she was gone into the shadows.

I watched the empty space where she had been for a moment, then cautiously stepped forward, fiddling awkwardly with the mask. Quietly, with sharpened attention, I began to prowl though the night. Any hope of actually 'tracking' anything in the mile or so of Mile End Park felt pretty futile, but it turned out that I didn't need to, for, a few minutes later, it found me. A sudden commotion broke out a few dozen yards away and I hurried in that direction. Two figures came staggering out of a side path—Star and the Butcher, I eventually decided. However, the cockerel definitely hadn't scored a hit. The masked figure of Star Girl seemed to be dancing in circles around him, a capering silhouette in the darkness, whooping with triumph and waving a long thin tree branch. Then she grabbed him and dragged, literally shoving him face first into the bushes and dancing away again.

So much for the chicken, I thought with a smile.

Then she saw me. I could make out the eyeholes in the mask as pinpricks of ultimate darkness in the already dark face of the marten. Her body registered sudden tension, arms held warily—and then she took off at full speed. I stared after her and sighed—but at least I had a fix on her direction now. And I followed quietly through the night. Not rushing. I knew I didn't have the strength to run for long. I would have to follow at my own pace—accept my weaknesses, yet still try.

I suppose it was no surprise that the moment I came on her again, crouched quietly under a tree, she saw me. Why the heck was I wearing a white mask against a dark background at night? The Beggar had given me a disadvantage right there, I realised with a frown. Star gave a sharp hiss and leapt to her feet—then to my surprise, she charged me in a flurry that made me back away, capering round and waving the same branch at me. Then it impacted my shoulder with a terrific whack. It was definitely not a play stroke—catching me unawares, it nearly knocked me over and it came with a blast of pain.

"Ow," I yelled. "What the heck was that for?"

Even as I said it, I realised I had broken an unspoken rule by allowing human words into this game. She gave a firm shake of her head and growled provocatively, daring me to attack. She jabbed at her eyes and her ear, then even mimed a clumsy plodding tramp through the grass for a few steps, the meaning of which was unfortunately clear. Then, in a flash, she was gone again among the bushes and flowerbeds. The dark left blank and as though untouched by human presence.

I stood there with my face burning for a moment, then set out after her with even more determination. A shrill whoop came drifting back and I focussed on it, hoping to get some sense of direction. But then another wild figure came bursting out of the darkness, no more stealthy than I was. When only half seen, the surreal dinosaur face of a cockerel is really quite terrifying. He skidded to a halt, angling those staring mask eyes for a pointed stare. A clash of steel and lightning, before I backed away. Never mind the cockerel. There wasn't much I could do about him, so I carried on stalking through the night in the direction I hoped Star Girl had gone. Every inch of my skin was prickling. I had to do this now I had taken it on—whatever 'this' was.

And Star had to be somewhere . . . over *here*.

To my fury, the exact same thing happened. She saw me before I could get anywhere near—my white mask presumably looming out of the night like a will-o'-the-wisp. Again that shrill alarm call rang out and again she danced round me, just out of reach. It is hard to register fun or playfulness in a masked figure you can hardly see—and for a moment that capering form looked genuinely unnerving. Again she waved that branch of hers. This time I could guess what was coming and had a moment to brace myself—but this time the whippy length of branch landed across my arse, even harder than before. There was a thwack that could be heard across the park and a pain that echoed through my body from head to toe. In response, I wheeled round with a low growl and charged her—by far the most aggressive move I had made yet. I was gratified to see her drop the branch and bolt—less so to see her vanish almost instantly, leaving me lost yet again in the luminous London darkness.

I swore briefly, but very loudly. I was getting fired up here. The fury of the chase had taken me over. I wanted to do this. I wanted to triumph here, not mess around and make a fool of myself. There had to be a way. I was the White Bear, for heaven's sake.

As if to underscore it, another massive commotion soon began nearby. This time, the squirming shadows revealed themselves as Clay Man, in his handsome silver mask, staggering out of the bushes with the Beggar literally on his back, clinging there with arms and legs. He staggered and fell and the Beggar gave a loud whoop of triumph, sitting astride him. Staring at them both, I met her masked eyes for a long moment, and was astonished at the energy in her body. It was telling me to wake up wake up wake up wake up . . .

I stepped away quickly, putting a few areas of bushes between us. It was time to get serious and work out how to crack this problem. By now, this was definitely no longer a game. There had to be a way. I'd show them. *No one* messes with the white bear. I had to move around in this world of grass, bushes and paths without making a noise and as invisibly as possible. I glanced round cautiously. The grass seemed soft and pleasant, well maintained without much alien matter, so I slipped off my shoes and left them leaning against a tree trunk. This was a little risky. Even though it looked the sort of place kids might happily play in the daylight, almost anything could turn up in a London park, with dog shit and broken glass far from the worst. But right then I didn't care—I was happy to take the gamble. This simple act had silenced the scuff scuff of my shoes completely and now I was walking as we were meant to walk. I quietly made my way forward, placing every step with caution. I carried on in the vague direction of where I had last seen Star, hoping she would still be nearby. A brief glimpse of what was probably the Butcher in the middle distance only made me feel more determined. No way was that bastard getting her first. No fucking way.

And there she was. She was sitting by a bush, glancing round cautiously at the dark undergrowth. I had seen her, but she hadn't seen me yet. That was a massive triumph. Immediately, I froze—then backed away out of sight again.

My mapping skills were coming into play now, I realised. I knew Mile End Park—I could put together a precise image in my mind of where the bushes and paths were and what route I could take to get close to her without actually opening up to her line of sight. There—and there—and there . . . a circuitous route that should bring me out directly behind her own bush.

I set off as quickly as I dared. I paced through the grass, occasionally wincing as my feet found something a bit noisier or harder. It took a few minutes but eventually I stole up behind the bush and came to a stop again. If she was still there, she was on the other side, out of line of sight. After a few moments waiting I caught a small shift and a tiny sigh. Every muscle and nerve in my body was tense and straining. So now it was all about silence and infinite caution, trying to stop my clothes from rustling as I worked my way round until I could just see her sitting there—the very tip of her shoe faintly visible in the dark, which I focussed on with pure tunnel vision. For a moment I felt alarmingly like some kind of sexual predator and I hoped no strangers were out there in the dark watching me. And for that matter, no strangers out there that I might descend on out of the dark by mistake. That would be fun. I forced myself to shrug that off, though. This was just play—just play like any young and inexperienced creature might partake in. A quick scan of the terrain I would have to cross—grass—and a quick preparation of every muscle in my body, a little like a cat's infamous bum-wiggle . . .

. . . and then I erupted out of the night at her, blasting through the edge of the bush and descending on where she was sitting like a smiting hand.

She actually gave a shriek and was on her feet in a second—but this time I had too much advantage—I was too close behind her. And I charged after her faster than I could ever remember running in my life—and grabbed her easily, pulling her down into the grass with a screech. My mask had gone askew and for a moment I could see nothing. I was hanging onto her purely using touch and instinct. I shoved the damn thing up onto my forehead, before renewing my grip. She was strong—and it's always a little startling to be reminded of the physical strength of another human body, as though with that comes a realisation of a reality that we are usually cut off from. But she couldn't escape now. We rolled over together for a moment until I got her pinned down securely on her face, one knee in the small of her back, most of my weight on her in a bizarre replay of that first meeting on the railway line. With a wild growl, I sank my teeth into the back of her neck, then bodily rolled her over and, as she scrabbled at me and squirmed, delivered the killing bite right into her throat . . .

She gave a shrill squeal.

Well, it wasn't an actual bite, of course, but it was hard enough to leave faint marks in her skin. And . . . I had her. I had succeeded. I had made the kill. Star Girl's suddenly flaccid body acknowledged that—and I wanted to scream, to howl at the moon. Or whatever equivalent thing it is that bears do. I'm no expert.

But no—it wasn't over yet. Of course it wouldn't be that easy. Something massive suddenly slammed into me, sending me sprawling off her—and I quickly recognised the silhouette of the cockerel mask against the night sky. The Butcher crouched beside me, squatting on his heels with hunched tension, looking less like a bird than like some lethal monkey.

"Mine," he yelled.

For a moment I froze with shock—then I saw red. This was my moment of triumph—and he had to come barging in? I was up again in a moment and facing off with him, feeling a glitter of combat. Then he sprang at me. I grappled with him with all my strength, vaguely aware of Star Girl sitting up and watching with a whoop of excitement. And no—no way was I letting him win anything here. He was the good-looking one. He was the fit and strong one. He was my natural enemy, I saw it now. The type of person who is always standing in my way. Whereas I had only one thing going for me—and I used it. I gave a grating yell and hurled all my weight against him, sending him staggering backwards. Then we crashed over, me on top, and he gave a winded shriek.

"Holy crap, Train Man," he cried. But I was already up again—and now Star Girl was standing before me, eyes huge and shining. And in that moment of celebration, she was no longer the quarry, no longer the victim. She was a fellow celebrant. She stared at me for a moment, arms spread wide, then ran. And I ran. I wasn't sure why, since I had already killed her once, but this game apparently wasn't over yet. Again, I was running harder than I was used to, my lungs screaming in agony at the exertion—but I couldn't help it. I had to follow her.

We dashed through the trees, leaving the Butcher far behind—on and on, round and about until I had lost track of where we were—my maps failing me for once. I only knew that she was ahead of me. Then I crashed round a bush and nearly fell over her, a shadowy figure no longer running but down on the ground. She was crouched on all fours now, staring at me eyes gleaming in the low light—and now I understood. And I landed beside her in a grassy skid. She responded with a shrill growl, driving herself backwards against me. And a moment later we were dry humping. I had her by the hips, driving myself against her buttocks while she grunted and gasped and clawed into the soil with her fingers. I honestly can't remember, but I think I might have been every bit as noisy. I could feel the soft skin below her ribs where I grasped her, the globes of her arse grabbing at my dick hungrily—arching her back downwards with almost ridiculous provocation. And yeah—it would be fine to go and go like this until she came, right there in her camouflage trousers—and . . .

And *what the hell was I doing*?

Reality caught up with me then like a freight train and I came to a stumbling halt, Star Girl's arse still pressed hard against my crotch. For a long moment we remained like that in a tableau, then she quietly disengaged, crawled forward a few feet and sat down on her heels.

"No?" she asked, looking back at me—and behind that mask could have been absolutely anything.

I sat back against a tree, shock and exertion suddenly catching up with me, the freight train finally running me over.

"I would have, Train Man," she said. "If that was part of the game." She tugged at her trousers thoughtfully.

I stared at her—actually wondering whether to restart. But the others were closing in on the racket. The plague doctor had removed his mask (magpie I think) and reverted to the familiar Philosopher, his eyes wide with curiosity. The Butcher still looked winded and pained and I didn't know what I expected behind his bird face. This was the first time I had got a proper look at

Clay Man and he was especially striking in his suit contrasted with a handsome grey and silver fox mask. The Beggar had also removed her mask and was staring at me with a mix of worry and unease. For a game, there was a weirdly serious and complicated atmosphere surrounding us now. How much of that had they all seen? Or heard?

"Game over?" Clay Man asked with a small smile.

Star Girl jumped up, brushing herself down and tugging her trousers straight. "I guess so," she said, removing her mask with a grin. I stared at her. In a very real sense, Star Girl had gone somewhere else for the last half an hour—and it was disorienting to see her back again. In another sense, she had gone nowhere—had been more visible and more there than ever.

"You okay, Train Man?" Clay asked me.

"I . . ." I could barely speak. "Yeah . . ."

"And are you okay, Star?" the Butcher asked, with a weird tone in his voice. I couldn't even bring myself to look at him.

"Absolutely fine," Star said, her voice warm and humorous. She looked at me and nodded. "Barefoot—nice touch."

"That was quite a spectacle," the Philosopher said. "You intrigue me, Train Man—I am starting to think I could write an entire thesis about you."

I didn't answer—indeed I hardly heard. I was staring off into the distance, remembering the recent party now—dancing with Tea on the roof. Maybe that wasn't so different to whatever it was that had just happened. I had a similar feeling of touching something primeval and very dangerous.

I scrambled to my feet slowly, staring from face to face, finally settling on the Butcher.

"Did I hurt you?" I managed at last. It was barely more than a mumble.

"I am going to be taking a few bruises home with me," he said dryly, "but I am sure I will live. I'll tell you something, though. You may be a lard-arse but you are pretty fucking strong."

"I am?"

"I suppose even a cockerel wouldn't have much chance against a polar bear."

"Yes—and that's not the only way you just made history either," the Philosopher said.

"What?"

"I'm pretty sure that's the first time a polar bear ever had sex with a pine marten."

"The mind boggles," Star said with a happy laugh. "And I can't wait to see what weird hybrid we produce."

"Possibly even more terrifying than either," the Beggar murmured.

"Group hug," Star called.

Even that hug had a slightly weird dynamic. I could feel both women very clearly—the Beggar trying to latch onto me, yet still staring at me with a very odd undercurrent. Me, though, I focussed on the Butcher and hugged him tightly. I felt I owed him.

"I feel better for all that," Star said at last.

"What now?" Clay Man said. "Shall we get back?"

"No," I said, surprising myself as much as anyone. "Now we do it for real. Right?"

"You mean go on a hunt?"

"Yes," I said firmly, while a part of me stared in horror and frantically tried to drag me back down to the land inhabited by sensible sane people. "We can try. Let's separate and have a look round, see what we can find—then meet up back at the wall in an hour or so?"

I have to say, the expressions on their faces were rather satisfying. I'd show them. Don't you dare think of me as the useless weakling, the miserable, mixed-up loser ever again. Just don't you dare.

"I agree," Star Girl said.

"I guess we could," Clay Man said. "But carefully, okay? London may be going mad but it's also tight as a drum."

"Yes."

"Very well," Clay said with a shrug. "Give me your masks. I'll pack 'em all away—and let's go."

As the group prepared to separate, the Beggar grabbed my arm. "What are we going to do? You going to join me?"

I hadn't actually thought that far ahead, but I nodded. "That would be good," I said.

"Where should we go, though? I suppose we are not so far from the marshes on the bike . . ."

I looked around the park. In the dark, the bushes and the city as a whole seemed to glitter—that same sense of the Polyhedron underlying everything like a web. And the polyhedron in ourselves as well. My mind was full of images. The rabbit. And Star Girl's words. And my own rage.

And I was hungry.

"Let's see what can we find right here," I said. "Let me just find my shoes . . ."

"Huh?"

"I feel a crack somewhere," I said as we walked. "There are waterbirds here, I believe."

"Are you serious?" she asked dubiously. "This is all a bit . . . public, Train Man."

"This place is as silent as the grave," I said. "I can sense nothing here with us. London is a ghost city tonight."

"If anyone sees you . . ." She gave up and shrugged. "Oh well . . . but carefully. Right?"

"Right," I said, dragging my shoes on and lacing them up. "Let's go."

I was trembling slightly but determined. Insanely so. Maybe this was something about needing to know. Or maybe to taste—experience—feel. Something totally raw. To find out what may lurk down in my depths. I suppose it confuses me as it no doubt confuses you. But I needed to experience this, I had decided. Right then I wanted—needed—to kill. To feel death in my fingers. As if that act would somehow clear the confused stink out of my brain.

I stared briefly round at the clustering buildings.

"Fuck sanity," I yelled, loud enough to make the Beggar flinch. "And fuck nature as well. I *am* nature."

I paced off through park, the Beggar hurrying after me nervously, and soon we were passing moored narrowboats. We walked some considerable distance through Mile End Park and soon I could see waterbirds, poking around on the riverbank as though it was daylight, as temporally confused as the human beings of this city. We kept walking, though, until we arrived at some areas with more cover—where the narrowboats could be left at a safe distance. And here I finally came to a stop and allowed the Beggar to guide me away from the path and in among the bushes.

"Okay," she whispered, "let's see what we can find—but be careful."

"Just keep an eye out for me, please. Make sure there is no one else about."

"You want to . . . ?"

"Yes—this one's mine."

"Very well," she said slowly. "But don't forget there may be people in the boats. Let's just listen. Always listen first to get a picture of the world."

I felt her move up against me, as though using her body to keep me in place there in the dark. We remained as quiet as we could. There was little to hear, though. Little from the outside world, anyway. Standing there with the Beggar beside me, I could actually hear her heart beating—rapidly—as well as the faint sigh of her shallow breath leaving her mouth. I could hear the infinitely quiet scuff of fabric as she breathed. While behind it all, the wind toyed with a million tree leaves. I remembered a strange concert I had heard while at college—even though I wasn't studying an arts related-subject, I was interested enough to follow it and this time a friend had taken me to see a performance of some experimental American music. Among them had been John Cage's 4'33"—literally just four minutes and thirty three seconds of complete silence, with the performer doing almost nothing at all. At the time, it hadn't done much for me, being a somewhat tense period listening to an uneasy audience trying to keep quiet—which, of course, was the whole, slightly jokey, point. Trying to draw attention to the sounds that are always around us. I do remember the shock that came when it was over and the applause started. It seemed very loud and dramatic in contrast. Now though, that whole thing suddenly seemed to make more sense. Silence was indeed impossible—another of those absolutes that humans just cannot find. Always there will be some noise, somewhere. If nothing else, then noises from yourself, from your heart and mind. And what we call silence is thus rendered powerful, with a very good example being these icy few minutes straining our ears for any sound that could be threatening.

But as far as I could tell, we were alone. There were no alien noises. And my attention began to focus. I remained frozen studying the various birds in sight, analysing them. There were ducks and a few geese, no sign of the usual moorhens, though—maybe they had the sense to be sleeping now. Could I trust my body to do this? Even though, compared to any fully natural hunt, this must surely be easy—these trusting birds, so used to humans in the middle distance.

The tension was increasing in me as I watched them—a hunger. A real, urgent, primal, deep-down need. And I allowed that need to quietly take charge of my brain, not blanking out conscious thought but making sure it knew who was boss. Eventually I made a quiet move—not forward but back the way I had come. The Beggar watched me curiously, then followed, but I was skirting round, as before—aiming to come through the trees and ornamental beds to a point much closer to them. It was a creepy raw feeling that was utterly alien to me—a feeling of vestigial instincts battering at the conscious mind. And the strange part was that I could see the exact same forces pushing at the Beggar—detectable in every jittering movement and gesture, and her fast breathing. Indeed, this whole incident, as so many had lately, was turning into a study in communication and awareness on a level other than words. And even as we paced through the bushes, I found myself wondering yet again how much we had lost as we became more and more dependent on our words and language. In a way, they were a bondage, not a liberation, however much they enabled us to discuss and define. Wordless communication was like ice and fire flowing through us—an almost terrifying intimacy.

After a few moments, I was where I planned to be; the birds were still there, close by. I tried to think of myself like the cat—like the hunting spider—like any other hunting animal that I may have seen at one point or another. But still I wasn't sure.

Nothing physical ever seemed to work well for me. At the same time, though, I knew that the one thing that would guarantee failure was to assume I would.

I looked up and down the waterside. London was submerged in quiet—not a trace of other human life. Barely even a murmur of traffic from the distance. So I gathered my muscles together—time to taste blood and violence . . .

. . . and I launched myself forward. I honestly had no idea what I was going to do when I got there, no idea whether I had any hope at all of making a catch—I struck like a spider, coming perilously close to running right into the canal in the process. The birds jumped away in shock as I slammed down, one hand brushing feathers but not getting a hold.

"Go," the Beggar whispered from somewhere—and I went. I don't think my body had ever moved like that before in my entire life. To be honest, I would not have believed it was possible. I had no conscious idea what I was doing, but maybe that's because all this functioned below the level of normal consciousness—vestigial withered instincts that we all possess, creaking and groaning as they were finally allowed to function. I plunged after that bird—a brown-speckled female duck. It stumbled through the grass, wings flapping, trying to get airborne as I followed in a pouncing run. Then it actually lifted itself into the air—and I pushed myself for one last effort. I hurled myself forward, I think actually leaving the ground myself for a moment, and my two hands squarely impacted the duck and dragged it down again in a flurry of wings. It fluttered and squawked as I landed in the grass, my fingers clawing for a hold.

And I had it. There was a massive flurry, wings flapping crazily. I stared down at it for a fraction of a second—then sank my teeth in.

Chaos. Feathers in my face, a clamour of anguished squawking, which was quickly echoed by every other bird in Mile End Park. Feathers in my mouth, tangled in my teeth—then a wash of blood. And I was actually growling as I crouched over that bird—a dull noise in the back of my throat worse than anything the white bear had produced—as I tore at flesh, spitting out mouthfuls of down then going in for more. A snap of bone between my teeth.

And then something hit me very hard on the side of the head.

I tumbled over sideways, with a yell and the bird staggered away a few yards, too wounded to fly or even walk properly.

"What the heck are you doing?" the Beggar hissed—seeming little more than a huge pair of eyes staring down at me, holding her hand awkwardly. I registered her, registered that I had been punched—and then the freight train of reality was thundering down on me again . . .

I slowly scrambled up onto my knees, blood and matter dribbling down my chin, spitting out a few last feathers. She had hit me with her open hand, hard enough to knock me off balance, but I felt as though I had been hit by a wrecking ball. A mental wrecking ball that had taken down my mind in one smash.

The Beggar turned away then as though remembering something. She swooped on the duck and there was a flash of metal. In a second, she had decapitated it, chucking the head away into the bushes. To my amazement, the body went struggling away in spite of the lack of a head, legs jittering and trembling. Then it slumped into stillness. Another stroke of the wrecking ball. Swinging like a pendulum.

There was a long silence.

"Train Man?" she managed at last, worried caution in her voice.

I couldn't speak. I thought for a while then that I might be dumb for the rest of my life. I managed to shake my head, flapping my hands uselessly. "I . . . I'mmng gooinngg," I managed at last, staggering to my feet. "I'm sssssss . . ."

Where was I? I needed that train NOW. *Please. Train. Anywhere. Train train train TRAIN.*

"No," she said sharply, eyebrows up and eyes huge. "Wait . . ."

I ignored her, though, and made to move away, such a tension inside me that I think I was twitching uncontrollably.

"Wait," she yelled, grabbing my arm and yanking me to a halt so hard that I almost fell over again. "For gawd sake—come here."

She was dragging me away, pausing only a moment to shove the dead duck out of sight under a bush with her foot. We walked some little distance, me not resisting, before she sat me down on a bench. I stared up at her dizzily, wondering what the heck was going to happen next. I was expecting all sorts of crazy things for a moment—that she'd hit me again, even that her knife would flash a second time and go right into my chest. Even her long nose looked aggressive—a bird's beak that could inflict a serious wound. Such thoughts made my skin burn in horrified deranged anticipation. I cringed as she reached into a pocket and pulled something out—a small square packet—then again at the sharp little rip as she opened it—then leaned back in panic as she approached.

But all that came was a dabbing at my face and neck—the cool flash of a wet wipe.

She worked for a moment in silence, then turned to my hands. I watched forlornly, feeling not unlike whatever fictional murderer it was whose hands were stained with blood that would never wash off. I wondered if these stains would likewise ever go. But of course, they did. Quite easily.

Then my shirt.

I could hear her breathing—almost a language in itself. Still uneasy. Slightly deeper as her eyebrows contracted in a frown. *Harder. Not coming off.* Rub rub rub. Then a relax as she paused a moment. Scrape with fingernail at some bloody debris. More rubbing. A slight sigh.

"Okay," she said at last. "Your clothes aren't perfect, but it's less obtrusive now. You might not be wearing that shirt again, though."

I just stared straight ahead.

She drew a deep, hollow breath, then sat down heavily beside me. Her hips were lightly touching mine—only a few square centimetres of fabric but I could feel the tension in her, clashing with mine in ways that ought to have caused a flash of light. "Train Man?" she murmured.

I couldn't answer. I couldn't even move my face. I still felt utterly frozen—as complete an ice-up as anything I could remember.

"Train Man . . . ?"

She finally turned to stare at me.

"I had to stop it," she said. "That's not . . . you looked as though you had gone somewhere very strange for a moment. That's not what it's about."

More silence.

"Okay," she whispered, sounding weirdly matter of fact, as though she was an instructor determined to be modern and reasonable, no matter what. "I always thought . . . this stuff . . . killing . . . is nothing to do with being brutal and macho and aggressive—it can be gentle. Respectful. Even loving. For our sake as much as anything, I admit. It's just a simple experience of the way the world works and our place in the circle of nature. It makes you think about your own mortality as well—and makes you appreciate your own life more. And it definitely makes you feel more connected to the natural world—more a part of it instead of some weird spectator. That's what I always thought, anyway."

"Please don't," I muttered. "Don't . . . sssssay any . . . thing . . ."

"For gawd sake, Train Man," she muttered, looking even more uncomfortable—and that tiny moment of intensity was enough to make me flinch away again with a jolt.

Silence stretched out for a few more eternal moments.

"Talk to me, please," she said, looking really scared.

"Fuck nature," I yelled, unexpectedly loud, my voice going shrill.

I had yelled that before, I realised.

"Why?" she echoed, still keeping that carefully reasonable tone of voice.

"I think nature is the evil one," I muttered. "Nature doesn't care. If that was my animal nature . . ."

"I dunno," she said. "Instincts you have never used before can be ferocious. They can run into overdrive simply because you never learnt to use them. You repress things, never learn to do anything other than hide them, and that only makes them explode more violently."

I stared at her—and yes, looking back on it, I know that was true. These were dead instincts. Or rather atrophied ones. And thus almost impossible to control. It's the same with everyone—we all have these big powerful instincts of various kinds that no one ever teaches us how to use. And when they end up taking the driving seat, you realise you have no control and they can end up going off like thunderflashes. If you have never had to fight or attack before, when you are finally on the spot and need to, or when your temper is pushed so astronomically far that you snap, you might well respond with spectacular screaming overkill simply because you don't know how to measure it. Sex is the same. You grow up with no guidance whatever, in a world that is totally confused—and when the instincts are finally activated, the flash and the bang can be cataclysmic. You end up losing it completely, clumsily reaching out and trying to grab, making bungled attempts to connect or seduce that are seen as aggressive. You don't know what you are doing simply because you never learned to control these things—because those instincts have never had any chance to stretch and flex.

Such thoughts weren't much use at the time, though.

"Are you okay?" she said.

The Beggar slid a comforting arm round my shoulders. I tasted the sensation for a moment, then guardedly allowed myself to relax. Not much, though. I felt as though I had done something unforgivable. But her touch was soothing. "Calm down, Train Man—it's okay. There's no sense in getting any kind of moral standpoint on nature—what is is, that's all. And whatever you do, don't think in black and white. Haven't we convinced you of that yet?"

"Okay," I breathed. "But then what's our place in it?"

"Hmm?"

"I mean . . . are we supposed to be the same? Or are we something different? Is there something wrong with me? Or are you the freak for caring? I just don't understand . . ."

"I don't know either," she said yet again. "It's a contradiction, isn't it? I was aware of it ever since those old days when I started hunting out of desperation—and I don't know what it means. But maybe sometimes one has to be the compassionate human—sometimes one has to be the great bear. And one has to control both."

"So—a balancing act?" I said earnestly. "Two . . . things. Won't comfortably sit side by side? The logical brain can't process it, the heart can't process it. So—what else is there?"

"According to the Philosopher, there's navigating by the seat of the pants?" she suggested with a grin. "Remember? It's not just the head and heart that you have to keep in balance. It's your arse, too. And maybe sometimes you have to let your heart and brain do the following."

That got a small smile from me—shaky but grasping at normality again. "So when Dorothy went to see the Wizard," I said, "maybe it was a shame that there was nobody with her who needed to find an arse?"

She gave a relieved laugh and patted her backside. "I guess this knows as much as any other bits," she said. "It's a good enough symbol of something, I am sure. People who forget their arses are doomed to incompletion." She gave a shrill laugh. "What the heck am I talking about, Train Man?"

"Makes sense," I said gloomily. "In some weird way." Now that the talk was just about flowing again, my voice was sounding a little closer to normal. But in spite of her presence leaning against me, her body in contact from thigh to shoulder, her breath in my ear, I still couldn't let the tension go.

"Come on," she said at last. "Let's get back home. Or whatever that place is."

"Are we just going to abandon that duck, then?" I asked expressionlessly. Part of me wanted to do precisely that—not wanting to deal with the bloody results of my outburst—and even less wanting anyone else to see it.

"Of course we fucking aren't. I just didn't want it near while I was trying to bring you back down to earth."

We walked back through the park to where a huddle of brown feathers waited under the bush. I stood there while the Beggar dragged it out and turned it over thoughtfully.

"It's not too bad," she said. "I seem to have cut off most of the mess when I took the head off."

After a quick look around, she bundled it into several layers of plastic bag, and in turn into her rucksack.

"Star Girl has brought back worse," she said brusquely. "Right—let's go."

I didn't bother saying anything as we found the bike and mounted it—or as we made our slightly unstable way back down the canal towards the watergate. I didn't want to start moaning and agonising any more—there seemed no point. It had all been said, by me and by her. I suppose I could have asked her to repeat things and repeat things until my muddled instincts somehow started making sense again—maybe I should have. But I didn't. Instead there was nothing to do except spend a lifetime trying to sort out which parts of my thoughts and reactions were real and which were fake. And even that may have been a pointless exercise.

✧

"Oh dear," the Beggar said, flashing a lighter and lighting a candle. "We forgot to clear up the rubbish last time."

Bowls were still arrayed on the boxes and on the floor, a few knocked over and scattered. The stuff we had put in rubbish bags had been ripped out again as well, proving that we were not the only things with access to this place. Maybe it was birds, since it was hard to imagine foxes scaling the ladder down here. Scraps of cooked meat and bones were everywhere.

"That was clever."

I stared round, feeling even more discomforted. But she just shrugged with a grin. "I suppose we had better clean this mess up," she said.

I gave a restive nod. This was almost the same smell that had haunted the roof of my home. It was a smell that got under my skin, especially now.

"Fuck," I muttered, uncharacteristically for me. "That is not nice."

She dragged out a rubbish bag and started casually picking up the bits. There was nothing for me to do except join her, gritting my teeth slightly at the touch of those stale morsels. But it was okay—she bustled round, as though it was the most ordinary thing in the world—and maybe it was to her. That helped me shrug it off. We loaded up the bag quickly enough, then sealed it.

"Better already," she said, cleaning her hands with a wet wipe. "Don't worry about it now—we'll take it back with us tonight and dump it. I'll just double-bag it so it doesn't smell so . . ."

She did so.

"I wonder where the others are?" she said at last, flopping into the sofa next to me, Clay Man's unfinished artwork looming above her.

"Maybe we are the only two nuts enough to have tried anything so close to home."

"Maybe," she said with a smile. "They might be a while yet—but hey, that could be kind of nice too." She grabbed my arm and I glanced at her, feeling a prickle. She had been rather quiet for most of the journey, I realised—which was undoubtedly a humanism for being very loud indeed, but in ways that didn't include words.

"You know it's fucking weird," she said at last. "The people who mean more to me than anyone else in the world, by a long long way, and I am not even allowed to know who they are, what their names are, where they live . . . fucking weird. I'm not sure I like it. But Clay Man—he's cautious." She sighed. "I don't even know who you are, Train Man," she said.

I was tempted to tell her my name and address right then, but there was a scuffle of footsteps, and Clay Man, the Butcher and the Philosopher came clattering in all at once. I have this feeling that I saw the faintest glimmers of annoyance cross her face at the interruption, but it passed in a moment and then it was all eager greetings.

"What's that smell?" Clay Man demanded uneasily.

"Like a bunch of idiots we went and left the rubbish here last time," the Beggar said cheerfully. "We got everything except that, it seems."

Clay Man looked taken aback. "Did we?" he asked in surprise.

"The remains were all over the floor."

He sighed. "Oh well—hopefully we can forgive ourselves that one blunder," he said with a smile.

Then Star Girl dropped in and came scampering down the ladder. It was immediately clear that she was still as full of furious energy as she had been an hour or so ago, and she almost immediately dragged everyone within reach into a group hug. It was an enthusiastic one even by Star's standards—she actually left the ground, trying to wrap her legs around whoever happened to be within range. She ended up falling through the clutching arms and landing on her back on the floor, laughing and flushed.

"Good old Star," the Butcher murmured, giving her a poke in the ribs with his foot.

"Any luck, anyone?" Clay Man asked. "I have two bottles of wine and some treats here. So even with that we can relax nicely."

"Nothing from me," Star said sadly. "There wasn't that much time . . ."

The Beggar and I exchanged glances and she gave a grin. "Worry not," she said. "We have a little something here."

"You got dinner?"

"Indeed we have," the Beggar said, opening her bag. "One duck for you layabouts."

"Nice one," the Butcher said. "Well done, Beggar."

"Actually, it wasn't me," she said with a smile, while I screwed up my face. I would have been quite happy for her to lie about that.

"Really? Congrats, Train Man. Nicely done," Clay Man enthused.

I found myself blushing in extreme embarrassment and the Beggar gave me a sly look. But I have to admit, it seemed nice, in a way. It really was, whatever you might think. The group was going to eat, and I was the one who had provided. Not in the cloying sense of making money or tramping to the shops, but in a much purer and more personal sense.

Oh well.

"Nice one," Star Girl said, leaping to her feet again. "Let's get plucking."

"Allow me," the Butcher said. He placed the duck on the table and put a pot of water on to boil. Star and the Beggar sat down beside him and the rest of us followed. I am not sure now precisely what he did—the details of butchery are rather a blur to me. I suppose I could have used anonymity systems and stealth browsing to 'go dark' on the internet and research this—I could have provided a full how-to here for you, dear reader, in the unlikely event that you ever find yourself in this situation. I could have made this book into an underground cookbook in the true sense of the term. A really dedicated writer might have done just that—but hey, the internet makes me nervous these days. I wonder what it was like in the heady free days when you could research almost anything, when it really might have changed the world—before the collective humanity realised that the absolute last thing it wanted was people able to research almost anything. Knowledge = perversion, they decided. Nowadays you might as well watch TV because wherever you look, all you see is a drip-feed of controlled news and facts. But anyway—all I remember was him dunking the bird in the hot water, presumably to scald it, and then the feathers were flying. A sodden, wet mess. And I watched with predictable mixed feelings—among which I won't deny a dose of curiosity.

"Come on, Train Man," Star Girl yelled, making me jump out of my skin. "You look like a lifelong prude who is trying to have sex for the first time."

I glared at her in surprise. She still seemed to be in an exceptionally wild mood—a look in her eyes that I was starting to recognise. A look of one who seemed capable of anything.

"You need to find that white bear again," she cried, slapping me hard on the shoulder. It was still very slightly sore from the whack she had given me with that branch and I flinched. For a brief moment, I wanted to growl at her, but I quickly swallowed that.

"Maybe, maybe," I said. But did I? I had *found* the white bear—or at least I thought I had—and I felt as though my soul was never going to recover from the shock.

"Yes maybe," Star said, jumping to her feet, suddenly blazing with energy. "You must be ready to stand up and bellow in the night—then tear the world to rags." She was dancing round the room again now, a frenetic and jerky motion closer to performance art than anything else. Even the Butcher came to a halt, feathers in hand, watching her. "Unlike those fuckers," she said, glaring at the ceiling as though everything that crushed her down was literally overhead.

"What fuckers?" the Philosopher asked.

"Those fuckers," she said, gesturing at the whole world. "Those fuckers who took my revolution and turned it into a load of insane people mooning around like entranced fairies. You could have smashed it all—destroyed those in power instead of trashing a few buildings and wandering round in tears. We could have kicked the fucking lot of them into the Thames and destroyed this stifling mess once and for all. But instead we all just wandered about, weeping and wailing, then went meekly home, got a day off work and listened to the fucking mayor telling us what cowards we are."

She actually shook her fist at the ceiling, breathing heavily and with a wide grin on her face.

"Fuck*errrrrrrrs*," she yelled at the top of her voice.

"Gawd, sit down," Clay Man exploded. It was an unexpected outburst—not very loud but forceful enough for all our eyes to jump round to him.

"Huh?" Star demanded.

"Sorry," Clay Man said. "I'm starting to feel as though everyone is going mad tonight. Myself included. I'm not sure I can cope with yelling right now."

"Oh, fuck you," Star muttered, but she did as he asked and landed heavily in the chair beside me.

"Seriously," Clay Man said. "What the fuck is going on? Does anyone know yet?"

There was a very loud silence. The Beggar and I exchanged glances. Then the Philosopher coughed quietly.

"It's as if all our normal instincts have broken down somewhat," he said softly. "Or rather—not our normal instincts maybe, but our cultural restraints and self-censorship. And something is being carried between us all. Throughout the city."

The silence returned while we digested that sonorous yet not very informative comment.

"If it leads to us getting naked and dancing around then maybe it's no bad thing," the Butcher said with a smile, delicately plucking a last few feathers from the now nude duck.

"A naturist is born," Star Girl said with a grin.

"And you fucking loved it," he retorted.

"Alright—two nudists are born."

"Actually," the Beggar murmured, "maybe three." She gave a slightly bashful grin.

The Philosopher shrugged. "Things carried through the air," he said, staring off into the distance. "Like germs. Diseases of the emotions. Or weather phenomena of the human soul."

It was obvious there was something he wanted to express, and these teaser phrases were just skating round the edge of it.

"What are you blathering about?" Star demanded.

He smiled. "Does anyone remember the stories of the demon-haunted schoolgirls of Kyoto?" he asked.

Everyone looked blank. I had seen people doing a lot of things in the last few days, but demonic possession had definitely not entered my head.

"It's one of those strange stories that get shared around occasionally," he said with a smile. "A decade or so ago I think."

It was ringing faint bells, actually. Somewhere in my directionless wanderings online, I had seen this. "Girls' school?" I murmured, trying to remember. "Epidemic of fainting?"

"Right—or more accurately seizures and other strange behaviour. If I remember correctly, about three hundred pupils were affected and the school was temporarily closed amid talk of demonic possession. Tsukimono or something. That means the 'Possessing Things'. And yet, they could find nothing wrong."

"Mass hysteria?"

"Right," he repeated. "The pressure was intense, as you can imagine. I am not a fan of exams. They are bad enough anywhere but we can imagine what the, shall we say, somewhat rigid social framework of Japan would do to them."

Everyone was staring at him in silence now, waiting for him to get to the point.

"What probably happened was that the stress became too much and eventually someone experienced a form of breakdown. That is no surprise. The curious part was that it acted as a nucleus for others. An excuse, if you like, but not a conscious one. The same symptoms of fainting, seizures and fits hit more and more people in a chain reaction until the school was shut down in a panic. But as I said, there was nothing physically wrong with them, it seems. It was a contagion—but not of anything physical. You might call it a disease of the emotions. Pressure finding a chance to release energy the moment it got something to latch on to—like opening a bottle of fizzy water."

"So . . . you think this is something similar?" Clay Man asked with a frown.

"I do not know. I am thinking aloud. I might be talking nonsense."

"It's not such an unusual story," Star Girl said. "I remember others . . . uncontrollable laughter that just went on and on, spreading through a community?"

"Yes."

"Contagious crying. Even contagious dancing? Or am I going nuts here?"

"No. There was the famous dancing plague way back in the 16th century in Strasbourg. This seems to be just some barely known way that the human animal responds to what is going on around them. A physiological and psychological reaction to the environment."

"Yeah, but what's this got to do with . . ."

"When you get down to it, how different is a riot?"

There was a silence.

"Yeah, but people riot for a reason."

"Well—sort of. Sometimes. It's a release of tension, with or without a direct immediate cause. The Tsukimono-haunted schoolgirls were reacting for a reason, as well—to release the pressure and defuse an increasingly impossible situation. And there must be reasons for the others if we could only see it."

In the silence that followed, the Butcher flourished his knife with a theatrical gleam. With a certain perverted delight, he was making quite sure I was watching him again before he moved on to the next stage of the butchery—the knife slicing through flesh. And I was watching, albeit with a certain tension. A part of me was determined to watch every part of this now.

"You know," Clay Man said, "for all its cold heart, London does still have an identity. If you are here for any time, you are a Londoner. You are a part of this place—it holds you in its hands. And if you wound the city, we all feel it. Whether we love the place or not."

"And oh boy has it been wounded," Star said sourly. "For years. And years. And years. It's practically the living dead."

The Philosopher nodded. "That's what I was wondering about," he said. "Maybe anger is actually the easiest thing of all to transfer through this circuitry? But other things, too. Even, in some bizarre way, a liberation of our natures. A sense of letting go. Wandering around naked, leaving doors open, strange predatory behaviour—and a million other things that follow deep and faded instincts. They are all a kind of . . . letting go. Even us, maybe. After all—we have also been going pretty wild, right?"

There was a silence again for a while as we tried to digest that, tried to decide whether it was genius or nonsense—and whether we could ever know.

"The news should be interesting over the next few days, that's all I can say," Star Girl muttered. "God forbid there's any kind of liberation of our natures in this world. They won't like that."

"It will be interesting to see if anyone learns anything from it," the Philosopher said, "or whether it will just be shoved out of the way as an aberration."

"Who knows," Clay Man said gloomily.

By this time, the Butcher had his hands deep inside the duck and was quietly extracting various parts of it. It seemed a messy, squishy job—surprisingly bloodless, but not fluidless. As he was working, to my mild shock, a couple of gleaming orange spheres fell out onto the table. They looked almost like fruit.

"Cool," the Beggar said picking one up. "A nice little bonus, Train Man."

"The Duck that Laid the Golden Eggs," Star Girl said happily.

Without any warning of what she was about to do, the Beggar had put one to her lips and sucked the contents out. I stared at her, feeling a twinge of gag reflex in my throat.

"Eggs," Star Girl explained. "Very very young eggs." She also took one and sucked it dry, with an approving look on her face. "It's egg yolk, basically."

"Oh . . . right," I said, still feeling a little clobbered.

The Butcher was still ferreting around inside trying to get everything out that might conceivably come out—whatever mysterious organs life had seen fit to place inside us all. And eventually, it seemed to be done. Star Girl held up the duck with a smile. "And the anatomy lesson continues. Behold what we all are in essence—a tube filled with tubes."

I stared down at the squidgy mess that had been extracted. The miracle of life reduced to a slightly gross pile of wobbly bits.

"And just remember," Star Girl said, "if anyone tells you you've got or need to have guts or need to be gutsy, this is what they mean. Squidgy, formless, slightly smelly and full of shit . . ."

"This especially applies to the military," the Butcher added, "and possibly to that crap about faint hearts and fair ladies."

"Noted," I said dryly.

"I wish we had a fresh water supply," he said wearily, as he grabbed another bottle.

"Well, beggars can't be choosers," the Beggar said with a grin, picking over the guts, sorting out various other parts that, in my anatomical ignorance, I couldn't even begin to identify. Presumably they were edible. Indeed, when she was done, there seemed very little left in the waste pile. A small squidgy heap, which she shovelled into a bowl.

"I will get rid of this stuff," she said, jumping up and making for the exit. "Feed the gulls."

"Good," the Butcher said. "Now—ideally we should leave it for half a day or so to age—that makes it tenderer. But we don't have the time for that so what say? A fairly long slow roast in its own juice? I think we have enough gas. Maybe we can grab a few hours' sleep even . . ."

"That sounds divine," Star Girl said, "but crisp it up at the end, right?"

"Of course," he said. "What kind of cook do you think I am?"

"I can't even think of a joke to answer that," she said. "I'll set up the chimney while you finish off."

The Butcher started slinging seasoning around, rubbing it into the bird then wrapping it tightly with foil and arranging it in a baking dish.

Meanwhile, Star had attached the long exhaust duct to the oven and run with it to the entrance hole. There was a whir as the extractor fan came to life—the only bit of electrical kit in the hideaway.

"One day we are going to gas ourselves to death, I am sure of it," she said, returning. "Clay? Your detector in working order?"

"It is," he said. "All sorted?"

"Yup."

"Detector?" I asked.

"Uh-huh—gas detector. We're in a rather badly ventilated space here. The last thing we want is to be suffocated by exhaust gasses."

I glanced round uneasily. That hadn't occurred to me before, but yes, with only one small opening high up, a mishap with the stove would not be good. Already some faint smells of cooking were starting to permeate this little home of ours, though. The Beggar rejoined us, drying her hands, and we passed through into the next room and sat down. Clay Man poured out wine and we sat there and relaxed, chatting idly about various things that I don't really need to relate here, as the night crept further and further into emptiness and darkness. Then Clay Man raised his glass. "Okay my lovely friends," he said. "May I suggest a toast of some kind? Not quite sure to what, though. Would anyone care to nominate?"

"To the London Madness?" Star Girl suggested. "May it not just fade away but usher in a whole new world."

Clay Man gave a quiet smile.

"To London?" the Butcher suggested. "Our crippled, bigoted, gangrenous but still rather irresistible friend?"

"Sounds good," Star said with a grin.

"It's survived for long enough in spite of everything—I don't think we need to worry about it too much," Clay Man said.

"To doing the undiscussable and discussing the unthinkable?" the Philosopher suggested. "Or in my case—watching people do the undiscussable."

"Train Man?" Clay Man prompted.

I hesitated.

"To curves," I said with a smile. Everyone gave me puzzled looks, but I ignored that and took a quiet drink. The Beggar chuckled and did the same.

"Aah fuck it," the Butcher said. "We all know what our own toasts should be." He drained his glass in one. The Beggar did likewise, then lay back in her chair, leaning against me and giving me a tipsy look, eyes shining in the candlelight.

"To that," Clay man said with a smile. "And to whatever the fuck is going on in this world."

The rest of them drained their glasses.

We must have talked more, but it was low-grade stuff, and I think I or we fell asleep somewhere soon after that, only to be wakened again by the beeping of the Butcher's alarm clock—meaning that it was time to eat. Or rather, time to sit around in increasingly hungry impatience as the Butcher fussed over the duck. He was a perfectionist, no doubt about it.

When he finally brought it to the table, it looked truly like a grand centrepiece from the old days when a fine roast dinner would be among a family's most glorious moments. He had prepared various vegetable dishes as well, including mashed potato, spinach with peanuts and mushrooms in garlic butter—and even a thick classic gravy. The smells were, I have to say, exquisite.

"Wow, Butcher," Clay Man said. "I think you have outdone yourself."

"A vote of thanks to our resident great chef," Star Girl said happily. "And of course—to the hunter that caught it with his bare hands . . . thanks Train Man."

I glowed at that, I really did.

Food was doled out—lots of food. Slices of duck and crispy skin. And again I felt that twang—the flesh-phobia that I would probably never escape entirely. But I shooed such thoughts away as well as I could—watching with interest as Star Girl eagerly reached out and took a slice, the others following her. I watched the oil running down her chin as she engulfed it whole and chewed. I watched her rub it away inelegantly and send me a big-eyed grin.

"Beautiful," she said. "Oh gawd—food orgasms. I am having food orgasms, I swear it." She squirmed exaggeratedly in her chair.

The Butcher gave a loud laugh. "Then my life has meaning."

"I have to agree," Clay Man said. "You can't beat a duck. You two have brought us a treat."

And it was the resulting glow, coupled with Star's dramatic reaction, that saw off the last of my unease this time. There was an energy in the room, a strange but simple energy of predation, and I wanted to be a part of it. I was not going to crumple and waver and be pathetic—not going to let my nerves interfere with the almost sexual look on Star Girl's face. So I took one—and ate.

The taste itself as I chewed was striking—a much richer flavour than the rabbit. I closed my eyes and tried to analyse it. The flavour made me feel as though I was swallowing something from the earth itself, and suddenly it clicked. The earth, nurturing and fertile, stinking and powerful—I could imagine it, heaving with decay and life. And then the plants, drawing on that—ruthlessly sucking that life up into themselves, only to be food in turn. The earth made leaf made flesh. The red blood that had been alive just hours before was a life essence, not a death essence—it had nurtured a powerful and beautiful animal, building this flesh that I now chewed. And now the life essence was flowing into me as well. Its energy and strength, far beyond my own. I was eating the earth itself, assuaging my own hunger and predatory instincts, like the wolf, or the lion—or I suppose like the white bear—and with that thought, I relaxed. And the mouthful of meat slipped down my throat as easily as you could wish.

"You guys don't mind if I masturbate over my next one do you?" Star asked, taking a second with a cheeky grin.

"Be my guest," the Butcher said. "I am sure it's the reaction any chef secretly hopes for."

I took another slice as well.

"Wow," I murmured seriously.

"I wish I had a boyfriend waiting at home," Star said with a smile, when she had made it vanish. "I have literally—managed to turn myself on now." She gave a shrill giggle, her face a little flushed. "I think I am still a little fired up." She flashed me a very brief grin.

"Well if you will talk about masturbation at the dinner table," the Philosopher said with a smile.

"Maybe you will have to make do with a more casual arrangement," the Butcher said, equally cheekily.

"Maybe, maybe," she said, staring dreamily off into space.

I watched her curiously—feeling a slight thrill. She wasn't kidding, I could tell. You can't be a lonely guy with an internet connection without developing quite a good sense for such things. I glanced round and saw that the Beggar was also watching her with interest, before meeting my eyes with a wry grin.

"Have some more, Star," the Butcher said happily. "I have *never* had this kind of reaction to my cooking before."

Star sat up, her face going even redder with humorous embarrassment.

"Okay—okay," she said with a laugh. "Sorry folks—normal service will be resumed very shortly."

We continued eating in silence until, a good many slices later, Clay Man put the empty plate of bones on the floor. Nobody really seemed inclined to talk. Instead everyone looked thoughtful and serene.

"That was quite profound," Clay Man said with a smile. "Thank you, duck."

"Yeah," Star said with a smile. The flush on her face had mostly faded now, but she still looked serene.

✧

A few minutes later, the Beggar shifted with a frown. "Maybe it is this strange night, but I feel restless now," she said lazily. "I need to move. Train Man, would you like to see a secret?"

"Flashing your pussy again, Beggar darling?" the Butcher asked dryly. "I thought we did enough of that last time."

The Beggar gave him a glance. "Real secrets," she barked, then laughed.

"Some secrets are born of necessity, some are born of cowardice," the Philosopher intoned solemnly. "And some of total illusion."

"Shaddup," the Beggar said. "Anyway, you are forgetting one, my dear Philosopher."

"I am?"

"Secrets born from sheer forgetfulness. And that is the case with what I would like to show you, Train Man—and not the case with my pussy."

"If you say so," Star Girl said dryly.

"The pussy is a part of the anatomy that is never forgotten, this is true," the Philosopher said. "And nor is it a secret from any kind of necessity, as far as I can tell."

"It's not a secret at all," Star Girl said with a laugh, framing a lewd triangle between her legs with both hands. "Sorry Train Man—scintillating conversations we have around here."

"Train Man knows," the Butcher said, leaning back elegantly. "Train Man knows everything. I bet he's got your pussy mapped as clearly in his head as the Sea Wall Rail Line."

I found myself grinning. There was a warmth about the banter, whatever the subject, that left a pleasant glow inside me—a glow of friendliness.

"Though I still need to learn the schedule of services," I murmured. Star Girl gave a shrill giggle and crossed her legs.

"Train Man makes a dirty joke," the Beggar said with a quiet grin. "I guess that means you are finally one of us."

She jumped to her feet.

"Come on," she said. "Never mind these dirty-minded tossers."

I was a little reluctant to move at all, the atmosphere was so tranquil. The glow of the candles had never looked warmer. "Where are we going?" I asked with a smile.

"You'll see," she said.

Star Girl gave a quiet laugh. "Come on, Train Man—just shift your arse, okay?"

The Beggar hurried into the next arch and I reluctantly downed the last of my wine, hauled myself to my feet and followed her. She gave a quirky and faintly challenging glance back at the others, then we set out—up the ladder to the platform, carefully through the curtain to hide the light, along the wall, down to the rough concrete below and out across the Soak—broken slabs and mud hollows, soon fading into scattered areas of seagrass and barnacles.

"Have you ever been out here before?" the Beggar asked. I shook my head. For all my knowledge of London, I had never ventured into the forbidden places until the day Star Girl had gone arse over tip on top of me on the railway line. I had them roughly mapped in my head, of course. I knew the layout, knew some of the buildings that had been left to stand forlornly in the mud of the encroaching Thames. But that was all. I stared up at the looming ruins with interest.

"Very few people ever come here," the Beggar said. "Cut off by rail and water, but I like to explore. I like to find places where I can be. And you know, private places in the city are so rare. Even the others don't come out here much."

I looked at the increasing mud warily. It was deep and soft—not inviting.

"It's fine if you keep to the concrete and the patches of shingle," she said, reading my mind. "This way."

We slowly picked our way out across the Soak through the darkness, our way lighted by nothing more than the Beggar's faint torch. The water quickly invaded my shoes, which paid only a token lip-service to waterproofing, and I winced at the feeling. But at the same time I was looking round curiously. The buildings loomed around us like massive tombstones, old brick and plaster and concrete, black with sea growth. We passed through them, then crossed an ancient footbridge over what had once been Limehouse Cut before the sea invaded. The mud and sea life deepened as we progressed, looking more and more like a tidal zone and less and less like a city, muddy channels and green algae sliming over everything. I was wary at first, carefully following the Beggar's footsteps, but as we progressed I began to get more of a feel for this strange land. More of a sense of which areas would support me and which would suck my feet down into black, squelching caverns. My eyes were getting used to the darkness as well. Many of the buildings around us had been bulldozed, seemingly at random, but plenty still remained like rotten teeth. There was no sign of human life here—only the sea wall behind us topped with its garnish of railway catenaries and the cluster of lighted windows poking over it from beyond.

I was stunned—stunned at these strange ghosts of the old city—the London that had been before. And I found myself wondering then whether it might be possible to explore further—the vast areas of Soak beyond Canary Warf, for instance, stretching as far as Grays and the endless marshes to the east. What were these places like? Somewhere out there, even the remains of the old city airport lay caked in mud and brine . . .

We arrived at a road . . . I am going to guess it was the remains of Narrow Street on the older maps, now eaten away in a mess of potholes. We didn't linger, though, just passed through an alleyway of exceptionally squelchy mud between the old buildings.

And then—there was the Thames. The original old bank of the Thames. I stepped forward, then stopped, realising that the solid ground ended here. Deep black water, rippling tranquilly—the rusting half-dead remains of a fence. And the view suddenly opening out to the galaxy of lights on the far side.

It was a disorienting feeling, stumbling around in the dark through this mud and concrete wasteland, such narrow ways and ruins, and then having it suddenly stop and dump you in the vast river. A few more steps and I might have gone right in.

"There was never any promenade or river walk here," the Beggar said. "At least—I don't see one. All this was private. And we—go in here."

She led me along the very edge of the water for a few yards, flashing her torch around, until we arrived at what had once been a door. It had been sealed off like most of them here, but the bars and chains had been busted open again and now it was nothing more than an oblong hole slimed with algae. We passed inside and the Beggar snapped on a tiny torch. Further holes spelt out the windows, but aside from that, the room within had been stripped utterly. Nothing but bare walls. On them, a startlingly regular banding of sea growth rose up—black seaweed at the lowest level, studded with mussels, segueing abruptly into filamentous green, segueing again into a dull green-brown dusting studded with the grey of barnacles. Then, above that, nothing but ruined plaster. It was a place that gave me a curious feeling—a sense of a singingly beautiful ruin, for all it had been an ordinary house. Like a dream, the intrusion of this brutal sea growth into the familiar lines of a home came with a surreal jolt and I stared round in awe.

The dark here was intense—a rare darkness in the city. But I could make out a staircase climbing up one side of the building, vanishing into the ceiling, and the Beggar gestured at it with a flash of light. Up we went, our feet tramping through those layers of sea life, sending winkles tumbling to the floor. The next storey was more mundane, still an almost stripped ruin of a home—just a few amorphous piles of debris and fabric left over from what it had once been. Away from the sea, there were hints of a delicate blue on the walls as the torch flashed around the rooms that opened off the landing—the remains of long forgotten paintwork. There were also a few spray-painted images—tags and graffiti art.

"One more floor," she said, and we continued up the staircase. I could remember a time not so long ago when even this small climb would have left me puffed and miserable, but now I was managing it fine. I can't thank my few cycle rides for that yet, but I can thank the energising effect of having connections to people—and of relaxation, of no longer fighting with the pavement every second of my life. We arrived at the next landing, presumably the last since there were no further stairs that I could see, and here the house was even more intact. Of the two rooms leading off here, one even still had a door on it, which the Beggar pushed open.

"Here we are," she said, shining the torch around. "Welcome home."

"Home?" I said, peering round the room in amazement.

"Well—in a way," she added. "It's a lot nicer than the one in Camden I spend my life scrounging round the city to pay for."

It had once been a bedroom, obviously—and there was even a bed in it—an old wood frame containing what looked like a much newer foam mattress and bedclothes. One wall of the room was given over to a massive floor-to-ceiling window that let in a dull city-glow. It was now completely glassless. Presumably it had once let onto a balcony, which had completely vanished, so now it was a dizzying gap into space. And beyond was the river. The Thames stretched out black and sombre with its glittering and cluttered jumble of buildings beyond. Directly in front of the window and positioned for the enjoyment of the view was an old sofa, one of several items of furniture—some ancient and fading to nothing, some showing signs of repair and renovation. Once this place must have belonged to a rich Londoner, a luxury riverside apartment worth more than most people would earn in a lifetime, but now it sat forlorn and empty—nobody to absorb that view—the Thames somehow disgraced and abandoned. And yet to me, this weather-worn room and glassless window could only be more beautiful than whatever opulence had been here in the past. This was what underlay everything we have ever achieved. And humanity, which so likes to glorify itself, is continually brought down again, yet rendered more real by this ruin.

"What do you think?"

I was at a loss for words. Even then, expressing superlatives was not easy for me.

"More beautiful than any suite in a grand hotel," I murmured, and she flashed me a curious look, then squeezed my hand.

"I'm glad you think so," she said. "I sometimes think I should get all my stuff and move in here permanently—I would except that some arsehole would no doubt immediately come along and put iron bars over the door—'for my own protection'." She shrugged. "Anyway—sorry, I am whinging again. Take your shoes off. Let's sit down and be comfortable."

I did so with some relief, wringing out my wet socks and draping them over something nearby. She sat down, reached under the sofa and produced a battered old lantern. A snick of a lighter and the candle within quietly flamed into life, replacing the torchlight with a faint but warm illumination. It spilled upwards over her as well, giving her a slightly eerie appearance. She gestured me to join her and I did so happily, appreciating the tranquil atmosphere. The sofa emitted a faint smell as of too much exposure to the open air and creaked painfully, but otherwise it seemed sound.

In the distance, shipping could be seen, approaching or fading away into the sea-distance. The cool sea-scented wind drifted in and ruffled our hair.

She gave a melancholy sigh, then a twisted smile. "I suppose when you get down to it, not many people have much more . . ." she struggled for the word. ". . . ownership of where they live than I have here."

"Yeah," I said. *Or Feather in her cave system with her underground friends . . .*

She was silent a moment, then shuffled round on the sofa to face me. "Now we are away from the others," she said, "I just wanted to . . . ask you a few things. Sometimes it is easier to talk one to one . . . right?"

"Yes."

"I wanted to ask how you were."

"I . . ."

"When you first came, you pained me," she continued. "It was as if all the humanity had been washed away from you—all emotion broken down. You were the unreal one, and everything that makes people real—affection, care, empathy, connection, kindness—that was missing."

I stared out at the rolling Thames. It had honestly never occurred to me to think of it that way, I had been so obsessed with being sealed away in my own little world where nothing could get in and cause yet more pain. I didn't say a word, but I was feeling a sensation on my skin that I couldn't remember ever feeling before, as though this person beside me was emitting an invisible energy.

"But maybe the irony is that those who are the most real, those who have the warmest hearts are the most prone to having that reality damaged. I still wonder what brought you to that state," she murmured. "Anything specific—or just, life?"

Outside, London continued. The lights of an airplane passed slowly across the sky, a moving mirror of the lights below.

"I don't think there was anything specific," I said. "It all seemed much colder and greyer than that. I just—knew I shouldn't be here. That there was no reason to be here. No reason at all."

She nodded.

"Me," she continued, "I suppose, I also came very close to being destroyed as well. Through hate and fear. Maybe a similar kind of thing? What I have to do just to keep alive . . . I don't usually like to talk about it, even to . . . us."

She sighed.

"I was fifteen and on my own," she said softly. "A self-taught scavenger and shoplifter . . . You know—there's all sorts of things you pick up that most people don't know about. You quickly learn how to shoplift and nick stuff—just a little. Keep things under the radar. Not enough to get into serious trouble. How to scavenge from the bins in any kind of safe way. That you need to keep your coin box a good distance away from you if you are begging because people don't want to get too close—don't want to catch your poverty or something, I don't know. You learn to be creative—that a joke is far more effective than a sob story. You just hope they can't read what's going on in your eyes. Keep moving, that's another one. Get out of the city centres at night otherwise you will only be hassled by the council's hired thugs—even arrested on fake charges if you don't do what they say. Then again, ironically, I even figured out how to commit minor crimes so I could spend a day or two inside without getting into too much trouble. It was warm in the holding cells—and they'd only occasionally beat me up or whatever. It was better than being beaten up outside at minus three degrees. Trust me on this."

She reached out and rubbed my arm, a smile on her lips that was trying to be cheerful, while I stared at her with ice crystals forming inside me. I returned the gesture with what I hoped was a bit of warmth.

"And of course, other people were always the worst part of it. Feeding out of rubbish bins is nothing compared to that. Those bastards were so beaten down by their own fear that all they could do was blank me out—pretend I didn't exist. I suppose I can't even blame them for it—but there's no room for rationality and thoughtfulness when you are stuck staring at that wall, I can tell you. I really came to hate so hard—everyone. Humanity as an entity. You have to sit there, feeling the entire weight and effects of people's judgement, their utter lack of interest, both the public walking past and the people in charge. I mean . . . it's one thing to feel someone being a judgemental prick when you can blank them out and go home, quite another when they stand between you and a possible meal—or any chance of ever having somewhere to live. Once you have seen that, there's absolutely no way you can ever be the same person again, and no way you can ever really forgive them. The human race as a whole, I mean. That hate used to be the beginning and the end of life. No way out of it, and everyone that surrounds you is not only ignoring you but actively working to keep you down with your face in the shit . . ."

I squeezed her hand again. The ice crystals of sheer horror were growing.

"Why I am telling you this? . . . it's not that I want your pity, Train Man. These days pity makes me want to hurt people. It's no bloody use unless you are prepared to accept that pity equals a need to change the world. I just . . . I just wanted to make the point that pain and despair and fear and—that feeling of worthlessness—they are not lonely things. In a way they only make the power of connection stronger. Because—all you need is one proper human connection and human feelings within yourself and then you can survive. Because if you lose all sense . . . or ability . . . of, of that connection and love, then the forces that are trying to destroy you, well, they've won. And maybe you might as well be dead. The hate never goes away but at least you have something you can put on the other side of the scales to balance it."

A tear moistened her cheek.

"And this group . . . suddenly I had four connections. And then the trampling mass of people didn't matter quite so much. I could let their poison flow away from me."

She leaned forward, staring at me for one very brief moment with brittle grey eyes that seemed to fill the world, then her head banged against my shoulder.

"Maybe five connections?" she murmured, looking very fragile.

Embrace. Her leaning half on top of me and gripping me with shocking strength.

"D-definitely," I stammered, struggling to get the words out. "Definitely five connections." It was all I could manage, but the hug was also communication of a far more powerful kind. "Why do you want to connect to me, though?" I asked awkwardly after a long minute. "Sorry but . . . I have to ask."

She gave a scolding groan, and then to my amazement, craned up and kissed me with a shock of moisture. She remained in contact for a couple of seconds, frozen completely still and very tense, then pulled away.

"You don't need a fucking qualification for fondness," she said with a shaky breath.

There was a fumble somewhere below my chin. For a moment I didn't know what she had done—maybe just some random emotional muscle movement. But then my collar popped open. She was trying to unbutton my shirt, I realised with a massive prickle. I stared down at that hand for a moment, and she followed my gaze and froze again.

"What are you doing?" I whispered, feeling a shock of what I can only call terror.

She stared at me blankly. I didn't say anything else—and nor did she, but it was one of the most complicated silences I have ever experienced, with almost an entire novel's worth of narrative and information. Questions were exchanged, fears were communicated, eagerness became disappointment and acceptance—and I saw something die in her eyes right then.

She slowly let her face drop onto my shoulder, then pulled away and sat up, staring out at the Thames. We ended up sitting there for an agonisingly long time, as though a freak ice storm had blown in and covered us both with a thin immobilising layer . . .

This is another of those sections that is proving hard to write—another one I keep leaving aside and coming back to, staring at, then going off to write about parties and riots and whatever. It's also another section where I have to be honest, even to the mystification or disgust of anyone reading this. I can hear you now . . . *What are you doing? Desperate to connect, half or wholly in love with the girl, and when she wants to shag you, you behave like this?* Believe me—I know. But all I can do is relate what happened. All my life, fat or thin, sickly or healthy, my flesh had been nothing more than an encumbrance, my sexuality nothing more than an embarrassment and a problem, drummed in time and again by the world around me. Feelings for people are an insult or an inconvenience or worse. Fuck romance. It's as if I was oozing some kind of black slime called love and I very quickly learned to keep it to myself. Love more repulsive than shit—than pus out of a gangrenous wound. And me that birthed it needing to be hidden and self-effaced out of existence. A kiss—no way, that slime probably tastes like battery acid and human excrement. Bare skin—no way, who knows what horrible things it has been doing while I wasn't looking? Sweat—stench—like the skin of some oozing, pustulating monster from a horror movie. I have a hard time even finding words to express this utter revulsion and if I let anyone get close, I would only have to endure yet more pain and humiliation. That's what it is like when you have managed to beat yourself down almost to death. That's what it is like when you have been this close to catching a train.

I have been called a lot of things in my life. Some people call me 'strange'—as if there's something strange about having emotions. Others wonder jokingly where I have buried the bodies. I have overheard people speculating that there is maybe something wrong with me—some form of autism or mental damage—and others have publically wondered whether I was castrated as a child in a freak accident—whether I am gay, or asexual. None are things I particularly like hearing because I don't believe any of them. I don't even believe the 'strange' one. There's nothing strange about me. I am just a normal human reacting in a normal way to the forces that surround me.

And now what? In that frozen silence, you might say that a weather phenomenon had caught me. I had bungled it massively, whatever happened now. Maybe I had made an enemy of one I cared about far too much. Maybe I had wrecked my place in this little group. Maybe I should just go. Get out of here. Slip away back into the mad London night. But if I did I knew that it would be such an ocean of self-hate that I would go running to catch, even embrace, that train. And yes, maybe that would be best . . .

"I'm sorry, Train Man," she said at last, her voice a little stiff—maybe even a hint of petulance hidden deep down there. "I thought . . . I mean . . . are you okay?"

"Yes . . ."

She finally looked away from the Thames view and returned her eyes to me. It was chilling how much those grey eyes seemed to be able to read. I didn't want to be read. I didn't want her gazing into the horrible depths. Then she shook her head with a small smile.

"Give me a hug?" she pleaded. "Prove it."

My heart flipped at bit at that—a shock of relief I suppose— and I quickly hugged her close. This was something I could do. I don't know why a hug should be so infinitely easier than sex, when the only real difference is about a millimetre of clothes, but there you have it. It's possible that I can somehow kid myself that I am safely not there.

"Maybe I am just an idiot," she said. "I thought—I really thought . . . I didn't want to upset you. I . . ."

"No . . ." I stammered urgently. "It's just . . . I . . ."

I couldn't speak—why do I even *try?* I let my head drop against hers, feeling her hair against my cheek. But it came through to me then, with great suddenness and clarity, that she was sitting here almost as insecure as I was. Not annoyed or frustrated—actively scared. Sometimes my fear reminds me very clearly that it is one of the most selfish forces that can ever take root inside you.

"Maybe you were right."

The words slipped out before I could analyse them in any way. She actually flinched.

"About what?"

"I'm just . . . I suppose . . . not used to people . . . showing affection." That was about as incomplete an explanation as it was possible to get—but at least it was something. Maybe it is easier to talk to people when you are hugging them. "It's been . . . so long," I continued, "just stuck in my little room, hating myself and living like some kind of sea creature in a crevice . . . Only the bickering internet for company."

"Well," she said, "I'm not exactly used to . . . showing it either."

She hugged even tighter for a moment.

"So—should I be showing it?" she asked at last.

"Yes," I whispered hollowly, tears suddenly in my eyes. "If you . . . if you want . . ."

"You mean that?"

"Yes."

"Gawd, Train Man," she said, squeezing even tighter with what sounded like a sob. There was a lot of strength in those arms—it was close to painful. "I'm confused," she said. "If you don't want to fuck me then that's fine but . . ."

"It's not that. It's just . . ." I gave up again. There seemed no sane way to explain this.

"I mean—I know I am a bit ... damaged," she said, "and . . . maybe that's . . ."

I backed away—then gave a shrill groan.

"No," I said aggressively. "You are beautiful. In every way . . . Almost unbelievably so. How you move . . . who you are . . ."

She gave a tiny smile. "Now you're talking," she said. "That's more how one is supposed to talk to a woman."

"It's me that's the fucking problem," I said, stroking her hair. "The last time I needed to find romantic talk was about seventeen years ago. And every fucking experience of my life tells me that if I sit here telling you how extraordinary and sexy you are, you would only hate me for it."

The Beggar had blushed crimson. "Oh boy—no. No—I promise you I wouldn't."

She shuffled forward to reclaim that hug—and it was that little gesture of wanting contact, coupled with the feeling of her rather sharp nose against my neck again, that finally caught me. There was a reality in that nose on some level, however comical it sounds. I could cope with her nose, even if other parts of her were rather beyond consideration—and right then the presence of her nose seemed more erotic than any other image or memory that I had of her.

And she noticed it immediately.

"Train Man," she murmured, deliberately squirming herself closer and applying pressure right there, "I think your body is wiser than you are."

"That's not hard," I said, every inch of my face burning with blush and pun completely not intended. She giggled into my shoulder.

"Okay then," she said. "So . . . is this a good moment for me to ask again, one last time?" she said with a smile, tugging at my shirt playfully. "Shall we? My cert's up to date and I had the op, you know. Years ago."

"You did?"

"Of course. I made up my mind pretty early on."

"Me too. I . . . don't have a cert though . . ."

"Something tells me—don't take this the wrong way, but maybe you haven't *needed* a cert for a while?"

" . . . "

"I think I trust you, that's what I am saying."

"Yeah," I said slowly. "Not for a . . . few years."

"Well then?"

"Oh gawd," I said with a sudden laugh. "I suppose it's good and dark. Okay, you've got a deal."

And thus my doom was sealed—and she finally released me from that eternal hug.

"What's wrong with us?" she said with a laugh. "I feel like some bewildered little kid now, doing it for the first time. It's all your fault."

"Shouldn't we . . . sign something . . . or . . . ?"

"No we shouldn't," she said with a frown that also paradoxically helped to clear the air. "Those things are an obscenity."

I nodded, eyebrows up.

"I think we need to get drunk," she said. "Maybe it would help us relax. I should have brought the wine. And maybe some of those masks."

"Maybe you should," I said with a chuckle. "Then I might not be making such a twit of myself."

That little laugh we had shared seemed to have had a massive power to it, though. It had somehow cleared the air even more. She physically towed me across the room to the bed. The lantern was left on the floor by the window, so it was a bit darker here—a fact I was seriously grateful for. And then, instead of my shirt, it was her own that she was unbuttoning. And with no way to avoid it, I had to follow.

"Yeah—where's that raging bear that rampaged through the park, laying waste to the world?"

"If it comes to that, where's the wildcat?"

"Stripping naked," she said with a smile, kicking her trousers away. "No cat—no bear. Just human. Some crap about the truth beneath the masks."

"Powerful stuff," I said.

"Sexy stuff."

"Yeah—very sexy."

She had got rid of more than her trousers now, but the fact that she was leading the way wasn't helping. By that point though, I had decided I was going to shut up. Sick of the sound of my own voice trying to explain the unexplainable and sick of worrying, I had found a tiny hint of defiance. For gawd sake get on with it, Train Man.

And two pairs of underwear landed on the floor—more or less simultaneously.

"Come on," she said, pulling the bedclothes over us both. "Let's make a nice little nest in here . . . That's nice, right?" she said with a smile. "I think our bodies know what to do better than we do . . ."

She was right about that, at least. Star Girl aside, it was so long since I'd had a proper erection—as opposed to some lazy half-uninterested stirring—that I was quite surprised. It almost hurt. That at least was functioning okay—and one failure point was crossed off the list. Only about a thousand to go . . .

And I could feel her legs wrapping round either side of me.

And then a sudden shock of wet heat . . .

And now I am wondering what the heck the reader wants here? Some kind of soft porn but without going into too much detail or reality otherwise some of you would run screaming? Or sniff in disapproval? Or get embarrassed? If you're not already. All I remember is a weird blundering motion that in the cold light of day would probably look every bit as odd as dancing without music. Somewhere in the back of my mind is the factoid that there is a phenomenon known as 'air-sex'—think air-guitar but with an invisible something much less irritating. I am talking about a solo, fully clothed, performative event undertaken by either gender, and one that, let's face it, makes about as much sense as many. But all I can say is that anyone who can stand up and do something that awkward in front of watching eyes gets my admiration. Half of the challenge of sex seems to involve getting over prudery and fear, while the other half involves getting over how bloody ridiculous it can all be.

"It's hot under this thing," she complained at last, tugging at the quilt. I had to agree—it was a relief when she kicked it off us both and on to the floor. And the dance continued. And yes—she came, probably as much from her own work as mine. Orgasm. Climax. Whatever word you want. And that's another funny thing about sex—we seem to be devoid of any kind of normal language for it. Nothing mundane. All we have is either painfully scientific or beyond dumb—do you have a *vulva* and *vagina* down there complete with *labia minora* and a *urethral erogenous zone* or do you have a fucking hoo-hee or hot pocket?

No wonder people have trouble communicating. But whatever the damn thing was called and whatever you want to call what it did, it was a spectacular outburst of energy that left her sprawled out on her back, looking stunned. Left me rather stunned, too.

"Oh wow," she said, arms spread wide. "That's the way to relax." She lay for a long moment getting her breath back and cooling off. "You didn't come, did you?" she asked at last.

I felt myself blushing crimson. "No, but . . ."

"You need to," she said. "Otherwise there is no balance in the universe."

"If you say so," I said, aware of the humour of the situation.

She gave a relieved smile and hugged me.

"I do say so. Get that thing back inside me," she ordered, "and get on with it."

And I suppose—well, I did. You don't need a blow by blow account. I suppose I was indeed starting to relax. After all, I had got this far and hadn't caused the universe to implode or the Beggar's eyes to melt. And I suppose it must have been a relaxant because afterwards the giggles caught me. The Beggar also cracked up. We didn't say anything. We hadn't even bothered to separate, remaining tangled sweatily together, my dick still inside her. For some unknown reason, I gave it a twitch, which she responded to with a cheeky squeeze. This was repeated a few times until we both cracked up again.

"I don't think I have ever been hugged before the—the way you hug me," she said. "I could hug you forever . . ."

That was quite high up on the list of nicest things anyone has ever said to me and I was quite silenced for a while.

"That's fine by me," I said at last. "If we could get food delivered or something—who needs to stop?"

More giggles. Eventually I scrambled off her—and in that relaxation, I finally allowed myself to look at her properly in the low light. Her stretched out, spread, excited, heated and cooled, bedraggled, sweaty and erotic. The body I had watched in action many times, now being seen in a totally new way—maybe a reality of perception that had never been there before. I put my hand over my eyes for a brief moment. "I am finally allowed to look at a human being?"

"I thought you got quite an eyeful before," she said with a laugh.

"Stolen glances," I said with a smile. "Very nice, but not quite the same as looking."

The Beggar had gone crimson again, but she made no move to hide herself, even her scars—indeed she seemed to stretch herself out on the bed even more. It was clear she was much less shy than I was, fortunately. It was such a sight that I ended up scrambling down.

"What are you doing?" she asked with a twitch of hope in her eyebrows.

"Just—things," I said.

I am sure I was still awkward and clumsy as I put my tongue to work. It's like playing a musical instrument. You can study theory and fingering charts as much as you like, but that's only so much use when you finally pick it up and play. At the same time though, this seemed weirdly easier than what had gone before—a little like reading a book aloud was easier than trying to engage in conversation. And it seemed to work because, a few minutes later, she exploded again—with considerably more violence than last time, almost twisting my neck. From where I was standing in the world, feeling that explosion ripping through her body was a very precious thing. As precious as bringing home that duck—as, let's finally come out and say it, as waking up that day surrounded by friends and realising I had missed that train after all . . .

SUNDAY

I would not have expected to fall asleep, not with a fellow human being so close by—not even after nature's greatest relaxant. Sleep has always felt a little fragile and all too easily lost. A popped soap bubble. A fractured snail shell. I must have managed it, though, because the next thing I remember was waking up with a jolt and a thrill of urgency. It was nothing exciting, just my body clock reminding me about the mundane reality of my first job of the morning. It was still dark. The lantern had burned out. I had no idea of the time, but my mind was urging me to move—don't be late—get on with it—shift for gawd sake. And I believed it. My body clock is usually right about these things, even with my sometimes crazy schedule.

The Beggar was lying beside me, though, sprawled out on her back, mouth open and one bare leg hooked over mine. In the dark, she looked almost creepily asleep, her face blank and expressionless—and I hesitated to disturb her. Yet I couldn't just slip away either. It was a conundrum and I looked round the room for my clothes. In them somewhere would be my phone, my only timepiece. I could just see them scattered on the floor and I shifted and leaned over, trying to extract myself from under her . . .

"Train Man?" she murmured with a sleepy squirm.

Damn.

"Sorry . . . I just need to . . ."

She rolled over, reeling in her various limbs and releasing me. I finally snagged my shirt, then the phone, and got a look at the time. Yes—my body clock was somehow correct—even allowing for the extra travelling time. Bravo, bodyclock.

"Okay," I said regretfully. "I have to go soon."

She gave a sleepy groan of protest.

"Sorry—but I need to work or I'll be pilloried. In the stockade. And I have to collect a few things from home, so—umm..."

"Oh dear," she said, sitting up and rubbing her face. Tiredness was heavy in her eyes—as it probably was in mine. We had only slept for a few hours, after all.

"I... I mean, what are you going to do?" I asked. "Can I... I mean when shall I see you again? Are we still on no-name no-personal-life terms here?"

An enigmatic smile.

"Perhaps you should take a look outside," she said.

I couldn't read the expression on her face at all and I frowned, then scrambled out of bed, forgetting for the moment that I was still naked. I hurried to the picture window and looked out—then froze. Down below, the darkness was wrong. It seethed and swirled like some kind of disruption of space-time or dimension rip—as if the world itself was disintegrating into primal goo around us, consuming the city. A glimmer of reflected light came back to me, rippling, slimy—and I realised what it was. The black, heaving Thames directly below, slopping against the walls. The building was surrounded by it, dull and strangely menacing.

It had never occurred to me to think about the tide.

I gawped at that black ocean, then spun round and stared at her, still lying comfortably in bed. She gave me a knowing grin in the faint city glow.

"You... oh gawd," I cried.

"Go on, call me something horrible," she said with a delighted laugh. "How long is it since you lost your temper at anyone?"

"I can't remember," I said dryly.

I leaned out of that glassless opening as far as I dared and stared down again—but no, that black water didn't look remotely inviting. It was impossible to tell how deep it was. It might have been shallow enough to wade but I had no desire to find out in this darkness. It seemed we were trapped here until the tide went down again. My job had gone to another place. Did that mean

I was doomed? Or, given what was happening in the city, did it even matter? Did anything matter now?

"You did it on purpose, didn't you?"

"I'm sorry, Train Man," she said with a smile.

"I've never seen the water so high," I muttered.

"It's a spring tide—or thereabouts. When the tides are at their most extreme, this place can be quite seriously flooded."

I stared out of the window. That was true. Spring tides were days the sea wall was made for. Add in a nice storm surge and it could take quite a battering.

There seemed to be the faintest of faint hints of grey in the sky now—reminding us that morning was not so far away.

She scrambled out of bed and joined me at the window. She was also naked, of course, and that did two things: A) engendered that vague sense of shock and delight and what I can only call the 'correctness' of the naked state that one feels—and B) reminded me that I was as well, which came with that vague sense of awkwardness, panic and what I can only call the 'incorrectness' of the naked state. Gawd, what a fucked up species we are.

"At least we have a bit more time to relax," she said with a grin, grasping my hand. "I hope you are ready for round two because I sure will be?"

Again the sheer unreality of it all made the world shimmer—unreal enough for me to accept her hug, clutching her close, skin against skin before the glowing lights of the city. I felt slightly stale after a night's hot sleep, but so did she and, weirdly enough, it didn't matter. It was superficial, beneath which was something that it would take a lot more than this to obscure.

"Yes," I said. "Shame on you for trapping me exactly where I want to be. How will I ever get to that place I utterly loathe now?"

That got a chuckle and she disengaged, then crossed to a shelf. She found a fresh tea light, soon getting the lantern glowing again and casting that flickering warm light over the room—and over us.

"I have some cold duck in my bag. And salad and bread and a few bits and bobs, so we should be comfortable. We could go back to sleep—but you know, dawn over the Thames is rather special. I am tempted to just sit here and enjoy it."

I was also tired. There was much lost sleep to catch up on. But her words came with a little thrill and I nodded.

"Want a wash, now we're up?"

"Can we?" I asked in surprise.

"Sure we can. Just a moment—I have some supplies." She ran back to the shelf and extracted a few things from somewhere.

"Sponge bath," she cried cheerfully, holding one up. "Pass me the water in my bag would you?"

I quickly found the one-litre plastic bottle and handed it to her.

"This is clean," she said, sloshing some water over the sponge and squeezing it lightly. "I left it here last time. I hope you don't mind sharing?"

"N-no—not at all."

"Oh and another thing . . ." She handed me a packet of mint chewing gum. "No toothbrush—but this is good stuff. It's a whacky morning routine, but it's the best I can do."

She popped some in her mouth as well, then to my surprise, began scrubbing herself.

"You're looking at me as though I was dancing the can-can," she said with a grin, and I blushed crimson. "Hey—this used to be routine for me. You would not believe some of the places where I have given myself sponge baths in the past."

It wasn't the fact that she was giving herself a sponge bath that was making me stare in astonishment though, it was the complete lack of self-consciousness. Again, it seemed almost miraculous to me. Even though the light of the single candle was dim, I still felt uneasy with reference to myself—yet she didn't seem to care at all, scrubbing at her various nooks and crannies as though I wasn't there. If sex was a kind of performance, for good or ill, then now I had been invited back stage, and in some way, that seemed even deeper.

"Come on, Train Man," she said with a laugh, slinging the sponge at me and towelling herself down with equal vigour. "Get on with it. Save a bit of the water for us to drink, though."

"Oh—oh, right," I said, sloshing the bottle over it with a mental shrug. I set to it, trying to enjoy the process, trying to just shrug it all off as unimportant—trying to believe the Beggar's seeming acceptance of me as a physical entity. "Such as?" I asked at last, to keep the conversation going.

"Such as what?"

"The places where you've had sponge baths."

"Oooh—bloody hell . . . inside blackberry thickets, in café toilet cubicles, actually on the canal towpaths at night when there was nobody around to freak out, on the train, on the railway lines, in the tents of some other homeless sod . . ."

"Wow . . ."

"You do what you have to, Train Man," she said, slinging the towel across to me. I also towelled myself as dry as I could—and I have to admit, it felt good. Cool and clean in the very slight breeze from the glassless window.

"I wonder if the others have gone home," I said at last.

"You know, you can see the hideout from the windows on the other side. We are quite high up and the missing buildings leave it quite open."

She grabbed my hand and headed for the door. I looked longingly at my clothes but there was no chance to access them and I had to accept that as we made our way through the building, wincing at the rough floor. We entered what had once been the main corridor, which was extraordinarily dark, then through another door. This rear apartment contained no amenities whatsoever—only empty and slowly decaying cuboid rooms that echoed any sounds we made back with a gentle reverb. Again I was thinking about what this building had been before—who might have lived here. I could easily sense the toxic pecking order and polite jealousy that must have existed—the people at the bottom of the building jealous of the people at the top—the people at the back jealous of the people at the front with their Thames views. And now all gone—human vanity as dust. For a moment, it made me shiver, but that soon passed as we approached the window. This was a much more modest one than at the front, though still glassless. We leaned against the sill and yes, the flooded Soak was spread out before us—a vista of demolished buildings and standing decay, as bleak a view as I had ever seen. With the city clustering behind its fortified wall like a concentration camp filled with frightened children, this wasteland again seemed a fundamental image for London. The city's dark heart and the grinning skull awaiting all of humanity, if some but knew it.

"I think they are still there," she said. "Maybe asleep. There's a chink of light—someone must have left the curtain open a tad. I hope it wasn't us."

"Good eyes," I said, focussing on a familiar section of the wall. "I hope they are not waiting for us. Or worrying. I mean, if the tide came in and we didn't come back then maybe . . ."

The Beggar gave a small smile. "I think they know," she said. "I bet you they do."

One hand trailed down my back.

"Know . . . ?"

"Why I dragged you out here. Or at least Star Girl does, and she never keeps quiet about anything. They know precisely what we've been doing. I somehow don't think they are worrying about us."

She gave a shy grin and leant her head against my shoulder.

"Let's go back," she said. "It will soon be dawn. And dawn over the Thames—it doesn't get much better than that."

We made our way through again without a word, again treading carefully across the rough and ruined floor. Back in what I can presumably call the bedroom, she bent down and blew out the lantern, bringing the darkness again. Then we settled on the ancient sofa before the big window, the Beggar positioning herself very close indeed. And by this time I was inclined to reciprocate, tugging her into another massive embrace as though trying to convince myself that she was really there. Outside, the city lights were beginning to realise they had competition—beginning to look a bit faded as the dawn crept closer. And it was indeed an amazing sight, even allowing for the macabre presence of the Soak. Given the way the Thames bends here, we could see across to Rotherhithe and also right down the river in both directions.

"Touch me, Train Man," she whispered with a mischievous grin.

"Hm?"

"You've got an entire body to play with—you don't need to just rub my back."

Again the surreality, and again the strange communication. There was a beautiful sense of freedom here—from time, space, self, other, everything. It seemed as though voices that had been nagging and chattering at me for years had finally shut up, leaving an extraordinary sense of mental silence—soothed by skin and the heartbeat of another, blown away like cobwebs before the most powerful sense of all. And over time, the grey spread in the sky, bleaching through the clouds—washing like liquid round us in two great arms. As though the sky itself was joining in the embrace. I suppose about twenty minutes must have passed in which we never said a word and never needed to. Communication by words is rather basic, after all, as I have said before—an almost trite froth on top of the true communication.

Then, intruding on this peace and magic, there was a faint hum of a motor. The Thames was sheened a gleaming metallic grey now, and through that grey, a black line was crawling—a black line originating from a black shape studded with a few lights. A small boat, just a rigid-inflatable. And yet it was a sound and a silhouette that I recognised somewhere in the strange encyclopaedia of London I kept in my head.

"River Police," I said with a frown, and the Beggar flinched, her body going tense.

"Oh gawd—let's keep out of sight."

She was still lying half on top of me and I could feel the tension in her body increasing as the boat progressed across our field of view. For a while I was a little surprised because I felt pretty much unknowable up here. We were sitting in the dark—we would surely be utterly invisible from out on the water. But then the boat changed direction. I could feel everything that happened next in the Beggar's body, almost as clearly as I could see it with my eyes. I could feel the muscles in her shoulders and legs suddenly clenching as it veered in towards the shore—and then vanished behind the buildings some way to our right. It looked as though it had pulled directly into the old Limehouse basin through the long-removed tidal locks.

The Beggar's eyes flashed from the grey river to me and then back again, then she quickly scrambled to her feet. We didn't need to say anything, we just hurried through the building, almost running to the back window again. And yes, there was the faint sound of the motor. And yes, there was the boat playing peekaboo in the slots between the abandoned buildings—now there, now gone, now there again as it pulled into what had been the Limehouse Basin area. It didn't even stop. In a moment it was in among the buildings themselves, riding the tide. My stomach sank in utter horror and I could feel the Beggar suddenly trembling as the boat approached as near as it could get to the hideout in the river wall, picking its way carefully through the ruins. Then it beached on the very concrete flow we had been playing around on not so long ago. The Beggar made a panicked movement, but there was nothing we could do. We had no contact—no phone numbers—nothing.

Then I realised there were more figures visible on the railway tracks as well.

"Are they still in there?" she demanded shrilly. I stood flattened against the crumbling wall as the scene played out, rendered almost mundane by distance. The uniforms on the railway line, with little experience of this environment and no idea about our one easy path, were trying to scramble down onto the parapet that lead to the entrance hole. Meanwhile some of those on the boat were trying to get up. Somehow though, the alarm had already been raised—no doubt the sound of the boat engine had carried down into the hideaway. There were a few faint shouts and a flurry of activity—and then someone was running along the parapet. I couldn't make out who it was at this distance, save that it was grey. Clay Man? The Philosopher was next out, looking round calmly. Guns were aimed at both of them. More shouts. The Philosopher didn't move but Clay Man just kept on running.

Then a pop. As dull and insignificant as anything else in this ghostly dawn environment.

The figure flopped down off the wall. It was a long fall with a dismal shingly splash at the end of it.

The Beggar gave a faint wail under her breath.

The police in the Soak went running in that direction, while up above the invaders had finally managed to get down onto the parapet. Some grabbed the unresisting Philosopher by the arms while others went scrambling into the hole in the wall. A few moments later, Star Girl was dragged out brutally, yelling what sounded like an incoherent stream of obscenities that reached us as a faint shrill murmur—looking ready to precipitate herself and everyone else right off the wall in her rage. The faint chaos still going on inside must have been the Butcher. In my mind I have an image of him elegantly brandishing his big kitchen knives like a crazy old English gentleman in some desperate last stand against a flock of unlikely and no doubt deeply racist *boys own* savages.

The Beggar swore quietly and I glanced sideways, still not processing it. No—I hadn't seen that. It was too far away. It was all a dream, or some daft scene on TV. It couldn't be real. The Beggar's face mirrored a similar confused shock, but she got through it quicker than I did and her fingers clawed at the window frame hard enough to break fingernails and splinter the old wood.

And in the distance, a small piece of grey flotsam that the police were now circling round with a strange caution, as though afraid of vengeance from an undead corpse.

✧

The mob withdrew with its trophies, though uniforms still picked around both on and below the wall like hopeful animals wondering if there were any more food scraps to find. Then, some indefinable time later, another boat arrived—and another. More people bustling around, up to who knows what. It was hard to see at this distance. No doubt they were making sure they had collected all the traces that three people who made up their own minds about life and one corpse could possibly leave. Of course, I tried to remember whether I had left anything of my own there. I was pretty sure I hadn't—but you never can know.

The Beggar hadn't said a word. Just stood staring, mouth open slightly but teeth clenched. And eventually I gave up. I took her hand and this time it was me doing the towing, leading her quietly back to the bedroom. Still without a word, I reached for my clothes and put them on again. Right now I needed all the feelings of security I could possibly get. The Beggar, though, just stood there, still naked. It looked as though she had forgotten completely.

"Are you—" I began, then stopped myself. I had been going to say *are you okay*, before it dawned on me that was probably one of the most stupid possible questions in human history. With no other options suggesting themselves, I ended up staring at her helplessly for a while.

"Uh-huh," she whispered. Meaningless.

I sat down and stared out of the window at the view—at the hazy day that was dawning.

"I'm going to blow," she said, barely audibly.

"What?"

"I'm going to . . ."

Almost exactly then, with the drama of a great romantic poem, there was a dull gleam of light as the sun cleared the buildings across the river to the south-east—a pale ghost of a sphere, coyly clothed in tassels of cloud. The Beggar stared at it for a while.

"Okay," I muttered, trying to find my way back down to earth. "So . . ."

And then the Beggar just exploded.

It began with a long rising tone, startlingly like the electric motor of a small train pulling out of a station, then a screeched swear word. Then she was raging. "What's the point?" she screamed, hammering at the wall. "What is the fucking point? In all the shit that is going on in this city, why do they have to hassle us? What is the fucking . . . point? What is the point? What is the . . . fucking point? I'll . . . I'll . . ."

She was practically dancing round the room now, totally out of control, waving her fists and occasionally banging them against the wall hard enough to dislodge the old paintwork and plaster. It was a bizarre and terrifying sight as she spelt out the things she would like to do to those uniformed figures if she only could—and to everyone else involved, up to and including the King, the prime minister, the BBC and the great British public. It was an outburst that outdid anything Star Girl had ever come out with, both in terms of rage and gruesome imagination. And I sat there uselessly and watched. I had never seen anything like this before in my life. I had never even dreamed of such rage.

She finished with her voice sliding so loud and high that my throat twanged in sympathy, then she collapsed in the corner, looking precariously close to falling out of the picture window. She crouched there trembling for a few minutes, then abruptly gave a squirm and a stream of piss impacted the floor with surprising force.

"Oh fuck," she muttered, reversing awkwardly away from the puddle and flashing me a weird look that was half guilty, half utterly insane—one that I will never forget. She dragged herself to the bed and flopped out on it, face down, her shoulders heaving as the rage abruptly transitioned into hysterical sobbing.

Of course I tried to soothe her, though the shock of what had happened and her explosive outburst had left me even less effective than usual. My stomach was roiling. Every part of me was trying to tremble, yet remained frozen. I suppose I also wanted to scream and cry. And yet here I was trying to calm her down? I should have joined her in a screaming match that would have brought that frail old building down. Instead, she lay there, occasionally tearing at the quilt with frantic fingers and screaming some expletive in an increasingly hoarse voice. It took at least twenty minutes before she finally began to collect herself a little.

And about an hour later she was sitting on the sofa in a hunched ball, still naked and staring woodenly out of the window. I could smell a slight tang of urine and sweat.

"Sorry, Train Man," she muttered and I glanced round in surprise. That was the first time in a while she had even acknowledged my presence.

"Don't apologise," I said softly. "It's—well . . . doesn't matter. But . . ."

"For the first time in my life, I think maybe Star wasn't angry enough," she said. "I would never have believed it." She gave a brittle laugh—a very very slight return to her normal humour. "Of course—all that rubbish was probably still there in the bag. And the duck. Why didn't I get rid of it when I had the chance? Maybe they can talk their way out of it—but . . ."

"Well, you could hardly know . . ."

"It's just basic security," she said. "The sort of thing Clay Man was always going on about."

She shook her head and stared out of the window. The Thames now looked much less ghostly—much more mundane. A boat was making its way downriver in the direction of the sea—just a river bus taking early commuters down the Thames.

"How soon before we can get out of here?" I asked at last.

She leaned over and grabbed her phone. "The tide will be down in about two hours—but I dunno. Maybe we should wait till dark again after . . . after . . ."

"Yes—I suppose."

"There's only the one way out of here that I know of and it's rather exposed during the day." She abruptly buried her face in her hands again. "Why didn't we choose somewhere with a bolt hole—a . . . another way out?"

I hugged her, ignoring the faint piss-smell that still clung to her. "It's going to be okay," she muttered shrilly. "We'll slip out of here—and they know exactly what to say to . . . to . . . make a good impression and deny involvement. I just hope Star Girl didn't start sounding off . . . oh gawd . . ."

She was silent for a moment.

"Sorry, Train Man—you must think I am completely cracked."

"No, no . . ."

She backed off and looked down at herself.

"I should probably get dressed. I sort of forgot I was naked for a while there—and I am a fucking mess . . ."

"Really—it's okay."

"Thanks . . . um . . ." She looked around awkwardly. "If we are here all day then I'd better not use any more water. So . . . I think I will nip downstairs. The sea is the only bath around here."

"Right . . ."

She left the room—a pad pad of footsteps tramping downwards. Alone again, I found a part of me that I hadn't even realised was tense relaxing a bit and I picked up my phone. A quick look at the time told me that my work would soon be starting. The work I might well be sacked from right now, the way things were going. A wholly mundane desperation clamoured in my brain for a moment. Maybe I could go to the doctor, tell him about my suicide attempt and ask for help—even though there was little any weary doctor or exhausted health service could do about that. But who knows, maybe some signed document would enable me to wriggle out of this. Of course, I would have to play the game—all sorts of blather about having gone off the rails, being eager to find my way back to normality through therapy or drugs, I need help but I'll be fine, pretending that wanting to lie on the railway tracks wasn't the most natural thing in the world . . .

Or would I just get arrested for trespassing?

Feeling very tired, I wandered through to the back of the building again—but there was nothing to see. The sea wall remained deserted and silent.

Leaning against the window, I made a quick phone call. *Sorry guys but due to various um problems I am stuck kind of literally so won't be able to make it to work today ummmmmm . . .* To my relief, though, I had been right. It barely seemed to matter. Work was at a standstill, I was told, the transport was still shut down and only two or three people had even made it and some bastard had kicked the window in during the night and thanks for at least managing to call with some excuse or other. I ended by promising to come in tomorrow—and yes, I absolutely essentially meant that. I couldn't let my income dwindle for more than a day or so. Then I resumed staring out of the window. Outside, I could just catch the sound of traffic now—and distant sirens that sent a chill down my back in a way they never had before.

A pad on the stairs reminded me of the Beggar and I hurried back through. She looked at me bleakly and I could tell she had been crying again. She reached for her clothes and put them on, then settled on the sofa beside me.

"Gawd," she muttered with an unhappy laugh. "If you still like me after that performance, I promise you I will never ask you for a contract as long as I live." She gave me a look with huge eyes, and then cautiously laid her head on my shoulder.

✷

We did wait till dark, though it was frustrating. A day is a long long time when there's nothing to do but exist filled with unease and despair. A span of time that elsewhere covered tens of thousands of words, I need to pass over now in little more than a paragraph. Neither of us talked much—no profound discussions or deep, deep healing philosophy. Sometimes we lay curled up together in bed, sometimes one or both of us would be pacing around restlessly, or hurrying to the back of the house for another look at the wall. There was little to see, though, beyond silence and inactivity. There weren't even any trains. We also spent a long time watching the changing view of the Thames—the way the directional light made it switch from deep grey to blue to silver and back again. Watching the ships pass by, watching the few clouds overhead as the hazy sun climbed higher for its daily assault on the world. We also ate the food the Beggar had brought—carefully splitting it into three meals, which was considerably further than it was intended to stretch. There was about half of a bottle of water left as well—which was even more of a trial.

When we had finished, we very carefully took what little meat scraps were left and slung them out of the window into the Thames, cleansing ourselves of any evidence, just in case.

Maybe a little bizarrely and in spite of our dark dark mood, we had sex again at one point—sort of sex, anyway. Nothing else to do, I suppose. It was hot, rather sticky and we had drunk far too little water to be sweating. My mouth felt hideously stale, maybe hers, too, but to my relief there seemed an unspoken understanding about that and steps were taken to keep that out of the equation. It was not exactly happy but even so it reaffirmed a bond of some kind. A bond that we really needed. And afterwards I found myself studying her again, trying to read her flesh. The marks and scars that covered her skin—that subtle disordered chaos that covered the white of her like writing.

"I don't think you want to know," she said. "Beat up—kicked—stabbed—attacked by the police—someone even set me on fire once while I was trying to sleep rough."

She turned over, indicating her side, and I realised there was a very faint unevenness and discolouration there—and my skin prickled.

"Why would anyone do that?" I whispered innocently.

She shrugged. "That's what people are, that's all," she said. "Whatever ideals people have, basically we are a species that thinks it's fun to pour petrol over homeless people and set them on fire. That's what the Philosopher is after . . . the reality underneath all the high-sounding crap that people like to imagine. Because all of that is wrong. He wants . . ."

She broke off.

"Was after," she corrected shrilly. "And Clay Man . . ."

"He might have only been wounded. The police can't just execute people they don't like. Even now."

She gave me a look that I didn't like much.

"How high is that wall?" she demanded.

"I . . . don't know."

"Pretty damn long way to fall, right?"

"Into water," I said, wondering why we were on the point of arguing over something like this.

"You know damn well he was probably dead before he even hit the ground," she snapped. "They know how to shoot—once they make up their mind to do it they make bloody sure."

"All I am saying is . . ."

"You want to bet on it or something?" she demanded with a touch of hysteria.

"No," I mumbled, actually feeling rather hurt. "I just want to . . . to work out the probability of—of whether . . ."

She stared at me for a moment with big eyes, then seemed to deflate. "Sorry," she muttered. "Please keep hoping—I lost mine years ago."

I shrugged it off and sought for something else to talk about.

"High-sounding crap?" I asked. Looking back, that probably wasn't the best subject change in history.

"Oh, you know what I mean," she grumbled. "That we are somehow creatures of justice, fairness, compassion, intelligence, reason . . . it's all bunk. How can you take a look at the world for any length of time and believe there's anything good about people? It's just stories some people make up about themselves to massage their egos."

I stared in silence. Right there, trapped in that room and in that horror story, I couldn't really disagree. History ancient and modern seems like an eternal fight against a hydra—lop one head off and three more grow. But we are the hydra. Not some mysterious external force, as the horror novels and myths would have you pretend. Ourselves. We creep and crawl through the stinking blood-soaked mud of our own devising, constantly screaming for relief, screaming to be allowed to live, while simultaneously perpetuating that mud for all eternity—while the knives that disembowel us are held in our own hands. And in the midst of that, we dream of 'meanings' to life? Maybe the only reason we dream of meaning and destiny is because we are so utterly incapable of escaping that self-made swamp—the only reason we dream of afterlives is because there would not be enough trains in the world if we accepted that this is all we have.

These were bitter thoughts, and by sheer force of contrast I found myself hugging her so tightly that it must have been verging on painful. She didn't protest, though, merely grabbed me back with equal strength. There has to be something precious in all this existence—and there it was, on the smallest and most personal level imaginable, while everything on a greater scale founders. As I have said before, it was a little knot of momentary warmth—a little flicker of light in an infinity of darkness . . .

And afterwards, I was stroking her scarred skin again sadly. In comparison to her, my own was almost pure, silky smooth, which gave me a slightly weird feeling. She returned the gesture, stroking my soft stomach and I felt a flash of tension. It was still going to be a long long time before I was going to be able to relax over that kind of thing.

MONDAY

There are gaps in my memory then, so I think we must have fallen asleep or drifted away into a half-doze—no great surprise after our disturbed nights. The next thing I remember with any clarity was a touch on my shoulder that woke me up with a massive, disproportionate flinch.

"You okay?" she asked, looking startled.

"Yes," I mumbled. A quick look round revealed that it was dark again. Deep night. Or morning. One or the other. The room was glowing with the flickering light of a single candle.

"The tide is nearly out," she said. "I checked the wall a few minutes ago and it all seems quiet. We should get out of here."

"Right—right, yes . . ."

I brutally grabbed my soul and dragged it back into my sleep-shattered and aching body, then managed to sit up. That was good news. I was feeling desperately thirsty and it would be a great relief to be back in the city again—back on the 'legal' side of the wall. A nice hot shower, one of the greatest pleasures in the world, within reach. I grabbed my clothes and hauled them on, then found my socks. They were dry now after a day in this heat, but that was hardly relevant because I knew what would happen the moment they encountered the mud again. The rough fabric was harsh with salt and I forced my feet into them with a few muttered swear words.

We shared a quick drink of water—now reduced to less than a quarter of a bottle—then the Beggar blew out the candle and flashed on her torch. We hurried down the stairs, through the well of darkness that was the desolate middle storeys and to the sea-slimed ground floor. A fresh layer of mud had been deposited, obliterating any traces of our footprints and we squelched into it. Outside. Through the narrow alleyway—into the ruined Narrow Street.

That was as far as we got, though.

With what seems an unfortunate coincidence looking back, a drone of machinery started up in the middle distance and we came to a halt. We didn't say anything, but we didn't need to, for it was clear an identical unease had been seeded in us. It could be coming from anywhere, but in our situation . . . well, *paranoia triumphans*, you know. We hurried on a few more metres with a bit more urgency until the view opened out, then came to a stop again. The whole light environment of the sea wall had changed—in fact it blazed, thanks to a series of floodlights up on the tracks themselves. And under them, on the railway line . . . machinery. A host of figures in fluorescent jackets. It might as well have been a tableau of dancing devils.

"Ohhhh," the Beggar said miserably. "What the . . ." She was silent for a moment, then gave a painful wail: "*Why?*"

"Track workers," I muttered.

I studied them, at least as far as the buildings would permit. They were scattered the whole length of the sea wall between the watergates, a generator thrumming in the background. I couldn't see what they were doing, though. The machinery was heavy but I could recognise no familiar track maintenance vehicles.

"No other way up?" I asked, my voice cold and precise.

She shook her head.

"So—what? Back to the bedroom and keep an eye on things? Hope they go?"

She gave me a dispirited look. Her hand was shaking, I realised—the expression on her face not so dissimilar to the previous night when she had lost it completely.

"We can't spend another day here," she said nastily. "I am famished, and we're almost out of water. Why do they have to come barging in tonight—of all fucking nights?" Her voice was rising and her hand slapped hard against a nearby wall with a blow that could have done nothing but hurt her.

I was silent, not expressing the obvious nagging thought that had arisen in my mind—that just maybe it had something to do with us. Coincidences are more common than we sometimes think, but even so, if there are clear possible reasons or connections, then the chances are that's what's going on. Occam's razor.

"Fuck it," she muttered and turned away, stamping back down the ruined Narrow Street. She was almost running and I followed as quickly as I could. I was anxious now for her sake, but also trying to use my brain. Trying to see if there was anything in my London maps that could help us. But as far as I was concerned, the sea wall was an event horizon—an absolute beyond which there was nothing. To the west, it followed the railway as far as Limehouse Station, then angled away and soon rejoined the old riverbank. Nothing there but water and mud. In the other direction, the Soak continued until it hit the deep channels around Canary Wharf island—or the moat as I always thought of it. Nothing there either. Canary Wharf was not a good place to go.

"Are you . . . relatively okay?" I asked as we re-entered the penthouse, aware that it was a stupid question but unable to find any other way of putting it. She nodded, but her hand was still trembling. I quietly removed my shoes and wrung out my socks for the second time. I could also feel a panic trying to well up from the deep places, but I was repressing it brutally. Must be calm. What can't be influenced can only be endured, after all.

"How much water is there left?" I asked at last, purely for calculation reasons.

"That much," she said, still a little short, dragging out the almost empty bottle. "Not bloody much."

I glanced at her a little warily. Her grim attitude was understandable, of course, but it was starting to get under my skin. Right now I wanted to be talkative—to help pass the time and to maybe get everything clear in our heads. Analyse the situation to the last detail—plot and plan—cut through the panicked haze. It didn't seem to be happening, though.

✧

Lying on the bed side by side, allowing the time to pass and staring vaguely out of the window—little to do but watch the night and resist the temptation of the almost empty water bottle. We didn't even need to keep checking the sea wall, because we could hear the work progressing—the occasional shout or bang over the humming generator—the drone of other machines. Anyone trying to sleep in the vicinity would have been clutching their pillows—but the railways always were a law unto themselves. The black gleaming Thames slowly rose again like some ultra-speeded-up vision of the chaos that had happened here when people first realised that the sea was not just going to go away again—that the city could not continue as it always had. I only vaguely remembered the horror that gripped London when this wall was built—when after years of arguing, lying, ignored science and increasing floods, we finally accepted that there was nothing we could do except work with it. I remember the fury as the once-lucky or once-affluent riverside residents were shunted out and moved into far lower standard housing. That was vaguely satisfying in a malicious sort of way since by that time the hatred of the well-off was getting very intense indeed, but I also remember the sense of something close to tragedy as we abandoned whole areas that had been a part of us for thousands of years. There was no particular redevelopment—that was the thing. At least not here. The wall barged through in a panic and the Soak was left to its own devices. Whether due to some profound psychological reason or merely due to money, the same mess was still there now, years later.

"Does your phone have any internet connection?" she asked.

"No—I shut that down. Couldn't afford it. It's only a basic one anyway. Why?"

She gave a melancholy shrug. "I was wondering what was going on in the city. Are they still running wild, do you think?"

Looking out of the window, it was hard to get any clue. The city looked the same—the same fungal growth of buildings dotted with endless lights.

In the distance there was a flash. Lightning. The Beggar looked round and focused on the dark view again. It's impossible to ignore lightning. We watched in silence until, a considerable time later, a mutter of thunder followed it.

"Maybe the heat is breaking at last," she said.

"Mmm."

A second flash. The storm was obviously a long long way away, but even so its presence was a relief. Maybe if the heat broke, other things might break as well. That was the hope. Maybe it would even return the world to normalcy.

We sat and watched as several more flashes lit up the sky—hulking masses of clouds standing out like vast black mushrooms.

✿

Time passing.

✿

"I need a wash," I said. "I am a mess."

The far-off storm was soothing but I still felt dark and gruff.

She nodded. "Me too. Doesn't take long in this heat. I suppose . . . downstairs. The tide's in. I . . . maybe I could come with you?"

I wondered why she was asking me instead of just, well, coming. Then I caught the echoes of the tone of voice I had used. There was not exactly much friendliness and warmth in the air now. Thirst. Impatience. Fear.

"Of course," I said with a smile, rubbing her arm. "Sorry—mustn't let this get me down." In my head, of course, 'me' actually meant 'us'—a little message I was barely consciously sending.

"Yeah," she said looking a bit relieved. "Things are getting weird. I can feel my hunting instinct—sharp as a fucking razor. I want to stalk it and pounce—even if it's just a glass of water . . ."

"Powerful. Can we then?"

"What?"

"Stalk and pounce on a little teeny tiny sip of water?" I asked plaintively. Can we trail and hunt the mighty bottle?"

She gave a sudden laugh and took it out of her bag again. "Why not?" she said, rolling it across the room away from us. She bounded to the floor and dropped into an all-fours crouch, staring at it, then wiggled her arse exactly like a cat—and launched herself across the room. Not surprisingly, the prey didn't put up much of a fight, but she rolled over with it nonetheless, hissing briefly, then came leaping back onto the bed with it. It was just a bit of fooling, but it seemed to clear the air a lot.

"That was strangely unfulfilling," she said, handing it to me with a giggle. "I wish it was a rabbit."

"So do I," I said—and that time I meant it. Oh boy did I mean it. Right then, I would have happily drunk its blood and eaten it raw. I remembered some of the scenes of the recent past—the rabbit and the duck, and with the hunger inside me, they brought a strange, glittery, urgent feeling that I could never remember feeling before. I think this was the first time in my entire life that I had experienced real, serious hunger—a reminder that no matter how unendurable things might be, there was always a long way further down the rabbit hole of suffering. Those on the streets, those forced to go without food for more than the usual few days a month to afford the rent . . . compared to them, I had it quite easy. And I will say that in the face of this rampaging need, the world now seemed an extremely simple place. Food hang-ups evaporate utterly at such times and you soon rediscover what is in charge of you.

"Anyway—wash," she said, bringing me back down to earth. "Nice and cool. Right?"

We stripped off again—this time with barely an awkward feeling. She grabbed the lantern and led the way down the staircase, right to the bottom floor, where we found the indoor sea waiting. I have to say, this was one of the most surreal moments of our stay here in the Soak. You have to picture this scene. We stepped down the last flight of stairs, only for the candlelight to reflect off the almost flat-calm water below. The darkness was intense, only a faint glow coming in the window from the lights of the opposite bank. The water barely moved, disturbed only by the tiny waves from the doorway. She put the lantern down on one of the steps and we walked on down into the Thames as though entering a swimming pool, wincing at the barnacles and other rough sea life. It must have been almost a metre deep and it came with a blast of beautiful coolness. We sat down side by side on the stairs, the faint light gleaming round the room.

Outside, distant lightning flickered again, lighting us up like two white ghosts.

"How are you feeling?" she asked quietly.

"Pretty much exactly the same as you, I suspect," I said with a smile. She returned the smile, then pulled me into a hug. I have to say, what with skin against skin, that watery environment and the occasional lightning outside, that was probably the most extraordinary hug I have ever known, and one I definitely didn't want to end.

"We'll be out of here soon," she said at last.

"I hope so."

"Then we can get back to normal again—can we? As far as possible with just the two of us . . . assuming it is just the two of us."

"I hope so."

She hugged me tighter.

"Gawd, Train Man," she muttered. "I am a mess. I feel in love and I want to cry and I'm horny and totally broken and enraged and terrified . . . All at once. My mouth tastes as though I've been drinking tar and my pussy feels as dry as an old book," she said with a shrill laugh. "When all this is over, after we've had a huge meal and a barrel full of water, maybe we can find somewhere really soft and comfortable and just be there for a few . . . days?"

"Sounds good to me."

"Maybe that would help me . . . help us get back to some kind of solid ground."

"I'm not sure I've ever found that solid ground in my life."

"Then it's about time we did. Question is—where? I live in a box in Camden—I mean literally. It's up by the ceiling—on legs."

"What do you mean?"

She gave a small smile. "It's something we put together—a wooden room thing, just big enough for a mattress and stuff—up on the ceiling. It's on legs and my roommates live underneath behind some curtains. I'm not sure why I got lucky and got the box. Maybe because there's only one of me."

"That's almost as good as my friend's fridge."

"Your friend's what?"

I briefly explained.

"Got to love people's creativity," she said with a grin. "My place—it's not exactly soundproof though," she said. "If I move too much, it starts creaking. When my roommates . . . I live with two girls in a fairly long-term relationship, and when they get going, I swear I can hear every squelch. I don't know whether to lose my temper or get my lube. It would be good to have my revenge, but even so—what's your place like?"

"It's . . . okay," I said. "Just a single bed—and it's in a little room with two girls living outside the door. I guess I have had to put up with them when they 'get lucky' so they can't really say anything when I do."

"Sounds like yours is a better bet than mine then. So—are we agreed?"

"Yeah—I'll tell them I have a lot of lost time to make up for."

"Something to look forward to," she said with a suddenly sad look on her face. "I hope," she added.

We stayed there for quite a while—there certainly wasn't any hurry for anything—enjoying the blissful cool and watching the distant storm fade. The time between the flashes stretching out more and more, the city returning to the nearest it ever got to darkness.

"Naked is nice, right?" she asked with a smile.

"Yeah—right," I agreed, wishing now I hadn't been such a coward a few nights ago. It now felt as though I had missed some vital chance to commune with these people that I might never see again. We should all have exchanged a few slaps on the arse and had a good roll in the mud. I think that would cure quite a lot of the problems facing humanity . . .

TUESDAY

As dawn crept over the sky, a new sound intruded into the world—the rumble of a train. Darting through to the back, I watched it—a simple eight-car commuter train. I wondered what it meant. Was the London Madness over or had they just realised that they couldn't cripple the city forever? Either way, it didn't mean the sea wall rail line was clear, for the machinery was still there on the other lines. I watched as the carriages rolled slowly east along the wall, playing peek-a-boo among the buildings. I could even make out people sitting inside, an early morning trip out of the madness to one of the Sussex or East Anglia destinations. An enviable journey.

As it disappeared beyond Canary Wharf, I returned to the Beggar who was curled up into a comma on the bed. It was obvious now that there was no sense hoping to slip out before it got light. The light was here, the light was now and any walkers along the tracks would be visible from a hundred windows. We slept a block of time away somehow, then awoke in bright painful daylight, feeling seriously unwell. The storm hadn't washed the temperatures away much and the familiar dull heat was right there to greet us. Ever-stretching time. A logarithmic spiral of dwindling water. No food. It was all starting to have its inevitable effects—all the symptoms of dehydration and intense hunger. My mouth felt dry. I couldn't swallow—even with the help of the occasional sips of water we allowed ourselves. My skin was dry as a stone. Dizziness and headaches. Deep deep fatigue that left me barely able to walk. And yet, when I was awake, my senses felt startlingly clear and aware of everything around me. All the details playing like an orchestral score. Every movement on the river. Or in the city beyond. The little boats. The river buses. The cars on the opposite bank. The birds in the air around us. My eyes followed them all. The Beggar too. Every move she made was shouted in my brain. I tried to just keep lying there with a faint smile on my face. Trying to keep calm.

☼

And . . . night came. Even after that interminable day, night came. The relief was immense. The silence on the Sea Wall also.

No matter what, we had to get out of here this time. We didn't even need to discuss that—it was burning in both our minds.

Again we made our way downstairs, somewhat as though in a dream, fumbling cautiously in the minimal light of the torch. Energy must be available to power my muscles . . . somewhere. Then she snapped the torch off and we stepped outside into the wet mud and concrete. The instant soaking of my feet. Barely noticed. Then it was through the ruined alley to Narrow Street.

"First thing when we get out, we go straight to the all-night supermarket down the road in Bow—and buy most of it, right?" I said. "Empty their drink cabinet."

"Oh yeah," she said with a grin. "I want at least three big bottles of mineral water and a carton of beautiful fruit juice . . ."

There was still no sign of anyone as we crossed the ancient ruined bridge over Limehouse Cut and arrived at the concrete flow by the wall. Still deserted. We felt very unsafe, though, as we scrambled dizzily up and approached the hideaway.

Then the Beggar drew a hissing breath.

Fumbled urgently in her bag and dragged out the torch.

Flashed it upwards . . .

At the top of the wall, coils of razor wire billowed along the parapet—but far worse than that, some of the crucial ruined brickwork that had served as our pathway up and out was quite simply no longer there. Gone. Demolished. Smoothed off into a sheer vertical face, a safe distance from the wall.

We stared at the sight, a feeling in my stomach that I am having a hard time finding words for. The pain in my head suddenly much worse. There was very little surprise, however. It was more a sort of leaden feeling of having fears realised—the knowledge that a half-expected doom is right there waiting for you. A glance at the Beggar revealed a similar dull inevitability. No doubt I wasn't the only one to have been quietly thinking this exact scenario. Of course, the first thing they would do is seal off the way in. Even amid all the chaos that had overtaken the world.

"Oh fuck it allllllll," she said, incautiously loud.

I just nodded dizzily.

"Okay," I said. Again my voice sounded weirdly casual and calm. Utterly failing to reflect the horrible feelings inside. "We have already established that there's no other way up. So . . ."

"Not that I know of." Her voice sounded slurred and shaking. "There might be something further along. A ladder somewhere."

We looked round the Soak helplessly, searching for an idea, but there was little to see. The Sea Wall stretched away in both directions, an impassable vertical metal surface. There were a few boats still moored in Limehouse Basin, some still in use, some apparently abandoned, but all locked and chained up very securely and no use to us. People had to be able to access these somehow, though—and boats could still come in and out through the Limehouse Cut and Regent's Canal watergates to get to the Thames. But that was also useless, as I well knew. The massive gates were a dull metal wall, decked with machinery. Big enough to be somewhat unnerving, in fact. There was indeed a way in, high above, but it looked like the gate to a concentration camp—more heavy metal, more razor wire.

I rubbed at my face urgently. "Can you spare a sip of water?" I begged. "It's getting hard to think. And right now we need to think."

She gave a frown. "That is mine, you know," she reminded, hunching her shoulders slightly.

"Huh?"

She blinked. "I mean—oh gawd. Sorry—yes, I . . ." She handed me the bottle at arm's length, not looking at me, and I took a microscopic sip. Just enough to moisten the mouth. I watched her carefully for a moment, then shrugged it off. I reached for my phone in the little pouch on my belt. There wasn't much battery left, but a bit.

"Can you think of anyone I could phone for help?" I asked. "How many degrees of separation are there from any given human being and a boat? Or maybe someone could sling a rope down?"

"I don't know," she said, her voice sounding almost devoid of hope now. "Let's . . . I dunno. I dunno. Let's just look around a little. There may be something."

That did indeed seem the only thing to do. We forced ourselves to walk, me holding a silent monologue addressed to my legs, begging them to function for a little while longer. We made our way through the Soak following the wall as far as Limehouse Cut. Then there was nothing to do but follow the old waterway back to that little footbridge. But before we could get far, we got the second shock of the night.

To our horror, we rounded a corner of ruined building and came face to face with a figure. A human figure, that is. Dressed in a florescent yellow uniform. He gave a startled exclamation and flashed a torch in our faces with a painful glare. For one long agonising interminable frozen moment, nobody moved and I had plenty of time to take him in. He wasn't a policeman—probably he was inspecting something or surveying something—or inspecting an inspection or whatever it is people do these days.

Then chaos erupted.

"Run," the Beggar hissed. "Keep with me. Come . . . where I am going. Just . . . keep with me."

She bolted. I followed without any hesitation whatsoever, adrenalin momentarily overriding the dull agony in my legs and sending me stumbling wildly through the broken concrete and paving slabs.

"Hey," the figure yelled behind us, dragging out his phone and moving in our direction. In spite of the panic—or because of it—I remember all this very clearly. I remember the Beggar moving like one of her own victims in the chase, dodging, darting, weaving, trying to get out of sight and throw the pursuit off our trail. We couldn't actually go very fast as the ground could hardly have been worse for running—slippery, slimy concrete strewn with stones and sucking mud, broken masonry everywhere. But our pursuer had it no better and he gave up soon enough. We kept moving, though, until we were back at Limehouse Basin, then staggered to a halt. That burst of exertion had utterly wrecked me—my muscles were screaming and my heart was racing at incredible speed. A glance at the Beggar revealed that it was the same for her. She had slumped over an old railing with a faint moan.

Then she abruptly turned away, bent double and threw up with a choking sob. It was not far off a dry heave but it must have undone at least a few sips of water.

She straightened up with an effort and looked at me expressionlessly, her face sallow and sickly.

And then, faint but unmistakable . . . the sound.

What you might call the icing on the cake of all this.

The sound of an engine in the distance. A very familiar engine.

The Beggar looked round uneasily—and my urgently scanning eyes soon found a moving light in the distance. Heading directly towards us. I grabbed her arm.

"It's the MPS helicopter," I said urgently, trying to shrink back even further into the concrete behind me. The Beggar swore loudly at the approaching light, and I didn't need telling why. The infrared eyes in the sky would be no friend to us.

"Now what do we do?" she said, looking close to despairing. We had to get inside, anywhere where the night vision eye couldn't see us—but there were only seconds to do so, and no passable doorway in sight. Everything seemed bricked up or locked or shut away behind welded bars or chains. "Come on," she said at last, her voice shaking. She ran—stumbling, ungainly and exhausted but still managing to move surprisingly fast over the slippery ground. I followed, thinking she was aiming at some building or other, but instead she led me straight to the Basin itself and, with an almost spookily quiet movement and no hesitation whatsoever, vaulted right in, feet first. I staggered awkwardly, but momentum made me follow with barely a thought, dropping down into the water almost as quietly.

This had once been a swanky marina protected from the Thames by the now vanished Limehouse Tide Lock. Once it had been a sophisticated, somewhat elitist place where picturesque boats had moored at some of the most expensive moorings in the country beneath the gaze of even more unaffordable flats. Now, though, it was a deep, black tidal pool of brine, only used by the occasional boat exiting the London canal network to the Thames. The cold grabbed me instantly. For a moment I panicked, since my feet could find nothing below. But then I realised I was floating. I watched the Beggar sink herself down as far as possible in the water until only a part of her face was exposed, and squeeze close against the old metal wall of this drowned harbour. There was a small concrete overhang and she tried to get underneath it—get what little of her face had to remain above water right up against the edge, and I quickly followed. There was nothing to hang onto but swimming gently against the metal helped us keep our position.

And then, with a shocking noise, the helicopter was right overhead, air hammering down. The Beggar grabbed my hand under the water and I remember hanging there frozen, troubled brine slopping agonisingly over our faces, pleading with some appealing yet doubtlessly non-existent power in the world to make that helicopter just go away without seeing us. Please go away, please go away, please get the fuck out of here . . .

There were red lights flashing up there, and they twanged at the world with an uncomfortable touch of familiarity. Yes—this was all very polyhedral. All so very, very human. It seemed for a moment as though threads of red light were spreading and populating the world again with that roaring machine as its nexus— red and brine confusing my eyes. Measuring.

Overhead, the constellation that was the aircraft drifted gently above the Soak. It passed backwards and forwards over the whole area for several minutes—at least I imagine it was several minutes rather than several lifetimes. Then to my shattering, giddy and almost erotic relief, the sound was fading again. The black aircraft was drifting away in the direction of Canary Wharf.

We didn't move, though, save for allowing ourselves to bob a little bit higher in the water. For a long while we stayed there, feeling the cold eat in. I'll tell you, the water makes some weird noises when the world is silent, when your ears are straining for the slightest invasion . . . it slops and slaps and kisses and pops like some weird and affectionate living thing.

And the red lights of that helicopter still seemed to linger in my eyes like afterimages. The Soak was gleaming red.

Polyhedron?

As time passed, though, and we saw no movement and heard no sound that could possibly be human, we began to relax. Maybe they thought we had slipped away in a boat or something and given up. After all, they could have no idea at all who we were.

"Come on, Train Man," she said. "There must be some clue in that vast database of yours that can get us out of here?"

I shook my head. I had no idea. If this was a different kind of book, then no doubt I might have been able to come to the rescue at the eleventh hour. I could have been the hero and you all would have loved me for it. Maybe I could have remembered some nook or cranny or outlet pipe that could allow us a way through after suitable adventures. But the simple fact is that there is little point to a sea wall with holes in it, and a combination of sea wall and main line railway isn't going to have many ways over it either. Not in London.

I rubbed at my eyes again in a desperate attempt to get the tinges of red out of my vision.

With nothing better to do, we remained in the water and slowly began making our way across the basin, following the metal wall westwards. West seemed a more friendly direction since it was away from the forbidding and all-seeing surveillance of Canary Wharf Island. Occasionally we had to detour around a boat—and then swim across the channel before the rather terrifying face of the watergate itself. Eventually we reached the western end of the dead marina and scrambled out with the help of what had once been a wooden jetty, now little more than a half-drowned woodpile. The Beggar, black and gleaming, slopped down into the mud and shingle like an exhausted pile of rubbish. Her face looked strange in the low light—barely human in this barely human situation. And still tinged with red, I realised uneasily. I looked round, then froze completely as more red lights deliberately winked on around us. Connected by ghostly threads. Far too familiar. It was very slow—you might even say leisurely. First one would appear, looking like just another warning light for ships. Then another, a minute or so later. Then another. I stared at them—no longer feeling particularly frightened. For some reason, as more and more of them appeared, my methodical brain even had me counting the seconds. 22, red light, 8, red light, 47, red light, 34, red light, 12, red light—somehow like a very slow musical composition, as though each light was a new note, slowly building up into a dense, tranquil atonal chord.

"What are you looking at?" the Beggar managed faintly. I just gestured.

"Do you see lights?" I asked, genuinely unsure and barely caring how the question might sound.

The Beggar stared for a moment. "Yeah—what's going on?"

That answered one question, at least—these mysterious lights were not only in my head. I looked at her—her features very faintly etched in red now. She looked scared and bewildered, underneath the exhaustion.

"Polyhedron," I muttered, too tired myself to say much more than that. "World Polyhedron."

"Oh," she said, hunching down again and looking at nothing.

After a few minutes' rest, though, we scrambled up and slowly walked onwards, following the red-tinged sea wall towards where it angled away from the railway near Limehouse station. There was still no way up, however. Now, instead of a railway line, it was topped with a red, iron fence.

Up ahead, we were running out of Soak. The reddened shingle was dwindling to nothing as sea wall and old Thames came together. The wall reached the old river bank and turned another sharp corner—and then there was only a small strip of shingly mud, a couple of feet wide, before even that faded out and the wall sat directly in water.

We walked as far as we could, here at the end of the world—a place as forsaken as anywhere I could imagine. To our right, the sheet piling towered up like an impassable fortress. To our left, deep deep mud and a river that looked like a river of blood. Up ahead, central London leaned directly over the Thames in a constellation of lights. The windows of Shadwell and Wapping staring out with uneasy defiance at the river that had already consumed so much of their neighbour. Beautiful yet utterly out of reach.

Red lights.

The Beggar was shivering.

"Fuck," she said. "I am actually cold . . ."

That was true. I could feel every atom of heat being wicked out of me by my wet clothes, just in case our exhaustion and thirst weren't enough.

18, red light, 6, red light, 28, red light, 4, red light . . . there was an acceleration here. I could still see the city clearly enough, but as though a superimposition was taking place and it was clear that if the current progression continued, there would come a point when the dominance would shift over—when the world of the red light and the world of the familiar London would change and it would be London itself that seemed the pale ghost hidden somewhere behind a red reality. I didn't know what would happen then.

"Fuck it," she muttered again, dropping to her knees with a squelch. She sat back against the metal looking totally defeated. I glanced at my phone, but of course the immersion had killed it. In the end I sat down beside her, my head running into overdrive, yet again analysing every snippet of information that I could call to mind, trying to find any possible way out of here. Red light or no red light, there had to be something. Some ladder somewhere allowing access. Some steps. Some jetty. Maybe we could swim for it—keep working our way along the edge of the Thames until we came to something. Anything. Though what, I didn't know. So many of the old access points to the Thames had been closed off or shut away behind impassable gates when the wall was built. Humanity's fence fetish had never seemed so domineering.

"Fuck it," the Beggar said a third time, much louder. Indeed, it was almost a scream and I could distinctly hear it echoing around the banks of this old, black, slithering Thames. She punched the mud and glared at nothing. I looked at her gloomily—but the outburst had put a thought into my head. What exactly was stopping us from screaming for help and concocting some story? That we had fallen in? That we had swum here and were trapped? Could such things work in modern London?

"The tide will be rising again soon," she muttered, fumbling for my hand, which I quickly gave her.

I was still thinking it through, the cogs of the brain chewing over the only hope I could possibly find. Now—sites where you could theoretically fall into the Thames. I was on rather firmer ground here than with places to climb out again. The miserable fence on top of the wall here was hardly a high one, and it didn't continue that far up river. Indeed, about 50 yards down, the wall formed into a promenade. The question was, could we have managed to swim or splash all the way up here? And what would happen if our screams were answered by the same fluorescent uniform that had chased us earlier? Maybe we should never have run away. Maybe if our wits had not been so scrambled, we would already have been out of here. Maybe . . .

"Not much use, are you Train Man?" she growled. I refocused on her with a flinch and hastily let go of her hand. In my shaken, dizzy and sickly state, that remark came like a punch in the mouth and I stared at her in shock. Really hurt.

"What use would you like me to be?" I demanded at last, my voice sounding cold. "Blow up like a balloon so we can just float away? Telepathically call to my train friends and summon a railcrane to lift us out?"

She was silent, staring at red nothing, then wearily buried her face in her hands. "I'll apologise for that when we are safe out of here," she muttered.

The thoughts came clamouring round, spinning in circles—horrible thoughts, that I really didn't need right then. Maybe this had all been a mistake. How could I ever have expected to find a human being I could connect to? No doubt she was also starting to regret it—starting to hate me for being there. What else could I possibly expect? Blah blah blah . . .

I gave a weary sigh, on the point of putting my suggestion into words, but I guess she will never know because, with beautiful timing, we were interrupted.

We are now coming to the point in all this when I have to choose what I say with some care—and where you will have to choose what to believe. Or . . . you know, maybe not. Maybe I should just continue in some loopy red acid-high and have done with it. I don't know. By this time, thirst and exhaustion were catapulting both of us into dreamland, no question. Was that why the red was invading the world? Was that why we were sitting in a London that looked like a vision of hell? You decide, because I don't fucking know. And I know even less about what happened next.

"Hello?" a voice called from the middle distance, and I stared round in confusion. It was not an aggressive voice. It was more, well, more like a fellow cautious denizen of the dark. A human being rather than an agent of the city. And it was not coming from behind us in the Soak but apparently from in front—out on the red darkness of the river. I stared in astonishment.

Surely I recognised that voice.

There was a movement somewhere nearby in the red-stained black. Even the Beggar flinched and stared, half scrambling to her feet. If the voice was an enemy, this last vestige of mud and shingle was not a good place to be trapped.

There was a soft splash and a large canoe slid out of the dark, drifting sideways onto the muddy shore alongside us.

"Hello," Feather said again—a greeting now. She stepped out neatly, then bent and hauled the boat further out of the water. I just, well, stared at her. If she had been a tentacled monstrosity out of the depths of the netherworld, I could hardly have given her a weirder look. She was dressed in her uniform of fisherman's waders up to her thighs, a mud-stained shirt and a wide-brimmed hat held on with a ribbon of some kind—and the familiar small rucksack on her back. There seemed to be a lamp on her forehead as well, held on with an elastic strap—not switched on. And as before, *something* over one eye. Something sophisticated with a lens, which she shoved up onto her forehead as she greeted us. Night vision?

And tucked in the boat beside her was an array of tools, including a large pair of wirecutters or bolt cutters, and a spade.

"What the fuck are you doing here?" I demanded in a slightly hysterical whisper, scrambling to my feet.

"Just mudlarking," she said. "Beautiful secrets, remember? Paying a twentieth of your living by picking up beach rubbish is no different to any other activity these days so I have to keep it stealthy sometimes."

Somehow I knew that was a lie. Don't ask me how.

I glanced at the Beggar, who was sitting squarely on her arse, legs apart, staring up at us as though we were both ghosts. And maybe we were.

"Um—who . . . ?" she managed.

I could barely bring myself to say it; it all seemed such a ridiculous coincidence.

"This is my neighbour." The Beggar just blinked.

"Have you been following me or something?" I demanded. Feather gave me an innocent look.

"In this?" she said, kicking the canoe with a dull thunk. I wasn't convinced. Don't ask me for precise details how or why but I wasn't convinced.

"You heard something, right? Your—radio—thing? You . . ."

Again the innocent shrug.

"So what's going on?" she asked. "I can smell that something is."

"We're stuck here," I said, still with that same curious casual tone, as though chatting in the hall at home. "The place is crawling with police, or something—whatever they are—and there's no way over that bloody wall."

"Uh-huh," she said as though that was the most normal thing in the world.

"We've been stuck here for three nights. Oh and . . . do you maybe have any water on you?"

Feather's eyebrows went up, then she produced a bottle of the most precious substance in the world from her rucksack. I stared at it as though it was emitting a heavenly glow, then took it with trembling fingers. It was a litre and close to full—gleaming dully in the red light that filled the world. I stared at it for an entranced moment, then handed it to the Beggar. She took it with wide eyes, as entranced as I was, then juggled the top off and was gulping it down.

"You two look in a real state," Feather said. "I'm glad I found you when I did."

"Can you get us out of here?"

She looked round at the canoe uncertainly. "Well, there's not really room in here—but do you think you could hang on?" She patted the rope that was strung round the gunwale. (Do canoes have gunwales? I don't bloody know.) "I'll take you to somewhere you can climb out. It's not far."

"In the Thames?" I asked.

"Yes. The water's calm."

"I don't think I could get any wetter," the Beggar said wearily, handing me the half-empty water bottle. I quickly downed the rest of it and . . .

No, that's not right. I put that bottle to my lips and almost moaned aloud at the sheer bliss of feeling cool fresh fluid flowing into my mouth. For a moment there, the rest of the world retreated, kind of like a really, really good kiss, and it was just me and that bottle in perfect union, around which the universe revolved in a dizzy spiral. Until, far too soon, it was empty. It was over. It was gone.

. . . and Feather nodded. "Good," she said brusquely. "Let's get out of here—just in case there's anyone still looking for you. You can tell me more about it later." She shoved the canoe back into the water and climbed in. The Beggar gave me a huge-eyed stare and scrambled to her feet. We squelched out into the mud.

"Kneel," Feather ordered, and we did so—the bewildered question flickering through my mind of what we were supposed to be worshipping here. But Feather quickly directed our hands to the rope gunwale. "Hang on tight," she said. "It should be comfortable enough—and not too far. Just make sure you don't come loose. I don't want to lose you in the dark."

We grabbed the rope and each wrapped it around one wrist as securely as we could, using the other to hang onto each other closely. I could feel the Beggar shivering still—a wet and cold body under her clothes, which were swirling around her like seaweed.

She gave me a haunted look.

"I'm out of my depth," she said, then gave a shrill giggle, kicking at the mud we were kneeling in. "I mean . . . all this . . . is just so strange . . . Where are we going?"

"No idea," I said sadly. "I don't know either."

"Ready?" Feather called.

"I . . . I suppose . . ."

Feather shoved the oars into the water with a couple of powerful strokes, dragging us further out. It was a strange sensation, feeling the mud and stones trailing away beneath us, the water getting deeper and more supportive. I wanted to help by kicking with my feet or something but I wasn't much use. The exhaustion was too great and Feather pretty much had to drag us, grunting with the effort. And then there was nothing. We were floating.

Feather gave a sigh of relief. Out of the mud it was much easier and she paddled up-river, keeping fairly close to the shore, oars driving through the water quietly. I looked back at the retreating Soak, mentally saying goodbye to it with no great fondness. Something had closed here—a chapter had ended with an ending I could feel right through me. Of course it had. Under this red light, the ruins looked cinematic, like some improbable fantasy backdrop on a dark stage—more like a deliberate human artwork or diorama than lingering survivors of a chaotic process.

We hung there, water swirling past us, little more than dead cargo. In the dark, I could hardly see the Beggar or see where her eyes were, but I could feel her free arm locked around me almost painfully. Every so often, I'd still feel the river bed brushing at my feet, or a collision with some debris down there that made me flinch. It was an extraordinary feeling and actually, in spite of the cold, in spite of our exhaustion, in spite of the red that gleamed all round, I was feeling quite tranquil. I don't know if you have ever sailed down the Thames at night? Or indeed any big urban river? It is a beautiful thing—and somehow even more so from the water surface itself. And here, in this dreamland of hunger and exhaustion, this strange viewpoint with all the lights of the city leaning over us, and the red web covering everything like a vision of space, it was breathtaking. I stared up at the looming walls as they passed by in the middle distance, wondering if anyone or anything was watching us. Late night wanderers? Security cameras? The Measuring Men?

A massive ruin loomed up out of the dark. I recognised it as the old Free Trade Wharf, a forgotten relic on the edge of another of those unaffordable Thames-side housing estates, now little more than a surreal monument of pilings and decayed wood. A few warning lights still glowed sadly to keep the shipping away—yet more red to add to the mix. Feather guided us carefully through the narrow gap between it and the wall, a claustrophobic red avenue of ruin. There had been a connecting walkway here once, now no more. I felt us impact some fallen timber with a jarring thud and the Beggar gave a faint groan and rested her head on my shoulder. I glanced uneasily at the rope round her wrist, visions in my mind of her coming loose and slipping away forever. If that happened, I might just go mad.

But then the ruin was behind us, the Thames opened up again and Feather picked up speed. I could see her looking round at the red city with an intent expression on her face, her body language conveying a hint of unease. Any hope of timing the lights as I had been was totally gone now—they were winking on at the rate of dozens every second. It was a red galaxy—the infinite lines and infinite angles of the Polyhedron filling the world. Indeed—they may have been starting to replace the city itself as I had suspected, as though it was the buildings that were transparent and insubstantial. It was as if the Soak had been the centre—the birthplace, from which the phenomenon was radiating outwards into the surrounding city. But of course, that could just have been my perception.

Through it all, though, the Thames itself remained as a black corridor—constrainable but untameable.

"Feather," I called, sounding almost casual. She stopped paddling and glanced round. "What's going on?" It was a simple question—such an obvious one, yet it hadn't occurred to me to ask it before now.

"I don't know," she said, and I could hear that same touch of unease in her voice. "It can't be the entire city . . . can it?"

She was silent a moment. "Maybe something has finally broken somewhere," she said at last. "I have never seen anything as big as this before."

I stared down into the dark water, trying to rest my bewildered eyes. Unreality was spiralling round me, its centre point a glowing singularity that threatened to consume my brain from within. It was all a dream, of course. Somewhere, I had segued into sleep—maybe I was still lying there in the penthouse with the Beggar. Or maybe I had never left the hideaway. Or maybe earlier still. Maybe I had fallen asleep on the railway line, with this whole story just that final dream you dream when you are dying, as the train roared down. There might well have been an equation between these red lights and the thrumming, buzzing vibration of the rails as the wheels approached.

"I don't understand," the Beggar said, almost under her breath. I had no reply to that beyond momentarily tightening the arm I had locked around her.

"It's not perfect," Feather said, as though confirming what she had been searching for. She dragged the night-vision monocular thing over her eye again for a moment, then returned it to her forehead. "Look. Over there."

I followed her hand to the shore to our right, but could see nothing.

"And there. The Polyhedron is broken," she said. "All over—it is in tatters." And I could see what she meant. If this was a spider's web, it was in a sorry state. There were places, many places, where it hung and sagged. Disrupted. Snapped. Curved. Feather started paddling again, driving the canoe in towards the bank, aiming for one of those areas. In my head I was trying to place which part of the city was located there. It must have been somewhere in Wapping, but aside from that, my mental maps had shut down as well. The city barely existed now.

We came floating up to one of the broken areas—and then actually passed into it. We drifted right in amongst the lights, which made no sense because surely that meant we had passed through where the bank would have been and left the Thames behind us. And as we did, the city seemed to fade away completely, leaving nothing but blackness. All I was aware of was water immediately around the boat, picked out with dull red highlights. Aside from that, there was nothing but the polyhedron, passing overhead. The lights gleamed a deep red, each with a powerful core of white shining through. I could feel no heat from them; they made no sound; no visible movement at all. They were just glowing points connected by threads that looked like hollow luminous tubes of pure energy. Like stars in a galaxy, there was actually plenty of space between them now we were up close. The connecting threads either hung loose, letting us through, or passed overhead like bridges as Feather continued lightly skimming the water with her paddles, propelling us forward.

I now had the even more surreal image in my head of the canoe drifting lazily down some east London street, passing between the tall and cluttered buildings supported by nothing at all—the strangest ghost yet on these crazy London nights. Who knows? Maybe that's what happens when you break the angles of the world. Maybe you really can row down the streets or fly across the rooftops—or sail the seas of dreams wherever you like . . .

Feather looked over her shoulder at us, and now there was a curious grin on her face. "It's awesome," she whispered. "No fighting needed, merely rejection. London seems to be tearing the Polyhedron apart. Because ultimately it's alien to what humanity is—so the rejection is instinctive if we let it."

"Right," I mumbled, too tired to match the glow of excitement in her face. I glanced at the Beggar, seeing her clearer now—but she was hanging there with her eyes closed, her free hand still gripping hard enough to hurt.

"Madness always was the ultimate revolution," Feather said solemnly. "Even the madness of a summer night."

She tucked the paddle in the canoe beside her and stood up, wobbling for a moment but soon finding her feet. From our vantage point, directly behind and below, she looked shockingly tall and somehow glorious in spite of her mudlarking gear—or because of it. She was staring ahead through that red world with a face filled with hunger and power. Feather the pilot, Feather the ferryman, still driving us onwards . . .

And we were still moving, yes—carried on by our momentum or by something else, I'm not sure. The water seemed to have a slight flow to it. A sense of life. Eddies and swirls. Water that seemed infinite, as though the Thames was just a visible sliver of a vast ocean.

"Are you okay back there?" she asked, not looking round.

"Yes," I said, wanting to laugh. "Yes, fine."

The Beggar gave a faint murmur of assent as well.

Ahead, the broken area of the polyhedron came to an end—the threads taut again now, directly in our path. I watched them uneasily, not at all sure what would happen if we actually touched one. Images of spiders' webs were large in my mind, but surely that was a totally facile comparison? They weren't going to stick us in a trap until the Measuring Men came crawling. Were they? Feather watched in silence, and then, to my surprise, she bent and picked up her wire cutters—short but tough-looking blades with long handles for maximum leverage. She held them out before her, a small smile on her face . . .

And *snip*.

The thread collapsed—not quite vanishing, but flashing darker and falling away. The Polyhedron sagged around us, the whole network shifting from the released tension.

A moment later, another came within reach—and *snip* again. And again. Feather gave a happy laugh. And then our journey became a surreal progression, drifting forward, Feather standing there, cutters at the ready, cutting our way further and further through the maze.

"Death to the Polyhedron," she muttered under her breath. "If I'd known it was this easy . . ." She paused and looked round. There was a vertex approaching now—one of the red lights suspended a few feet above the water. I could see Feather watching it, eyes glittering. Then she opened the cutters again with a grin. "I wonder."

She leaned down and reached out with that device as it approached, then plunged the blades into that red light, closing them with a clash right in the middle.

The results were dramatic. It was as though she had tried to cut through a high-voltage electricity cable. There was a nasty snapping bang and a blinding flash—white, with a hint of green. To my astonishment, I got a momentary image of city all around us—the classic dull east London buildings looming tall overhead. They were only there for a second and then gone again, but it was enough to make my mind and stomach swirl. Maybe my vision of paddling down the street had been spot on. The shock knocked Feather over backwards with a shriek and she pretty much landed on top of us. The canoe turned over, plunging us into chaos. Feather came splashing into the water, still holding the wire cutters. I remember struggling with the ropes that we had wound round our wrists to keep us attached—but the boat pitched down beneath the surface, far too fast—as though it was being pulled. Pulled by a violent current of water that had appeared from nowhere. I heard the Beggar give a choking screech as we went under, kicking feebly but not really able to do anything except be dragged into the suffocating black. I didn't dare try to breathe, expecting nothing more than the final flood of water if I did. So I held my breath as long as I could until my lungs were screaming. Something slammed against me—or rather I slammed into it. It felt hard—very hard. Maybe metal hard. And it was all round me. An imprisoning tube. I was in a tube, being swept along with no idea which way was down or where we were going. I could see nothing. I was not the driver here, only the passenger. No doubt in my dream on the railway tracks, these were the final seconds— the train wheels only metres away, my whole body shaken by the vibration. Or maybe it had already got me—my head taken off cleanly and sent rolling and tumbling down the line, still clinging to some confused form of consciousness. All I can say is that I have never in my life wanted to scream such a scream as I did then, but I couldn't because to do that would mean releasing my precious breath.

Then with a blast we emerged from that pipe, not in a waterfall but in a slackening and spreading flood. And for the first time, I felt something solid. A flat surface that instantly established itself in my mind as downwards. The world had a floor again. And I was lying on it feeling a blast of reality that had me thrashing and choking and spitting out water, struggling for breath, my saturated clothes slopping around me. I opened my eyes and stared up with a shriek, registering little but the same dazzling red of the Polyhedron. Overhead arched a network that seemed denser than anything I could remember from before—like the core of a galaxy. A massive ceiling of lines and angles. And as I stared upwards I realised that there was something else there. And I froze in complete skin-crawling shock.

There was a circle of figures surrounding us. Or rather not a circle—let's be clear. A circle of figures is only points on a polygon after all. Vertices. They were little more than dull black human shapes, silhouettes against a backdrop of red, but where their faces should have been was complete madness. I could see . . . well, there was only a blank. Utter blackness. In which a single white spot or disk was located. And that disk was moving. Orbiting. Engaged in a slow spin in the vertical plane around that black face-like space, taking several seconds to complete each orbit. You can't read expressions in a face like that. They are intrinsically inscrutable, yet I could tell that they were looking down at me—at us, for I could see the Beggar also lying nearby in a sodden heap. There were tears in my eyes of some kind of horror—yet at the same time I could hardly bring myself to care anymore. I had been dragged far beyond caring. So I curled up on the floor and lay there waiting.

What did it feel like to be finally measured and found wanting?

Then there was a screech—and Feather erupted into my field of view. She looked a sight, wire cutters still in one hand, her hair a wet explosion. She said nothing, but in that silence I could see a rage that eclipsed even that of Star Girl at her wildest—focused, deadly and under control. She was staring round urgently, turning in a full circle, still trying to analyse the situation. Then she looked up and there was a flash of alarm on her face. Following her gaze, I realised why. It seemed to me that the Polyhedron was being repaired. Don't ask me how. Some—thing—was hard at work, bringing together the damaged areas of this web. You can imagine a spider-thing if you want. If it helps. But to me, everything was so diffuse and so otherworldly that any attempt to compare it is going to make little sense. The train nut in me wants to compare it to a multidimensional electrical wiring train crawling through the countryside, but going in every direction at once. Or maybe it was a dream of a manufacturing robot wittering away in a car factory with inhuman precision, and at least a few extra dimensions, reaching and grasping.

I stared up at it with a heavy feeling in my stomach—the sort of feeling you might get when watching some vital process disrupted and trampled on. It was like the agony of political wrangling, as people bitterly argue ideologies while people die in the streets of neglect. It was the same feeling you get when you watch the vampires manipulating the housing market. It was like the fight between sexual liberation and prudery. It was like watching the neo-Nazis or the worst kind of bigotry winning out in the human consciousness. It was . . .

Even though I still barely understood this, it was fucking horrible.

And Feather menacingly opened the cutter blades.

She stepped forward—and to my surprise, the Measuring Men retreated. She stepped again—and again they retreated. And it was at this moment that my fear started to fade away. These beings, whatever the heck they were, didn't seem particularly dangerous. In some way, conveyed entirely by their gestures and postures, they looked scared—confused . . . The word 'childish' is trying to attach itself to them in my mind. Stupid infantile things. Primitive. Vestigial. They watched Feather as she approached and an enormous grin spread across her face—then a massive screech as she broke into a run. The Measuring Men scattered, then swarmed after her, leaving us behind entirely. They followed as she ran to the edge of this open space, brandishing the cutters.

"How quickly can you rebuild this thing," she demanded loudly, reaching out and casually snipping a thread, "when there's a million of us whose minds can no longer fit your angles? And then two million? And then a billion?"

I could almost feel the place itself quail—shaking and blurred in my dizzy mind as the battle started. As the blades flashed again, cutting thread after thread. Snip. Snip. Snip.

And I wanted to burst out laughing.

"You can't do anything really, can you?" Feather said. "Just like those morons on the surface who can only fucking stare and frown. You only have power if people want you to. And you know what? I *don't* want you to."

It seemed to be true. The Measuring Men were able to do little to actually stop her. They just stood there gesticulating like defeated politicians, their bodies radiating panic, those absurd orbiting disks spinning pathetically. Under other circumstances, very other circumstances, I might even have started feeling sorry for them. There was a horror in this, though—the 'evil forces' revealed as nothing more than pathetic children. Pathetic, deranged, infantile, yet still there they were—the driving force in a world that throughout history would sooner crush you than save you, and until it does, refuses to even register your existence or your suffering. A world that I certainly couldn't change. A world that I had only managed to find some strength against by stepping sideways through the cracks to somewhere else.

Feather was scampering around through the web, still cutting with dizzying energy. Yet even so, neither side seemed to be gaining an advantage. The repair process continued implacably, yet rushing seemed impossible—and again I wanted to laugh. Was this a steady state? Or was there indeed a tipping point, as Feather had said? Whatever stupid war this was, fought with wire cutters and childish dread, could it ever be won? Or was the conflict between the angle and the curve somehow eternal? An inbuilt contradiction in us all, just like all the other contradictions that make us human?

In the end, I lay down again beside the immobile Beggar and shut my eyes, exhausted beyond awareness—too tired to cope with this any longer. The whole world was blurred and draining downwards inexorably. The same dwindling of my severed head on the railway line, if that dream was indeed true. With Feather still furiously cutting and the Measuring Men gesticulating like shocked children, it all faded away into a haze of moving shapes. A red spiral that shrank down to a point and vanished.

☼

Why is it that the dominant feeling of civilization at the moment is the sense of loss? So much seems to have fallen by the wayside in recent years, from the fundamental pillars and supports of society to any sense of human decency. And for what?

On a shingle beach under a grey sky, something I always saw as far more representative of Britain than any pomp and circumstance, we gather to say farewell to sense and reason, to humanity itself. Such a sea of hate and pain, of poison. But while the leaders and legislators crawl and squirm in their eternal mud-wrestling, people fade away and die, life becoming impossible. It is not and has never been a game.

And on the beach, it is as though an endless parade of floating coffins drifts out to that point where the sea becomes one with the grey sky. Hundreds and thousands and hundreds of thousands, each one filled with stories of human despair and death. Rest in peace, sad cast-offs in the dance of death. Souls lost to the endless and eternal rot of humanity.

WEDNESDAY

Again my head is tumbling down the railway tracks, catapulted far harder than a football. The eyes cannot focus. The world is a blur. No particular pain, just an ultimate shock that comes as a white silence, as my lord the train settles over me like the softest quilt. Indeed, being bodiless is a kind of release. I feel light—feather-like. Out of control but it hardly matters—as green rays shine up from the earth like a sunrise, soothing and tranquil . . .

And in this dream, death is nothing to fear . . .

Until my eyes jolt open.

I don't know where I am. I panic. I don't know if it is day or night. I don't know if I am alive or dead. If I am dead then the absolute last thing I want is an afterlife. All I wanted was to cease. Such an utter cessation that, as far as I am concerned, I had never existed.

I think I must have yelled something out loud, for I remember hands on me. Cold, almost startlingly cold. I fought them for a moment, but the touch was reassuring and I soon calmed down. And with the calm I registered light, which played potential reality like a trumpet—a great blaring bell of clear thought aimed directly in my face.

And yes, I was lying in bed—in a room as round as a bubble. A familiar face was looking down at me.

"You two were in quite a state," Feather said. "Just take it easy for now. You can sleep here as long as you need."

"Two?"

She pointed over to the other side of the room and I saw another figure, nothing more than a huddle under a blanket. The

Beggar. The relief was extreme. The fact that she was there and not vanished like a phantasm helped focus my mind—gather my memories. Again, it was a matter of sorting them all out into the correct order in my head, and again I won't bother you too much with that since I have already related them. Let me just say that it all came with a huge sense of closure, though not of the good kind. Closure of the chapter of life that had opened so recently on the railway line and then continued in the arches under it. Things always change. Implacably so. That hardly seems a profound realisation, but right then it seemed so and it came with a deep desolation.

I sat up with an effort, adding the fact that I was naked to my small compendium of awareness. Naked, muddy and stinking of river water and worse. Maybe Feather had removed our sopping wet clothes so we didn't freeze, but I could also imagine them abandoned somewhere in the depths of the city while two more deranged, naked phantoms crawled around in the dark. There was no sign of them, anyway. My memories could find nothing to help me there either.

"Okay," I said, my voice even softer than usual. "Where are we?" The room was round, or, more correctly, dome-shaped, and there were no windows. Art decked the walls—basic furniture. Even a computer system. I was lying on a rough mattress on the floor and beside me were several empty water bottles that I had presumably drunk at some point in a wild orgy of rehydration. At least, I wasn't feeling thirsty now.

"Where are we?" I demanded again, in wonderment.

"We're back in the caves," Feather said with a smile. "You don't recognise it?"

"Oh—right."

The place finally slotted into my mind then, of course—another room in Feather's underground complex. I nodded and felt some part of me relaxing. That seemed a good place to be.

"Seriously—what's going on?" I begged. "Please, Feather—this is hurting my head."

"I thought it was the best place to make for last night," she said calmly. "My housemates are good people. It's as safe a place as you are going to find in the city."

"Okay, but what about . . . I mean, what happened? How the fuck did you know I was there in that Soak?"

She shrugged and smiled. "Hey—I'm just a mudlark. Just a normal permit-carrying mudlark. I poke around, pick up crap and scavenge, that's all."

"But—the Measuring Men? The . . . Polyhedron thing?"

"What about them?" she asked.

"Didn't you . . ."

"They are just a metaphor," she said soothingly. "Just a symbol of what is wrong—what we have to fix in humanity before we can ever progress—or to avoid our own extinction and invalidation."

"But . . . you showed me . . ."

"You were in a sorry state," Feather said. "No wonder you are a bit confused."

She was playing mind games. She had to be. But I couldn't even begin to work out why. Such thoughts were like a mountain and, right now, I couldn't even make it over the foothills.

There was a movement across the room. In response to our voices, the Beggar sat up with a faint vocalisation and a feral look in her eyes. She was also naked—also muddy and bedraggled.

"Where are we?" she asked, her voice hoarse.

"This is my home," Feather explained again. "You are safe here."

"Oh, thank fuck for that," the Beggar said. She stared at Feather for a moment, as though trying to find something, anything in her head that could help her out—then she shrugged it off. She scrambled out from under the blanket and jumped in beside me, grabbing hold, arms going round me like steel bands for a moment before slowly relaxing again. For a moment, there was a blast of self-consciousness, well aware of how much I stank—but under the circumstances that seemed almost ridiculous. She stank, too. It was a very raw moment—two gruesome, naked animals clinging together in their filth, her face pressed into my neck, the feel of her long, pointed nose against my skin, slimy hair trailing over me. And I grabbed her in return and held her tight.

"All I can remember are dreams," she said, sounding close to tears.

Feather stared down at us expressionlessly—and it must have been quite a strange sight. Then she nodded. "You can go home whenever you are comfortable. Your own bed. Or stay here. As long as you need. You are very welcome."

"Thank you," I mumbled.

"There's dinner cooking in the common room," Feather said. "When you are ready for some food, it will be there. You can also take a shower up in the main building. Until then, rest a while."

"Food?" the Beggar managed blearily, as though wondering if that phrase had any meaning.

Feather smiled. "Yes. We do okay—a bit of creativity goes a long way. Do you mind a little meat? Sorry if yes, but we've got some in today. Down here we get what we can, of course, and it's all good."

I saw a flicker of surprise on the Beggar's face.

"No," I said. "Not at all, that's fine."

"Good. Let us feed you something nice before you go."

"Can't we stay here forever?" I asked forlornly.

Feather gave a laugh—then a thoughtful look. "Maybe," she said with a wry shrug. "I might be wrong, but I think you would fit in. Are you two a unit?"

I looked down at the Beggar helplessly, and she met my gaze with a similar gleaming question. Were we? I had always looked on the more formal declarations of love—exchanging rings, betrothal, whatever—as rather strange. No doubt they always felt too bound up with outmoded thought processes for comfort. But now they seemed to make more sense. At least you know where you stand then. Maybe one can make up one's own rituals—no need to be a slave to tradition—but whatever those rituals are, whether it's going off and having sex under a waterfall, sharing the two halves of a geode, giving each other a zen spanking, or even simply talking about it and shaking hands, at least they make an emphatic point. As it was, I just stared down at the Beggar feeling totally stunned again, unreality flooding me. I wanted to ask her what she thought we were, in spite of her dull grey eyes, but again, I couldn't even find the words.

"I—suppose . . . we are," I said.

The Beggar rested her face against my shoulder again. What a fucking romantic way to declare a relationship.

"I have to say it again, though—you need to remember that you will be living through the cracks. It's a different world. Where we do what we can and what we need. Some things will be awkward. Illegal. And also, you may hear things and see things—beautiful secrets, I suppose. And you will need to leave the surface behind you."

"I left the surface behind years ago," the Beggar said. "So I am past caring, to be honest. Put me where you like." She was silent for a moment then gave a sigh. "The only thing that kept me going was knowing beautiful people I could escape to . . . and now they are gone. Except you, Train Man. So—"

Feather gave her a worried look. "There's a lot of darkness flowing here," she said sadly.

"Yeah," I agreed, aware that she couldn't know the vast majority of our story. But there was no doubt she could read a certain amount. The Beggar had every limb wrapped round me now and she showed no sign whatsoever of letting go. It was almost an erotic embrace, trying to get as much skin in contact as possible—yet there were certainly no sexual instincts going on at all. Instead it was purely a matter of contact and desperate intimacy. I looked down at her, her eyes dull, her body tense, and it dawned on me that she was completely in shock. Far more so than I was. I suppose the bonds that had been severed for her a few nights ago had so much more time to strengthen than in my case. I was still the newcomer, after all. And of course, any shock to the mind requires its healing process, its recovery, its scar tissue, just like the body.

Don't question it, I told myself. *The last thing she needs is for you to be scared or stiff.* There was nothing to do but to stay there, using the pressure of my muscles to provide whatever comfort I could.

"Can I also tell you something a little gloomy, Feather?" I asked, stroking the Beggar's slimy hair.

"Of course?"

I hesitated, some part of me calling myself an utter idiot for the words that were starting to form in my mouth—something I never expected to say to anyone. But now I realised that I needed to get this out of me, somehow.

"I tried to kill myself the other day."

Her eyes flickered round at me with a sharp look, and she nodded silently.

"I suppose you could say—more than anything—I was just tired. On the most fundamental level you can imagine."

"What made you change your mind?"

"A chance encounter," I said and left it at that. She nodded, apparently accepting that as sufficient. "I don't mean that as a sob story," I said, suddenly my familiar awkward self again. "I just mean that . . . well, I know what you mean about exhaustion. I think we are all far too close to the edge of possibility."

She patted me on the shoulder. "I know you do," she said soothingly. "If you were somewhere comfortable, you wouldn't even have seen this place. The question is, are you sure?"

"I'm sure," I said quietly. "Thank you."

I glanced down at the Beggar, but she made no response.

"Very well," she said. "I will talk to the others—actually, I already have, but I will talk to them again. And . . ." She looked at the Beggar. "I'm sorry—I don't know your name?"

I froze, eyebrows up. It was almost a shock to be reminded about that. We had got about as close as two people could get without surgery, but she hadn't told me her real name yet. I suppose it barely seemed relevant since, in our heads, we both had names already. We'd exchanged, them, we'd learned them—they were what we were.

The Beggar gave a small smile, then finally rolled over, blinking hard. The toes of one of her feet gripped at my leg. "Oh yeah," she said, looking very casual. "I am . . ."

And there it was. She quietly introduced herself. Her toes gripped my skin a second time. I stared at her, feeling a very weird feeling.

"Good," Feather said. "But anyway—let's get you some food. Are you ready to come through or shall I bring some?"

The Beggar glanced at me for confirmation. "We'll come through. I think we'll feel better for that, thank you."

Feather nodded and indicated two gowns or robes hanging on a peg. "You can wear these—and come when you're ready."

She left the room. For a moment there, the Beggar had looked a little more energetic, but now she just burrowed down in the bed again.

"The dilemma," she said at last with a small laugh.

"Hmm?"

"I never want to leave this bed again. I want to just lie here until the world no longer exists. But . . . I also haven't eaten for three days. So . . ."

The fact that she had cracked a small joke was an extreme relief. "You're right, we'll feel better for some food," I said.

"Yeah."

It was still several minutes before we untangled our lethargic limbs and scrambled to our feet. It was impossible not to wobble and we supported each other as we dragged on the robes—basically helping each other to dress. Then we stepped outside into the passage and started the short walk down to the common room. I could see the Beggar looking around curiously as we went, taking in the little rounded rooms with a gleam of interest in her eyes. I could read the same questions in her face as had no doubt been in mine when I first saw this place.

"We . . . stay here?" she asked at last in a small voice.

"I was thinking, yes," I said after a moment. "I mean, I wanted to . . . move in here if . . . it's possible. I don't know, though. I hope so—I am so sick of the surface. But . . . I I I know you have a place of your own—but maybe . . . you also . . . if you liked? That is, if Feather can . . ."

I stumbled to silence.

"Moving in?" the Beggar asked dizzily, looking around at the rough tunnel.

"Yes."

"Oh—right . . . thanks," she said and quietly slipped an arm through mine. She might have said more, but by that time we had arrived at the common room and I pulled aside the curtain.

"Hey," someone called as we peered in—a young, black-skinned woman with beads in her hair wearing what looked like overalls. "You okay? How are you feeling now?"

"Yes—thank you," I managed. I gave a brittle laugh. "Just trying to work out what the fuck happened in the last few days."

"Do you need anything else to drink—or?"

I consulted myself thoughtfully and was surprised to find that the answer was no. I must have downed a lot of water at some point in the recent past. But before I could say so, I unexpectedly wobbled on my feet and leaned hastily against the wall. The woman looked at me with concern, but then Feather was by my side, taking my arm and guiding me to a chair. Then the Beggar beside me.

"Sorry," I muttered, feeling embarrassed. In a cosmic sense, maybe it hadn't been that much of an ordeal, but I still felt totally wrecked.

"Don't worry—just take it easy," Feather said—and then she was introducing me. Telling them who I was. I watched her carefully, then glanced at the Beggar, knowing what was coming and, for some reason, feeling uneasy—as though a mask was about to be removed. It was a stupid thought, though, and I swallowed it—and when my name was tossed out there, I just nodded. "They would like to join us here, as you know," she said. "Move in."

"Oh yes," she with the beads in her hair said with a focussing of interest. She looked at us both analytically. "Well you certainly look as though you have been spat out by the world. You look as though you need a place like this."

"Yeah," I mumbled.

"Anyway—let me get you some dinner."

"Thanks. Very . . . very kind of you . . ."

As the woman hurried away to the small kitchen area at one side of the room, the Beggar turned to look at me with a tiny smile. "So that's your name?"

"Yup," I said.

She nodded, and leaned her head against my shoulder again. And thus it was that almost without noticing, almost casually, we finally found out who we were.

A few more of the residents were gathering round, examining us with interest. We were both so tired that we could hardly be very social, but fortunately that didn't seem to matter. I was impressed by the seriousness and friendliness everyone was showing.

"So who are you all?" I asked at last with a smile.

The black woman gave a quiet laugh.

"Who are we? If you are moving in here, I suppose we had better introduce ourselves properly," she said, looking around. "I'm a web designer," she said. "I have a business putting together glitzy flash animations and websites for people." She glanced round the room.

"I'm a hairdresser," another woman chimed in, "so if you ever need to look sexy, I'm in room fifteen . . ."

"I'm a surrealist painter," a young man said with a nod.

"I make jewellery."

"I write poetry."

"I do palmistry at Camden Market."

"I'm an electrician."

"I'm a chef."

"I'm nothing at all—and that suits me fine," someone said with a laugh.

In my mind, I was back at a certain other bizarre introduction just over a week ago. It came with a sense of déjà vu—from one weird underground community straight into another one. Maybe. Then the cat—Fitzroy—was there, giving me a calculating look, sniffing at my fingers and rubbing against my leg in greeting. I scratched his head. The Beggar next to me hadn't said a word.

Then that same friendly web designer handed us plates with a bizarre collection of food on them—some divinely cooked spinach and mushrooms, what I think were Jamaican festivals, some kind of sweet-savoury rice with nuts in it. I stared up at her warm smile feeling another surge of emotion that I would have to analyse later.

"Do you mind a little meat?" she asked. "Sorry if yes, but down here we get what we can, of course, and it's all good."

"No, not at all, that's fine," I said feeling slightly dazed again.

A few cubes of white flesh were added to my plate. Tasting it, I was pretty sure it was rabbit. I saw that same flicker of surprise on the Beggar's face as she also accepted some.

"Maybe," she said, "if I can really move in, I can help you . . ."

SATURDAY

Arriving back at my little appendix a few days later with the Beggar beside me felt truly strange—as strange as anything that had happened recently. No doubt it was the fancy of seeing the familiar place and familiar world through her eyes—my dreary home something alien and new and exotic with every detail to be absorbed and analysed. For example, at one point on the appendix, there was a short stretch of mesh fence, and some person or persons had tied a whole array of coloured ribbons through the links. They had been there for a while, I remembered, and they hung weather-beaten and faded like seaweed—but I had never before really seen them. If there was a language or meaning to them, if there were codes in the pattern of colours, then I had no idea what they were. We didn't comment on it. I'm not even sure if the Beggar saw them, for she still seemed to be going through life in a haze. They gave the appendix a curiously exotic feeling for a moment, though. That's the way London works—and the way people work. A substrate of ancient crumbling brick invaded by gleaming and sterile developments, then inevitably invaded again by details like this.

My clothes and wallet never had showed up again so there was nothing to do but wait outside, with more details standing out like glowing runes. The door to my building was also pretty much invaded by languages of various kinds—scrawls of spray paint and stickers advertising unknowable things. There were even a few dreary racist or classist symbols that I had barely noticed before—little extrusions from the gloomier parts of the London hive-mind. Now, though, I saw them with a chill of embarrassment, wondering how well all this was holding up. Fortunately, it wasn't long until some neighbour appeared on a mission of her own and let us in. And then it was a matter of banging on my own door. To my relief, it quickly opened, but the look on Aceline's face as she peered out was fearful. "Oh it's you," she said, looking relieved. "Come in. Where the heck did you get to? I was getting worried."

Tea also sat there, dressed in a night robe, her hair messy. She was still bruised, though much recovered compared to a few days ago. She gave me a smile, then bowed a small bow, fluttering her hands in the air, gesturing from me to her with a quirkily questioning expression on her face. I bowed slightly in return.

"I haven't got my key," I said.

"Oh tut," Aceline said. "Well, I'm glad you're back. This place has been going insane lately—I wondered . . ." She screwed up her face, looking at the Beggar curiously as we stepped inside. I wanted to retreat immediately to the quiet of my room, but politeness demands its sacrifices.

"This is Aceline," I said, "who lives outside my door. And Tea, who lives down the hall. My place is—through there. Don't get too excited."

The Beggar gave a tiny smile and I waved at her introductorily.

"This is the . . ." I stumbled to a halt. No no no. No she wasn't. She had a name now, but my tongue had tangled around it completely. "This is a friend of mine," I said before I could stop myself—and that was even worse. For a moment, complete vocal shutdown threatened as I tried to work it out and I could feel every muscle going tense. It was the same problem: every word that floated into my head sounded ridiculous and totally alien. Girlfriend, lover, partner—all sounded like nonsense and I could hardly bear to even think them in case the world decided to prove me wrong. The Beggar couldn't possibly be a *lover*. She was just someone I had accidentally bumped genitalia with and who now happened to be walking in the same direction for a while before wandering off again like a random particle.

The Beggar gave me a brief glance that I couldn't read—for good or ill. Aceline must have seen something in my face, though, for she grew a huge grin. "So that's where you've been," she said. "Contractual formalities? You might have let us know, though. I've been worrying."

"Aaaah," Tea cried, mirroring the grin, and I could feel myself going crimson.

"That's not quite what . . . I mean . . . well yes, but . . . that wasn't why . . ."

To my surprise, the Beggar gave a brief giggle and I glanced at her hopefully. To my even greater surprise, she winked a small wink. "Alright alright," I said, raising both hands and trying to save the situation. "I could probably rephrase all that."

"What happened then?"

"I don't really know how to explain," I said truthfully enough, sitting down on Aceline's bed with a sigh. The Beggar also dropped politely onto a chair. "It's a long story. We got stuck somewhere—trapped. Lost my wallet. That's why I had to bang on the door."

"Fuck," Aceline murmured sympathetically. It wasn't much of an explanation, but it was all she was getting for the moment.

I looked longingly at the door to my room again. I still wasn't sure what was going to happen now. So far there had been little serious talk—little planning or discussion. I had no idea whether I or she or both of us would be staying here for the next few days. I had no idea what the sleeping arrangements were going to be. My bed was tiny, so presumably that meant I would be on the floor, which wasn't appealing.

"How are you now?" I asked Tea.

"Ah yes," she said, looking faintly embarrassed. "I'm . . . fine. I'm a tough nutter, as they say, and trying to be as cheerful as ever."

"There hasn't been any sign of Tad," Aceline added. "Hopefully he doesn't want to come back here any more than we want him to, the bastard."

"That's good," I said. "Maybe it's just another part of the insanity going on at the moment . . ."

"Or maybe he's just a bastard," Aceline said. I shrugged. Maybe.

"What has been happening here, then?" I asked. There was no reason to believe that my own familiar home would be somehow shielded from everything that was storming over the city, but the thought of the London Madness roaring through here was still a somewhat strange one. Aceline sat down next to me and poured herself a glass of wine—and I could see the exhausted jittery tension that filled her.

"Oh, it's been mad," Tea muttered. "Absolutely mad. You just won't believe what's been going on. I was nervous about opening the door. The police were in . . ."

"Why?" I demanded, looking up. "Not looking for me I suppose?"

"No—why? What have you been up to?"

I shrugged that off with an impatient wave.

"Just rowdiness," Aceline said, hunching down and staring at the floor. "Lots of arguments, fights. Lots of people running wild and making a noise—a few who were involved in the riots. Oh and . . . we found out who killed the cat."

"The bones?" I asked, waving vaguely at the ceiling and aware of the Beggar giving me a curious look.

"Yeah—can you fucking believe it?"

"Who?" I demanded.

Aceline shrugged and named a name—not someone I knew in any detail, like most people here.

"And they arrested him?"

"Yeah," Tea said. "I thought everyone was going to chuck him off the roof for a while—they were fucking out of their minds. But fortunately they called the cops instead."

There was a silence while I digested that one. And here, one peripheral story finds a kind of closure, anyway. A better story and I would no doubt have been there—a proper sub-climax in the narrative. Then I could have taken a look into his eyes to try and see the mystery. I doubt they would have revealed anything remotely alien, though. People love to pretend that those who do things they find repugnant are somehow different, changed, warped, other—but the truth is that we are all basically the same.

Look into the eyes of a cat killer and I'm pretty sure you won't find much that you can't also find in the mirror.

I nodded. "I can believe it," I said, feeling filled with weariness. Aceline shoved the wine bottle in my direction and I in turn offered it to the Beggar, who shook her head with a brief smile. I didn't take any either. I was not sure I trusted myself to be drunk right then. It might have soothed the tension in me—or it might have sent me completely nuts. "I dunno what the news has been reporting," I said at last, "but . . . there have been a lot of strange goings on."

"Yeah," the Beggar said, speaking for the first time since we had arrived. "Eating pigeons. Killing pets. Running round naked. Crying in the streets. Leaving doors open . . ."

Aceline stared, eyebrows up. "Oh fucking hell," she muttered. "That's mad. I don't get it."

I shook my head. For a moment I wondered whether to try and repeat the Philosopher's theory of communicated emotions, but I had no idea yet whether any of that made sense. "We've missed the news the last few days," I said evasively. "I don't really know anything more."

Aceline reached over and obligingly woke up her laptop—and the news page.

. . . the over five hundred British scientists who have signed a letter calling for the immediate closure of the London Labs. Meanwhile, another massive and increasingly aggressive crowd had gathered, also demanding closure. The police have arrested some 80 protestors for public order offences, including petrol bombs and slingshots. At least . . .

"They're really hammering that place now," Aceline said.

"You . . . think it will work?" the Beggar asked with a hint of desperation. My eyes fixed on her, understanding why perfectly well. The unspoken thought was in both our minds as the crowds seethed—the thought of just who might now be inside those dull metal gates. It left an agonising coldness inside me that must have mirrored her own and I found myself watching that crowd, silently pleading with them. Yes—just rip that place open once and for all—overrun it—tear it to shreds—liberate the place . . .

For gawd sake, there has to be *some* humanity in the world. Surely?

"I wish," Aceline muttered. "But . . . we've been yelling about these things for years. They never really change, unless it's to get worse. I just don't understand how so many people can support this level of cruelty. I mean—everything, not just this. *Why* do people just keep right on . . . It just never ends . . ."

She rubbed at her face urgently.

. . . whereupon the riots shifted to the police station and the surrounding area, with considerable damage to shopfronts and several cars set on fire. The damages caused have been . . .

"Put that off," the Beggar said suddenly—soft, but I could instantly see the tension in her.

"Huh?"

"Please," she said. "Put that . . . off." She was shaking, a hint of tears in her eyes. She was trying to preserve some kind of normalcy but it was easily seen through.

Aceline looked worried and closed the page quickly. "Are you okay?"

"Yes . . . yes, sorry," the Beggar lied. I slid a little closer and squeezed her shoulder, which I desperately hoped would be of some comfort.

"Well, I was just going to say that though those fucking labs are still causing rage, everywhere else it seems to be tailing off now," Aceline said. "The Madness has lost its momentum. Something like ten thousand extra police in London now—and they are appealing to the public for help in dealing with it all."

"How?" the Beggar demanded with a frown. "If we see someone running around with their arse out, we're supposed to tackle them and drag them off to the Tower or something?"

"They were asking parents to check their kids' shoes to see if any of them were suspiciously new—or any other odd items turning up out of nowhere. Looking for looted stuff. Or keeping them at home at night . . ."

"Are you serious? It's not just a bunch of kids running wild," the Beggar said, her voice heated.

"Well that's what they were saying," Aceline said with a shrug.

"London has gone mad and they are trying to pass it off as a few badly behaved brats?"

"Tell me about it. There's literally nothing else on the social media—millions of pictures. Fire everywhere. Burning buildings. Shops ransacked, people swarming, riot police, taser attacks and truncheons . . ." She sighed and stretched—the stretch of one who has not had enough sleep for too long. "Ah well, it's over now. Hopefully."

"But will we learn anything from it?" the Beggar asked. "I doubt it."

"What things?"

"I dunno," the Beggar said. "That it was more important than a few brats running around, for starters."

Aceline shrugged.

"What about the deep levels?" she asked with an awkward stare at the floor—and for a moment I could almost hear the Philosopher talking again. "I mean, all this stuff . . . it must be important. There must be clues in it. But you can bet your arse no one will fucking care. They'll just dismiss it as an aberration. They always do."

There was a silence and the Beggar continued to stare down gloomily. Her obvious anger actually made me feel a bit better, though—it was a lot more alive and human than the quiet hazy gloom that seemed to be her dominant mood at the moment. Aceline watched her as well. It wasn't really an argument, but she looked slightly discomforted nonetheless. I decided to step in and change the subject. There was one piece of important news that I hadn't even mentioned yet. And there was no obvious way to lead up to something like this.

"There's something I need to tell you," I said.

"Oh?"

"I might . . . I mean I am . . . moving out," I said with an embarrassed smile.

They both gave me startled looks. "Really?" Aceline demanded, while Tea spread her hands with a mock-tragic grimace.

"Yes," I said. "I . . . might have found somewhere . . . cheaper. And . . . easier."

"We shall miss you."

"I am moving in next week. It's being worked out at the moment."

"Where?"

"That's a rather long story," I said evasively. "I . . . can't really say—yet."

They both stared at me with what I can only call knowing frustration—and yes, they knew what was going on, I realised. Maybe moving into hidden housing was almost mainstream these days. Again the question of how many people were doing this floated to the top of my mind—doing it with varying degrees of efficacy and sophistication, but still managing to escape. And I do wonder. If enough people simply step away from the familiar system of greed and artificial illusions, then what actually happens? Is there a tipping point? Would the familiar vampiric system just become irrelevant or would things crumble? Would the whole thing tip over like the revolution in *Animal Farm* and become as poisoned as its predecessor? I wish I knew. I wish the Philosopher was here to talk about it. Maybe in the end, we all just ride this world, forgetting that nobody and nothing is actually in charge of it. Forgetting that most of what makes us suffer is arbitrary . . . that there's no driver to this train as it races round the sun. Even the Measuring Men are just passengers.

"Well—you'd better bloody visit us," Aceline said. "Even if we can't visit you."

"I will," I said—and I meant it. In a way, I was going to miss these people, neighbours and those outside my door—not to mention Tea, my partner in silent language. I looked at her, feeling a strange warm sensation—a release as the last tinges of earlier attractions drifted away into whatever land of ghosts such things inhabit. Not exactly gone, for they never go completely. Just . . . superseded. *Look at me,* I thought childishly, *I am free of you . . .*

"In the meantime—how about some dinner?" Aceline said. "I got some of the new flavour mycofillet—and I'm sure there's enough for two more. Piri piri flavour."

The Beggar gave a sudden giggle and I glanced at her. "Thanks," she said. "That would be very kind of you."

☼

"What happened to her?" the Beggar asked, sitting down on my bed. "Those bruises looked horrible."

Maybe I should have lied, but such things don't come easy to me and the truth just came walking right out of my mouth. She muttered something under her breath, looking even gloomier. I watched her anxiously, but she simply lay back on the bed and gently dragged my arms around her into a hug—a gesture that was surprisingly similar to Fitzroy wanting attention. More proof that at the end of the day, no matter how disconnected we may end up, humans are animals too, with the same basic needs and instincts. This was typical of her these days. We would lie together as though we never wanted to be more than a few feet apart ever again in our entire lives. Even when she wasn't hanging on to me, she seemed to be carefully maintaining at least one point of contact—holding my hand, her foot hooked over mine, her arse against my back. At first that had been worrying—I didn't like the blank unhappy look on her face. But as time passed and the fits of melancholy and disturbed nights began to recede slightly, her need for physical contact only seemed to increase. I guess this was just the way she was. After a lifetime of being trampled and marginalised, maybe she had some catching up to do—as indeed did I. And I was only glad that she could find and act on this need, rather than becoming sealed off in a dark place with no trust left at all, as happens to so many.

"Are you . . . I mean how are you feeling?" I murmured.

"I'll live," the Beggar said. "I feel so helpless, though. Do you think . . . should we be there in that crowd outside the gate? Should we be making petrol bombs?"

"I . . . dunno."

"I never did that before in my life," she said. "I wasn't Star Girl. But now—I dunno. I kind of want to at least try. Even though we'd probably just end up inside with them . . ."

She sighed miserably.

"I . . . really want to find them again, you know . . ."

"Maybe we can," I said. "Maybe there are ways."

"You mean when the labs are done with them? You have ideas?"

I nodded slowly. Yes—maybe. Maybe I could track down the Philosopher by researching the London colleges and universities. Maybe I could find Star by searching around Hackney Wick for clothes makers. Or maybe they would be looking for us at one of the few places we all knew—the New Sea Wall. Clues could be left. Spray cans could leave messages. Ways could be found.

"That would be nice," she said, before falling silent again. It wasn't much—but it was something to think about.

Something to hope for.

I lay there feeling her hair against my face, my eyes idly drifting round the room, trying to analyse what state I had left the place in. I had given it quite a tidy shortly before my first trip to the railway line, so I hoped that it wasn't too bad. Hopefully no suspicious bottles or leftover food. But anyway, what did it matter? The world had changed now. Changes upon changes. The result was that I felt less disposed to apologise for myself than ever before. I found myself squeezing the Beggar harder. She responded in a kind of contest of muscle strength that came with a surge of warmth.

"Was it you, Train Man, who was always going on about the angles?" she asked at last. "About the polyhedron? Or did I dream it?"

"I . . . I think it was me."

"I feel as though I've got one vertex of that polyhedron . . . straight up my arse and about to emerge from my throat."

She gave a long groan and rubbed her face with her free hand.

"I've been dreaming about that damn polyhedron," she said, somewhat to my surprise. "I remember making paper models when I was young—star-shaped . . . pointed. Tetrahedron, stellated icosahedron, cuboctahedron . . . but now that regularity was turning itself inside out like . . . like some kind of nest. And every turn was taking me with it—turning and turning."

"Have you seen it?" I asked, still genuinely unsure about that.

"Seen . . . ?"

"The Polyhedron. The red lights."

She stared at me blankly.

"They drift," I murmured—no idea where the words were coming from.

"Hmm?"

"Turning in space—the perfect angles. Shining. Flashing lights that dazzle all our eyes. I never realised that they were dripping blood."

"What the heck are we talking about?" she asked with a smile.

"The angle and the curve," I said. It felt as though I was taking on Feather's role as the teller of weird fantasies here—but once you have the idea of the polyhedron in your head, every story becomes bound up with it. "The angle represents the tight, rigid, controlled—the curve is the organic, the blurred, the indefinable, the free. And I suppose . . . in nature there are angles and patterns, but they are slaves to the curve . . . I mean to the organic. With us it's the other way round—we are trying to enslave the curves to the angles. And that's when things start to hurt. One day the angles have to go."

"I don't have a clue what you are talking about," she said after a pause, "but I kind of like it."

I had to laugh. "It probably doesn't matter that much," I said.

"I need a shower, I think," she said. "I stink. Then we can go to bed?"

"Yeah—me too, I suppose."

She gave a small smile, though without moving. "Share?"

"Um . . . um . . . sure."

"Please bear with me," she murmured, burying her face in my shoulder. "I still feel as though someone kicked me in the stomach. I just really don't want you to—well, just give me a little time, that's all."

"Of course," I whispered, feeling relieved. "Me also. I kind of want to say the same thing." There was a hint of dread in the back of my mind that the awkwardness I felt would remain for so long that the Beggar would lose patience and simply not be there any more before the transition was complete—if indeed it ever was. We are layered like onions, layer after layer, each one deeper and harder to access than the last. Like the ocean. Like the internet. Like the universe. And teaching those deeper places new lessons was easier said than done.

But in the meantime, nothing to do except get on with this thing called life. Nothing to do but keep riding the train.

"For all sorts of reasons," I said. "Bear with me as well."

"We shall bear," she said with a smile that I felt rather than saw. "This new home . . . Just so you know, I'm really pleased about that, even if I don't show it."

"I'm glad . . ."

"It reminds me a little of our space in the New Sea Wall—but permanent. And somehow . . . ours." Her face suddenly fell. "You think it will be—fairly permanent?"

"It seems as permanent as anywhere I've ever been," I said, hoping that was true. How could you ever know? Throughout history, human beings have always yearned for permanence—something that can safely be trusted to always be there. Weird then that history has done nothing but rip that away. Some of that was natural—an increasing awareness of the transitory nature of all things, but in the world of things humans can actually control, there was nothing natural about it and it remains one of the biggest mysteries of life why we have moved in the exact opposite direction to what we yearn for so determinedly.

She stared wanly at nothing for a moment, briefly goosed by memories—then shook it off with a smile.

"We'll have to consecrate the place after we move in," she said. "A bed is not a bed and a home is not a home until you have had sex in it."

I glanced at her curiously. That was the first time she had shown any interest in that since the disaster.

"Can I eat you out again?" I asked. "That was way way waaaaayyy the best bit."

She gave a blushing grin. "Any time, my dear Train Man—any time."

She stretched herself out flat, one arm still locked around mine, and stared at the ceiling dreamily.

"I . . ."

The words stuck in my throat. I had been wanting to say *I love you,* but was left following her eyes to the ceiling instead, so used to those words being poison. I literally couldn't say them. Instead, I gave her hand a squeeze, which I hoped would convey something similar. When she squeezed back again, it was a relief.

CODA

We sat, the Beggar and I, in the grass by the water, staring out at the colourful scene. The sun was low in the sky, painting the evening a sombre red glow, as though the city was still burning.

I still call her the Beggar—still think of her as the Beggar, as well, even though I know her name. Just as I am still Train Man. They say names have power, but it appears they can also be shaped at will. And maybe when you get down to it a name that is also a tag has even more power than merely an arbitrary word assigned before you are even born. The Beggar is a strange moniker, not exactly a happy one, but I don't think it will be going anywhere just yet.

She rolled over lazily and rested her head on my leg. She was on the mend now—less the unnerving ghost of herself while her mind healed from the shock and despair she had experienced.

"I remember when I lived here with my mother," she said out of nowhere, "long ago now. I always thought it was a friendly place. It's hard to keep that notion up when you don't have the safety of a home of your own, of course. But once . . . well, there was something curious one night."

I looked at her with interest.

"You know—when you are homeless, you need to keep moving. But that one night I somehow ended up sleeping in the centre of Hackney. I had a sleeping bag and a padlocked rucksack that I always tied to my hand or foot. Not that there was anything of value in it, but you know, people will always try. I was in a doorway—some sort of public building not so far from here. But that night it was hot, so I fell asleep on top of the sleeping bag—

and I didn't notice anything, certainly didn't wake up. But when I woke, I found . . ."

She gave a smile—an unusually broad smile, which warmed my heart a little.

"I found that someone had tied six helium balloons to my belt," she said. "They were just there, bobbing overhead when I opened my eyes." She gave a laugh. "And then . . . well, I shrugged it off. But when I opened my bag . . . my locked bag . . . I found someone had slipped a hundred quid in there. I still don't quite know how. Or why."

She was silent for a moment. I reached out and took her hand and she squeezed it with a smile.

"You know—that haunted me for a long time afterwards. You don't see much nice stuff out on the streets, but when something does stand out, it really stands out."

"What did you spend it on?" I asked. She shrugged.

"Just food," she said. "And clothes. Lasted me quite a while. Though I did manage to buy some slightly healthier stuff for once."

She glanced up at the sky, which was now almost fully dark. I followed her eyes, taking in the scattered lights of London. It was a beautiful sight—an unending complex, filled with possibility and horror, magic and despair, all preserving some kind of balance that felt to me to be unique, rightly or wrongly.

In the distance, among the buildings, one single red light gleamed. I studied it for a moment with a slight frown. And as I studied it, I had the feeling that it was studying me back. Like a specimen under a microscope.

"Talking of that," she said, "perhaps we had better go and look for some? We have thirty-three mouths to feed now . . ."

I blinked and dragged my eyes away. No doubt just a warning light . . .

"Okay," I said, scrambling up. We made our way into the quieter areas away from the water and she reached into her bag, feeling for her snares.

A PARTIAL LIST OF SNUGGLY BOOKS

G. ALBERT AURIER *Elsewhere and Other Stories*
S. HENRY BERTHOUD *Misanthropic Tales*
LÉON BLOY *The Tarantulas' Parlor and Other Unkind Tales*
ÉLÉMIR BOURGES *The Twilight of the Gods*
JAMES CHAMPAGNE *Harlem Smoke*
FÉLICIEN CHAMPSAUR *The Latin Orgy*
FÉLICIEN CHAMPSAUR
  The Emerald Princess and Other Decadent Fantasies
BRENDAN CONNELL *Clark*
BRENDAN CONNELL *Unofficial History of Pi Wei*
ADOLFO COUVE *When I Think of My Missing Head*
QUENTIN S. CRISP *Graves*
QUENTIN S. CRISP *Rule Dementia!*
LADY DILKE *The Outcast Spirit and Other Stories*
CATHERINE DOUSTEYSSIER-KHOZE *The Beauty of the Death Cap*
BERIT ELLINGSEN *Now We Can See the Moon*
BERIT ELLINGSEN *Vessel and Solsvart*
EDMOND AND JULES DE GONCOURT *Manette Salomon*
GUIDO GOZZANO *Alcina and Other Stories*
RHYS HUGHES *Cloud Farming in Wales*
J.-K. HUYSMANS *Knapsacks*
COLIN INSOLE *Valerie and Other Stories*
JUSTIN ISIS *Pleasant Tales II*
JUSTIN ISIS (editor) *Marked to Die: A Tribute to Mark Samuels*
JUSTIN ISIS AND DANIEL CORRICK (editors)
  Drowning in Beauty: The Neo-Decadent Anthology
VICTOR JOLY *The Unknown Collaborator and Other Legendary Tales*
BERNARD LAZARE *The Mirror of Legends*
BERNARD LAZARE *The Torch-Bearers*
MAURICE LEVEL *The Shadow*
JEAN LORRAIN *Errant Vice*
JEAN LORRAIN *Fards and Poisons*
JEAN LORRAIN *Masks in the Tapestry*
JEAN LORRAIN *Nightmares of an Ether-Drinker*
JEAN LORRAIN *The Soul-Drinker and Other Decadent Fantasies*

ARTHUR MACHEN *N*
ARTHUR MACHEN *Ornaments in Jade*
CAMILLE MAUCLAIR *The Frail Soul and Other Stories*
CATULLE MENDÈS *Bluebirds*
CATULLE MENDÈS *To Read in the Bath*
EPHRAÏM MIKHAËL *Halyartes and Other Poems in Prose*
LUIS DE MIRANDA *Who Killed the Poet?*
OCTAVE MIRBEAU *The Death of Balzac*
CHARLES MORICE *Babels, Balloons and Innocent Eyes*
DAMIAN MURPHY *Daughters of Apostasy*
DAMIAN MURPHY *The Star of Gnosia*
KRISTINE ONG MUSLIM *Butterfly Dream*
YARROW PAISLEY *Mendicant City*
URSULA PFLUG *Down From*
JEAN RICHEPIN *The Bull-Man and the Grasshopper*
DAVID RIX *A Suite in Four Windows*
FREDERICK ROLFE (BARON CORVO) *Amico di Sandro*
FREDERICK ROLFE (BARON CORVO)
　An Ossuary of the North Lagoon and Other Stories
JASON ROLFE *An Archive of Human Nonsense*
BRIAN STABLEFORD *Spirits of the Vasty Deep*
BRIAN STABLEFORD (editor)
　Decadence and Symbolism: A Showcase Anthology
COUNT ERIC STENBOCK *Love, Sleep & Dreams*
COUNT ERIC STENBOCK *Myrtle, Rue and Cypress*
COUNT ERIC STENBOCK *Studies of Death*
MONTAGUE SUMMERS *Six Ghost Stories*
DOUGLAS THOMPSON *The Fallen West*
TOADHOUSE *Gone Fishing with Samy Rosenstock*
JANE DE LA VAUDÈRE *The Demi-Sexes and The Androgynes*
JANE DE LA VAUDÈRE *The Double Star and Other Occult Fantasies*
JANE DE LA VAUDÈRE *The Mystery of Kama and Brahma's Courtesans*
JANE DE LA VAUDÈRE *Syta's Harem and Pharaoh's Lover*
RENÉE VIVIEN *Lilith's Legacy*
RENÉE VIVIEN *A Woman Appeared to Me*
RENÉE VIVIEN AND HÉLÈNE DE ZUYLEN DE NYEVELT
　Faustina and Other Stories

CPSIA information can be obtained
at www.ICGtesting.com
Printed in the USA
LVHW041522100619
620736LV00004B/881/P